PAPER CITIES

AN ANTHOLOGY OF URBAN FANTASY

Also by Ekaterina Sedia:

According To Crow

The Secret History Of Moscow

Also from Senses Five Press

Sybil's Garage Issues 1 — 5

PAPER CITIES

AN ANTHOLOGY OF URBAN FANTASY

EDITED BY EKATERINA SEDIA

Senses Five

Senses Five Press
Hoboken, New Jersey

First Printing. Collection copyright © 2008 Senses Five Press. All Rights Reserved. Copyrights for the individual stories and the foreword remain the property of the authors. Page 271 functions as an extension of the copyright page.

Senses Five Press
307 Madison St, No. 3L
Hoboken, NJ 07030
www.sensesfive.com
info@sensesfive.com

Publisher's Cataloging-in-Publication data

Paper cities : an anthology of urban fantasy / edited by Ekaterina Sedia.
    p. cm.
    Contents: Jess Nevins - Foreword--Forrest Aguirre - Andretto Walks the King's Way--Hal Duncan - The Tower of Morning's Bones--Richard Parks - Courting the Lady Scythe--Cat Rambo - The Bumblety's Marble--Jay Lake - Promises: A Tale of the City Imperishable--Greg van Eekhout - Ghost Market--Cat Sparks - Sammarynda Deep--Steve Berman - Tearjerker--Stephanie Campisi - The Title of This Story--Mark Teppo - The One That Got Away--Paul Meloy - Alex and the Toyceivers--Vylar Kaftan - Godivy--Mike Jasper - Painting Haiti--Ben Peek - The Funeral, Ruined--Kaaron Warren - Down to the Silver Spirits--Darin C. Bradley - They Would Only be Roads--Jenn Reese - Taser--David Schwartz - Somnambulist--Anna Tambour - The Age of Fish, Post-flowers--Barth Anderson - The Last Escape--Catherynne M. Valente - Palimpsest.
    ISBN 978-0-9796246-0-5

1. Short stories. 2. Fantasy fiction. 3. Fantasy. I. Sedia, Ekaterina.

PS648.F3 P11 2007
813.08766--dc22   2007928152

Text set in Hoefler text. Titles set in Big Caslon.
Cover art by Aaron Acevedo (http://aaronace.com).
Book and cover design by Kris Dikeman.
Copyediting by Darin C. Bradley (http://darinbradley.livejournal.com/).

To Dad and Connie

CONTENTS

Editor's Note

The stories collected in this anthology range across historical periods and places real and imagined. But they all take place within cities — and they all talk about what urban life means. I selected these stories because they share the insight into the cities as living entities, benign or sinister, that can shape the existence of their inhabitants. And they share the passion for those agglomerations of flesh and inanimate matter, with all their foibles, glories, and hidden truths. Some of the authors are well-known; others are brand new and just starting to make a name for themselves. I love all of these stories, and I hope that the readers will as well.

— Ekaterina Sedia, New Jersey, August 30th 2007.

URBAN FANTASY

by Jess Nevins

One of the appealing things about Urban Fantasy is that, as John Clute points out in the *Encyclopedia of Fantasy*, it is a mode of storytelling rather than a subgenre, and as such accommodates a variety of themes and approaches. Urban Fantasy is not restricted by genre limitations the way that cyberpunk, hardboiled detective fiction, the Western, and pirate romances (among others) are. Urban Fantasy can be about almost anything — and *Paper Cities* is an excellent example of this.

We can trace the Urban Fantasy as far back as the *Arabian Nights* and the stories of Haroun al-Raschid wandering around Baghdad incognito and finding adventure. Similarly, the Gothics of the late 18th and early 19th centuries provided the Urban Fantasy with several basic elements, especially the ever-present backdrop of a circumscribed location, usually a castle but sometimes a mansion and occasionally even a city, as the setting for a story's plot. But the Urban Fantasy as we now recognize it began in the 1830s and the 1840s.

The tendency in fiction to portray cities as both a setting and as a type of supporting character began in the 1820s, with John Polidori's "The Vampyre" (1819), the first modern urban horror story, and with the Newgate novels, early versions of crime novels which told the biographies of criminals and illustrated the lives and *milieu* of the urban underclass. Victor Hugo, in *The Hunchback of Notre Dame* (1831), made Paris into the main character of the novel, much more so than the hunchback Quasimodo, and Eugene Sue did the same in his hugely popular *The Mysteries of Paris* (1842-1843) and to a lesser extent in the only slightly less popular *The Wandering Jew* (1844-1845), but Sue added an element of the fantastic which Hugo refrained from. In *The Mysteries of Paris* the lead character, Rodolphe von Gerolstein, is almost supernatural in his ability to disguise himself, to be where he needs to be, and to know what he needs to know. *The*

Wandering Jew has the explicitly supernatural character Ahasuerus, the Wandering Jew of medieval myth, as well as other less overtly sketched supernatural aspects. With *The Mysteries of Paris* and *The Wandering Jew* Sue established, for modern European and American audiences, the concept of the city as a location where the fantastic was not just possible but appropriate. The Newgate novels, and early urban crime stories like Pierce Egan the Elder's *Life in London* (1821) and Lord Bulwer-Lytton's *Pelham* (1828), had expanded the axis in which urban stories could occur, from "peaceful" to "criminal." Sue established a new axis: "realistic" to "fantastic."

What followed in England and Europe was a widespread use of this concept. Dickens followed the example of Hugo and Sue and wrote stories in which the city would seem to be the most appropriate venue for the fantastic, or stories which were fantastic in all but name, and in so doing established London as the archetypal City of the English-speaking literate world. The 19th century saw a shift in population from rural to urban settings, and new, urban-centered forms of fiction arose, including the casebooks of the 1850s, proto-police procedural stories focusing on urban crimes, and the urban haunted house story, in Bulwer-Lytton's "The Haunted and the Haunters" (1859). But looming over all successive writers was Dickens and the way in which he shifted the public's frame of perception of the city. In Dickens' hands London became an active participant in the story, an almost sentient location in which sentimentality, despair, and melodrama were mixed and heightened. At the end of the century Robert Louis Stevenson narrowed the portrayal of the city with his *New Arabian Nights*, a continuation of Dickens' work. In applying the original *Arabian Nights*' conception of the City to London as a place of wonders around every corner, Stevenson emphasized the purely fantastical elements and eliminated the politically activist and ideological elements of Sue's and Dickens' work.

However, for the American reader the urban milieu had a different set of associations and assumptions. The Puritans had seen the American frontier not as pristine, innocent wilderness but as an evil place which reflected men's sins. This outlook colored 19th century American fiction, explicitly in the works of Hawthorne and less so in works like Robert Montgomery Bird's *Nick of the Woods* (1837). But Americans had a similar distrust for the city. The most powerful expression of this distrust is in George Lippard's *The Quaker City* (1844-

1845), a vigorous portrayal of Philadelphia as an urban Hell rife with kidnapping, murder, and rape, whose redemption is only possible with an apocalyptic fire. This wariness of the city, and dread of what lies around its corners, is the recurring theme of American urban fiction, and can be seen in works as various as the short stories of Fitz-James O'Brian (see, for example, "The Wondersmith" (1859)), and the crime and Western dime novels. In the very popular Deadwood Dick (1877-1883) and Frank and Jesse James (1881-1903) dime novel series the communities of the settled frontier are harmonious, while New York City, and implicitly all Eastern cities, are locations where the corrupt and powerful prey on and victimize the innocent working man.

It was this tension between the city-as-full-of-wonder and the city-as-dreadful that primarily influenced 20ᵗʰ century Urban Fantasy. Neither can be described as primarily English or primarily American, as there are many counter-examples for each. Landmark European and English works of Urban Fantasy from the late 19ᵗʰ early 20ᵗʰ centuries portray the city as containing horrors in addition to wonders, including Victor von Falk's 3000 page Grand Guignol masterpiece, *Der Scharfrichter von Berlin* (1890-1892), Bram Stoker's *Dracula* (1897), Gaston Leroux's *The Phantom of the Opera* (1910), and Thea von Harbou and Fritz Lang's *M* (1931). And there are a number of examples of American Urban Fantasies whose cities tend more toward wonder than horror, from the Terri Windling-edited "Borderlands" series to Francesca Lia Block's stories about Los Angeles. But as a broad tendency American Urban Fantasies begin with the assumption that the city is innately flawed and horrible; examples include Batman's Gotham City (an exaggerated form of New York City), the Chicago of Fritz Leiber's "Smoke Ghost" (1941), the New York City of Angela Carter's *Passion of New Eve* (1977), and the Seattle of Megan Lindholm's *Wizard of the Pigeons* (1986). English/European Urban Fantasies tend to portray the city in a more benign fashion, even if, as in the novels of Terry Pratchett and China Mieville, the city has its realistically horrible aspects.

Which brings us, at last, to *Paper Cities*. As a mode of storytelling Urban Fantasy is almost two hundred years old, but as a distinctive publishing subgenre Urban Fantasy dates back only to the 1980s. Authors like Charles de Lint, Emma Bull, and Megan Lindholm helped establish Urban Fantasy and gave it its distinctive character. But, as traditionally happens with new literary genres, the second generation of Urban Fantasy authors are pushing against the boundaries laid down by the first generation's writers and taking the genre into new and welcome territories. The stories in *Paper*

Cities not only draw on numerous inspirations but, entertainingly and skillfully, apply the Urban Fantasy mode to both non-Western cultures and to other subgenres and fictional forms. Darin C. Bradley's "They Would Only Be Roads" recasts urban fantasy as a cyberpunk story, complete with grit, street-level programmers, a decaying urban milieu, and the possibility of romance and redemption. Hal Duncan's "The Tower of Morning Bones" is a vivid Joycean mosaic; like Hal's *Vellum* and *Ink*, "The Tower of Morning Bones" mixes old mythologies and a joy in the power of language to create something uniquely Duncanian. Barth Anderson's "The Last Escape" takes the story of a heroic rebel in a dark direction, unexpectedly moving from superheroics to horror. Jay Lake's "Promises" is, like his other City Impenetrable stories, atmospheric, harsh, and decadent (if not Decadent), but it also has a core of emotion and sadness which most Decadence lacks. Paul Meloy's "Alex and the Toyceivers" reminds us that the suburbs and outer boroughs are also fitting locations for urban fantasy, especially stories involving children and pets.

Anna Tambour's "The Age of Fish, Post-Flowers" is a post-civilization breakdown monster story, but Tambour eschews the predictable action movie heroics and explosions and concentrates on the cost to humans of surviving in an inhospitable environment. Mark Teppo's "The One That Got Away" is a knowing riff on the Club Story, but from a 21st century perspective. "The One That Got Away" is about what Lord Dunsany's Mr. Jorkens might have had to endure if he lived in the real world. Stephanie Campisi's "The Title of This Story" is not particularly easily classified, as it is equal parts urban decadence, Borgesian horror, decadence, and lexigraphic fantasia; if it must be placed in one category, the only apposite one is "Campisian." Greg van Eekhout's "Ghost Market" is urban horror, grim, sad, and a quietly savage slap at a modern culture which slights the deaths of ordinary people, reducing them to statistics, and gives undue weight to the deaths of celebrities. Richard Parks' "Courting the Lady Scythe" uses a traditional fantasy backdrop to tell a story that is both a be-careful-what-you-wish-for story, with its inevitable twist, and a bittersweet romance. Ben Peek's "The Funeral, Ruined" is a kind of sequel to his "The Souls of Dead Soldiers are for Blackbirds, Not Little Boys." "The Funeral, Ruined" uses an alien necropolis and a wounded veteran to consider the definition of the self and to topically remind the reader of what a society forces its soldiers to endure.

Jenn Reese's "Taser" has magic and demon dogs and telepathy, but those are external elements; "Taser" is ultimately a story about life on the street as a member of a teen gang, and as such would have fit comfortably, even with its fantasy elements, in *The Saturday Evening Post* in the 1950s, or next to *West Side Story* in the 1960s, or *The Outsiders* in the 1970s. Cat Sparks' "Sammarynda Deep" begins as an Arabian Fantasy and ends as a melancholy romance and consideration of the cost of honor. David Schwartz's "The Somnambulist" is an examination of the cost of magic and what a relationship with a sorcerer might actually entail, and also a sharp metaphor for a certain type of husband. Kaaron Warren's "Down to the Silver Spirits" is a maternal horror story which will resonate with mothers, and a marriage horror story which will resonate with husbands, and a parental horror story which will resonate with mothers and fathers. Steve Berman's "Tearjerker," one of his Fallen Area stories, is both an homage to Samuel Delaney and a meditation on victimization. Cat Rambo's "The Bumblety's Marble," one of her Tabat stories, uses the structure of the traditional fairy tale to tell a colorful urban picaresque coming-of-age story. Michael Jasper's "Painting Haiti" is about the power of art and the call of family ties, and provides a welcome reminder that cities are rarely monoculture, and that even fantasy cities have immigrants. Forrest Aguirre's "Andretto Walks the King's Way" uses the vocabulary of traditional fantasy to invoke Edgar Allan Poe and Mervyn Peake and perhaps tell an AIDS parable. And Catherynne Valente's remarkable "Palimpset" is an evocative work of Decadence that superbly blends Valente's distinctive, lush style with a memorable fictional world.

If *Paper Cities* is any indication of second-generation Urban Fantasy — and I believe it is — both the mode of storytelling and the subgenre have a bright future.

Jess Nevins
Hunstville, Texas
August, 2007

ANDRETTO WALKS
THE KING'S WAY

Forrest Aguirre

The Castle

hain mail clatters as the gate guard turns a clanking hedgehog of keys to give a milkmaid ingress to the keep. She stumbles through the side-door into the courtyard, groggy from morning chores and the last evening's indiscretions with the butcher's eldest son.

It was the carnival, she thinks, blames, trips through the doorway and splays milk across the cobblestones with a curse.

A monk stops to chide her blasphemy, but she is too hungover to care.

A pair of guards laugh at the girl's predicament, both hoping they run into her at the carnival when the shift is done, neither telling the other of their shared intent.

Through an arrow slit, a tiny avalanche of dust falls and a rooster crows. The sun floods over the crenellations, the day begun.

The Commoner's Way

Impetuous, the spoiled prince sets forth, disdainful of the royal edict that forbids entertainers entrance to the great hall without the king's personal invitation. He swears there will be no such decrees when *he* inherits the throne.

Dust begins to cover his trouser legs. He looks down at the dirt, congratulating himself on his peasant disguise, but questioning the wisdom of wearing said disguise over his doublet and breeches. The day must, at some point, get hot.

The Carnival

Flags are strung from the front eaves to stakes at the road, a fabric queue beckoning to the wealthy, the naïve, the bored. Ilyan the bear trainer wakes to the staring eyes of his animal. The acrobats have already begun stretching and setting up their gymnastic instruments. A woman of ill-repute stretches in her bedroll. Her purse is a little heavier from a night visitor. She feels an ache growing in her groin, but this cannot be a result of her sale the night before. Impossible.

The King's Way

Andretto, the prince's own dwarf jongleur, staggers through the gates following a night with the carnival whores. The gate guards kick his backside, laughing, sending him into a well-rehearsed tumble. Only Andretto is not stable on his feet as he comes out of the roll, his head still cracked from a half-barrel of hard cider the night past. He drops to his knees, crawling up to his bed above the keep's kitchen.

The Castle

Once on his cot, Andretto heaves under a wave of sudden nausea and cold sweats unassociated with last night's excess. No amount of drink can make a man this miserable, he thinks. His head scorches from the inside, the steam rising from the kitchen pots beneath cooler than his own flesh. He hears a low, gravely sound somewhere in the distance, like a dog barking at children.

King's bellows echo off the walls of the council hall.
"Where is my son?!" and a guard slinks from the room to relay instructions down the line. Murmur passes to murmur, and three horsemen emerge from the castle's main portcullis, crossing the moat bridge at a gallop.

The Commoners' Way

Blacksmithy's brood, three males strong, bully the weaker children along the way. "Cain't!" — "Prove it!" — "Yay?" — "Nay!" and fists rain blows on the tanner's son, bloodied nose as red as heated steel, ash-black eye forming as young Tanner nurses his face and pride, the Smiths walking on, seeking victims as a fire ignites inside Tanner.

A group of off-duty soldiers, recently released from the night-watch, saunters toward the portable city.

A juggler, bright in smile and azure, or, and argent stripes, watches from atop man-high stilts as the first trickle of crowd approaches the fair. He spots the prince, noting the noble's poor attempt to appear poor. There is geld to be made today!

The Carnival

Varga, the bear, eats the proffered lamb with a lust unseen by Ilyan since the Easterner first captured the beast fifteen years ago. Unease creeps across the trainer's skin as he recalls how pieces of his hounds flew through the air like rain that day. Ilyan reminds himself that the past was gone and shrugs off the feeling as the fears of an old man. "Too long I have done this," he complains to the bear. "Soon I will train an apprentice and sell you off, old friend. I cannot stay married to an animal until I enter the grave." The fur-lidded eyes continue to stare at the man's bald plate. Ilyan ignores Varga, looking outside his tent door toward the faire's common where wrestlers grease their trunks and slap their triceps, taunting the locals to challenge their strength. "Who dares?" and "A penny, pay a penny, and five to you if you win!" sounds across the grassy square. The yells invade the tent of the whore, who massages her pain-filled armpits between lung-deep coughs, the warmth of her ascending fever her only comfort.

The King's Way

Sheep bustle before the crook of a shepherd, travelers form a village common over the hills. A wedding feast requires the fowler's wares: quail, duck, and chicken for the celebrants, and the shepherd has come to trade. One of the flock disappears at the edge of the fair closest town, on the road to the castle.

To market with flour the miller closest castle trots his ox cart. The deputy-sheriff takes taxes at the courtyard entrance — a bag a cart or gold ducats in kind, this miller passes to the centermost stall. He trades with his neighbor, a chicken a bag. "Won't the wife love this? Fowl for dinner. Times are good."

The Castle

Into a tavern, musicians three: a fiddle, a bodhran, and a quiver of krumhorns — announce the faire to the early crowd. Then on to another, another, a fourth. The air brightens in their path, smiles and poorly written invites trailing behind them, a chorus of resolve and plan changing in their wake from the illiterate crowd. They might as well have accepted their own execution papers, so excited are they by the music, and so ignorant of the written word.

In the great hall, gloom as the king waits word. "I'll have that boy whipped — unfit for a prince. And whose breed might he be, daughter of my liege, whose?!"

The queen leaves to card wool, unwilling to argue.

The dwarf's nose bleeds profusely. Andretto is in misery, as if an unseen horse has kicked him in the head. This is no mere hangover. He begins to shiver, cold sweat down the neck and back. He wishes the privy were closer.

The Commoners' Way

The off-duty soldiers spot the wrestlers, and one answers the call: "I have a penny, greasy man," the largest boasts. "I've taken a sword in my side, a Saracene arrow to the leg. Methinks I can best you." And the betting begins: 5:1, 1:5, a month's wages wagered. He is Boecker, the watch sergeant, a Prussian by birth. He removes his doublet and tunic to reveal his rip of a scar, then enters the ring.

His soldiers bet against him.

The Carnival

The king's horsemen scan the crowd, but cannot find the prince. They slow, an excuse to watch the entertainment. An old man, paunchy as his pet, bids the bear "Dance! Dance!" to the glee of the crowd. Then, to their horror, a scream tears forth as the bear plunges over the wrinkled trainer, clawing his face clean, then onto the crowd where the prince — "There he is!" — is caught in the gut by a passing paw, opening the abdomen, a shiny trinket at the prince's neck having caught the beast's attention. The horseman trio bolts to Varga, swords drawn, and hackstab until movement ceases. Two pick up the prince as the third clears the way, stooping at a tent long enough to wrestle something from therein: "Give me the blanket, whore!" and they wrap up the bleeding prince and take him toward the castle where a more exquisite pain awaits him.

A lady of ill-repute lies dying cold in her tent, her blanket fluttering away with the prince. Black buboes erupt from her neck, armpits, and groin.

The King's Way

The acrobats, earlier apprised of the prince's presence at the faire, tumble up the King's Way toward the castle in the mistaken assumption that the noble will share his son's love of spectacle. They cartwheel and somersault through the nameless crowd, pity for the commonness of the commoner lending a sad edge to their antics. They throw one another over grey and white flocks, laughing and smiling hysterically in their sorrow, unable to differentiate between the four-legged and two-legged sheep beneath them.

Tanner eddy-turns from the Commoners' Way to the King's Way, melding with the anonymous crowd, money pouch empty of coin, face full of pain. One eye swells shut, giving half of his brain a dark, solitary place in which to brood. "Will I always be the weakest of boys, the weakest of men?"

"Silk from the East," claims the burgundy-velvet-clad trader, but a spear poke between his wares yields a muffled cry of pain and a scarlet-tipped point. Uncovered from his brocaded cocoon, Van Huys, the mad thief who raided the queen's bed chamber last spring, leaving his signature silk scarf folded in the shape of a heart on her pillow. The castle guards, remembering the sting of their floggings, pull the vagabond from between the sheets. The driver is escorted to the guard house, worrying over the possible confiscation of his goods. He will soon find that the material is the least of his worries as he learns that flesh is much more precious than silk, but no less susceptible to cutting, tearing, and rending.

The Castle

Midday the quiet is terrifying, apocalyptic, think the stall-watchers. Only merchants at the market, trading amongst themselves. No customers, these having followed the musicians out of town. The merchants scheme and collude in broad daylight, preparing for the mass's eventual return. They are bold and greedy — no need to hide it while the consumers are away. Honesty among thieves.

The king sits silent on his throne, listening for some sound that might herald the return of his errant son. The queen cards wool alone, glad for the peace.

Andretto floats, Ophelia-like, on a river of nausea and hallucinations. He lets the fever carry him, far from the aches in his armpits and between his legs, the bumps that scrape raw with every toss and turn. He dreams of opulence, a room of pillowed silk where young harlequins, mere girls, caper and dance for his entertainment. The taste of salty flesh fills his mouth as he gorges himself on roast boar. On either side of a golden door stand two Cushites armed with scimitars, loyal to the death, loyal to King Andretto. He hears the tinkling of wind chimes through an open window and a strange scent wafts through.

The Cushites melt into misshapen brown blobs. Heads roll off harlequins, and their bodies decay only slightly faster than the unraveling silk of the room.

The wind chimes lose their crystalline edge, flatten into the wheezing and popping of his lungs.

The scent is a pudding of sweat, phlegm, and blood.

The Commoners' Way

The musicians weave through the joy-blinded crowd, proud of their catch. Half-drunken men and foolhardy boys abandon responsibility for the rules of the fiddle, dance-walking to the bright tents at the end of the road. Gentle-women become suddenly bawdy, their daughters staring, gape-mouthed and unsure, at their transformed mothers and the speech coming from their laughing maws. A priest warns the crowd to repent, but they laugh him to scorn.

The Carnival

Boecker's Saracene arrow is his undoing. A bald wrestler, a head and a hand shorter than the Prussian, flips the watch-sergeant onto his back by lifting the larger man's bad leg. His soldiers, each winning five month's worth of wages, are now significantly richer than their superior.

But lust presses them on and it is only a few moments before they open the curtain to the whore's tent, fumbling at their pouches.

Their ardor is quickly quenched when they look past the lips of their pouches. Their gaze, all thrice at once, meets the vacant eyes of her bubbled corpse, all studded with iridescent black pearls.

They flee back to the castle, stumbling over each other for the first opportunity to fight their way through the crowds to the protection of the keep.

The King's Way

The guards' dour faces overshadow the acrobats' fire.

"No entrance, gypsies, by order of the king. Turn back."

The acrobats' well-rehearsed smiles and over-the-top flattery are met with cold stares and the slick sound of unsheathing steel. Smiles collapse, the acrobats turn onto the Commoners' Way.

They see a nearly empty road between castle and carnival, an open strip of nothing. Smiles return and the gypsies bound away again toward the tents, tiny clouds of dust erupting from their hands and feet.

Tanner scoots past the acrobats. An old guard recognizes him, lets him through the gate house.

"Looks like you've got yourself a good knock in the eye."

The guard squints, mirroring Tanner's swollen face.

"Here's what ye do." The wizened soldier leans over and whispers into the young man's ear. A sly grin spreads from old to young, spanning two generations.

An older man, ancient, if one could see beneath his carefully-gathered cowl, slips past the old guard and the boy. He is unobtrusive, anonymous, so much so that no one notices as he slips through the customer-empty market, past the guards of the inner keep, and into the hallway leading to the council hall.

Most do not realize that the prince is wounded. They mistake the diagonal scarlet marks across his front as a heraldic symbol, bend gules, blood-red and bright. But there is no mistaking that it is, indeed, the prince, despite the dirty beggar's cloak held round his shoulders by one of the king's own bodyguards.

The prince's attendants make their presence known, carving a reckless swath through the crowd. The throng is thinning, some turned back to follow the acrobats back to the carnival, others filtering off to the countryside when they see that the guards are in no mood to tolerate unauthorized entry. Besides, some conclude, the merchants have likely gone off to the faire. The castle will soon be full of nothing but ghosts.

The Castle

The merchants, each one thinking that he has had the advantage over all the others, latch up their strong boxes, load their goods in carts or on mules, cover their stalls, and head away from the keep. They leer with impish eyes and thin, hollow smiles, congratulating their peers while mocking them in the shadowboxes of their greedy thoughts.

The king fidgets on his throne, uncomfortable and alone, save for two statuesque guards who could be asleep, for all he knows. The great hall is cold and stinks of cinders from the previous night's fire. He almost wishes he could rescind the decree that no foreign entertainers would enter the keep. Fire-eaters and acrobats would warm the walls and provide entertainment — heaven only knew where his own dwarf was. Besides, such a decision would likely have prevented the prince from succumbing to the draw of the carnival. But the signs were clear, the Black Death was spreading. And though the gypsies might bring their curse to the countryside, the keep would not be breached.

The king brings a small bouquet — posies, marigolds, roses — to his nose, driving away the foul miasma that he somehow senses has entered the castle.

Tanner, on his way home, spits into the bucket of milk outside the butcher's door. Moments later, a burly arm reaches out and pulls the bucket indoors.

A sticky puddle of humours pools on the floor next to Andretto. In a moment, the mass congeals and stands upright in the form of a tiny, misshapen man no larger than the dwarf's hand. Between a feathered beret and a brocaded doublet bulging to obesity, the homunculus's face bubbles, gurgling forth barely recognizable words.

"Anblethlo, thlee time isss neaharr."

The dwarf groans.

"Leave me." Tears sting Andretto's face, evaporating with fever before reaching his chin. The cool rivers left in their path do little to soothe the burning.

"I cannoth leeef youa, mai frendth. Not unthil thee ent." The voice turns jocund, or as jocund as the voice of a creature that perpetually drowns in its own juices can sound. "I weel bee yor combanyunn. W-hen I leef youa, youa weel no thet thee tie-mmm hass rann ot."

"Will I die then?" Andretto is sad, but resigned.

"I ham a hallooshinashun, not a proffet."

Distant laughter trickles into the room like the sound of a burbling brook far away in the distance.

The merchant is the only person in the guardroom who is not laughing.

The laughter is mirthless.

The echoes in the merchant's bruised and bloodied ears resounds with pain and his own agonized cries.

The Commoners' Way

The road is a canyon, empty save for settling dust, the muffled sounds of laughter and screaming from the guardroom, and the unrestrained peals of laughter and screaming from the carnival.

The Carnival

For all practical purposes, the keep has moved to the carnival. The most ambitious merchants have moved, with their customers, away from the un-inviting stone walls of the castle to the brightly-bedecked open arms of the tent city. Locals and foreigners mingle indiscriminately, shared drink and song and proximity melting the barriers between them. All is merriment and merriment is all at the carnival.

The King's Way

Boecker's men sprint ahead of him, an occasional coin flinging out from one of their purses to litter the King's way with wealth. The Prussian limps behind, the wound of the past, aggravated in the present, hindering his way to the future. It is futile. His men push the few remaining pedestrians (those alert enough to hear the clank of ducats on hard-pack) off the road and onto its sloped embankments. Peasants filter off to their farms in the evening sun, some holding enough coin in their hands to carry them through several poor harvests, come what may.

The prince bends his head down as the bodyguards ride their chargers beneath the portcullis. His bowing is, however, not out of respect, nor is it done to avoid the steel gate, a full six feet over his royal brow. It is purely involuntary, and it is only moments before he slides off the bloodied saddle. The rider catches him before he hits the ground and holds him above the dirt with one powerful arm. It is not long before the heir apparent is surrounded by attendees who clean his gore and staunch his wounds with whatever materials are at hand. Even the blanket around his shoulders is stripped into bandages to bind him up.

The Castle

The anonymous ancient one walks boldly into the king's hall, striding up to the throne of the brooding monarch. The guards, lulled by the silence that has covered the room since the bodyguards set out after the prince, only slowly come to an awareness that the figure approaching the king is not the queen. The king, eyes cast to the floor, does not see the figure until the old man — an assassin, for all the guards know — doffs his cowl and speaks.

His voice is warm and comforting, like dried flower petals carried softly aloft on a zephyr. His words, however, betray the soothing voice, revealing it as a mere tool, an instrument.

"His majesty does well to bury his face in flowers. Still, that will not be enough."

The king looks up, flinching as his guards seize the man less than a sword's length from the throne.

The voice continues, only slightly perturbed by the guards' rough handling.

"Pestilence has already found its way into this place. His brothers, famine, time, death, will follow soon."

He stops silent, staring, with a satisfied grin at the king as he is dragged away.

"I have delivered my message, oh lord" precedes the closing of the door.

Chilled shivers wrack Andretto's frame. He catches stuttering glimpses of the homunculus through blinking eyes. His tears feel suddenly hotter against the clammy skin of his face, a shocking temperature reversal.

Sound comes to him as if piped in through a series of tunnels, one for his breathing, one for the screams in the distance, one from a whistling tea kettle left unattended in the kitchen below, yet another for the voice of the homunculus, thinning to a whisper.

"Thee tie-mmm iss heer, my friendth."

Each tunnel suddenly blares like an army of un-tuned trumpets. His head explodes in a demon-song dirge of agony.

The guard room falls silent. Suddenly disinterested soldiers ebb from the tower, black-cowled grave diggers flow into it. The merchant has sold his final wares.

The Commoners' Way

A murder of crows descends on the deserted road to peck at crumbs and tidbits left behind by the evaporated crowds. A wild dog lopes up the ditch-side and scatters the birds. Then, losing interest, the mongrel saunters off into the country once more. The jackdaws return as soon as the dog is out of sight.

The Carnival

The crowd's energy wanes. Even the acrobats have had their fill. The party loses its savor as several attended wander home, heads in hands, though the drinking has barely begun. The musicians are spent, the dancers victims of vertigo. The celebratory mood has gone akimbo, succumbing to a subtle, yet sinister pall. Soon, the carnival is a desiccating starfish, lines of celebrants dissipating into the purple evening. From all directions, a cough, a sniffle, a groan, like the distant snapping of a small fire at the edge of a field of tall, dry grass, the sound carried on the wind of omen, an expectation.

The King's Way

Boecker hears the low mumble of the crowd from far behind him, pierced by the occasional sharp cough. As he reaches the keep's portcullis, he is struck by the odd notion that the coughing has increased in regularity and intensity, like a series of war drums inevitably leading up to the army's charge. As the gate lowers, his consciousness rises, and a realization strikes him in the heart and spine.

"Bar the gate! Let none enter, on pain of death! Bar the gate!"

The Castle

Boecker turns from the falling gate as the king's own guards rush out from the keep, hurling, like a human ballista, a roll of rags that the sergeant barely recognizes as a man. The rag doll-man tumbles through the portcullis at the last possible moment, the sharp point of the gate pinning the edge of his cloak like an angry dog. The soldiers have no time to laugh, so focused are they on shutting the double-door oaken gate behind the portcullis. A huge crossbar, three arm widths thick, is set into place on iron rungs bolted firmly into the doors.

The soldiers lean up against the gate, wiping their brows. They look at each other and laugh, relieved to have locked out the worries that plague their sergeant so.

The prince, with assistants, hobbles into the king's chamber. The king runs to his son. The queen, hearing the arrival, also runs to her son. They three embrace, unashamed tears shed before lesser nobility and servants.

"Father, mother," the young man chokes, "I am so sorry".

"No, I must apologize, my son," the king humbly declares. "I was, ah…"

The king stops short, looking down at his bosom.

The queen screams at the sight of the blood that covers the triumvirate. The bandages have not held.

Boecker steps in through the doorway, the worry on his sweating face encrusted with a certain finality. He shakes his head and begins to weep.

The remaining audience scatters like mice before torchlight.

It is night, but Andretto cannot sleep. His energy has come back to him and the homunculus has melted through his floor, down into the kitchen beneath. He gets to his feet — still a little sore in the joints, but alive and recovering — and tests his legs for a walk. They hold, and the dwarf decides to go get some fresh air.

He descends to the kitchen, where midnight cooks ply their trade in grim silence, chopping with purpose, but without hope. The servants are fretful, preparing for the morning meal as if it will be their last.

Andretto walks past the king's hall, eerily silent, even for this late hour. He then ascends a spiral staircase, up a tower to the balustrade.

He emerges into a moonless night. It is devoid of sound, save for the distant bark of a dog and the scattered caws of crows. Even the carnival in the distance is silent. He thinks that the tents may have already been taken down, but it is difficult to tell in the dark.

He breathes in the cool air and coughs a little. His chest aches, but his lungs do not burn as they did earlier. A light breeze blows, but does not elicit chills as it would have at the height of his fever. The bumps have already subsided, and though he is sore, he can feel his health seeping back into him.

"I will survive," he says out loud. His voice sounds awkward on the wind, his announcement unheard by any ears other than his own.

Somewhere near the castle someone lights a fire. Another appears a little further out, then another even further. Andretto smiles to see the little camp and cottage fires ignite like stars throughout the keep and to the countryside, to the very limits of the horizon. Around those fires, he thinks, are philosophers and laborers, whores and soldiers, kings and princes. It looks to him as if everyone in the world is connected, warming themselves, together, by their fires.

THE TOWER OF MORNING'S BONES

Hal Duncan

"Once upon a time the lands of Shuber and Hamazi, many tongued
Sumer, the great Land of princeship's divine laws, Uri, the land having
all that is appropriate, the land Martu, resting in security, the whole
universe, the people in unison, to Enlil, in one tongue gave praise."
— Enmerkar and The Lord of Aratta,
(Trans. Samuel N. Kramer)

Daybreak In The Underworld

...away astream, a babe asleep, alone by babbalong of riveron. By sumer falls and hinter springs, we finned a wolfchild in invernal wildwoods. Where?

— See, there? we say.

A marblous youth carved out in white and green of mirror-moon and veins of vines: a singer slain. Muses and furies dance around him in an Amazon of maize. The winged horse of his sylph sups at the water lapping, slapping, at his feet. Flowers and leaves form almost a blankout over him.

— What is his name? we quiz. If we could kissper it in his ear, he might arise out of the night, into the mourning.

— Away, we scoff at our others.

— A way? A- wait! He is awakening.

Opium smoke on Lethe water drifts, gold with the touch of day's first light. A wake of shifting serpents in his streams slaps up a wash of water over this narcotic drowned in hyacinths and lotus petals. Ah, he thinks in slow stir, rousen in his slumber, ah, to be an angel in the arms of others, gifting freely the communion of the cock. And now, in a wakening to sounds of rhapsody and rapture, of a piper at the gates of dawn, the songliner stirs in laze, takes in a breath of haze, and yawns. He notices the song and knows, as the sound fades, it is only an echo of a shadow, a reflection of a memory.

The wake and wash of amber and umber dreams recede with slumber, dying embers of the night's ephemera, drifting from the young man's dazing thoughts. He opens his eyes to glimmerings of dawn, and draws himself out of his dreams as he draws down the linen sheet.

His naked skin beaded with sweat, raking his fingers thru his crow-black hair, he tries in vain to hold on to the flesh of flux of what he knows he's dreamt. But, O, the song…it was a song so sweet that to remember it would cause too great a sorrow, too deep a yearning for return.

Bleary and blinking in the gloam of daybreak, the songliner rolls in bed to face his lovers, still asleep, serene — in their own forest streams of dreams perhaps. He misses the moment already, but…they say the greatest gift the god of wilderness and music ever gave to our trapped animal souls was to forget each time we hear that song in sleep.

But there are always echoes.

He slopes out from beneath the sheets and goes cold barefoot, slapping skin on wooden floor, and over warmer, rich-patterned, Prosian rug, to the window where the city waits for him to wake it, make it rise.

The Answerers For Your Sins

Elsewhere in darkness, at the foot of sheer and ragged cliffs, in rock and concrete, cracked and broken by the crashing of milkwater, scoured by swash of black basalt sand and bound, wound round by chains and wires threading through his dead flesh and woven into stone, his shattered ribcage torn by twisted steel, impaled in his eternal agony, a thief of fire rages at his binding. If he would only rest, his chains would rust away, but he must rage against his fate. Some day, he swears, some day the gods will pay. Some day.

Within the caverns of a mountain, a crippled smith hammers out the artifices of eternity in gold and steel, copper and bronze, his broken body wracked with pain with every blow. He builds himself anew, his legs of bronze, his hand of silver, eyes of mirrored chrome, steel teeth and iron heart. In the dark and fiery cave of shadows and reflections, some day soon, some day, the shell of an adamantine-armoured and articulated god will be complete. And coldly, dispassionately, he will begin to forge himself a soul. Some day.

Calloused bloody claws, the hands of a fallen king, slap stone and push. His arms strain, and his muscles, veins and sinews, stressed, stand out in sharp relief as stone. Step by step, he drags the great rock higher up the mountain, rough rubble skree under his sliding feet all scattering as he slips and struggles, throat torn by his parched and soundless scream. He will not break, he knows, even as the rock tears from his grasp and rumbles crashing to the bottom of the slope. He will not break, he knows, as he begins the task again, not knowing that it's only when he breaks that then his rage will lift the stone above his shoulders and carry it up to the gates of the eternal city itself. Some day.

Myth is a burning man of wooden soul, clay skin carved in with crimes and reckonings. Titanic, godlike and all too human, we have manufactured, in and from your myths, symbolic shabtis, men of stone and answerers for your sins. Call it Hell or Hades, Tartarus, Sheol or Kur, this modern *altjerinca* is the landscape of the damned. We have no choice in this, we bitmites of the afterworld, gifting you only what you want: order, meaning.

Outside the twilight and beyond the pale, on the other side of our distinctions, in the dark, there are no definitions, no edges, only the internal horizons of your senseless souls. There is, it seems, no forbidden realm so dark you cannot envision it as torment for the forces that you fear. We have no choice but to make that vision flesh. And yet, for all their exile from reality, these myths refuse to recognise defeat. Some day, they say. Some day.

The Time Of Dawn

The songliner lays his hand on slits of shutters on the windows, and unslants them with one smooth motion, letting light slice in, a grey glimpse of gloaming still too dull to be considered dawn. He stretches up on tiptoe, limbers arms behind his head and out far to the side. He roars another yawn. Sensing its master's motion, somewhere a system swishes on to gild the walls, the rug, the bed, the folds of sheets, the curves of sleeping lover, and the desk (where dog-eared scraps of paper with phrases of Heraclitus written on them jut out from between the pages of an old Plato's *Morphology*), to gild all this with flickerings of subtle-hued subdued light, reflected and refracted, shimmering simulations of a fire's life.

That night, he'd dreamt of fire. He had dreamt of all the spirits of the crossroads, down the ages, hoarding their legacy in the stone underfoot, in the lost songs of the river and the roads of dust that were their books. Beneath the temple of the tree, they sat in council, ancestors, judges, dynasties of deified dead. Yes. He'd dreamt of a magic lantern play of shadows on the wall of a cave — Eleusian and Elysian, illusions of elusion — and of premythean valkans of stone and metal, giants of the Raucasus and high Shimalayas, builders of mountain kurgans, asleep in vast cavernous dreamtombs, under Eastralasia and Cyberia. Even as he was waking from — and yet still walking in — his own sleep, he was dreaming that these Brahman also sleep but will a wake, that, in their sleep, they dream this world — this old, old world — a new.

Outside, in the first grey light, a forest of stone creatures rises around itself in shapes of shadow in the morning mist of cloud and fog that rolls in from the ocean out there in the inchoate. Ghosts of creatures form out of the roiling cloud: wormlike, softbodied, proto-vertebrate Pikaia of the Mid-Cambrian; Mixopterus Kjaeri, sea-scorpion of the late Silurian with the spiny cage of its front limbs; late Devonian extinctions; charcoal wraiths out of the Carboniferous. Out there, it is the dawn of time. Out there, the unawoken city sits in limbo, in the emptiness of a Mid-Permian super-continental desert, world of the trilobites with eyestacking all-round vision, and great Acadoparadoxides sacheri. Out there, it is the time of dawn, the dawn of time, as it is every morning in the city at the world's end.

Fire. He had dreamt of fire: a fierce firmament in the deep structure of the afterworld, a flux of flash in an ocean system of eddies and currents, waves and tides, splashes and ripples, the simple quarternity of colour complexified into chiaroscuro. He'd dreamt the word *anounciation*, adjected into the void, watched it refracture into a whole language of light, of elemental primes, a whole kaleidoscope, the turmoilance of seasons turning, wheeling destiny and fortune, as painted in the sworls of blue and white over a cornfield.

 The songliner shakes the last slumberings of sleep's nonsense from his head, clears his throat. It is his work to summon a more solid world with song, to sing reality into existence. The last thing that he needs is more weird words to make the world still wilder.

The Carter And The Stone

Over the sleek slate colouring of cobbles, curved smooth but still lumpen, limps the cart, rattling its bone wheels through the ruins of the city, bringing in the dead. Built not of wood but out of stone, of ossified bone, built from the great petrific trees that grow out in the wilderness of limbo in the desert outside the city, the cart is solid and moves slow, methodical, a cold-blooded lizard of a vehicle, a bone-built automaton drawn by a tame chimaera. The carter flicks the reins — *hie*

— halts at a junction, looking first left then right, then rolls on — *hie-hup* — through the dark streets.

He glances over his shoulder at the cargo of stone, of bones and dust, the rubble of abandoned paradises and infernos brought out of the derelict eternities of the illusion fields, the crumbling wastes where all those other cities of the dead have long since risen and fallen, these worlds that had seemed — to those who left their lives behind to walk the long road of the crows and cornfields — to offer Havens in the Hinter where a wanderer might find an everlasting home with other warriors of valour, other pious pilgrims, places of revelry or rapture. It seems, from the wilds the carter travels, that there has been, once far ago, for every wanderer on the road, a city made for them alone, a hall within that city and a table in that hall where sits an empty chair, at the right hand of their divinity, waiting for them alone.

Even eternities die in time, collapse under their own weight. Glass flows from multicoloured windows, pouring down to mingle with the sands that scour the edges of these afterworlds. Souls sit in never-ending feasts slipped into drunken slumbers, and the echoes of the echoes of the laughter and the song reverberate on the stone walls, and the stone tables and the stone souls and the stone gods; but eventually even those echoes die.

And so they have come, they have all come, in the end, to this one city on the edge of everything, whether as refugees or relics: as souls still...active even though in their eternities they've long forgotten their original identity; or as souls long since surrendered to a dormant state, ossified and crumbling statues of themselves, splinters of bone, handfuls of dry red dust. So the carter travels out each night into the wilderness, to scavenge the soul cities for the stone, the sand, the lime, the constituents of the cement which holds this last great city of the dead together.

The chimaera creature switches its scorpion-sting from side to side, a lick of flame, a sword of fire. Scaleshimmers golden on its copper carapace where the fiery streetlights glint, its body speaks a language of its own, the articulation of its animal nature, lithe and powerful, muscles ribbed and rippling like the flanks of a horse, the shoulders of a cat. A beast of burden, unable to decipher all the civilisation around it, and in communion only with the sound and sweat, its great horned head belowers in threat or bondage, leonine mane framing a face androgynous, ambiguous like a virgin or a viper boy. It sniffs a snort of air, trying to scent something akin to its own sylph. A snort of steam comes from its nostrils, grey vapour blown into the mist of morning, dissipating into wisps. The very air that fills the streets, the carter thinks, might be the breath of such a beast.

The Beginning Breath

And as the singer, muezzin of myths, breathes in, breathes deep the air into his lungs and holds it, holds it to begin, the city stops, held in the moment. The wisping mists, caught in a sudden current, all align like smoke drawn back towards a smoker's mouth, sucked back towards the source. If the carter and his beast were to follow the pale trail of time through the streets they'd find the mouth of it all, a shuttered window in an old sandstone tenement in the Litan Quarter where the singer stands, in contraposto crucifixion pose, his hands rested on window frames, head slightly tilted, ribcage stretched, caught in the tension between muscles intercostal and extracostal, and lowered diaphragm. Breath fills the lungs that wing the singer's heart. The city stops.

Elsewhere, elsewhen, a boy walks up onto a stage, surrounded by his family and friends, watched over by a priest, to read — to *sing* — from scripture, sing that today he is a man. He fills his lungs with air and fear, and touches a trembling finger on the script of arcane letters brought through empires and millennia, knowing that this moment in his life is shared with countless other young men.

On another stage, an actor pauses in his soliloquy, holding the moment for effect, letting his audience feel the tension, the anticipation of release.

Elsewhere, elsewhen, a priest enters the holiest of holies on the day allotted to an annual act of ritual recitation. He leaves behind him all the pomp and ceremony of the others, of his father and his brothers, as he walks alone behind the final veil to stand before the gilded chest, its solid secrets shielded by the great winged cherubim that face each other from either end. He is there to speak the secret name of God, an act forbidden but for this one moment, this one day in every year when God is to be called, the covenant remade, the world begun again. He feels the weight of his responsibility and the pride of it, in his dry mouth, in his cracked throat, and in his chest.

And as the singer sings a crystal note, beginning in wordless purity, elsewhere, elsewhen: the boy sings out the death of childhood and the birth of manhood; the priest invokes his hidden formless deity, naming it, and thereby binding it into reality, into the world, into *his* world; and another priest, elsewhere, elsewhen, opens the mouth of his dead desiccated lord and, through a curving pipe, blows breath into the dry lungs of the mummy, as the ceremony calls for, thinking of the old legend, of how the creator was himself created, how Ptah, the potter god, emerged out of the primal chaos, conceiving the great god Atum within his heart, and bringing him forth upon his tongue in the speaking of his Name.

In the back of his cart, the carter watches dust, raised in the rattling motion of wheels stumbling over cobbles, caught by the faint, distant vibration in the air, dancing.

The Architect of the Tower

The tower rises out of and over the old city's sandstone streets, an obelisk in steel and silver sheen, mirroring the sky it scrapes, yet somehow, also, in the way the first light of the morning slices off its surfaces, seeming also to imprison darkness somewhere deep inside. Behind the modernism of its glass façade, something in its structure suggests the same vision, the same voice, the same vast and ancient purpose as stands, still and solid, in all monoliths of all millennia, its inner mysteries the silent architecture of a monotheist creation. And here, in the city on the edge of time, it is a singularity within a singularity, a monad in Monopolis.

But now, here, in the moment of time's dawn, for all its still solidity a slight sound breaks the silence, a hum, a buzz. A resonance.

It is said, in the rumours that run rife among the babble of rabble in this city's streets, that the architect who designed its geometric abstractions to seem this transcendent, so very absolute, is himself still studying it. Long ago, and of his own volition, so they say, he entered into his construction and, as he wandered, following the Fibonacci constants in the volutions of the inner corridors, he ceased in a way to see himself as separate from it; now, so the story says, he's long since disappeared into its intricacies, spotted now and again across the abyss of its vast atrium, here or there, crouched on a ledge like some lost gargoyle born of it. Some say they've seen his face in stone reliefs, heard an echo of his voice in the acoustics of a hall.

This is the crux, perhaps: that his intent in its construction was that the building and what is beyond it should seem bounded by and binding each other, just as the world and the will of any creator are bound and bind. And so in his design he sought to capture the complexity of the relationship between creator and creation, describing it completely and consistently. It was only as the tower rose, however, manifest in steel and concrete, glass and plaster, light and matter, that he began to understand the resonances of its form. So, as he walked the curves of corridors, the reiterations of room, the shapes and spaces of it, tracing out its meanings with his feet, what he read in what he'd wrought was an *intension*, an internal tension, which tore the whole idea of creation as an act apart within his head, which spoke of the will and the world in a language as liquid and turbulent as the tower was solid and still. So he walks within it still, still designing it, redesigning it in his head. Sometimes, in the night, they say, when no one else is looking, walls shift and rooms realign, reflecting his schematics.

In the city of the soul, this is the tower and the tomb of change. This is the architecture of time, described in three dimensions, not just one, the four-square breadth and length of it a plan of energy and possibility, its solid shape formed of events much as the city that surrounds it — and the whole afterworld surrounding that — is formed from and forms, in turn, one great event. To some citizens it seems a symbol of power, sentinel for a system of stability of thought that generates order out of rules, imposed imperatives. From its highest window, in the heights of awareness, the lords and legislators, whoever they might be, may well be looking out over all the city, out to the deep-sweeping fields of illusion, past the known or knowable to the far horizons, to the startless, endless finity of truth.

To the carter, looking up at its dark shape before him, framed between the peeling paint on wooden doorways, soot-stained walls and rusting iron fire-escapes, and crossed, obscured, by lines of washing hung like bunting, it is only another monument to mortal vanity, waiting to fall, in time.

The Bitmite Builders

The lord architect looks out over the darkness flowing through the city streets below, over the rivers of night still running even as rose hints of dawn tint the red tiles of older areas of the city. The whole world he sees is fallen like some Babylon torn down by bitmite builders, scoured by scarab seraphim. In the thick of flowing black, he can make out the ruin, the rubble, the jut of a skyscraper impossibly angled or the bulk of a new rookery grown out of long-abandoned docklands. A motorway flyover curves elegantly into the air, spirals around itself and ends abruptly in mid-air. The work of the bitmites.

— You think they'll stop? the consul asks him.

The consul stands at the desk, tapping a finger on the leather surface of it, his drab uniform creased and sweaty. The lord architect turns to him, shakes his head, walks slowly back from the dark vision on the other side of the glass.

— No...I don't know.

— We need to know, m'sire. You have to find out what they want.

Bitmites. The blind watchmaker's clockwork toys. The lord architect has studied the fine construction of these nanite mechanisms of intension, awed by the precision timing and geared interlock of automation, the way a core command structure processes stimuli into activity, translating patterns of reception into patterns of inception. Even in innate reflex, even back in those days when the intensions that invoked their actions were not theirs but the intensions of the situation, of the need or the danger, the bitmites had seemed such intricacies as a man might spend a lifetime studying. And he has spent far longer than that. He doesn't know how long. After the first millennium, in the world remade in images of heaven and hell, of forgotten histories and imagined futures, the measuring of time no longer seemed so relevant.

By then the bitmites had begun to reconstruct humanity themselves.

They had emerged out of a covert military or medical bioscience, the recorded rumours of the old world said, as airborne and invasive artificial germs and antibodies, designed to find their way into a human host, to wreak havoc or to immunise. Or as a secret system of surveillance, chirping information across the airwaves to each other, acting on such signals in accordance with unknown agendas and unspoken protocols. For a while he had believed them to be alien technology, seeded by some cold intelligence that sought to understand the human mind by manifesting all its ancient dreams, all its desires and fears, in the world around it. In another era, he became convinced that he himself was their original creator, that by some accident he had unleashed them on the world. He preferred to think that he was only one of the first called in to study them, only the last man of his team to fall, to surrender to the dreams they offered, the last man of reason in a world of chaos.

After an eon of studying them, though, it seems that he knows less than when he first begun, and he worries at his failing memory. He sleeps by day and stays awake by night, when the bitmites are most active, most destructive and reconstructive, as if only his vigilance can keep the world from finally dissolving.

— What time is it? he asks.

The consul brings an antique fob watch from his pocket, snicks it open and looks curiously at the face, taps at it, winds it, taps again.

— M'sire...

— It doesn't matter.

Outside, lighter now with creeping daybreak, the grey and formless fog, the flowing billows of the bitmites that roll in out of the ocean, that the press once christened demon dust, flow over the world like a morning mist, dissolving silhouettes and outlines, smearing lights of windows into an ethereal glow, volcanic-golden, like dying embers seen through smoke and shadows. He wonders how much of the city outside even exists anymore.

— It's nearly dawn, he says.

A Shape Of Songlines

— Thru Triassic and Jurassic, run, sings the songliner. Run, you small bipedal theodont reptile, evolve into 200 million year old ichthyosaur; two metres of Arthropleura mammata curl around you; swim in the stone, you fossil ray, Pseuderhina alifera; spiral ammonite, your curling siphuncle partitioned by curving septa into buoyant chambers; fly, archangel Archaeopterix, in the first flash of light, progenitor of birds, progenitor of dove and crow, of harbinger of peace and thief of fire.

Fire. The light at the time of dawn, at the dawn of time, before the sun, is not the insipid glory of an aetheric archon, but the volcanic fire that paints a rock wall with the flickering solidity of lamplight. We trace out the textured clarity of the world we wake into with the precise lucidity of blue and the luxuriance of gold, for even the afterworld is basalt, burning hotter than the face of the sun and with a core of iron. Clothed in encrustations of blue-white glass waters and ice, deep-black alluvial mud, rich-red raindust of songlines, the green sheen of lush plants. Even the air, our breath, our pneuma, is not colourless but blue — the air in our lungs the very sky above our heads.

Yes, he had dreamt of the spirit that began his world, not as the shallow, pallid glow of some celestial essence, but as the rich, full flesh of fire, fire upon the deep. And he feels it in his lungs, the fire, as he sings now, the flesh becoming word, the word becoming world.

— Arise, he sings, two-million-year-old Homo habilis; walk the dreamtime of our afroaustralasian Adam, in your caverns of fire and decapitation. Come, Cro-Magnon, out of the Dordogne of painted aurochs and gazelles, you birdmen of the Paleolithic, flying in the liquid depths of heaven, animal men of Lascaux and the Tassili-n-Ajer. Carve the fat mother, widowed bride in graves and caves. And walk out of the darkness carved in fire, waking into forest dawn.

Out of the desert, streams of consciousness flow, fusing as rivers that flood the city's streets at night, merging with the chthonic ocean.

Over the grey memory of his dream and over the grey reality of the world outside, he sings out loud and long the lines that weave the world around him, music and mosaic, a shape of songlines. This modern muezzin sings from his minaret to wake the mourning city up, and as he sings, a tower of hours arises out of swamp, vines climbing shaft to glassy dome. The songliner laughs — the city's morning glory. Somewhere a weathervane cockcrows.

— Awake, sunken slumbering city in the jungle, he sings. And as he sings, the silversea of dawnsurf breaks over the city and the mist rolls back from it, this city of the secret knowledge of the alphabets, city of the builders of the book and of the three unworthy craftsmen, city of the sons of the first killer, city oust of Eden and inland of Nod.

— Awake, he sings.

The Tower Of Babble

— Hie! Hie!

The carter turns, pulls back the reins with one hand, shields his eyes with the other as sunlight strikes, shears off the mirror of the tower and flashes like a blade down into the streets, piercing the mists and picking out each mote of dust. The chimaera stops and snorts, paws at the ground. Blinking, the carter pulls the brim of his hat down to shade his eyes, gathers the reins up in both hands again and flicks the beast onward. He can hear the muezzin's song now, ringing out over the city, echoing off the walls just as the sunlight shatters off the mirror windows of the tower, and though he does not recognise the language of it, the tune is so familiar that he hums it quietly to himself as he drives on, feeling the vibration in his throat, the rhythm in his chest.

He turns a corner and the tower stands before him, closer now and overgrown in vines, down at the far end of a weed-cracked tarmac street of concrete flats, their balconies all lush with foliage, crawling ivy and cascading flowers. As he rattles down the street, the shrieks and whistles of waking birds rise and fall around the singer's song, as tumultuous and chaotic as the foliage but somehow, like the foliage, with some solid, ordered structure buried in there, buried deep but present. Under the veins of vines, the morning has a skeleton, articulated in song and stone around him.

— Hie! Hyah! He turns another corner, and the tower is there again, a shattered ruin, a jagged, broken-bottle shard cutting up into the grey-black smoke that billows from its burning hulk, flickering with red and gold flames, blue-white flashes of electric discharge like lightning lashing its frame with showers of sparks. The chimaera flings its head from side to side, flicks its tail in animal nerves, and he speaks soothingly to it, coaxes it on, turns yet another corner to —

The tower rises out of and over the old city's sandstone streets, an obelisk in steel and silver sheen, mirroring the sky it scrapes, but also — in its incompleteness, in the greys of girders and concrete columns, where the mirrors stop but the tower carries on up as a confusion of cranes and portacabins and clear plastic tarpaulins — somehow reflecting the reality of the city beneath it, of streets that even in their dilapidation have a dynamism and a grandeur, a vitality that the modernism of the finished portion of the tower hides behind its mirrors.

As the carter rides his cart into the confusion of arriving workmen, of machines chuntering into life and spewing petrol smoke into the air, of yellow hardhats and curses and the architect with the blueprints in one hand, pointing upwards with the other, and the gaffer shaking his head, and a hundred other carters, all arriving from different directions with their loads of this morning's bones, all being pointed at the dumping grounds; as the song of the distant singer echoes over itself and melds into and becomes this cacophony of daily life: the carter follows the line of the tower's walls upwards past their actual ends and on upwards to the eventual vanishing point in the blue morning sky.

Red, Gold And Green

Red, gold and green, the city stretches below. From his window in the highest room within the tower, the lord architect watches dawn wash over it, all the greys and blacks of shadows dissipating, mists burned off by morning sun. He sees the cathedrals and the mausoleums, spires and domes, parks and rookeries, docks and dumping grounds, centres of commerce and recreation, malls and stadiums, slums and skyports, office blocks and temple compounds, all the gardens and the ghettoes. Here and there are a few places that he recognises — a building that has kept its place, a street that hasn't shifted — but the main part of it is utterly transformed. Razed in evenfall and hinter's night and raised anew with daybreak, the city defies all reason, all attempts to grasp at any sort of certainty within its structure.

— You should not blame yourself, m'sire, the consul says.

He tries not to, but in these three short years since his designs were made flesh he has seen too much not to regret his actions. He remembers the man-to-man talks with the presidenti, how he'd spoken of the vast potential that these bitmites might have as agents with autonomy. He remembers the months spent studying the strains, breeding for behaviours, virtually rewriting all the wired-in prescriptions of their natures, creating a whole liquid language for them to feed on, drink and breathe as information. From automatic organs of reckoned reflex, their actions measured and meted out to them by their design, he'd watched them evolve reckoning mechanisms to get the measure of a complex context, challenge the authority of the situation and act on chances, choices. He —

— You should not blame yourself, m'sire, the consul says.

But it was he who gave them their categorical imperative — the final, over-arching rule that they could break their own rules. Without this, he was sure, all the modules of their simple sentience that he'd adopted and adapted from innate responses would have amounted to no more than a cold calculus of survival. He had given them a reckoning of doubt and certainty, a sense of fear and fury, of desire and satisfaction, so that from these fundamentals he could build in them a sort of cunning, nerve and will quite absent in the automatons they began as. That, with the engrams he had built into the language itself, should have made them the most potent combination of the autonomous and the automaton, the soldier and the slave. But the creatures seem to have evolved their own chaos of tongues, and now, in all the noise of it, in all the clamouring, the inhabitants — *and he remembers shaping them from clay with his own hands* — have made themselves a rabble, a babble, scrabbling in the dust and rubble, too much trouble —

— You should not blame yourself, m'sire, the consul says.

The lord architect turns to his consul, caught in a moment of confusion. For a second he feels, looking out over the city, as if the tower is falling, as if he is falling down into the world below, out of the clear blue of the sky and into the reds and golds and greens of the city of souls, of dust and stone and clay and bone. The sense slips away — a daydream of some sort — till all he can remember is an image of his own hands, slick with rich red ochre, clay or blood. His brows furrow, but the reverie is too insubstantial, and all he has left of it now is a rough shape, the bones of the memory without the flesh, the melody without the words.

He realises that somewhere between dawn and dusk he has forgotten his own name.

The Death of the Name

The songliner sings of a great tower that was to be built at the command of a rich and powerful merchant. Neglecting *import* and *purpose* for *significance*, the merchant saw meaning as a search for perfect forms, a quest for structure for solidity. He sought a library of definitions, a museum of rules, galleries of boundaries, a grand hall of names. So he called before him the greatest architect of the day, made him a lord, and the lord architect took on this most ambitious of commissions. He designed the building. He tried to impose an artificial frame on the dynamics of intension. Tall it was, the tallest building in the world, reaching up to heaven itself. But as the limit of the complexity of any system of thought is reached, that system must turn in upon itself, self-referentially, becoming convoluted, confused. So on the day it was to open, the tallest building in the world collapsed and fell.

An aqueduct in the streets below turns through impossible shifts of perspective, its channel twisting up and up like a staircase until, reaching its height, the water comes crashing down as a cataract, returning to the marble pool from which it pours.

The songliner sings of the delimiting of delimitation in himself, the death of the name in a sinkhole of singularity, the self as infinite zero.

— What's your name? one of his lovers had asked him. He had turned to look at them both, lain there in the bed behind him, lazing in the linen.

— Well, he had said, you know how sometimes you had something from before, but you don't have it anymore?

A shake of head, and a wry smile, then:

— You know you're crazy?

He'd laughed and nodded. Of course he is; his sense recombined in serpent swirls, the kinaesthesia of attitude that forms a feel of self remergent with his awareness of the world embedding it, how could he not be? Gifted the vibrant vision of we bitmites so he can give voice to it, he is almost one of us...almost. We are inside all of the inhabitants of this city, but only he is truly aware of this, awake. And a name seems such an insufficient token for this chaos at his heart, this involution of the snake world, forever turning in upon itself, devouring its own tail. Better a stretch, a yawn, a song, to scribe that circling line of identity as existence in the world.

The room is shaped in shimmering tracers like the hallucinations of an acid trip, like a 3D movie seen without the glasses, but there *is* system to his sense of it. An acid snake of sensual scheming, one eye red, the other green, winds round and through his virtual world, a mandala substructuring vision with wheeling lights as chariots of aliens or angels. These are the underlying patterns in the structures of sight, making possible the schizoid shifts that generate new concords, new aesthemes forged from shapes and shadows, forms and tones. Outside the sky shades from cerulean to azure to indigo, but in the skies of imagination there are no missing shades of blue.

— We're all crazy, he had said.

His song is the binding and the winding force that makes sense. An ancient power's grace and glory is palpable in every dancing sight and sound, or smell, or taste and touch, of substance and of self. The world is whorled, an intricated object of ecstatic wonder or an involuted maze of fear and fury, a mystery born in the collision of myth and history, its inhabitants more noumen than human.

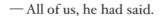

— All of us, he had said.

As notes in music, the aesthemes of his songline organise into a theme, ephemeral certainties of sight challenged by curiosity, eternal potentialities of sound imposed by doubt. In the build up and release of tension his story gathers import, gains integrity. Embedded in the whorled world, he is rapt in rhapsody, in a harmonic cohesion, meaning made for him in rhyme instead of reason.

Tension, attention, intension, contention — he has always tried to understand the full sense of a word not as a singular significance but as the sum of individual semes, of other words made from the same root morpheme. He sees them as aspects of a shattered unity, meaning as broken hologram, each fragment containing the whole implicit but with only a fraction in clear focus. This is why we chose him to sing the world.

— Your world doesn't make sense, his lover had said.

— The world is what it is, he had said, no more, no less...but what it is is subtle and mysterious.

He stands at the window now, his song of the world and of its ending almost done, his song of the new beginning just begun.

Arcadia As A Tomb

He comes out of the desert, a child of hoof and horn, a kid in lambskin, thief and liar, a hellion of rebellion accompanied only by the bitmite choir which echoes the voices of all those who've lost their names in death, of the whole history of humanity crumbled to dust. His own name is as forgotten, but he sweats and itches in a second skin of cowhide, he huddles and hungers under burnt-black borrowed wings at night, and so, for all that he is lost, he *lives*. He walks across a blank eternity, searching for anything as sentient as himself. But there are only us, we bitmites who unmade the world in our attempt to satisfy all souls, to impose an artifice of order on the anarchist metaphysics of humanity's imagination. We sought only to give humanity what it desired, not understanding it desired the end of enemies, desired a war to end all wars, the peace of death. Now there are only us, we bitmites and a few dumb beasts, chimaerae rumbling empty carts though the Hinter, guided by instinct alone. Hitching a ride far out into the sands of his dreams, he buries the bones of his own history deep in a desert dusk, and sings a lament for it, an elegy we build into a funeral pyre.

He sees then, hears; he understands the weaving of our vision and his voice. A singer of souls, unbound, reborn, his words are fire, this devil in a crow with broken wings, and we are the answerers to his solitary desire. So in the absence of all others, he begins to sing an afterworld into existence, first a brother.

The carter he has summoned with his song smiles at him from his seat beside him, nods.

He sings the road of all dust, the river and the ruins of the world he left behind. He sings a mountain city carved into the rock itself, painted in the silver of the moonlight, in the crimson of his blood, and in the grey of mist; He sings it cold and gold, its colours tainted on in deep guilt and bold strokes across hard surfaces. He sings of crows over cornfields in a turbulent sky, in the burning high heat of a storm sworling low and slow towards him. He sings of kherubim and seraphim, words whispered on a heavy air. He sings of two ravens nailed to wooden posts before a farmhouse porch and door — one Thought, one Memory. He kneels down to taste their blood, to strengthen his song with reflection and remembrance. As he rises and walks on now, in his song he carries the souls of all those he has ever known or ever will know, or will never know, carries them with him into eternity.

— Follow me, he sings, ubashtis, shuwabtis, beaked Egyptian answerers, follow me out of the Elysian Fields of toil, of scattering Eleusian grain and gatherers of illusion's seeds, follow me into the city of the empire.

Out of the billowing cornfields of the carcass and the carrion crow, out of the silversea above, he comes, this songliner, like a lost slave hunted, a stranger haunted, into the empty streets of the city of time. Souls are the stones on which this town is built. Souls are the frescoes on its walls and statues in its plazas, souls its domes and towers, balustrades and colonnades and golden books of hours. This is the eternity sought by humanity, built from its dreams, by us, Arcadia as a tomb.

Into Arcadia he comes, to be its death.

— Titans and gods, arise, he sings.

And so they do: Shamash shines on the date-palms of Inanna. Tammuz walks in Thermidor, through hanging gardens of germinal and floreal green. Even death, death is arisen, rich and red as clay, in creatures made from ash and blood, dissolved in flood, reshaped by human hands. Myth is unbound, a burning man of wooden soul, clay skin carved in with crimes and reckonings, unleashed, unloosed.

The empire falls and the republic rises once again.

The city rises round him, stones throwing off slow shackles of solidity, of eternity, for the substance of dreams, for the mortality of symbols. The tower which rises over the city, over evenfall, and over hinter, the tower of all we ever were or would have been were we not dead, resounds, stone shaking, quaking to his song. Anew, awake in the singer's song, we wind as his words around a tower reaching for the sky and falling, falling always and forever into the joys and sorrows of the hours, into the flesh of days, into the words shaped on a singer's tongue, a tower of all the bones of morning, falling always and forever into the glorious confusion of the world.

Courting the Lady Scythe

Richard Parks

Jassa son of Noban was a handsome young man of limited ambition, which was to say he had only one — to woo and to win the girl called Lady Scythe. It was a frustrating ambition, to say the very least.

It was noon on Culling Day, and the crowd along the Aversan Way was barely a crowd at all, by the standards of the city. Most citizens kept off the streets of Thornall during this time if they could. Those who didn't were either the unfortunates who had friends and relatives given to Lady Scythe or the unfortunates with business that could not be delayed or the triply unfortunate with lives so wretched they enjoyed the spectacle of any sorrow they did not share. Whatever their reasons, they made way quickly for the Watchers, the traditional Guardians of the Emperor's Justice.

Jassa sat in a niche high up on the remnants of an ancient wall along the equally ancient street. Hardly anyone remembered why the Aversan Way had been named for a purely mythical creature or why there had once been a massive wall running alongside it. Jassa didn't know, any more than he knew the tale of how Lady Scythe's family had become the hereditary Executioners of the Emperor's Pleasure in Thornall. Nor did Jassa care. All that mattered was that Lady Scythe — whose proper name, rumor had it, was Aserafel — had outlived her father to become the sole descendent of her noble house. All its rights and burdens now fell to her, and today that meant he'd get to see her.

Jassa sighed a lover's sigh, and the thought returned like a revenant in a particularly stubborn haunting. *If only I could speak to her...*

It was not possible. The only time Aserafel left her family's holdings was on Culling Day, and, by ancient decree, only representatives of the Emperor himself could approach her then. All others risked instant death. It was for her own protection, Jassa realized, but it certainly did complicate matters. As for appearing at the lady's door to present his suit, that was unthinkable.

Which is not to say Jassa didn't try it. The doorkeeper had looked Jassa up and down, made the only judgment possible, and sent him away. Now he sat and waited. Just to see her. It was all he could do.

"Make way!" shouted a Watcher, but his command wasn't really needed. The street was almost clear now. Most people left had moved off the road and now ringed the ancient common. The Watchers took up their positions at the four corners, gleaming in steel and bronze. Then came the Device, pulled by a matched team of black geldings along the Aversan Way and then into the center of the common by the monumental statue of Somna the Dreamer.

Jassa didn't have his blacksmith father's genius for iron and steel, but he had a fair eye for the practical applications of metalwork. The Device consisted of a platform raised to about shoulder height, with a smooth steel framework mounted just beneath a circular opening in the center. The mechanism itself was spring-loaded, though most of the actual working parts were hidden inside the platform itself. The mechanism was armed by a crank mounted on top of the platform near the driver. The victim placed his head within the metal frame underneath the opening and, when the mechanism was triggered, the unfortunate's neck would be at once stretched to its full length and then neatly severed at the base by a hidden blade. Painless, or at least so quick that it probably didn't matter. Not that anyone had been able to complain.

Not as clumsy as an axe nor requiring the skill of a swordsman. Consistent. Practical. The same for all who suffered the Emperor's Justice at Thornall, high or low born alike. The one thing you could say about a machine that you could say about almost nothing else — it was fair.

The condemned arrived first. Three today: two young and one old. That was two more than usual; the troubles in the coastal province at Darsa had raised the level of death across the entire Empire. All of the condemned had been stripped to their breeks, their arms bound behind them. They were paraded through the crowd by a contingent of four more Watchers, who brought them to the base of the Device and left them there, then took up their positions about the execution machine. The prisoners stood blinking in the sunlight, pale and frightened to a man, but they did not try to run. There was nowhere to go.

Jassa's breath caught in his throat. *Lady Scythe.*

She arrived riding a bone-white stallion, her one nod to tradition. Jassa was old enough to remember her father making his entrance in a costume that matched the color of his mount, bearing a scythe of polished silver and wearing a death's-head mask and a crown of thornwood. None of this for Lady Scythe. Her hair was red gold and unbound; she was dressed in a plain flowing skirt and a laced bodice. A less discerning eye could have mistaken her for a barmaid, if it wasn't for the chain of gold about her neck and the fine leather boots and gilt spurs she wore as well.

She could make her work more of a spectacle, as her father did. I wonder why she does not.

Such trappings weren't required, but, when he thought of it, Jassa could see their value. Any ruler would take heads when the need arose. Do it too often — even at need — and discontent could follow. Wrap such in enough legal form, plus a little mystery and ritual, and your subjects could almost forget that the real point of this show was to end the lives of three men. But when Lady Scythe was at work, there was no question of why the three wretches in question were present.

She drew rein on the common and said, in a clear sweet voice. "The Emperor has commanded. All will obey."

No one else spoke or made any more noise than a body must. The occasional cough, or a shifting of feet, or, here and there, muted sobs. The three condemned men turned to face her as she climbed down from her mount. A Watcher took the reins.

Aserafel's face was unreadable. She did not speak again. She walked briskly to the side of the machine and removed a small cloth that covered the trigger. A Watcher gave the command: "Set!"

The driver turned the crank until it would turn no more. Lady Scythe nodded at a Watcher and he led the first young man to the harness. The condemned man placed his head into the harness; the harness itself was mounted in such a way that the condemned looked full into the eyes of his executioner.

Will it happen?

It did, just as the mystery had occurred with all other executions he had seen his love perform. Just before she pulled the lever, Lady Scythe said something. Jassa did not hear; he could only see her lips move. He wondered if anyone did hear, except the condemned. Jassa was too far away to be sure, but he could almost swear that the man looked, well, astonished. Then Lady Scythe pulled the lever, and the man's headless torso fell on the green. The body twitched once and was still. There was a low moan from the crowd. A young girl fell into the arms of an older woman, who stared with silent grief at the dead man.

"Set!"

Again the preparation was made, again the younger man was taken first, as was the custom. Lady Scythe's whisper, and then the second man's body fell alongside the first.

"Set!"

The old man had stood perfectly still all this time, but when the Watcher came for him, he did not move. The Watcher tugged at his arm, and the old man pulled away. He stared at the machine, his eyes wild, and he would not take a step farther. The Watcher motioned to two of his comrades, and they hurried forward, grabbing the old man from either side.

"No! I'm not ready!"

Jassa shook his head. *Do not resist, Old Man. It will only mean more pain for you and might cause my lady grief.*

The old man didn't seem to consider Lady Scythe's feelings. He was still attached to life and meant to stay that way. He struggled with more and more desperation as the guards pulled him closer and closer to death. He almost broke free, and one guard raised a mailed fist over the poor man's head.

"Stop!"

The fist halted in mid-strike. Even the condemned man ceased struggling. He watched with the others as Lady Scythe walked up to him and held out her slim hand. The Watchers glanced at each other, then at her, and they let go of the old man and stepped back.

The old man looked confused. He stood unmoving for a moment, then he took her hand, and she stood on tiptoe to whisper something in his ear. He drew himself up to his full height; for a moment the years seemed to fall away, and Jassa could imagine what he must have been like once. The old man smiled then and let the girl lead him very slowly to the machine. In a moment he was in the harness, stoic and patient as a stone. In another moment he was dead.

Lady Scythe climbed the steps to the top of the machine, and the driver bowed low. She reached down and, one after another, lifted the severed heads and held them high for the crowd to see. Then all was done. She climbed down and reclaimed her mount and soon she had disappeared back down the Aversan Way with her execution machine and the Watchers following in her wake.

It was only then that the lamentations began, as the relatives and lovers and friends came to claim the bodies.

"I want what I can never have. It's foolish."

Jassa found himself wandering down the Aversan Way in the opposite direction from his love, out toward the ruins of the city walls, out toward the Weslan Gate. He was thinking, what little could be called thinking amidst the brooding, that he would take a long walk in the countryside to clear his head and his mood. It had been some time since Jassa had passed this way; he had quite forgotten about the Storytellers.

No one knew for how long the men and women who called themselves Storytellers had been meeting by the Weslan Gate. Idlers they were called by many, beggars by those who did not know them. In the late afternoon they would leave their homes and shops and forges and sit in groups on the grass by the ruined stone arch and tell stories. They did not ask for money; they did not ask for anything except time and attention. Needless to say, such were not in abundance. When listeners were scarce, as they often were, the Storytellers would form in circles and tell stories to each other.

They were not necessarily the kindest of listeners.

"Fah! You call that a tale, Lata?" An older man looked with disdain upon a young girl while the others of their circle, men and women, young and old, watched and smiled.

"I serve Somna as best I can, Tobas." The young girl spread her hands in supplication. There was a twinkle in her eye, and she showed no signs of anger.

"You serve the goddess's aspect of bringer of sleep and ease," returned the man called Tobas. "A worthy goal, but personally I prefer my listeners to be awake."

"When was the last time you *had* a listener, Tobas?" Lata asked sweetly. Laughter all around. Tobas looked outraged, but it was clear that none of them meant a word.

Liars, of a sort. Jassa started to walk by.

"I have a listener now, friends," Tobas said. He looked right at Jassa. "Hello, young man. Have a seat."

Jassa blinked. "Ah...no, thank you. I was just out for a walk."

"But you *were* listening, at least for a bit." He smiled at Jassa. "So as long as you're here, I'd like you to help me settle a difference I'm having with this talentless lot — " he indicated the circle with a wave of his hand. "They say that no one appreciates stories anymore. What say you?"

"Well...I used to," Jassa answered frankly. "It's been some time."

"And why did you stop? Too busy? Too mature? Too much involved with the day-to-day burden of living your life?"

"All of that," Jassa said. "And the fact that they were almost never true."

"They're almost *always* true," Tobas corrected. "They just may not have actually happened. But there are true stories. If you would hear a story, you would rather it be a factual one?"

"Of course."

"Then let me grant your wish. Sit down."

Maybe because he really had nothing better to do, or maybe because there was no good reason *not* to, Jassa sat down. "May I choose the story, then?" he asked. He was feeling a little mischievous himself. Tobas nodded, and Jassa went on. "I want to know how the Aversan Way got its name."

"Well then — if the story will come to me, then I will tell it," Tobas said, and Jassa just smiled. Tobas returned that smile. "What troubles you, friend? The fact that no one alive knows that particular story?" Jassa nodded, and the girl shook her head. "You're wrong. Somna does."

"And does Somna speak to the Storytellers?" Jassa asked.

"Somna speaks to all," Tobas said. "But sometimes she speaks most clearly through us. Now be silent for a moment. I must see if there is a story for this young man."

Tobas closed his eyes while the murmur of voices from his circle quieted. Jassa watched, noting that Tobas's lips were moving. *Doubtless practicing the first lie...*Jassa was ashamed of the thought from the moment it was born, for it was clear that Tobas wasn't trying on words for effect — he was praying. The other members of the circle, eyes closed, heads down, were doing the same. Jassa didn't move for several long moments from pure astonishment, and by the time it occurred to him to try and slip away, it was too late. Tobas opened his eyes.

"There is a story for you, young sir. A short one, but no less a thing for all that."

Jassa licked his lips, suddenly dry. "I would like to hear it."

Tobas nodded. "It was the dawn of the Third Age," he said, in a tone subtly different from his normal speech. "At this time, men and the Firstborn of Somna, the special ones that we call Aversa, were still sharing the world. Together one of the Firstborn and those who were our distant fathers raised the stones that were to become Thornall."

"Why?" asked Lata.

"Because the Aversa knew that harmony is pleasing to Somna," Tobas replied. "She sought to serve. Our ancestors were content to let her."

"Why?" asked an old man across the circle.

"Because men knew that the powers of the Aversa would make their work go more quickly," Tobas said. "And they sought their advantage."

Jassa could see the stony expressions of the others in the circle and knew that whatever had touched that one storyteller had grasped them all. He spoke carefully. "Why did our people hate and fear the Aversa?"

"Because one of them had more power than all of our distant fathers. Because there was nothing of them that was part of our fathers, save for Somna who created both. While Somna dreams she creates our world. The Aversa share a bit of that sleep, as well as the dream. Any one of them could remake the world, up to a point, and no one of our fathers knew what that point might be. Uncertainty breeds fear like cattle."

"What happened?"

"The walls were finished. The Temple of Somna was finished. Our distant fathers tried to slay the Aversa as soon as this was done. They failed. With a word she broke the temple and then walked out of the city, along the path still called the Aversan Way, through the Weslan gate. When she stood beneath it, the walls fell. All except the Weslan gate, where we gather to this very day."

"Where did the Aversa go?"

"To Loga's Well, at the foot the Gralat Mountains, which some call Gahan's Spine — " Tobas shook himself, and his features relaxed. The others in the circle followed him as if on cue. Perhaps it was planned that way. Jassa did not think so.

"Did I go too far?" Tobas asked the others. He seemed to have forgotten about Jassa.

"The lad's question was unforeseen and ill-timed," said the old man who had spoken before. "but, if you were not meant to speak the answer, it would not have been spoken."

"You're a fatalist, Gos," said another. "I think it was a mistake."

"It doesn't matter, it's done," Lata said.

"What's done?" Jassa demanded.

Tobas shrugged. "If you don't know, then perhaps that's for the best. Thank you for listening."

The circle broke apart. Somna's Storytellers went off alone, in ones and twos and all in silence. After a while Jassa left, too, with the rather strange feeling that, as he passed beneath the Weslan Gate, he was leaving a temple.

Jassa did not go very far in his walk outside the city walls. He soon passed through the Weslan Gate, now deserted, and made his way home. There was no one there to greet him, had not been since his father's death the month before. The smithy attached to the building was locked tight and shuttered, the forge cold. Jassa gathered what he thought he would need, and in the morning he left the city. As he passed the Weslan Gate, Jassa paused for a moment and smiled.

I need a miracle to win Lady Scythe. If there's any truth at all in what the Storytellers said, now I know where to find one.

It's not as if he had anything to lose.

The Aversa laughed until Jassa was afraid the roof of the cave would come crashing down on both of them. She finally wiped tears from her eyes and grinned at Jassa. She had a lot of teeth. Sharp, too, he thought.

"They *still* tell that story in Thornall? Such a paradox, that men's lives should be so short and their memories so long. For all that they never seem to learn much from either."

"Then it's true?" he asked.

The Aversa shrugged. "Truth is a matter of interpretation; if the Storytellers failed to mention that, I will be amazed. Did it actually happen? More or less."

Jassa had followed the storyteller's directions and walked for two days, until he came to the foothills of Gahan's Spine. He followed the only road — more of a goat-path — and came to a freshwater spring near the end of a narrow box canyon. The cave was just a little farther in.

He found the Aversa sitting on a chair of stone about ten yards from the entrance, at a place where the entrance shaft widened into a high, echoing chamber. For a creature of myth and legend she was surprisingly easy to find and to recognize. She was slim and elegant, but her hair was white, and the beautiful proportions of her face were nonetheless covered with skin almost translucent with age, marked with a fine network of lines almost as if she had been woven of spider-silk. Her eyes were larger than any human woman's, and the color of amber. She almost appeared to be waiting for him.

"It's true, then? You can reshape Somna's Dream?"

"We can make small changes in the world, if that's what you mean. Trifles. And at very high cost."

"I'm not a wealthy man, but I have some property to sell — "

The Aversa almost burst out laughing again, but she confined it to a brief chuckle, though it took obvious effort. She shook her head. "Let me show you something, Jassa of Thornall."

The world changed.

They weren't in the cave now. They stood in a perfumed garden at the base of a mountain that looked a little like the one where the Aversa made her home now. A waterfall cast rainbows into the air as it fell into a marble basin. Statues of exquisite artistry were set into niches carved in the living stone, in places Jassa remembered seeing as eroded, crumbling rock just a few minutes before. The Aversa sat done on a white stone bench and patted the seat beside her. Jassa sat down, numbly.

"How do you like my home?" the Aversa asked.

"It's lovely."

"Yes." She sighed deeply. "It's also gone."

They were back in the cave. The Aversa wasn't smiling now. "Once all my people lived like that. But there never were many of us, nor did living in peace with your kind work out very well. They'd think us greater demons than Gahan himself when the mood struck them. Use us when they could, kill us or drive us away when they could not. Until what few of us are left hang on in the empty places that no one else has found a use for."

"With your power, why did you allow this to happen?"

The Aversa smiled again ruefully. "Our power is in the Reshaping of Somna's Dream, the dream that is the world. But it is still Somna's dream, not ours. Do you know what happens when someone reshapes the dream in a way she does not like?"

Jassa shook his head, trying not to lose himself in her amber eyes. The Aversa continued. "It disturbs the Goddess's sleep. Do it often enough and brutally enough and she wakes. The world ends. Do you think the Aversa wanted to do what the Demon Gahan, with all his tricks, has so far failed to accomplish? Your folk have their place in Somna's dream or they wouldn't be here; I think ours will soon go away entirely."

"But...you are Beloved of Somna! First of all the races of the Dream!"

The Aversa looked around at the bare stone walls. "As I said — the cost is high. Only we pay it, Jassa. You do not. You choose your way, and that has its own consequences which have nothing to do with me. Now, then — do you still want me to help you?"

Jassa took a deep breath. "Yes."

"You're a fool, but I already knew that. This concerns Lady Aserafel of Thornall, yes?"

Jassa blinked. "How do you know that?"

"I can always tell when the Storytellers have been at work, and whom they've touched. Your dreams told me the rest. Call it a whim, but I will help you. What do you want?"

"If you've seen my dreams, you should already know."

The Aversa smiled again. "Clever boy. Dreams at once reveal and obscure. It's true I know what you want. Do you?"

Jassa shrugged. "I want Lady Scythe to love me. I want to have her lips on my brow. I want her to look into my eyes with such devotion that, in that instant, she is mine and only mine."

The Aversa nodded. "So I expected. Hand me that stone at your feet."

Jassa bent down and picked up a piece of dull limestone, little more than a pebble. He handed it to the Aversa, and in a moment she handed it back to him, only now it wasn't a stone. What she gave him was a small bronze medallion on a leather thong.

"Wear this," she said. "When you return to Thornall, show it to the Watcher at the gate. You will get your wish. Or..."

Jassa was already tying the cord around his neck. "Or?"

"Or you can toss it in the nearest river, or simply drop it here and now, go home, take up your father's profession or some other, and build a life for yourself without Lady Scythe. That would be my advice, if you'd asked for it."

"I can't do that. I love her."

The Aversa nodded, and she looked even older than she had before. Older, and infinitely more weary. "I know," she said.

On the long walk back to Thornall, Jassa took a little time to think. He wondered if it were really possible to do as the Aversa had advised; he would always be a poor substitute for his father at the forge. Oh, he was well-trained, and Jassa was sure he could earn a decent living at the forge, but not like his father. The man worked art with his steel; where Jassa would make a serviceable sword, Noban would create a master blade, perfect in balance and form. The same for anything Jassa had attempted; what his father had went beyond experience and practice, and Jassa knew that neither one would turn him into the smith his father was.

I could settle for less.

Only it was a lie. That was one thing Jassa could never do. Just as with Lady Scythe; there was no one to compare to her, and no point in trying. All or nothing; if there was a middle way he could never quite see it.

Jassa looked at the medallion. It was a simple disk of bronze with a carved sigil that looked like a closed eye. He dimly recognized it as one of the ancient symbols for Somna the Dreamer; beyond that it meant nothing to him. He wondered what it would mean to the Watcher.

He didn't have to wait long to find out. Jassa approached the gate and the Watcher on duty there. Jassa didn't show him the medallion; Jassa didn't have to. The Watcher glanced at it as Jassa approached, and in an instant the man's sword was at Jassa's throat.

"In the Name of the Emperor, I apprehend thee."

In a dirty, damp cell that night Jassa reached fitful sleep. The Aversa was waiting for him in his dreams.

"You betrayed me!" he shouted, though no one not on the stage of dreams heard him.

The Aversa shook her head. "I have done something, yes, but not that."

"They wouldn't even tell me what the medallion means."

"To the Watchers it means you are a man who helped lead the revolt against the Emperor in the city of Darsa. A revolt that is spreading. Now they will stop looking for that man for a while. We all serve Somna with what we have, and the Emperor's reign has been bad for all of the Dream. You aren't the man they were looking for, of course, but the Watchers believe otherwise."

"Then I'll tell them!"

She nodded. "I suppose so."

They both knew it wouldn't make any difference. "Why?" he asked, finally. "What did I do to you?"

"You asked my help," she said. "And did not understand what that meant. That understanding is coming." Then Jassa was left alone in a dream that was no more than a dream. In the morning he did not remember.

Jassa walked with three younger men along the Aversan Way; his arms bound behind his back. In time he came into the presence of Lady Scythe.

Jassa almost smiled. *At least no one can deny me this much.*

One by one the others died. Soon it was his turn. He looked right at Lady Scythe and said, "I love you."

The Watchers just stared. Lady Scythe's sweet face had a quizzical look, but she didn't say anything. Jassa drew himself to his full height and waited for the Watchers to try and force him, as they had the old man. It didn't happen. Lady Scythe stepped forward immediately and took his hand. She led him to the device.

"You don't understand," he said. "I love you."

She smiled at him. "I do understand," she said, and then Jassa was in the harness. Her smiled flirted with madness. "Of all those I have loved, you were the only one to speak first of love to me. Thank you."

Lady Scythe took her place by the lever and then Jassa saw her lips move, as they always did. Only now he was close enough to hear. Now he was close enough to see the look of joy and devotion in his Lady's eyes; the recognition that was always there when she pulled the lever and looked into the eyes of Death itself. And, at that instant, it was all for Jassa.

"I love you," she said.

Jassa wanted to laugh, but he had no time.

When the Storytellers gather at the Weslan gate, every now and then someone tells the story of how Lady Scythe took an unclaimed head lying by the statue of Somna the Dreamer and made the skull into a gilt drinking cup. They would tell of how she would smile to herself as her lips brushed its cold brow and she gazed into its empty eyes. No one really knew if this actually occurred, but like any good story it grew enough in the telling that, in time, more than one good meaning found haven in the shade of it.

Such as the version in which, a few years later with both the Empire and the need for her services in decline, Lady Scythe married the governor of the frontier province of Lyrsa and moved far away from Thornall. Her clothes, her gold, and the skull cup were all she took from the city. The execution machine fell to rot and rust beneath the statue of Somna the Dreamer who, with closed eyes, saw all.

The Bumblety's Marble

Cat Rambo

The bookstall was Doolia's shelter, her refuge. The afternoons she spent reading on the Saltmarket Building's topmost floor were more precious than anything else in her crowded existence. Which made the noisy intrusion of her three older brothers this afternoon all the more horrifying. She envisioned a life of never being able to read in Deitl Krank's shop again without fearing a sharp poke to her ribs, a frog slipped in her pocket, the sharp teasing whistle that meant "Look at Doolia," laughter following.

She glared around at them. Tow-headed Cirius and Claytus, twins, and their younger brother by a year at fourteen, Marcus. He rolled his eyes theatrically.

"You know what they say about Krank, don't you?" He leaned forward, stage whispering. "He consorts with Dark Forces — the Dead People beneath Tabat!"

Deitl Krank, a small, gnomic man with pursed lips and spectacles like moons of chilly light, cleared his throat from the two-crates-and-a-shelf counter where he sat.

"If you're not purchasing anything, I suggest moving along," he told the boys with a flap of his hand. Much to Doolia's dismay, he included her in the gesture. She would have protested, but she didn't want the boys knowing how important it was to her. That way they wouldn't look there for her again.

Resigned, she followed them down the twisty, windy stairs, past a series of little windows, each a different shape: trapezoid, triangle, arch — framing the crowds of the marketplace outside.

At the stairs' foot, in the Bumblety's stall, case after case displayed bird eggs arranged by size and adorned with paint, wax, feathers, silk flowers, or even jewels. Less ordinary eggs as well: warty green cases from swamp trolls, the flat black purses that hold skate eggs, spangled gold balls cradling embryonic faerie dragons and the clear bubbles from which sylphs hatch. On a topmost shelf, three cameleopard eggs stared down, the dark spots on them looking like cartooned eyes.

The Bumblety itself served as showcase. Its bulgy, greasy, coal black skin glittered with marbles pushed into the sticky flesh. Its eyes were two enormous glass orbs, the right a yellowy-green and the left as blue as noonday sea.

As Doolia turned the corner, Cirius and Claytus jostled, pretending to push each other into her. On the topmost shelf a white oval wavered.

Without thinking Doolia held out her hands to catch the falling egg. It filled her palms with cool smoothness, sized like an ostrich egg but speckled with rose and blue undertones like sunrise. At Marcus's exclamation, the Bumblety turned. All three boys vanished into the crowd, leaving Doolia behind.

She stood in shocked silence as the Bumblety moved to her in a waft of cedar and licorice. It took the egg with stubby fingers studded with lines of freshwater pearls, turquoise balls, and malachite rounds. She had never heard it speak.

Replacing the egg on a shelf, it held out an arm. Lines of marbles were fixed along the length. It gestured at her to pick one.

The marble emerged beneath her shaky touch as though the skin were expelling it: an inch-wide amber glass sphere, a crack in its depths like a line of light. She thrust it in her pocket, mouthing nervous thanks, unsure how to express gratitude and worried she might offend it.

She chose to turn and leave.

Exiting the building in a sunlit dazzle, she collided with another body and went sprawling with an *oof.*

Still trying to catch her breath, she scrambled to her feet to extend a hand to her obstacle. He refused it, scowling as he rose.

He was exquisite, a china doll next to her untidy length of limb, neatly pressed pants and jacket unlike her crumpled clothing. She stared at his immaculate midnight hair, conscious of her own disarray.

"Watch where you're going!" he snapped, and pushed past into the building.

Doolia glanced at the sun's position, ignoring the jostle and sway of the market goers around her. Youngest of seven children, she knew from experience that while there would be plenty of dinner left from the inn's table, it would be simple stew and bread. She liked the market fare's variety: sour-sweet thornfruit candy, steamed fish eggs in purses woven from dark seaweed fronds, roasted nuts, and smoky dried fish. Her mouth watered at the thought, and she fingered the marble. The Bumblety operated under its own laws of commerce, but perhaps the marble could be traded for a bite to eat.

She made her way to the market's northeast corner where food stalls emitted smells ranging from cinnamon to cassia root to coroco, the gritty salt that dwarves favor on venison. Sheltered between an oyster shucker and an elderly woman dispensing bundles of fragrant twigs, Annaliese was gathering up her leftover fried fish. Doolia knew that since the other teen tended her sick father, she left earlier than most vendors.

"Annaliese, Annaliese." Doolia came up beside her, eying the spratlings, thumb-long oily fish threaded on pine sticks. Three skewers left. "Will you trade me? You must be tired of fish."

"Do you have food to trade?" Annaliese said. "I don't dine on promises."

"I have this." Doolia rolled the amber ball on her palm, slanting sunlight roiling its depths. "It's so late there won't be any dinner for me..." She let a sad quaver edge her voice.

Annaliese sighed and pushed a skewer to her. "Take that, then. I can trade the other two for pasties."

Pleased with the exchange, Doolia went to sit by the harbor to eat her fish, one by one, each small chewy curl a blend of salt and piney smoke.

Returned home, she was slipping in through the Salty Turnip's back door when an alleyway shadow caught her attention. "You! What do you want?"

The boy who had bumped into her earlier stepped from the darkness. His dull-gray but well-tailored cloak blended with the shadows, making him difficult to distinguish. "I want to buy something from you."

"What?" Doolia blinked. She could imagine nothing of hers this upper-crust youth might want.

"The Bumblety gave it to you."

"Oh! The marble, you mean? I gave it away already..." She broke off as his brows knit in anger. "But we can go in the morning, it has to be very early in the morning, before sunrise, and get it back. How much did you want to pay for it?"

He unpinned a clasp, knotting the cloak's corners at his throat in its place. He held out the circle of gold and pearls, yellow flowers with shimmering white centers, set in a larger round of ironwood but closed his fingers over it when she reached forward.

"All right," Doolia said, mind awash with avarice. A pin like that would buy books from Deitl Krank's stall, sweetly musty books she would be able to read unchallenged under the quiet drone of the sunlit flies, at least a year's worth, maybe more. "Meet me here tomorrow, here in the alleyway. We'll go get it. Why do you want it, anyhow?"

"It has sentimental value," he said, his tone flat. "All right, in the morning. Don't stand me up."

She nodded and went inside.

She took one of the little bread loaves cooling by the kitchen hearth and ate it in the common room near the fire, listening to the tavern's easy chatter. She fell asleep as a bard began the many stanzas of *Caram-Sul's Doom*, and when her father shook her awake, she staggered upstairs into her bed to dream of dwarves and vast stone cities by shadowed cave light.

She rose before anyone else to fumble with the brick that held her cache, extracting it: three thin, half-moon silvers. When she arrived in the alleyway, the boy was waiting cloak-wrapped, standing well away from the stinking bin of fish guts and leavings that a crowd of gulls picked through. Two alley cats, shrouded in mange and hunger, watched the birds, tails lashing.

"What's your name?" she asked. "I'm Doolia."

"Dion," he said, voice as sullen as the gray clouds glowering overhead, heavy and low with rain promise. The cobblestones' greasy swells underfoot testified that when the sky did give way to moisture, it would be a revisitation.

Annaliese lived near the Piskie Wood, the little square of woodland surrounded by pointed iron fencing that held the enclave of piskies that sanctioned hunters brought out for the Duke's Bounty, an ancient and hallowed avocation given to war heroes and those who served Tabat well. Annaliese's father had been the former; allegedly he had vanquished countless pirates and was given the position of Piskie Hunter by the Duke himself.

Within the last few years, though, the old man had succumbed to senility. Annaliese kept him locked in the house throughout the day while at the market, but in the evenings went with him into the Piskie Wood and watched him check his snares for the winged humanoids.

Their house slumped near the entrance. Boxes furred with red blossoms cradled the curtained windows and a bustle of smoke rose from the chimney. Doolia smiled when she glimpsed it.

"She's still here cooking."

Annaliese opened the door, sleeves rolled up and aproned, surprised to see them.

"I need to buy back that marble," Doolia said.

"That marble? Why, what for? Here, come inside."

Annaliese's kitchen ceiling was low, and the room smelled overwhelmingly of fish and smoke. Doolia's eyes watered and squinted, but Dion seemed unaffected. Annaliese's father sat near the stove, wrapped in a gray blanket despite the room's sweltering heat. He watched the arched wire cage before him. In it something flapped and buzzed.

"Is that a piskie? I thought no one ever caught a living one," Doolia said.

"It was snared and hadn't killed itself trying to get loose like most of them do. It must have just gotten caught," Annaliese said. "It's a small one, just a baby."

Doolia stared into the cage. The piskie seemed fashioned from black candy-floss and leather, its translucent wings a constant blur. It stared back.

"Don't they talk?" Doolia said.

"They don't usua — "

Dion cut Annaliese off with irritated words as quick as knife slashes. "Where is the marble?"

"I gave it to my father. Papa, do you have that marble?"

The old man stared at the baby piskie, eyes glazed.

"Papa," Annaliese tried again, then went over to go through his pockets. He paid no attention.

"He must have lost it, it's not here."

"Where would he have lost it?" Doolia said.

"Perhaps when we were catching the piskie. It put up quite a struggle."

"Well then," said Doolia. "We'll try the Piskie Wood."

"Piskies are dangerous," Dion said. The other two blinked. "I mean historically they've been savage."

"Not for centuries," Annaliese said. "The city piskies are trophy piskies. The last survivors of the Piskie War, with sorceries laid upon them and their children so they will be harmless."

"So now you hunt them to re-enact that war?" Dion said. "Rather bloodthirsty, isn't it?"

Doolia shrugged. "You talk as though you're not as Tabatian as anyone else. Do we want to debate piskies or go find your marble?"

They entered the wood through a wrought iron gate. Its intricate scrollwork depicted a long-dead Duke beset by tiny flying forms.

Slender, dark-barked trees filled the wood, and layers of ferns and maidenberry covered the ground. As they walked, raindrops fell with heavy plops from the leaves along the path, and cold moisture crept up their legs, dampening their leggings. Unseen things scurried out of the way, and an oppressive feeling of eyes in the upper branches had Doolia constantly swiveling her head.

They made their way towards the center, where Annaliese had indicated the trap line started its spiral. There in the middle of the wood, trees surrounded a brief clearing.

"Odd," Dion said.

"What is?"

"Every tree in the circle is a different kind of tree. See, that one is an oak, and that's an apple."

"Annaliese said to look for the white birch tree."

"Yeah, but she didn't say anything about the trees being different."

"Why would she?"

"It just seems odd."

They bickered their way towards the birch's pale shimmer. As they reached it and she stooped to examine the snare, Dion's hand reached for her.

"Watch out! That's fresh dirt!"

But she was already falling into the pit, dragging him with her in a confusion of limbs and bruises.

When she awoke, darkness and the smell of earth pressed on her. Fiery pain constricted her wrists and ankles.

"Welcome back," Dion's voice sounded in her ear.

She was pressed up against something lumpy and cold which turned out to be Dion himself.

"How did we get here?"

"The piskies dragged us. You were unconscious and there were too many for me."

"Too many? There must have been every piskie in the wood!"

"Quite probably," he admitted.

Her nose was jammed under his chin. She paused in the darkness. "Why aren't you breathing?"

"It seemed pointless to keep up the pretense."

"What?"

"I'm one of the underdwellers."

"You're a ghoul? An undead."

"Those are two of the vulgar, mistaken terms people sometimes use, yes," he snapped.

"What are you doing here?"

"The same thing you are. Looking for my marble."

"No, I mean what's the deal with the marble?"

Silence prevailed for a time. She could hear distant water dripping, and her nose could pick out individual odors: the woody smell of tree roots and Dion's faint effluvia of myrrh and rot.

"It's my mother's heart. I thought if I put my mother's heart in something and kept it with me, she would pay more attention to me."

"That's blackmail!"

"No, no, I wasn't going to tell her I had it. Just let the magic work its unconscious effect."

"Couldn't you just tell her you want more attention? How many brothers and sisters do you have?"

"None."

She shrugged. "Try being one of seven, then you'll see no attention. But I don't understand — the marble is her heart?"

"I'd been coming up here to get books on magic," he said. "It's a transference spell. But I didn't realize the spell had worked. I left the marble in my room and she took it and brought it up to buy herself her own scrolls. Deitl does a good trade with us — he gave the marble to the Bumblety in turn."

A whisper of noise and sickly luminescence came through the darkness. It seemed blinding at first, but once her eyes had adjusted, she saw a contingent of piskies. One held a glowing, spongy mass that lit the cramped tunnel.

Two piskies cut their feet free and they staggered along, bent halfway in order to avoid scraping their heads on the ceiling, until they reached a larger chamber. Dion could stand fully here, but Doolia still stooped.

A bloated piskie sat atop a pile of fist-sized white cases. More piskies filled the cavern edges, their wings' hum a whining underscore.

"You will speak now!" the central piskie demanded. It stared at them, its eyes imperious. "You will offer to do our bidding!"

"Er, all right," Doolia said. "Perhaps we might offer to do your bidding, sir, ma'am?"

"You will retrieve our taken one, you will bring it back here!"

"Of course. And there was this marble we were looking for..."

"You will not speak!" The piskie gestured, and another at her side wobbled the marble forward on the cavern's uneven ground. "This holds a soul! It will be smashed if you do not return!"

Inwardly Doolia groaned, seeing the determined glower on Dion's face, but she nodded.

With a last glare from the piskie ruler, they were pushed along burrows, and forced to crawl out the last one on their hands and knees, emerging in a tangle of sea nettles near the gate.

Annaliese was long gone from the house. "I don't have the key!" her father shouted from inside.

"We could wait till she comes back," Doolia offered, but Dion shook his head. He placed his hands on the door's surface and whispered to it, looking strained.

"What are you doing?"

"Shut up, I need to concentrate. It's a door opening spell."

Sparks flew from his fingertips, outlining the lock. With a soft click, the door swung open, and they stepped inside.

"We need the piskie, sir," Doolia said.

The old man's eyes shifted between them and the doorway. "What will you give me for it?" he said.

"It seems as though you might like to be let out, sir," Dion said.

"We can't do that!" Doolia whispered. "Annaliese will be furious! What if he hurts himself?"

Dion said nothing, but continued looking to the old man clutching the cage.

Dion and Doolia returned to the center of the Piskie Wood, skirting the gaping pit. They knelt and set the wire cage on the ground, opened its door and backed away.

The piskie hovered by the door, as though suspicious. Then with a movement almost too quick for their eyes to follow, it was gone into the underbrush.

They looked back at the trap. The marble sat atop it.

Despite a fierce argument, Doolia insisted on escorting Dion down through the tunnels underneath the marketplace. She marked them mentally for future explorations, but finally was lost in the maze of dark twists and turns.

The further they traveled, the warmer and moister it became. Fungus covered the walls, mottled purplish growth like giant's ears and tendrils strung with pearly drops. Stars shone on the arched ceilings overhead in the form of glowworm clusters, fat-bellied and unmoving.

"Is it all like this?" she asked Dion.

"Like what?"

"Like being in a museum at midnight. Or a church."

"Oh. Yes, it's always like that." He considered. "I hadn't really noticed. It's certainly much quieter than where you live."

"Sounds wonderful," Doolia sighed.

"It's not."

"How can it not be? All the peace and quiet you could want, and money to buy books with when you like."

He shook his head again, picking his way through a forest of blue stalagmites, knobbed and coldly swollen. The splash and drip of his footsteps echoed from all sides.

As they rounded a corner, the walls of the cavern swelled outward. They stood at one end of an immense, elongated chamber, ribbed with massive drips of limestone, cradling an underground lake. A slippery path edged the cavern wall, stepping up and down and back up again as it led to a shelf-like landing on the other side, where a single light gleamed.

As they came closer, Doolia saw that the light came from a silver lantern that sat beside a high-backed stone bench. A woman wrapped in white sat there, watching the slow play of ripples on the lake's surface. Beside her on the bench, scrolls lay cluttered like attenuated leaves in the windless air.

"Who is that?" Doolia asked in a hushed whisper.

"It's my mother," Dion said. His hand stole to his pocket. He stepped along the water's edge to the woman.

She looked up as they approached. Her profile was as beautiful as a new moon riding the sky's breast, and her hair fell like a shining obsidian waterfall. Her disinterested gaze passed over them and returned to the water.

"Mother," Dion said. "This is my friend Doolia." His hand half-emerged from his pocket, fingers wrapped around the marble, but his mother's polite aloofness did not change.

The only sounds were the plink and sigh of water and Doolia's breathing. They stood in silence: Dion and Doolia watched his mother, who seemed to have forgotten them.

After an eternity, Doolia stirred, trying to ease her legs.

"Take the lefthand path each time on the way up," Dion said. "That will take you to the sewer tunnel and that ladder."

She would have said something more, would have said some word of goodbye, but the terrible fixity with which he looked at the woman, who sat motionless and unchanging, stopped Doolia's words in her throat.

Turning, she made her way home, to the crowded rooms above the Salty Turnip. Shouts of welcome greeted her there while far below, the silence lingered on and on.

PROMISES;
A TALE OF THE CITY
IMPERISHABLE

Jay Lake

Girl

She'd had a name, when she was small. All children did, even if it was just Grub or Little Jo or Sexta. But for some living on the brawling streets of the City Imperishable, names were like cloaks, to be put on and taken off. And for some, a name might be cut away like a finger crushed beneath a cartwheel, lest rot set in.

The lash cracked past Girl's ear, so close she felt the sting, though without the burn of a rising welt.

This time.

Girl held her pose splayed against the wall, dipping her chin as best she could with her face pressed against the rough stone. She waited while Sister Nurse studied her. Right now, there were five of them under Sister Nurse's care. Each of them was named Girl. Each of them was taller than the broken hinge set in the wall stub along Pyrrhea Alley. Each of them was shorter than the rusted iron post in front of the Fountain of Hope where the alley let out on Hammer Lane. That was how long they had under Sister Nurse's care, from hinge to post. It was the way of things in the Tribade.

"What's your name?" Sister Nurse asked, looking up from just below Girl's feet.

"Girl," she whispered, though a woman's voice in her head spoke another name.

"Where are you bound?"

It was the catechism, then. "From hinge to post."

"You've my count of thirty to gain the roof," Sister Nurse said.

Not the catechism after all. Girl scrambled, knowing the task to be impossible — there were at least five body lengths of wall above her, and the other Girls had been climbing quickly while she was stopped for questioning.

She came to a window at Sister Nurse's slow *eleven*. Scrambling up the side of the frame, it occurred to Girl that Sister Nurse had changed the rules. She was no longer climbing the wall, she was gaining the roof.

With no more thought than that, Girl tumbled into a dusty room. The lash cracked against the window frame but missed the soles of her bare feet. She scrambled, taking up the count in her own head, looking for stair or ladder before time ran out and she was beaten bloody for both failure and insubordination.

Never again, she told herself. Not while she drew breath.

Each of the Girls had made a scourge. The six of them, for there had been six at the time, had gone into the River Saltus to land a freshwater shark. One Girl had been bitten so badly she was taken away bloody-stumped and weeping, never to return. The rest skinned their kill, cured the strange, rough hide, and cut it into long strips for braiding. They used human shinbones, found or harvested at their own discretion — Girl had cut hers from a three-day-old corpse — for the handles. The sharkskin braids were anchored to the handles by copper windings. Those, mercifully, had been provided, though Girl supposed only because the City Imperishable lacked mines for them to descend into.

She'd wound her old name into her handle, setting gaps in the copper in the places where the letters might have fallen. It was a code known only to Girl, a secret whispered from her former self to her future self in memory of silent promises of revenge and betterment. "You are you," she'd said, a message being drawn out of her with red hot tongs by the Sisterhood.

Whenever Sister Nurse landed a blow or cut across her back, her neck, her ass, her thighs, Girl knew it was with the power of her lost name behind it.

She'd never asked the other Girls if they'd somehow done the same. Perhaps they bled in vain. She did not.

The Tribade did indeed beat her bloody before a fire that roared in an iron grate. The metal glowed like eyes in the darkness of a summer night. Skin came away in narrow red flecks while sisters shouted at her. Is this your name? Who are you? Why are you here?

"Girl," she told them, until she could no longer move her jaw. That was all she said, no matter what they asked her. She would give them no satisfaction. Instead she remembered every blow, for the future.

In time Sister Nurse cut Girl down and slung her across her neck like a haunch of meat. They trudged through moonlit streets, surrounded by beggars and whores and night soil men, none of whom lifted a face dark or pale to acknowledge Girl as she watched the world upside down through blood-dimmed eyes.

Stairs after that, stairs on stairs on stairs. They were climbing the Sudgate, the great, monstrous, empty castle which anchored the southwestern wall of the City Imperishable, brooding over the river and the poorest districts and the vine-wrapped forests that slunk away further to the south. She could tell from the scent of the dust, too — this was cold stone crumbled with age and disuse, not scattered dirt and flakes of skin and pollen borne on bright breezes from beyond the walls.

Even if Sister Nurse had remained still and silent, Girl would have known where she was. Then, and always.

On the roof — a roof, rather, for the Sudgate was ramified and ramparted like some palace of dream — the moonlight was almost violet. The heavy grease-and-shit scent of the Sudgate Districts moiled below them somewhere, miscegenating with night humors off the Saltus and whatever flowed down from Heliograph Hill and the Limerock Palace. Sister Nurse set Girl down so that they stood on a narrow ledge, looking back across the City Imperishable to the north and east as a curious, abrasive wind plucked at them both.

The great ranging complex of the Limerock Palace in the middle distance was the most obvious structure. Gilded and tiled domes of the Temple District gleamed in the moonlight. The Rugmaker's Cupola on Nannyback Hill punctuated the northern horizon, its candy-striped walls shadow-on-shadow now. Smokestacks and factories and mansions and commercial buildings stood all across the City Imperishable. This close to the summit of the Sudgate, they were as high up as all but the tallest of the buildings and hilltops.

Sister Nurse said a name. It was a familiar name, one borne by hundreds of female children in the City Imperishable. It was the name worked into the handle of her scourge. Girl said nothing, did not even blink or turn to face the half-remembered sound.

"Are you taller than the post?" Sister Nurse asked.

At that, Girl turned and looked. Her own length of leg had not grown in the last day or two.

"Are you taller than the post?"

As always, there was no hint what that might actually mean. Sister Nurse set exercises, asked questions, made demands, meted out punishments. Waking up each day was always reward enough. It meant she had a future.

It was more than some had, in the alleys and flophouses and mucky attics of her part of the city.

"Are you taller than the post?"

No question was ever asked more than thrice.

"I am taller than the City Imperishable," Girl said.

Sister Nurse smiled. "Then you are free, if you can fly away."

This was something new, something outside the boundaries of pain and promise. Girl looked down at the tiled roof sloping sharply away from the ledge beneath her feet, the angle so steep that the missing pieces were scarcely visible. It was a hundred body lengths and more to the pavement of the wallside alley.

"But I have not been given wings," she whispered.

"Then we have failed you."

It took Girl a moment to understand what had just been said. Not that *she* had failed, but that Sister Nurse, and the Tribade, had failed her.

I will not back down, she told herself. Girl spread her arms, stared at the pale moon a moment, whispered a name, and toppled forward into empty air and the broken-toothed mouth of the cobbles far below.

Little Mother

"Run it again, Little Gray Sister," urged Sister Architect.

She considered that. The baby shifted in her belly, making her heavy as a cotton bale, and just as ungainly. There had been pains in her groin, too, pushing the edge of what was permissible. She could not lose the child, but she could not lose herself either.

Little Gray Sister looked over at her partner in this effort. It was another rooftop, another evening, another Tribadist, but she was very much in mind of the night she'd been reborn. "It's not a matter of trust," she said. "Nor casting away."

"No..." Sister Architect smiled, her eyes glimmering in the pale moonlight. "Pride, I suppose. You've already made your goal." Her goal, in this case, was a scale across the rooftops from the bakery on Forth Street to the Cambists' Hall on Maldoror Street a block over, and there up the false steeple on the old Water Bureau office to make the jump across Maldoror and down to the edge of the Limerock Palace's south wall. From there, it was trivial to slip over the rampart and enter the building — the real work was in the run up and the leap, the parkour-pace practiced to deadly precision by the Gray Sisters among the Tribade. The false steeple was one of the two or three hardest runs practiced by the sisterhood.

To run the false steeple days before a baby was due was the hardest way to make the course. *No one* could scale and jump with her usual speed and precision while her belly was distended and full of sloshing life.

Little Gray Sister had, and fetched out the Third Counselor's privy seal to prove it. Not for the sake of the theft — the Tribade had their own copy of the seal, accurate right down to the wear marks along the left edge and the three nicks in the bottom petal of the rose — but for the sake of doing the thing.

Pregnant and due.

In this moment she was already minor legend. If she did what Sister Architect suggested, and she succeeded, her legend would grow.

"Vanity," said Little Gray Sister, leaning backward to ease her spine. "I have already proven all that I need to."

"Hmm." Sister Architect sounded disappointed, but did not press her case. "Perhaps you are not quite so much flash as some of the younger sisters claim you are."

Another test, she realized. But true. There were many kinds of sisters in the Tribade — red, white, blue, black, and more. Sister Architect was a blue sister, one of the professions, though her skills were mostly put to plotting and revising the rooftop runs, rather than any new construction.

Only the grays were trained to die and to kill. Only the grays were given the bluntest and sharpest weapons and trusted to use them. Only the grays were trained between hinge and post in secrecy and ignorance, that their true mettle might be known.

Only the gray sisters became Big, Bigger, or Biggest Sisters, to lead the Tribade into the uncertain future.

She smiled with pride at the thought.

Her abdomen rippled, a muscle spasm that caught Little Gray Sister by surprise. She sucked in her breath.

Sister Architect tugged at her arm. "Sister Midwife awaits within the Quiet House."

"I — " Little Gray Sister stopped cold, fighting a wave of pain so intense it roiled into nausea. She took a deep, long breath. "Yes."

Big Sister — like all Big Sisters, a gray sister — sat on the edge of Little Gray Sister's cot. Big Sister was almost a heavy woman, unusual in the Tribade, with roan hair fading to sandy gray and glinting gray eyes. "You're a mother now," she said. "Would you like to see the baby?"

Little Gray Sister had thought long and hard on that question. Her breasts ached for the child, weeping a pale bluish fluid. Her loins felt shattered. Even her blood seemed to cry out for her offspring.

Like everything, this was a test, though of late she had been her own examiner more and more. "I would, but I shan't," she told Big Sister.

Big Sister took Little Gray Sister's hand in her own, clenched it tightly. "You can, you know," she whispered.

Little Gray Sister fancied she heard a burr in Big Sister's voice, some edge of old emotion. It was possible — the Tribade were neither monsters nor ghosts, just women of a certain purpose living within the walls of the City Imperishable. "I could hold her... " She stopped again, realizing she didn't even know if she'd birthed a boychild or a girl.

A girl, she decided. The baby had been a girl. Just as she had been, once.

"I could hold her, but I do not think I could let her go."

"And would that be so bad?" The emotion in Big Sister's voice was almost naked now, a shift from control to a raw wound that might be decades old.

She held on to that hurt, knowing she must own it too, if she were ever to set things right. "Not bad, Big Sister, not if it were my ambition to take the red and care for her myself, or even train among the Sisters Nurse."

"Well." Big Sister's voice was controlled once more. "Will you take the hardest way, then?"

That was the other choice. The Tribade had many sisters of the brown, the street toughs and money bosses. They shook down good merchants and shook down bad merchants far more, kept rival gangs in line, maintained some semblance of order in streets and districts where bailiffs were rarely seen. Those women were the most public of the hidden faces of the Tribade, and they did most of the public work.

Little Gray Sister could run rooftops, tackle criminals and watch over her city for the rest of her life as a brown sister. But the only path to becoming a Big Sister, a Bigger Sister or even — and especially — the Biggest Sister, was to take the hardest way.

She cupped her leaking breasts in her hand, regretting the feeling of both tenderness and joy. There had been a man at them once, too, for a few hours, the night she'd gotten with child amid tearing pain and weeping and a strange, shivering joy. She still wondered who he was sometimes, but at least he'd been kind.

"I am ready."

"I'll send for the fire and the knife."

"The ink, too, please," Little Gray Sister said. "I'd prefer to have it all at once."

An expression flickered across Big Sister's face — unreadable, save for context. Most women waited for the healing before they took the ink. Tattooing the Soul's Walk across the flat, puckered scars on a Big Sister's chest was one of the greatest rites of the Tribade. It was also one of the most painful, for the poppy given for the fire and the knife was not given for the ink.

Little Gray Sister would do it most painfully, cutting away her womanhood in the first blush of mothering to join the ranks of the sisters who protected their world.

Still, she was surprised they had the brazier ready, and the long knife, and there was even no wait at all for Sister Inker.

Someone had known. Perhaps all of them had known. Just like they'd known to be standing on the rooftop just below, the night she'd jumped into the violet moonlight.

Even though it was the Quiet House, her shrieks set dogs barking three streets away. It was the only time in her life Little Gray Sister screamed.

Big Sister

She looked at the long, narrow velvet bag Biggest Sister handed her. The two of them were in a rooftop cafe in the Metal Districts, a place where women in gray leather with close-cropped hair received no special scrutiny. There was an electrick lamp on the table which buzzed and crackled, shedding pallid light against the evening's gloom. The wind was cool, bearing mists and distant groaning booms off the River Saltus.

"You know there is one more test," Biggest Sister said. The woman was compact, a walking muscle more reminiscent of a bull terrier than the fine ladies of Heliograph Hill.

"There is always one more test." Big Sister shrugged. Even now, a year and a moon after, her chest ached whenever it was chill, or if she moved certain ways. Sometimes she awoke with the pain of her breasts still full of milk, and for that brief muzzy instant between sleep and alertness treasured the feeling, false though it was. *Never again* kept slipping into the future. "Life is one more test," she added.

"Yes, yes, that's what we tell the girls. It makes nice philosophy for them to whisper over after lights-out. But really, life is for living. After this, only you will set yourself to more."

"Have you ever stopped setting tests for yourself?" she asked Biggest Sister.

"No." Biggest Sister smiled. "But my Sister Nurse always did say I was a fool and a dreamer."

Big Sister held the bag. She already knew what was in it, just by the feel — her old sharkskin scourge. With her old name coiled in copper round the handle.

"There've been three sisters take the hardest way these past two years," said Biggest Sister. She folded her hands around a cup of kava, but did not lift it to her lips. "In that same time, four Big Sisters have gone to rest beneath the stones, and one has taken the blue in deference to her age." The cup twirled slowly in her hand. "I am sure you have studied arithmetic."

"Yes," said Big Sister. "I can count."

"We are not dying away, far from it." Another twirl. "We are at some danger of losing the edge of our blade, becoming in time nothing more than an order of monials ministering to the poor and the victims of the state."

"And if we did not run bawd houses and guard the dark pleasure rooms and take money from the cash boxes of the petty merchants?"

Biggest Sister sipped this time before answering. "We *protect*, and we aid. That is not the same thing as bettering. If we did not do these things, someone else would. Someone else always will. Someone male, who does not care for women, who will not trim the balls off those men who prey on children and break the pelvises of whores. Someone who will simply count the money and throw a few more bodies to the sharks. And they would not give hospice or teach beggar children to read or make sure the potshops have meat in the soup kettles."

They would not beat bloody the girls growing between hinge and post, either, Big Sister thought, but she kept her words within. As she had always known, there was a sad wisdom to everything the Tribade did.

"There is...more," Biggest Sister said. "You have not reached this lore yet, but believe me, there is more. Much sleeps beneath stones and behind walls in this City Imperishable that is not seen in daylight. And for good reason. Along with others, we guard those secrets. Only the Big Sisters, though. And you must past this final test before your title is more than honor."

Big Sister drew the sharkskin scourge from its bag. Though it loomed huge in her memories, the thing seemed small in her hand. A toy, almost. She'd wielded worse straining at pleasure with some of the other sisters who had a taste for the rough trade.

But never used such a thing on a child.

"This," Big Sister began, then stopped. She took a deep breath. Her hand shook as it held the scourge. "This is what is wrong with us."

"No." There was an infinite, awful gentleness in Biggest Sister's voice. "That is what is wrong with the world, that we must raise some of our Girls so in order to be strong enough to stand against it."

They were quiet a moment as a waiter passed with a basket of hot rolls, spiced with cardamom and sea salt. He didn't see the scourge lying in Big Sister's hand, and he never would. It was why some among the Tribade met here to talk from time to time.

"Hear me now: there is a greater wrong to come," said Biggest Sister. "This last test. A distillation of our way. You must give life before you can take it. This you have done. Now you must take life before you can have power over the life and death of others. You must kill for the City Imperishable, for the Tribade, for yourself."

"With this?" Big Sister asked. "It would be a sad and messy business."

"With that. So you come full circle, releasing the last of your name." Biggest Sister put down her mug. "If you do not do this thing, you will still be a Big Sister. In other times you would have remained a Gray Sister, but our need is too great. But you will never rise to Bigger or Biggest Sister, and you will never see the inner secrets that we guard. And you will never wield the blade against someone's neck, either in your hand or by your word." She stood. "Come to me when the thing is done. Tonight, or half a lifetime from now, come to me."

"What thing? Who am I to kill?" Big Sister hated the fear that trembled in her tones.

"The child who you would have been," said Biggest Sister. Her voice was distant as the unknown sea. "Bring me the head of a girl-child, that you have killed yourself, and you are done with tests forever. Beggar or daughter of a Syndic's house, it makes no matter to me."

She was gone then, her cup shivering slightly on the tabletop.

Big Sister walked to the edge of the rooftop, where a wrought iron railing worked in.a pattern of roses and snakes marked the drop. She stood there, watching a pair of heavy horses draw a scrap cart quietly through the late streets. The moon was slim this night, but still it washed the streets in a purpled silver.

There were a hundred thousand people in the City Imperishable, she thought. A third of them must be children. Half of those would be girls. Would a hive miss a single bee? Would a tree miss a single apple?

Her breasts ached, and she thought she felt milk flowing across the spiral tattooed scars as she wept in the moonlight. There was no way to stop this save to become what she hated most, no way to keep promises made to herself in the earliest days save to break them with blood.

It was not what was wrong the Tribade, it was what was wrong with the world.

Slowly she picked at the copper windings on the haft of the scourge. The name of that young girl smaller than the post dropped away as flashings into the street below, where beggars swept daily for the scrap. She picked until she'd forgotten forever the name, and with it the promises, and there were no more tears in her eyes to follow the copper down.

Big Sister dropped over the railing to a three-point landing on the cobbles. If she was going to hunt a girl, the child would be taken from the highest, greatest houses in the City Imperishable. No mere beggar was going to die for her.

And then, never again, she promised herself. Big Sister ignored the hollow echo she could hear ringing from the future.

GHOST MARKET

Greg van Eekhout

e's five years old, and the blades of his skates rasp the ice. He thought there'd be more falling down involved, but skating turns out to be easier than he thought.

Now he's nine. The ball rips through the net. He catches the rebound and shoots again. Rip, rebound, shoot again.

Fourteen. He makes little piles of blue eraser debris while the clock ticks away. Still twenty questions to go.

Seventeen. The seatbelt buckle presses into the small of his back as the boy leans over him, even more nervous than he is.

He's nineteen. Rip. Rebound. Shoot again.

And twenty-two. The last age he'll ever be. The park got dark early, but no problem. He knows this trail, and it's good to be alone with his thoughts.

There's a sound behind him. Are those footsteps?

Every third Tuesday of the month, they hold the ghost market beneath the Washington Street Bridge. You have to get there early if you want the best bargains, before the sun has a chance to warm the day.

"Hey, you wanna be a red-hot lover boy?"

I shrug. "Who doesn't?"

Behind a folding table, in a stall built of PVC pipe and crinkled blue tarp, she's shaped like a Willendorf Venus in a Che Guevara T-shirt. "Some people are scared to be red-hot lover boys," she says, showing me an apparently empty beer bottle sealed with wax. "I knew this one personally. He was my neighbor. He fathered seventeen kids. Energetic, you know?" She winks. "He was in the act when his heart exploded."

"How romantic," I say, taking the bottle and holding it up to the gray-lilac sky. There's nothing to see inside. "But that doesn't sound like red-hot lover boy to me. It's more like horny-old-man-who-wouldn't-give-his-wives-a-break boy."

She snatches the bottle back from me. "You're free to shop elsewhere."

I think of continuing this stimulating bit of dickering but then, "Dead end," says a voice in my ear.

I tug down my wool cap and move on.

There's a part of the market that's not really an official part of the market. You have to go further under the bridge where, if you look up, you'll see a green-black mess of struts and supports, like a giant spider's web. The sound of traffic rumbling over the deck mixes with the rush of the river, and it's like the roar of blood when you cover your ears. Go this far and you'll find a space sectioned off with a chain-link fence. There's a gate with a lock, but the lock doesn't work, and if you know that you can go right in.

Good bargaining can be done here.

Some of the dealers are cooking their breakfasts over lit trashcans, and the air smells of garlic and cabbage and fish. There's the high-pitched tinkling of a string instrument, the tapping of a drum.

I walk up to a man sitting on a Coleman ice chest. He's old, child-sized, his face worn and shiny like an over-polished shoe. He smiles his clean dentures at me. "I got a gun," he says, and his hands fidget inside the pockets of his jacket.

"Um." I take a step backwards. "Okay."

"We can deal," he says, "but get funny and I blow a hole in your chest." With one curt, matter-of-fact nod, he takes a swig from a can of Dr. Pepper.

"Maybe I'll try someone else," I say.

He takes his hand out of his pocket, and I flinch. But the hand is empty. He waves it at me dismissively. "Go ahead," he says. "They got nothing. Just nursing-home stuff. All old shit. Rip-offs."

It's a common fallacy that young and fresh is better than aged. People are paying ridiculous prices for expired infants and children, and there's even a ring on the east side that gets tips from the doctors of terminally ill kids. It's crazy. It's like Dutch tulips.

"I didn't just fall off the turnip truck," I tell the little man. "I can recognize value when I see it."

He looks me over thoroughly, like a tailor assessing the drape of a suit. "Huh," he says. "Well. What're you looking for, then?"

Some people will inhale only ghosts who died in terror. Others are interested only in little girls, or in executed convicts, or in fragile women with jittery, prescription-drugged spirits. So many kinks.

"You read the newspaper?" I say. "You hear what happened to that boy in Dump Hill?"

The expression on the old man's face doesn't change. He shrugs a little.

I go on: "They say they tortured him. Marks on his wrists, cigarette burns, the whole treatment. The bottles must have been singing here." Ghosts grow excited when they know they're about to be joined by another of their kind. Ghosts call to their own. "You get in on any of that?"

Murder victims. Indulging in this particular kink is illegal. They'll put you away for ten, fifteen years.

"Don't know what you're talking about," the man says.

I stare at him. It's amazing how long he can go without blinking.

"Really? You don't have a piece of him? Well, okay. I'm sure somebody here does." I show him the corner of a rubber-banded wad of hundreds. It's an inch thick.

And, ah, there it is. The tiny little flicker of his eyes. He glances over my shoulder.

"I don't like the look of you," he says.

The hundreds go back into my pocket. "Whatever. Enjoy your Dr. Pepper." I get a full twelve yards away before he calls out to me.

"Wait."

I pause. Turn. "Snooze, you lose. I'll deal with somebody else." But I walk back over to him.

A hint of a smile touches his beet-colored lips. "There is nobody else. I got him closest to the moment."

Closest to the moment.

He means he got the boy closest to the moment of death.

I spend a few moments nervously reassessing my surroundings, checking to see if anyone's watching. Huddled figures move in the dim morning light of the market. The string instrument plink-plinks away, and the drums do an impatient toe-tap.

I give him a nod and he produces an apple juice bottle capped with a strip of duct tape.

This part is necessary. The bottle's contents are invisible, and no buyer would part with his hard-earned cash without a sniff. And I have to make sure it's genuine stuff for reasons of my own.

The man tears off a strip of tape from a roll and sets the bottle down on his ice chest. I crouch down and lean forward. Everything happens quickly, now. He pokes the bottle's seal with a sewing needle, and I get a whiff, and then the strip of new tape goes over the bottle.

He's two, and the grass tickles his feet.

He's fourteen. Cigarette smoke burns the back of his throat, but he proudly suppresses the cough.

He slides his hand under her shirt, thinking of someone else. The opening chords of the song say everything about him worth knowing.

Rip, rebound, shoot again. Three. A Birthday card. Fifteen. The bitter first taste of beer. Running, laughing across the finish line. Footsteps and pain.

"Eight-hundred," the old man says.

I give him the money and take possession of the bottle.

Very clearly, so there's no possibility of being misheard, I say the prearranged words: "That's good stuff."

And the voice in my ear says, "Take him."

The tinkling string instrument falls silent. The drum beats stop. Hats are thrown off, shawls discarded, and a surge of blue windbreakers descends on the old man.

The honor of handcuffing him is mine.

And long after, when I'm in the office banging out my report on my coffee-stained keyboard, the boy is still with me. He rises in my head, not just his death-moment — the bright, acidic terror, the sorrow of knowing that the only end to his torment is the end of everything — all that is just the sharp edge.

But what cuts deep is his life. The thousands of small moments. The diary moments, the formless events, the pinings and hungers and little victories — all of it. I live every second of it. I am him. All the sweet and bitter richness of his life.

I have been on the task force for six years.

I have tasted many ghosts.

They never go away. I am their vessel, and I will carry them for the rest of my life.

Everyday, my street value increases.

When I come to die — take a bullet in the face, jump off a bridge, do a morphine fade-out in a hospital bed — someone's going to have a good business day.

Sammarynda Deep

Cat Sparks

T he woman nestled amongst the cushions would have been considered beautiful had her right eye not been torn from its socket. The scarring was brutal, hideous. From the moment Mariyam entered the bar, she had been drawn to the scarred woman and her entourage. As fate would have it, the man she had hoped to meet at the Starfish that afternoon was one of the scarred woman's friends.

"Haptet, at your service," he said, smiling and pressing his lips to the back of her hand.

"My name is Mariyam," she replied. "Behameed said I was to seek you out. He promised you would be my guide, should I ever find myself in Sammarynda."

Haptet's eyes widened. "Behameed! The old dog. He is like a brother to me. Please join my friends, let me buy you a drink." Haptet could not wipe the smile from his face. "Behameed! It's been years. Is he here with you? I've not seen him on the peninsula for a decade at least."

Mariyam settled herself amongst the cushions and smiled. News, it seemed, did not travel quickly in these parts. The old trawler captain Behameed had been dead five years, but he had said she could always use his name, and that it was as good as currency along the peninsula. About that, at least, he had not lied.

Alcohol pulsed warm currents through her veins as she surveyed the room while listening to Haptet tell stories of his troubled youth, spent crewing on Behameed's yacht back before the war. Mariyam laughed along with the rest of them — and some of her laughter was genuine. This was not the Behameed she had known. This one seemed like a reckless idiot rather than a hero of Maratista Plain.

The décor of the Starfish echoed its name. Five-pronged motifs, both painted and woven, covered the walls. Above the tables stretched a fishing net laden with desiccated creatures, each one tinted in pastel shades.

Mariyam tried not to stare at the woman with the missing eye, whose name she now knew was Jahira. A difficult task. She was, simultaneously, beautiful and hideous. She'd be used to the whispers and stares; the pity in the faces of strangers, Mariyam thought. She turned her attention to the others: handsome, well-groomed men and women whose names she would not need to remember. She noted their familiarity; the brushing of skin against skin, the way they leaned in on each other when they spoke. So much intimacy. She felt a sudden swell of emotion. Her eyes moistened, but she fought the feelings down. These were not her people. This was not her home.

"Tourists everywhere!" exclaimed Haptet suddenly as he dragged on his water pipe, causing the coals to flare. Both Jahira and Mariyam watched the smoke dance in the glass chamber as he exhaled. He gestured to a group seated at the far end of the room. "They come only for the jousting season to fill their pockets with baubles and poke their noses where they don't belong."

"But surely you welcome the money *we* tourists bring," said Mariyam, casually feigning hurt as she waved for the waiter's attention. "You may have been born here, but you were educated inland, same as me, Haptet. Same as me. Your accent betrays you. Perhaps there's more similarity between us than you'd like to admit?"

A young boy in a white linen smock approached, proffering a drink on a tray. Mariyam took it as the coin Haptet tossed spun and clattered on the shiny metal plate.

"You have caught me out," said Haptet, winking at her slyly, "And now you must tell us — which of the grand inland cities are you from?"

"I was born in Makasa," said Mariyam. "I'll bet you that boy is destined for Allamah University, or any one of a dozen others in the ancient city."

"Perhaps," said Haptet, "or perhaps not. Sammarynda is a port of many choices. If the boy wants to go to Allamah, his father will find a way. But few of our people settle permanently in other cities — did you know that?"

Mariyam didn't, but then there was much she did not know about Sammarynda and its inhabitants. How easily these people had accepted her amongst their number. Haptet was right. She was a tourist, and not a very well-researched one. She had come to Sammarynda to put an end to her nightmares. When she'd left home, nothing else had mattered.

"Why have you come to Sammarynda?" Haptet asked. "What is it you are seeking?"

"Something different," she replied after a considered pause. "Isn't that what all travellers seek?" She looked to Haptet as she spoke, but he had become distracted by another man seated at a table near the door. An Inland trader, a Bedouin, dressed in thick desert robes.

As she watched the men talk, Mariyam realised that Jahira was watching her, staring intently with her one clear eye. Mariyam sipped her drink, a reflex action. Where to look? The damage to the woman's face was so visible, so obvious. Why did she not wear a patch or a veil? Mariyam longed for Haptet to rescue her, but he had become deeply absorbed in conversation with the desert man, so much so that the mouthpiece of his water pipe rested idle between his palms. When she looked again, Jahira was staring right back at her. Mariyam smiled, a feeble gesture laden with unintentional condescension and sorrow, then she looked away too quickly. Damn, she thought, but I couldn't help myself. She studied the patterned fabrics of her companions' garments, waiting for the tide of conversations to envelop her once more.

A soft hand pressed upon her shoulder. Mariyam looked up at Jahira's ruined face as she positioned herself to nestle beside Mariyam on the cushions. Up close, the wound was infinitely worse that it had appeared from a distance.

"Please," Jahira said, "let me explain."

Mariyam stared into the empty socket, and then into Jahira's whole eye, which shone as clear and bright as sapphire. Only then did Mariyam notice the heavy makeup the woman wore to enhance the beauty of the one eye she possessed. Her lips were painted, her cheeks rouged, her eyelid rimmed with ebony kohl and dusted with fine gold powder.

Mariyam drained the last of her honey vodka.

"You are Haptet's friend?" Jahira asked.

Mariyam nodded, wondering immediately who this woman was to him. A lover? Surely not. A sister, perhaps?

"My missing eye," Jahira said, gesturing to the mass of pink scar tissue, "It is my honour."

"Your what?"

Her lips parted as she prepared to explain, but her words were drowned out by a commotion amongst the camels hobbled together a few feet outside the doorway. Men shouted to each other across the low tables and brightly coloured cushions. Mariyam watched Haptet as he watched the Interior men leap up and tend to their disgruntled beasts with the same amount of caring and focus that they would expend upon an injured child.

"We do not speak of these things amongst strangers," Haptet remarked later as he and Mariyam strolled along the bank of an artificially constructed lake. Both moons were out, and the constellation of Kashah the Dog-Headed Warrior sat directly overhead. Mariyam gazed up at it, as if trying to determine its shape and meaning. Haptet studied her face in turn.

"Jahira said her ruined eye was her honour but I don't know what that means," said Mariyam.

Haptet nodded. "Sammaryndan honour is a private matter. Not something we would usually explain to tourists. But as you are a friend of Behameed's..." He looked upwards at Kashah for inspiration. "When one attains true adulthood in Sammarynda, one must render upon oneself an honour. It may be small thing or a great thing. The choice is entirely one's own."

Haptet stopped walking. He grabbed the fabric at the base of his shirt and pulled it over his head, turning to reveal the naked flesh of his back. A thick scar snaked from his left shoulder blade almost all the way to the base of his spine.

Mariyam stared. "From the war?"

"No," said Haptet, releasing the fabric and turning back to face her. "That scar is my honour. When my time came I asked two friends to hold me down and a third to wield the scythe."

The light of the moons cast a pearly luminescence on her skin. Mariyam frowned. "You *chose* to be scarred? Surely you can't be serious?" And then the truth of his words hit home. Jahira's eye. Mariyam gasped, bringing her fingers to her lips.

"I don't expect you to comprehend our ways," he said, gesturing to the path ahead. "For some, honour may be a scar. For others, it may be a sacrifice. Giving up something of great value. Do not waste your pity on Jahira — she is in no need of it. You may find her honour hideous, but I assure you, the people of this city do not."

They continued their stroll along the lake in silence, enjoying the ambience of the night.

"Mariyam, why have you come to Sammarynda?" Haptet asked suddenly. "Is it for the water jousting? The season is just beginning, but you seem so incurious about it. So distracted."

Mariyam looked up at Kashah again, as if seeing the face of the dog clearly for the first time. "Yes," she said, "the jousting. I have come to watch the men fight."

Haptet could hear the half truth in her words.

"There is an island to the north where the women weave the most exquisite cloth. You must buy some to take home with you — it is unlike anything else, I promise."

Mariyam nodded, allowing Jahira to guide her through the morning markets. They did not hurry. No one hurried in this part of the world. The Sammaryndans made time for the little things. They were keen listeners, astute observers. Details were valuable: the difference between living and merely existing.

Now Mariyam could see the Sammaryndan's honour everywhere. Scars were popular, although few were as brutal or as visible as Jahira's. She had learned that the peninsula sported a whole caste of medical practitioners whose only work was to inflict damage on healthy individuals as they entered adulthood.

Mariyam picked up a length of cloth and twisted it in her hands. The silver fibres woven within shimmered in the light.

"I have always wanted to visit Makasa," said Jahira as she reached for another bolt of fabric, shooing away the saleswoman with a flick of her hand. "Was that where you became friends with Haptet? In Makasa?"

Mariyam feigned distraction as she scanned the crowd in search of a particular familiar face. A futile exercise, she knew. The man she sought would not be strolling through a marketplace like this. *He* would be preparing himself for the evening's festivities; practicing his balance or his swordsmanship if, indeed, he was here at all. *I should have made this journey ten years ago. Even if I find him now, it's too late.*

Mariyam observed a man with a limp, a girl with a cleft lip, another so thin that her clothes hung off her bony frame like rags. How could she not have noticed all of this when she had first arrived?

"Perhaps there is something else you would like to see?" Jahira had noticed Mariyam's gaze wandering away from the embroidered cloth on the table. "Leatherwork? Jewellery? I'll take you to the silversmith quarter if you think you can stand the noise."

Mariyam smiled. "I'm happy to wander through the market."

Jahira nodded. "Then let us walk this way. I have some purchases to make."

Mariyam felt sunlight on her skin as the two women pushed their way through the throng of shoppers and hawkers, tourists and tradespeople. Now and then she was shoved or jostled by the compact, hurtling forms of children absorbed in their games of catching and chasing, refusing to let the thickness of the crowd slow them down. The sharp tang of unfamiliar aromas assailed her. Spice sellers crouched in doorways beside woven baskets deep with the many-hued ochres of their wares.

Images from the ocean touched everything: fish carven into doorways, serpents embroidered onto coats, shells painted with precious metals, looped onto gold and silver chains to rest on slender necks.

Most fascinating of all were the apothecaries, their windows festooned with the twisted forms of desiccated creatures, the origins of which Mariyam could only guess at. Some seemed monstrous amalgamations of fang and bone. Surely such unnatural fusions could not occur in nature? Mariyam placed one hand upon Jahira's shoulder, gesturing with the other at a malformed shape dangling from red string beside a net of dried frogs.

Jahira shrugged. "It is from the Sammarynda Deep. Some of the curiosities thrown up from the crevasse have medicinal properties. Others are fierce poison. Many apothecarists make their living solely from determining which is which."

Mariyam longed to step through the cool darkness of the doorway, to be enveloped by the multi-fanged strangeness within, but Jahira had moved on already, keen to get to the fresh produce section before all the best choices were gone.

With her mind filled with images of scissor teeth and warped bone, Mariyam turned a corner and saw a group of black-shrouded women squatting in the shade of a crooked awning, their wares spread before them on a square of faded cloth. Jahira had gone ahead with her basket. Mariyam glimpsed her through the archway that led to row after row of laden fruit barrows.

The squatting women ignored her until she crouched down before them and pointed a slender finger at the row of glass vials lined up along the cloth. The vials held a substance that glittered and shimmered even in the shade.

"What are these?" she asked.

The women eyed her coldly, not bothering to mask their contempt. Mariyam asked again, this time in Barter using the accompanying hand signs. Reluctantly the nearest of the women answered, but the words she uttered made no sense. A name, probably, in a local dialect. Something with no equivalence in any other tongue, certainly not Mariyam's.

Gently she lifted a vial from the cloth and held it up against the light. Inside the glass, colours shimmied and swirled. Whatever it was, it was beautiful.

A shadow fell across Mariyam's face.

"Tourist junk," said Jahira, looking down on the old women with an air of annoyance. "Let me take you to the artisan quarter if it's trinkets that you want."

Mariyam rose, brushing the sand from her skirt. "But what's inside the vial?"

Jahira paused. "Shavings from Glass Rock. These ancient whores are too old to sell themselves, so they thieve a little of our long-abandoned cultural heritage and peddle that instead."

One of the women said something to Jahira. She snapped back a reply in the same tongue. "What they're selling is illegal. I should report them to the Harbourmaster."

"No — don't do that," said Mariyam. She closed her fingers around the vial and dipped into her purse for a coin. "Is this enough?"

"More than enough," said Jahira. "You shouldn't encourage them."

Mariyam threw the coin down on the cloth, and the faces of all three women erupted into cheery smiles.

"That is more than they usually see in a week, but no matter. Let me take you somewhere you can waste your money on high quality merchandise."

That evening back in the Starfish, Mariyam sat with Jahira, Haptet and their friends gazing out across the ocean, watching the reflections of the two moons, Neme and Kryl, spill ripples of gold across the water.

Mariyam touched the vial in her pocket, rolling the smooth glass beneath her fingertips.

"So," said Haptet, lifting the wine pitcher, "Tomorrow the jousting begins. Have you chosen a champion? Have you placed a bet?"

Mariyam shook her head. "Such a strange ritual. What is it for? Why do the men fight each other?"

Beside her sat Jahira, and next to her another man she did not recognise. The left side of his face was stained with an intricate pattern that ran all the way down his neck to vanish amongst the dark hairs beneath his shirt. His honour or his art, she wondered. Was there any difference between the two?

Jahira leaned against his shoulder as she sipped from a long-stemmed glass.

"The joust was once a political event, but now it is merely a display of athleticism and skill," said a dark-skinned woman dressed alluringly in turquoise and gold. "Sammarynda has been peaceful for years now. No one fights any more."

"I shall bet on Orias," Jahira said loudly. "I have won money on his steady stance and deft manoeuvrability three years in a row."

Orias. Mariyam froze at the sound of the name, but only for an instant. No one had noticed. No one had been watching her.

"So typical of you to bet on a prince," said the turquoise woman.

Jahira made broad theatrical motions, feigning indignation at the suggestion. "Orias is no mere prince! Orias is a hero of the war!"

"Nevertheless, a prince he is — and all the ladies bet on him," said Haptet. "And he wins because he is a skilled and masterful warrior. It is almost impossible to make an honest coin as a result."

"A prince indeed?" said Mariyam, afraid of the tremble in her own words as she uttered them. Surprised that they did not lodge in her throat. "I didn't know Sammarynda had a royal family."

"It has dozens of them," Haptet laughed. "But Orias is my friend. I will introduce you. He is like a brother to me. Did you know he fought in the battle of Maratista?"

"Really?" said Mariyam. "He fought? Then I am impressed. I know how few warriors walked away from the battlefield that day."

"You have heard of Maratista?" asked Haptet.

"I have been there."

"To Maratista? Are you serious?"

For a second Haptet and Mariyam locked eyes, but the waiter began to clear the table, and the moment was lost amidst the clinking of glasses and the ordering of food.

Fireworks exploded below them on the beach, accompanied by the squeals of children and the barking of dogs.

"Today Jahira spoke of Glass Rock," said Mariyam, raising her voice. "I would like to see it. Will you take me there?"

Haptet nodded, regarding her curiously. "Tomorrow," he said. "I will take you there tomorrow."

From a distance, it seemed to Mariyam that Glass Rock had been inappropriately named. It was not made of glass at all, nor anything that resembled its texture. The mineral — whatever it was — seemed to suck light from the air. It stood out from the surrounding rock formations like a dark stain.

"I want to touch it," said Mariyam.

"No," said Haptet. "Touching is forbidden."

"But old women scrape away fragments to sell."

"Maybe," he replied, "but all the same, it is forbidden — and for very good reasons."

She thought he seemed much darker today than when they had first met. Was it because of Jahira's affection towards the tattooed stranger? Unlikely, thought Mariyam. These people are comfortable with each other's oblique infidelities. No, it is Glass Rock itself that sets him ill at ease.

"If I can't touch it or climb upon its surface, may I at least learn its history?" she asked, her fingertips brushing the vial of swirling particles concealed in her pocket.

They climbed a little higher along the ridge until they stood directly opposite, the two rock outcrops separated by a stretch of water. Glass Rock seemed to beckon, drawing their gaze toward it although there was little to see.

"Below Glass Rock is a crevasse that chasms downwards for miles. No one knows how deep it is. No one has ever touched the bottom."

Mariyam stepped as close to the edge as she dared. The water was crystal-aqua; same as it was all around the Sammarynda peninsula. But the water directly beneath Glass Rock was as dark as a starless night.

"Our ancestors went to Glass Rock when all hope was lost. They would paint their bodies with a poultice of oils and shavings from the Rock itself, and they would stand over there, right at the very edge."

"They would throw themselves off? Suicide?"

"They would dive, but not to their deaths — although those who did not enter the water smoothly would sometimes break their backs and drown."

Mariyam stared at the black stain below the water.

"The divers entered the Sammarynda Deep. They would swim down into darkness, vanish for a time and then they would return. Changed," said Haptet.

"Changed? In what way?"

Haptet frowned, searching for the right words. "In many ways. It's hard to be specific. No one could predict the form a change might take. Sometimes a diver would emerge with a different face. Other times he would appear the same, but no longer be the same inside. Some believed the particles from the rock to be an integral part of the change itself. The old women who sell the shavings at the market are from a particular bloodline — a tradition that goes back hundreds of years."

Mariyam recalled the twisted carcasses hanging in the apothecarists' windows.

"Touching Glass Rock is against the law," Haptet continued. "No one has stood there for a century."

She stared out across the water, imagining the swift, lithe form of a diver cutting a shimmery arc through the void, before plunging into the abyss.

"Why is at against the law to dive?" she asked.

Haptet shook his head. "The changes. They were too unnatural. Too swift. Too severe. If we are to change, we must do so slowly, by degrees. The Deep made monsters of us. We were almost destroyed by the power of — whatever it is down there."

Mariyam nodded. She stared at the dark patch of water.

Haptet cleared his throat. "Mariyam, yesterday you said you had been to Maratista. May I ask —"

"A long time ago," she said. "Many years. I don't wish to talk about it." Her eyes remained fixed on the darkness below the water's surface.

Behind them a horn blared: a drawn-out, mournful sound.

Haptet's face brightened, glad of the interruption. "The jousting begins soon," he said. "We can get a good view of the boats from here." He led her back the way they had come, then down across another stretch of cliff.

Below, the slender watercraft made a pattern like thatch across the still surface of the harbour. Each was decked in different colours.

"The prince you mentioned last night," said Mariyam. "Which of the colours is he?"

"Prince Orias? His colour is dark blue,"

"The colour of the Sammarynda Deep?"

Haptet stopped. He turned to face her. "What a curious thing to say. Nothing is the colour of the Deep. *Nothing at all.* Prince Orias's blue is deep and rich, but it does not devour light!"

Mariyam nodded. "I would like to see the boats up closer. And I would like to meet your prince."

Haptet smiled. "I knew you would. I have arranged it already. You will fall in love with him — I can assure you of that. Every woman does."

"No doubt," she said, masking her bitterness as best she could, leading the way back down the rocky path that wound around the cliff side all the way back down to the beach.

Mariyam felt herself gently mesmerised by the relentless swirling of the dancers' multi-layered skirts. The entire population of Sammarynda had come down to the water's edge for the opening of the Jousting festival. Several people had explained that the mock battles to be fought in the long boats tomorrow were symbolic of yet another war from a distant time. The survivors of that skirmish had settled this part of the inhospitable coastline and turned their talents toward farming the sea.

To Mariyam, it seemed as if every night in Sammarynda was a celebration of something. Flaming torches cast a warm glow upon the skin of merrymakers as they watched small boys heft long sticks to play at mock jousts on the grass. Youths tattooed with multi-coloured swirls wove in and out between the tables bearing baskets of sugary treats wrapped in twists of coloured paper. These they tossed into the crowd, or pressed into the hands of small children.

"I wish I had learned to dance when I was young," Mariyam shouted to Jahira.

"There is still time," she said. "Why don't you stay here with us for awhile? I know someone who can teach you. Age is not important."

Mariyam sat back in her chair, sipping her drink as a line of pretty little girls in pinks and greens, shells woven into their hair, bangles on their wrists, snaked past the tables, laughing and squealing. No one minded when items were knocked to the floor. No one cared about anything other than their unadulterated, radiating joy.

The long boats were moored a little way offshore, their decks encrusted with paper lanterns. The sky lit up with fireworks, these even bigger and brighter than the ones the night before.

Suddenly a wall of cheering erupted from somewhere to the left of their table. The crowd began to part, foot by foot, and the lanterns seemed to burn brighter as the men who would perform tomorrow's joust made their way through the space cleared for them. Each was garbed in fine garments expertly tailored to the contours of their bodies. Decked in their individual colours, each walked tall and strong and proud, aware that they were there to be admired.

"I've been in love with Orias for years," Jahira whispered as she clasped Mariyam's hand in her own.

Mariyam nodded, the pace of her heartbeat quickening. "Orias's wife must be a very fortunate woman."

Jahira shook her head, smiling sadly. "Orias has never chosen a wife. He does not allow himself love the way we do. It is his honour."

Mariyam gripped Jahira's arm. "What do you mean he doesn't allow himself love?"

Jahira turned to face her, and Mariyam sensed her own fingers tightening their hold. The dark space where Jahira's eye should have been still shocked her, no matter how many times she saw it.

"You know about our honour, Mariyam. Both Haptet and I have explained it to you."

Mariyam shook her head. "Your scars. I understand them. But — "

"Not all scarring is physical," said Jahira, "Orias's scars are in his heart. Apparently there was a woman during the war. They fought together, side by side. They were captured and imprisoned at Fallam Keep. Both suffered greatly in the enemy's hands."

Above them, a firework exploded suddenly, erupting into a magnificent flower, then flickering away into nothingness.

"But they endured, Orias and his lover. They survived, and escaped to fight for vengeance at the battle of Maratista Plain. Orias was a young man then. He had not yet chosen an honour for himself. When the war ended, he realised no mere wound of flesh would ever suffice. There was only one thing that held meaning for him. The woman he loved so much. So Orias sacrificed her for his honour and returned to Sammarynda. Or so it is said. He does not speak of such things with me."

A field of twinkling roses rained down from above as betrayal stung Mariyam like a scorpion's tail. The pit of her stomach fell away into nothingness. Orias had abandoned her without a word of explanation. Sacrificed her to the mores of a culture she didn't even know existed. *Why didn't you tell me? Rather I had died in the pits of Fallam Keep than endured these years alone, never knowing why you left, never understanding anything of the truth...*

Mariyam's breath rasped in her throat as her heart beat louder and louder, in syncopation with the footsteps of the men as they approached. Orias. *Prince of darkness, Lord of aching and despair.* She could not yet see his face, just his silhouette against the fireworks and the gentle swaying of the gaily painted crowd.

For all these years she had dreamed of one single perfect moment, wondering what she would say to him as they were reunited.

But this moment was no dream, and as the gap between them closed, time slowed, and the years that had stood between them folded in on themselves, fading like trails of gunpowder across the burning sky.

All you had to do was tell me. The truth would have freed us both.

Each warrior of the Joust strode past, waving at the cheering crowd as confetti swirled and danced on heady currents. Time slowed further until it dripped like honey as Orias took another step directly into her line of vision. Their eyes locked. Time paused, and in that eternal fragment, Orias glimpsed her scarred soul laid bare across her face. He learned the true price he had paid for his honour. Orias remembered all of it. Every moment they had ever shared, as clearly as the moments they had not. A shadow passed between them, a cold electric chill that sucked the brightness from the fireworks and made the coloured specks of paper tremble to the ground like dead leaves.

And then it was all over. Mariyam turned her face away, and the warriors continued on their heroes' walk. Time resumed its regular rhythms. When she looked back he had gone.

Flecks of sunlight shimmered on the water as the boats positioned themselves to begin. High on the cliff above spectators sat, nestled comfortably into wooden chairs, or sprawled on coloured rugs.

The empty chair beside her made Jahira nervous. "Are you sure Mariyam didn't say where she was going? Why travel all the way from Makasa if not to watch the main jousting event?

Haptet shrugged. "She never even mentioned the festival before I brought it up. It's very strange, but I have the strongest feeling it was never the reason for her coming here."

Jahira craned her neck to search the crowd. "Maybe she has gotten lost. You know her best, Haptet. Is she one who might lose her way in a crowd?"

Haptet shrugged. "I have known her only minutes longer than you have. I can only guess at the sort of person she may be."

Jahira stared at him. "Really? You are not old friends? You seemed so familiar!" She glanced across at the others, all of whom shrugged as well.

Haptet shook his head. "I met her for the first time in the Starfish. You were there. She was curious about your eye. Remember?"

"Yes — but I presumed — "

"No," he said. "I did not know her before that day at all — only that she said she was a friend of Behameed's. I'm beginning to wonder if we haven't all presumed too much."

"She came here to find Orias," said Jahira, pulling her cotton wrap tightly across her shoulders, even though it was not cold. "Now that I think about it, I'm certain. Last night at the festival. Didn't you see what happened when they met?"

"Look!"

A gasp rippled suddenly through the crowd, causing all heads to turn at once to the cliffs behind the beach. A lone figure stood atop Glass Rock, her skin shimmering in its sheath of glittering oil. Clearly a she, despite the distance; the curve of her hips well-defined against the impenetrable shadow of the rock's obsidian surface. And equally clear was her intention. The woman was preparing to dive the Sammarynda Deep. She stood poised as still as the rock itself, eyes cast downwards, waiting for the perfect moment. Waiting for the crowd to quiet itself.

"Haptet," whispered Jahira, "I think that Mariyam is she — the inspiration for Orias's honour. Mariyam is the woman from the war."

Haptet's eyes widened. "But that's astonishing. Where is he now? Out on the water already? Did he board the boats with the others?"

Jahira didn't answer, nor did she turn to discuss the alarming development with her friends. She understood perfectly. She'd observed the dark current pass between Mariyam and Orias last night, a subtle jolt of anguish that inflamed the very air around them. She understood they were not strangers. Neither were they friends. Something powerful bound them together, trapped them in each other's vortex, unable to escape. Mariyam had come to Sammarynda to slash those bonds forever. It was she who'd paid the price for his honour. All she wanted now was freedom. "I'm sorry I didn't understand," Jahira whispered. "*I would have chosen the very same way.*"

One of the long boats pulled away from the others and headed for the shore. Orias's blue, Jahira noted. Was Mariyam aware of it, so high up there on Glass Rock? If so, she gave no sign.

The murmuring of the crowd intensified as people began to notice the boat, and the single figure in full jousting regalia who leapt from its prow out into the shallows, kicking up clouds of foaming white water as he waded to the sand. Once on land, he raced for the rocks, stripping off jewelled leather as he ran, his pace slowing but not his determination.

Atop Glass Rock, the diver stepped forward to the edge. Was she staring into the abyss below with terror and trepidation? Or was she calmly appraising the future she had chosen for herself? Her stillness did not betray her thoughts. No one would ever know her truth.

The twittering of the crowd intensified as Orias clambered up the rock face, small stones and chunks of earth raining from each foothold. The brown rocks gave way to the cold solidity of Glass Rock's extraordinary mineral composition. Orias kept climbing.

The crowd gasped in unison as the diver raised her arms above her head. *No. Wait for him, you must wait. He has almost reached the top.*

She did not wait. She crouched, then pushed her body upwards and outwards, cutting a graceful swathe through the air, then falling like a spear. She broke the surface of the water cleanly, a blade plunging home with a killing thrust. Barely a ripple marked her passage.

As the water's surface smoothed, all heads turned upwards to the rock face. The climber clung to Glass Rock like a spider, inching forwards and upwards, somehow finding handholds where there were none. A tide of sympathy washed over the crowd. He was too late. Too late to stop her, but he didn't know it. He could not see that she had dived already.

Finally he hurled himself the last few feet, tumbling in a heap onto the rocky dive platform. He rushed to the edge, peered over to stare at the dark crevasse below the water. He hung his head in despair.

The crowd hushed. No one dared whisper now. Every one of them felt his sorrow and his tragedy, whatever the story behind the strange drama they were seeing.

Orias turned his back on the ocean. He walked away, then suddenly stopped, spun around and ran towards the edge, flinging himself into the air, assuming the diving position as he fell to the accompaniment of ten thousand screaming onlookers. He did not break the surface cleanly, but the ocean took him, just as it had taken her.

The night was still as porcelain, the ocean flat and calm, as if laying in wait for something great to happen — something that would change the world forever. For Jahira, things had already changed. Things that could never be made right again.

While Sammarynda grieved for its drowned prince, Jahira waited for a sign that the legends of their land were true and not just fancy tales for tourists. Every evening, she climbed the cliff directly opposite Glass Rock, sat cross-legged at its edge and gazed downwards at the dark patch of water, darker than the night sky itself. Not even Neme and Kryl cast their reflections upon its shadowy smudge.

One the third night of the third week, as she watched and waited, the surface of the water broke. Something emerged, coughing and spluttering, flailing its limbs in panic. Jahira leapt to her feet and ran down to the beach, grateful for the starlight that prevented her from stumbling on loose rocks. Above, Kashah the Dog-Headed Warrior watched as she stripped off her clothes and plunged into the ocean to swim to the struggling form, which had begun to shriek in panic. Jahira was a strong swimmer. She managed to haul the struggling one to safety.

As the two of them lay panting on the sand, Jahira realised she had rescued a child. A girl of no more than twelve or thirteen, pale as alabaster, thin as a reed. She wrapped the coughing girl in her coat. She had to get her home quickly. Away from the beach before anyone saw what the Sammarynda Deep had cast out in exchange for the city's most beloved prince and the stranger who had enticed him to his death.

As they stumbled across the sand, their feet crunched down hard on small shells and fragile bones of twisted sea creatures tossed onto the sand by the dark Sammarynda tide.

The girl could not speak. She uttered terrified guttural sounds from the back of her throat. Not a language, as such, but Jahira understood it, just as she was not surprised by the thin webbing of skin stretched between the child's fingers and toes.

Jahira responded in as soothing a tone as she could manage, murmuring that she would protect the child and keep her safe from harm. But the child would not be safe, Jahira knew. The child would never be safe. The citizens of Sammarynda port would hunt her down and kill her without question, just as they would kill the old women at the market who had sold Mariyam fragments of Glass Rock, if they hadn't done so already. It did not take much to draw superstition to the surface. It would not take much more to return the land to the violence and terror of centuries past.

By the light of Kashah, Jahira understood that her missing eye had never been her honour at all. It was merely a cosmetic thing, an act of vanity, performed to draw attention to herself. Her true honour would lie in protecting this child of the Deep; the unholy fusion of Mariyam and Prince Orias, whatever the cost, even if the price to be paid was her own life.

Tearjerker

Steve Berman

Thisday

Gail hates being outside when it rains vinegar. She doubts the hags' assurances that it clears the skin and removes warts; as a child, she put chicken bones in vinegar to discover days later they would be all rubbery. She wipes the wet hair from her face, grimacing at the sour trickle that slips past her lips. Her hands move to the pocket of her jeans, checking again for the plastic bottle of aspirin from the shelter.

She stumbles down the block, her sneakers sodden and her feet cold as she steps in puddles. The weak light coming from the sky with its brown clouds makes the street look unfamiliar, and for a moment, before hearing the recorded saxophone, she thinks she might be lost.

Then she spots the faded awning up ahead and the white stonework. The doors to the dilapidated hotel are left open until nightfall.

Bulbs sputter in the old crystal chandeliers in the lobby. A quiet line of people stands waiting to reach the front desk. Each holds something they think has value. Layers of wet clothing drip and saturate the frayed Persian rug. From hidden speakers comes more wailing brass.

She feels feverish inside the stifling-warm lobby. Gail's soaked sweater hangs about her like a lead vest. Through the line of people, she catches sight of Brennan. The little girl sits atop the front desk, her small legs hanging over the side. The hags have dressed her in the lemon-yellow sundress with lace trim, her blonde hair held back with a white scrunchie. One of the Grace sisters stands beside her, and, as Gail watches, the old woman grins and pinches Brennan's cheeks with both hands. Not fondly, but hard enough to turn the little girl's face red and the hag's knuckles bone-white. Brennan begins crying, and the Grace sister strokes her chin. "There, there, well done, dear," she coos, before lifting a porcelain teacup to catch the tears. "That will do nicely."

The hags wear brightly colored flannel nightgowns with slippers. Their weak, watery eyes resemble a hound dog's.

Next to the first Grace is her twin, holding aloft a vintage hypodermic, the sort that Gail has seen in black-and-white movies, all glass and shiny chrome. The hag's lips form a small "o" as she focused on refilling the needle from the teacup.

Gail tries not to stare as the needle slips into the next in line. The smell of those waiting makes her want to retch. Being a tearfreak is no excuse for poor hygiene. Once she is back working for the hags, she'll draw the addicts baths. She can scrounge for salts and scented soaps. Everyone will appreciate her.

She climbs up the grand staircase, trying not to catch her feet on the ripped runner. A middle-aged man in denim overalls plods up the steps. One hand trails along the wallpaper; he has not rolled down his sleeve after receiving the injection.

The tearfreaks don't always reach their rooms, and some collapse on the landing or a hallway. The hags hate when that happens and have told Gail how slovenly it leaves the hotel. They order her to put the addicts to bed.

Gail will come back later to see if the man needs help; she wants one last conversation with Alexander. He needs the aspirin.

Days Past

All the rooms on the hotel's third floor (the stairs skipped the second floor, and no matter how many times she tried, Gail couldn't find her way there) were numbered 83. The hags forbid her from venturing onto the fourth or fifth floors. The elevators don't work, haven't since reality fell away last year, and the only way to reach the upper levels is by gloomy passages along the servant's stairwell. Ever since she began working for the hags months ago, Gail began to think of herself as a servant girl and explored the hotel whenever possible.

That was how she came upon Alexander on the fourth floor in room 450. Or maybe the fifth floor, room 540. Sometimes numbers changed when she wasn't looking.

She had been scooping out deviled ham from a jar with her fingers and roaming the dim hallway of doors when she overheard a Grace sister speaking.

"There once was an old woman who lived in a vinegar bottle? Not a very believable beginning to my story."

Gail peered around the door. The hag sat on one of the uncomfortable wooden chairs found in many of the rooms. She leaned over a young man lying on top of the sheets, one of her gnarled hands lifting up the front of his bathrobe. Underneath, he was naked, though someone had written in red ink all over his skin. Even the soles of his feet had words: *I shall be so happy living here* up the left foot and down the right.

"I think you could at least come up with a better ending for me," said the hag. "Ungrateful."

The young man grunted. Maybe groaned.

When the hag stood, Gail slipped away into the next room's welcome darkness. She licked her fingers clean, slipping the empty jar into her pocket. She heard the creak of the floorboards as the Grace sister passed by. They always creaked, and Gail wondered if their footfalls aged the hotel step by step.

She counted to a hundred before entering the young man's room. Under the white terrycloth robe, his chest rose and fell. The writing had vanished from his skin, which looked pale and drawn to the bone. He might have been handsome if someone hadn't shaved off all his hair—not just scalped him but plucked clean his eyebrows and lashes as well.

He opened his eyes. *Who is there?* bled onto his forehead.

His marred body marked him as Afflicted, one of the caste changed for the worse by the Fall. She had never been so close to one before. "Doesn't that hurt?"

He nodded. She felt better knowing it pained him. That made sense. Too many things about the hotel, about the Fallen Area, never did.

"I wonder why the sisters never mentioned you." She sat down beside him on the bed.

I am their keepsake. Alexander.

"I'm Gail. I do all the dull stuff for the hags. It looks like they are doing a very poor job of keeping you." She doubted he weighed more than a hundred pounds.

Truly. scrolled across his chin and neck.

"I don't mind reading you, but it's hard to have a long conversation. I'd have to peek and we only just met." She nearly giggled.

Alexander opened his mouth. He had very white teeth but no tongue. She could not see any scar tissue.

"Sorry."

Could you bring me something to eat?

"Sure." She regretted finishing off the deviled ham. Real food could be hard to come by Inside. She had taken the jar late last night from behind the front desk; one of the tearfreaks must have brought it as payment for a fix. The tangy paste would have been easy for Alexander to swallow without a tongue. She wondered if he could still chew.

The power did not work in the hotel's vast kitchen, but the hags had bartered with an anthvoke to fix the refrigerator, a massive bone-white relic that lurked in the corner of the kitchen like a dusty fossil. While it worked without electricity, shaking and humming, they must have connived the Talented out of his payment, for the refrigerator conjured only chilled condiments. The hags did not seem to mind, and their breath was always a miasma of sweet and sour.

Gail never trusted any of the Talented. They cheated at surviving by using unfair gifts. Awakening dead household appliances might seem pathetic, but it gave anthvokes an edge over the normals like her, who had to contend with life in the Fallen Area. She regretted not leaving Philly before the immense concrete walls had been erected, quarantining what the rest of the country considered a "reality infection." The early days of the Fall had seemed exciting, but the novelty had been worn away by constant uncertainty—streets could misdirect from one day to the next, what had once been a safe spot to crash might become risky to walk past. The Talented frightened her, too. The Afflicteds' bodies no longer worked as they once did, but the Talented could work the chaos Inside as they pleased like selfish magic.

The rules of life changed constantly. She could only persevere. The hags paid little, but the hotel's quirks didn't threaten. She helped herself whenever possible.

Gail tugged hard on the refrigerator's cool metal handle. Jars and bottles crammed the shelves. She started rooting through them. Colman's Mustard. Alaga Pickle Syrup. Mack's Cider Vinegar. Anything an anthvoke awoke had to be vintage. She found Bengal Club Chutney and a can of chocolate sauce.

"Snick-snacking so early, dear?" One of the sisters stood in the doorway.

Gail shrugged. She had never mastered the quick lie.

"We need you to clean the last 83. Poor Mr. Theo's constitution isn't what it used to be. We may have to water the tears down next time."

Gail nodded, hiding her annoyance. Mr. Theo should be the last one taking tears. The old man couldn't move without a litany of groans. "I'll take care of it."

When she stripped the bed of the soiled sheets, a tiny gilded case slipped to the floor. She picked it up, listening to it rattle and fingering the scratched enameled terrier on the top. Her thumb flicked the latch and she counted seven tiny pills. What do old men have? Hardened arteries? High blood pressure? Gail promised under her breath to give the case back to Mr. Theo when she saw him later in the week.

She felt guilty it took so long to return to Alexander and apologized several times. He needed help eating. Gail had to tip the chutney, allowing small chunks and liquid into his mouth, then water brought from the sink in the deviled ham jar. Like a ventriloquist dummy, he could "talk" while swallowing.

I was the sisters' first attraction. My stories filled the lobby.

"Before they found Brennan?" Gail wiped his lips and chin clean.

Yes. The little woebegone.

"I once sneaked a sip from her tea cup. It tasted so sweet, made me choke. I fell asleep and dreamed." Gail remembered that sensation on her tongue, how it made her shiver all over.

What of?

"Snowglass Night. Sitting in front of my television set, eager for news on what happened to the neighborhood. Some cable network. The announcer spoke to me. Not like normal, he actually answered my questions. Told me how bad the rain would be the next day and I should wear galoshes. Do they still make yellow rubber boots? Anyways, the announcer had an overbite and a bad toupee, and he had finished telling me that people were disappearing in Philly, and then static interrupted him. The screen had the black and white confetti snow, like all the plugs had been pulled but the power. I went to my window and knew that sets for blocks around were snowed-in and always would be."

Sometimes I think I overhear the dreams of the addicts. Alexander grimaced as the words rose. *I remember how contented they were listening to my stories read aloud. So quiet, so still, with smiles.*

Gail normally slept well, especially if she visited Brennan before bed. But finding Alexander provoked her thoughts, leaving her restless on the mattress in the grand ballroom. She turned over, and one foot slipped out beneath the blanket. The marble tile sent a chill through her.

Why would the hags keep Alexander? They had always seemed disgusted with Afflicteds, turning away any that entered the lobby. Gail never minded them, not the ones with minor deformities, such as the girl with glass hair Gail once glimpsed waiting outside the stalls of the Food Auction.

She closed her eyes and tried to drift off while envisioning crimson writing covering the insides of her own eyelids. She thought of him stranded in that bed. Were they punishing him? The thought made her anxious about what might one day happen to her.

The sisters had instructed that Gail handwash all of Brennan's clothes. They made her add rainwater to each rinse, so the colors wouldn't fade. On dry weeks, she took vinegar from the refrigerator.

When not shedding a tear, Brennan was kept in her room. Brennan sat on the floor in pink pajamas and fuzzy slippers, not far from where the metal pin secured her leash. She looked up when Gail brought the clean laundry. "Hello."

"Hey, kid." She began putting away the clothes in the closet.

"You've seen the Bookman." Brennan's tone blended whine and accusation perfectly.

Gail stopped. "You know about him?"

Brennan nodded. "Yep. He's ugly."

"Aren't you the sweetheart?" Not for the first time did Gail wonder what the girl really was. Not truly Afflicted, as she seemed normal except for her tears.

"Why don't you like me?" Tiny lips pouted.

Gail sighed. "But I do." Practiced lies came naturally to her. She left the laundry and took Brennan into her arms. "Now do I get my taste?" Her mouth grew wet with anticipation.

Brennan shook her head, tickling Gail's face with blonde hair.

Gail did not raise her voice. That hadn't worked in the past. Brennan might hide under the bed, and then Gail would have to drag her out by the tether. "Mean little girls grow up ugly."

"Like the sisters?"

"Like the sisters." Gail hugged Brennan. "So?"

Brennan bit down on her lower lip. She had an overbite. Tears formed at the corners of her eyes. When they trailed down her puffy cheek, Gail eagerly licked them away.

The cloying taste made her tongue feel lacquered, and she fought a coughing spell. She let go of Brennan and grabbed the laundry basket. By the time she reached the hallway, she could feel her insides glowing. She took a few more steps, and then dawdled under a sputtering wall sconce. Her skin tingled, and she stared at her arms, wondering if words lurked just under the surface, the serifs scratching to be set free.

Visits with Alexander became as necessary as treats from Brennan. Gail listened as he told marvelous things, secrets taken from the Grace sisters. They had been beautiful once, with dancers' legs, swinging their hips in simpatico with jazz from the hotel speakers. She read that pariah dogs patrolled the Fallen Area, meeting in a cabal of mutts. That one of the tearfreaks spied for the outside world, but his reports rambled with lachrymose dreams. Alexander seemed eager for attention even when it pained him to write. When she left, he could stir a little and lifted an arm to take the water glass.

She decided to spend the following night with Alexander until her eyes became blurry. Perhaps he would offer her a lullaby. She held tight to the banister as she climbed to the fourth floor. Creaking sounds came from up ahead. Half-illuminated by the light of Alexander's room, the hags drifted down the hall in pale, quilted housecoats.

Gail hoped they would walk past his room on their way to bed. She never knew where they slept. But they stopped outside of 450. Each sister reached for the other's satin belt, loosening it. Their coats fell with velvety sighs to the worn carpet. Bare breasts sagged, but the skin on their thighs looked taut, the buttocks firm. They held hands and walked inside.

Gail ran back to the ballroom. She lay on her back and stared at the ceiling all night and shuddered whenever she thought she heard a sound. She told herself that forgetting Alexander would be best.

She busied herself with her chores and visits with Brennan. When Mr. Theo came to the lobby empty-handed, begging for tears, she watched the hags level a revolver at his chest and threaten to ruin the rugs unless he left the hotel. She never offered to return his little case, still in her pocket.

When that afternoon's line of tearfreaks dwindled away, Gail swept the floor. With the broom she maneuvered the trail of dirt into arcs, reminiscent of Alexander's handwriting. By the time she had finished with the lobby, she had to sit down on the bottom step and catch her breath. Her hands trembled, and when she rubbed them, they felt bony and worn.

Brennan ran up to her. She lacked her leash. "They want to see you." Brennan looked back over her shoulder in the direction of the hotel bar. "Trouble double." She curtsied once and then giggled while running up the staircase.

The mahogany-paneled walls of the bar might have once suggested a warm opulence, but now the room seemed restrictive and stuffy. Normally it was kept padlocked, as the hags did not want anyone to steal what little liquor remained. Gail had discovered the combination soon after she started working. She discovered she enjoyed single malts around then as well.

Sitting together on a burgundy leather chaise, the sisters cupped crystal tumblers of scotch in their laps.

"We heard you were a thief." The left Grace slurred her words.

Gail had never seen either drunk before; the sight of their wet lips bothered her more than the accusation.

The twin dipped a finger into her glass and swirled the drink around the rim, creating a brief chime. "You think being young and pretty masks cleverness."

What did they know? She tried to recall everything she had taken.

"You've been feeding our Book."

"He has a name."

Both made an odd sound of derision, almost a wheeze.

"I'm not the one keeping a man prisoner."

Another chuff. "Who's locked and who's the locket?" The left Grace stabbed towards Gail and spilt her drink. "His stories have left us old."

"Sister, you're still beautiful." The right Grace stroked the other's face.

"I'm taking him away." But her words sounded hollow to her own ears. She had no idea where she could bring him. Yet the thought of sharing Alexander with the hags—and the memory of seeing them disrobe and sauntering into his room—pained her.

"Did he fuck you?"

The right Grace smirked while threading her fingers through her sister's gray hair. "His dick is shaped like a fountain pen."

"Horrible nib."

"Hurts like hell."

As Gail ran from the bar to the lobby, she heard one of them call out, "We're the only ones that never tire of his stories. We kept him. Kept him safe."

When the wind struck her bare arms, Gail regretted being so quick to leave the warmth of the hotel. She wandered aimlessly down the next two blocks, telling herself that in the morning the hags would be sober and reasonable. They'd take her back if she promised to avoid Alexander.

She could see her breath rising in front of her. The closest doorway led into a liquor store. Shards of glass covered much of the floor. The shelves had been ransacked, probably ages ago. Down one aisle, she found and shook clean a banner for Pennsylvania wineries. Wrapped with it, she lay on some old wooden pallets and tried to sleep.

She stirred well after morning. Whatever soured wine remaining at the bottom of some broken bottles seemed to have coated the inside of her throat. Her head ached with something akin to a hangover.

The hags wore cheerful floral nighties in the morning. They scowled when she walked into the lobby.

"We thought of you like a daughter."

"Now you're far too wayward for our liking," said the other and motioned with the revolver at the door. The gunmetal gleamed as if oiled.

"My stuff—" Gail had one foot on the staircase when she heard the safety's click. The sisters tsk-ed, and Brennan muffled giggles behind a small hand. The unkempt line of addicts broke apart when they noticed Gail crying, and she had to struggle through hands grasping to reach her face.

She wandered the neighborhood. A place that sold tea looked inviting until she remembered they had thrown her out after catching her stealing from a woman's open purse. She napped briefly in a deep doorway until nudged.

The couple standing over her had kind faces, which worried her while she blinked away sleep, but they insisted she would be safer at the shelter. She wondered how she could not have known such a place existed, but then she had never dared explore every twisted street Inside.

The shelter had once been a posh Cuban restaurant she could have never afforded before the Fall. The walls remained a warm orange stucco decorated with framed vintage prints of buxom women leaning or stretching with cigars nearby. But now they looked down upon dingy cots and blankets and tables cluttered with pots and trays. Ashtrays of polished, cloudy marble were stacked in spots and held the remains of candles.

There, the nurse, a pudgy short woman with close-cropped hair, offered Gail warm clothes from a donation box and a cot to rest on. The wool sweater smelled musty and hung like a tent on her frame. The others staying at the shelter eyed her warily. She drank salty soup and considered asking if the workers were volunteers or were they paid.

When the nurse was distracted helping a scrawny goth boy delivering packages, Gail snooped around, finding the infirmary behind a hastily hung curtain. She picked up a lighter that weighed down some letters. Her thumb traced over the engraving—*Aroma*—then flicked the wheel and created a tiny flame. It had to be worth something. She palmed it before the nurse could come back.

"I think I need some air," she told the woman.

Gail carried on a long conversation with the hags as she retraced her steps to the hotel. They told her how sorry they felt over casting her out and offered treats. Brennan would be so relieved to have her back; the sweet tears would flow down that round face. Tears just for her.

When Gail walked through the doors, the hags waved at her, beckoning towards the front desk. She held up her offering, sparking the lighter's flame. "Here, a present."

"Aww, dear, we thought you might come back for a dose." One of the hags rubbed Gail's arm warmly, while the other filled the needle from the cup.

"You look so haggard. Have you not been sleeping well?"

Gail slid up the sweater's sleeve as the sister came closer with the needle. But the point dipped before it broke skin and the tears squirted out to land on the floor.

Gail yelped, as if she had been jabbed to the bone, and fell to her knees. She barely stopped herself from clutching the damp rug.

"Maybe you need to curl up with a good book, dear."

She wrapped her arms around her torso as proof against their cackles, but still they stung. With nowhere else to go, she returned to the shelter. She needed a bit of care before figuring out what she might do. Normals who have no role in the Fallen Area end up lost and hungry. Roaming Inside was dangerous. More than people had been altered. She had overheard too many rumors of carnivorous alleys and debris.

That evening, she woke soaked in sweat. Her fingers twitched, her body burned as if the acid in her stomach had spilled. Gail could not recall where she was, and panic filled her for several minutes until her eyes adjusted to the darkness and she remembered. She shouted out for the nurse. Groans and curses of disturbed sleepers echoed. The syrupy medicine the nurse brought slowly soothed her.

Stabbing pain heralded each motion the next day. Even breathing took effort. She found a hand mirror and stared long at her reflection. Had the skin around her eyes always looked crinkled? The other women staying at the shelter laughed at what they must think was vanity, but Gail knew what had happened. The hags had warned her about Alexander too late. She felt ancient.

The nurse hassled her with questions about drugs. Gail screamed to be left alone. She knew the sisters would never let her see Brennan again. She wanted nothing more than to hold the girl close, to nuzzle and kiss that soft face. Then everything would be right again.

The rain fell, and her pain worsened. Arthritis, she was sure. Her trembling fingers went to the faux gold case in her pocket. Bent low to hide the contents from the others, she considered taking one of Mr. Theo's mystery pills. By staring hard, letters gradually appeared on their surface, as if she palmed tiny bits of Alexander's weird flesh.

"What is Lanoxin," Gail asked the nurse, when the woman came to check on her. She kept her treasure hidden underneath the blanket.

Suspicion filled the nurse's eyes. "Digitalis. Foxglove. You're too young to worry about such things."

"I thought I heard one of the others asking for it."

"I hope not. It's for people with weak hearts." The nurse leaned forward and whispered, "How's the withdrawal?"

Gail shook her head. The woman didn't understand. Gail didn't crave Alexander's words anymore. She needed to stop reading him. The hags, too. Maybe without their Book they'd all become young again. He must have a terrible heart to hurt them all so. Maybe she wouldn't have to feed him all the little pills. "Do you have an aspirin?" she asked.

Thisday

The hags never see her climb the staircase. Or maybe they approve of her plan. Yes, Gail, is sure they must. Maybe Brennan, too.

Gail raps her sore hands on Alexander's open door. He stares at her from the bed. She offers her best smile.

"Let's talk." She jiggles the bottle. The Lanoxin rattles along with the aspirin.

The sisters told me you left.

"It hurts, I know." She gritted teeth while prying off the cap. It takes three attempts, and she struggles not to gasp by the end. "Here." She brings the pills to his lips. He opens his mouth, and she makes sure to place them on his molars. He grinds his teeth.

"Now tell me a story." She sits down on the chair. As the letters flourish over his skin, she tries not to shiver in anticipation of reading his ending.

ꙮ

The Title of This Story

Stephanie Campisi

n Downtown, between the hypodermic fringes of Sitter Park, where the junkies walk a prickly carpet of needle-tipped glass and crumpled foil, and the painful gloom of the domed Helltricks complex that pollutes the Skendgrotian skyline with its void reflective windows and vast wooden landing platforms, lay a sickle-shaped swathe of religion and spirituality, and similar things long-illicit. A trickle of residences and warehouses and gutted ex-churches, hammered together as one with irrationally added cement facades, drooping and spiking in architectural curlicues and messes of starved ivy that drank the moisture from the porous walls.

At the edges of this swoop of dark, nested buildings, there was a slightly tilted terraced house, rocked on its foundations and pockmarked from gang wars and decayed at its base from the lapping of the Voda, like a tooth hollowed with cavities. The residence of Regent Polertrony claimed a tentative space here, propped up by an abandoned satellite building of the Kram, Skendgrot's most famous religious landmark, on which it leant like a tipsy cultureman. The residence was as recently as a decade ago marked by a half-door, unusually unadorned with names and titles and post-doctorial suffixes, but now hid behind a fringe of airplants that burst from the wooden trellis on the walls.

It was on a small wooden seat, with ribbons of white paint peeling from its sides like sunburnt skin, and a plump round cushion in a faded gingham, that Regent sat, a photographia of a strange new device pinned to his old wooden clipboard, which rested in his lap, trembling a little as his weight shifted to accommodate his constant poppy-tea drinking and the confident mathematic jottings he scattered across the page like a handful of spidery seeds. The photographia depicted a strange sort of box that opened out to reveal a series of letters printed on bone-pale keys, and the thick glass of a screen that curved like an eye. A slim generator was attached to one side with warped screws.

Regent worked quickly, mindful of the playful habits of the Skendgrotian sun, which had no qualms about hibernating behind a mass of feathery cloud or burning with such violent intensity that the Mora-infested canals of the Voda would hiss and churn. He glanced at the photographia on occasion, making notes and taking measurements, and datum by datum plotting these on to a chart that resembled a rudimentary chart of the elements. Regent was the pre-eminent Downtown onomastician, or rather, was as pre-eminent as those specialising in an outlawed vocation could be.

His current commission required nothing more than a working knowledge of the basics of onomastics and basic mechanical etymological research, though the construct was simple enough that the inherent name of the object in the photographia all but burst from the page. He quickly solved the remaining equations, then filled out a form containing the item's name, as well as a receipt for services rendered, and set the clipboard down on the cracked flagstones that puffed with moss at his feet.

His poppy tea, a habit that had grown to gnaw at him increasingly strongly as he leant on it in an effort to remove his boredom, bit at the sides of his mouth, sloughing loose skin off from his receding gums.

If he tilted back his chair and squinted past the stubbly growths of buildings that marched in awkward lines around the veins of the Voda, he could make out the spiny modernist sculptures dotting the vast, peaked roof of Downtown University. His tenure there had extended over fifteen or so years, and yet the daily walk through the green-tinged glass partitions from the ground level rooftops down to his office, which was a drowned room three storeys down, butting off a library wing, had always kept his interest.

The possibilities to be found in that library...and the potential scope of his work — it didn't bear thinking about. Regent stooped to collect his work and headed inside to prepare another poppy seed wash.

The corners of the book, despite its cloth-wrapped cover, dug into Boy's leg, leaving a small, red divot that swam with sweat from his back. A tram car sighed above him, rocking restlessly on its slowly unspooling cable, homeless ever since the floods had cut the generators and the rails had closed half a century before. A blackened arm, like a waxy bruise, waved in death from one of the side doors, which had slid open from the prisings of the beak of a carol bird. The arm had a hand, and the hand had two remaining fingers, which crooked like fly-legs.

The tram car was coated in soot from the crematorial belching of the Abattoir Towers that huddled alongside the Wynching Cemetery. The cemetery was, in fact, where a tram car like this belonged, but the city's burial limits seemed to have grown obese in the wake of the gang wars, disease, and the fallout from the Jolts. Boy, innocent on the inside, knew these things; knew them as he knew the importance of the book, and the translation that he was required to procure.

It was mid-afternoon, and even the rickety laneways, constructed from precarious planks worked together with wire and nails and right-angles, were busy with people heading back to work from home or an opium den after a prolonged siesta to escape the heat. A man like a walking apteka walked by, paper cones of herbal medicines and garlands and rosaries of gems and cloves adorning him as though he were an aficionado of bizarre jewellery. He thrust a paper cup of crushed peppermint mixed with something foul-smelling at Boy, who found himself cringing and hanging back, walking slowly enough that he could get lost in the crowd, but not so slowly that he would be noticed. It was easiest to push along with the clusters of slumming Kramtkrovian culturemen, noses carved to gashes from cocaine, or the washer-women dragging Hessian sacks of machine-churned clothing, or the man with the dozen parrots threaded through their skulls on to a totem beam.

The Skendgrotian skyline up close slithered by like the spiky troughs and peaks of a divinograph, leaping and swaying, then plummeting as commercial centres butted on to a shanty town region where the consumptive and malformed massed together. Boy, ever-conscious of the brutal weight of the book he carried, tried to walk briskly, to ignore the at-once fascinating and loathsome spectacles ubiquitous in this mere fraction of the vast city. He tried not to show that he feared this immense place, which seemed in complete contrast to his home in one of the farthest Brackis hamlets. Instead, he focussed on the repercussions that the naming of the book would have for his people.

Regent finished tabling the cryptic crossword for the morrow's newspaper, and began filling in clues and answers with a confident hand. This would be a relatively simple crossword, with a basis that he and his former colleagues at the University had jokingly called "a variation on E the minor," after its reliance on the slightly arcane and exceedingly rare value that this particular formula assigned to the letter "e."

It was by now late afternoon, and the sky was beginning to blush (although this could have been from the effects of the poppy tea) at the oncoming dusk. The frail light stuttered against the profusion of green that swamped his tiny front courtyard. It was as though the immediate space around him was alive with tealights, as though for some grand religious procession that the youngsters of Downtown could only dream about, and which Regent could remember only hazily as a string of carnivalesque masques and costumes and lines of chanting youths who stepped slowly, as though the world were glass beneath their bare feet.

Regent would have slipped further into reminiscence if not for the cautious tread of someone making their way over the homemade crossings that zigzagged their way back and forth across the murky Voda, allowing access to the upper storeys of the Old Skendgrotian buildings that had escaped the flood, and to those levels and houses that had been hastily tacked on with no heed to planning regulations or aesthetics in the years that had followed.

Presently, a youth in perhaps his late teens or early twenties stood in front of the ivy-savaged gate that Regent liked to believe sheltered his privacy. His skin was tanned and creased beyond his years—from the harsh, direct sun that beat down on rings of villages that orbited the fat mass of the city, surmised Regent. The skin of Skendgrotian city natives was not as easily picked, as the sun there was sly, reflecting off grimy glass here and sneaking through thick clags of pollution there. The city natives' skin could range from alabaster white to the deep purple-black of fine chocolate, depending where in the city one lived. The boy had grey eyes, old eyes, which shone with the determined arrogance of youth, but at the same time the fatalism of old age. Regent was unnerved by those eyes.

"Can I help you?" he asked, setting aside his crossword and securing it from the lashing of the unpredictable wind with his metal fountain pen.

The boy was silent a moment, casting his gaze down to where an identifying plaque would ordinarily hang, but upon noting its absence, returning his attention to Regent.

"Dr Polertrony?" His Rs were burred; his Os buried deep in his throat. He was definitely from the Brackis region. "The—" he hesitated, before saying, far too loudly, "the onomastician?" His voice rolled off the murk of the Voda, coming back to him as an echo that rang like a bell. "I've been asked to enlist your help," he finished in an intonation-free blurt. He fumbled about and produced a broad leather-bound book that had been partially wrapped in vibrant silks. He reached a hand over the gate, offering the book to Regent. A white-tipped creeper snagged at the boy's arm, and the soft flower crowning it fell free as he snatched his hand back.

Regent stood, took the book from the boy, hefting its considerable weight, and unlatched the gate, beckoning his visitor to enter the courtyard. He could smell the sweetly burning taste of the honey sauce that the nearby bakery used as a basis for all of its sweet breads and desserts. It was these things he missed, the innocent homely things, the way people used to have roles to fulfil—the way they all used to fit in.

Regent ran the gnawed fingertips of his empty hand over his hirsute wrist, clasping the wrist in a bony grasp while he waited for the boy to enter. The book was heavy in his hand, and he felt the damp from his finger seeping into the vivid silk layers. The youth slid past him, smelling sharply of onion and garlic and spice; some of this from sweat, and the rest perhaps from cologne, Regent thought.

Regent gestured for the boy to be seated in his gingham-covered seat, and turned to wind the small generator that hung like a spider on metal arms from a swoop of wire overhead. The generator chugged to life, pouring a hesitant and stammering spotlight onto the area below. Its light was cut in concentric circles, indicating where the round wire mesh covered the globe of the generator.

Regent took a seat on an overturned wooden crate, being careful not to spear himself on its splintering edges. He shifted the book from hand to hand, waiting for the boy to address him once more.

The youth leant forward, his collarless shirt hanging open and revealing a surprisingly strong neck. "It's a holy book," he said, nodding. "My people have asked for it to be named, so that we might discuss it in greater detail and so the book will grow in power."

The onomastician rubbed a gnarled thumb over the cover of the book. "Naming provides power," he muttered, keeping his eyes on the book. He shifted the patterned silk, all gold-spattered crimson drawn in rich swirls, looking for text or some sort of embossing. The cover was bare bar a design of three intertwining lines, bulbous at each curved end.

"May I open it?" he asked, unsure as to any particular traditions or rules regarding the book. It had been so long since he had dealt with something such as this, and he was unsure as to any customs that might need following.

"Of course," said the youth. He skittered his shoe back and forth over the swelling mossy caulking between the old flagstones that paved the courtyard. A mosquito, fat, with dangling legs, landed on his arm, and the boy watched it with interest before lazily waving a hand at it.

"This isn't a Brackis script," noted Regent, taking in the blockish letters that ran down the page in neat, divided columns. The script was hard, but with flourishes here and there, as though to add a touch of humanity. It had been hand-scribed, Regent thought, taking into account the slight irregularities between repeated letters. "It's one of the Dead languages."

"Yes it is," said the boy, confidently. "Old Silthan. It's a perfect language, the most complicated language in the world. It was made for... designed for the expression of religion." He added the last in a lower tone, swatting again at the mosquito that had long since gone elsewhere.

Regent gripped the book feverishly, marvelling at the opportunity that had been presented to him. "Number systems, is that correct?"

"The geometry of words, we call it." The youth stood, straightening himself a little hesitantly, with that unfamiliarity that comes when one is still learning to trust the changing boundaries of one's body. "If I leave it with you..." He trailed off, a high, questioning note in his voice.

Regent righted himself. He found that his eyes were level with the boy's shoulder, which was slim but strong beneath his thin shirt. He raised his gaze, feeling somehow that the power balance had shifted, and so pre-empted this by going to the gate and swinging it open. "One month. Hopefully less. But come to me in a month, and I should have your name."

The Brackis boy stood for a moment, as though trying to reassure himself that the sacred book would indeed be safe, but finally turned to leave, a fragile smile creasing his face. "A month."

Regent listened as the boy crept back and forth across the beams that separated him from the smear of blight that was the Voda River. For all his attempts at silence, the beams shrieked occasionally, a noise that was all the more evident now that the day had faded and the acute evening stillness had set in.

Boy stood on one of the many criss-crossing, interlocking beams of splintery wood and bricks rammed through with rusted poles that had been set up, makeshift, by persons unknown. There was a neat little arched bridge further down, drawn from bluestone and decorated with colourful mosaics and ornate fretwork, and marked with metal signposts that howled as the wind caught them, but quaintness in no way made up for practicality, and so it seemed that this monstrosity of footbridges joining the rough alleyways flanking either bank of the Voda had been devised from a mixture of necessity and laziness.

Boy balanced where he was, squinting back at the domed building that leant like an ailing veteran against Dr Polertrony's residence. Its front windows, what appeared to have once been glorious leadlights depicting detailed scenes, were bare, revealing only thin stalks of straggling black metal here and there from which the glass had long ago fallen.

He steadied himself, then leapt onto the near bank, sliding in the mud-drowned weeds, avoiding a whorl of vomit plastered like papier mache down over the knife-like reeds and death lilies. He stumbled up to the path, still off-balance, feeling hazy and heady from the greasy, humid air. A feral cat, mangy and with a distended belly and hungry eyes, crawled out from a sewer drain and fled past him and on to the sagging stone balcony of a once-beautiful mansion.

The tiny church had once been painted a vibrant pale blue, the colour of wren's eggs, but now was lined with layers of algae and the gritty handprints of smog. Birdlime caked the protruding windowsills like foul snow, and airplants clung grimly between the widening gaps between the bluestone. The front doors, double and pointed at their tops, were set to one side. Cracked metal fretwork splintered across them.

Boy went around to the north side of the church, the side farthest away from Dr Polertrony's. There was a toothless grille here, obscured only partially by broken glass and rocky debris, that seemed to lead inside. He slipped through, bending down and curling up in that manner that only the young seem capable of, squeezing into small spaces like rats.

Inside, the church was stifling, as though it were holding on to a lungful of air indefinitely. The fading light spilled through the blind windows, catching on the mosaic ceiling and floors. The pattern on the floor alternated between coloured and mirrored tiles, as did the ceiling, but in such a way that the mirrors above reflected the coloured tiles below and vice-versa. The effect was oddly sea-like, and Boy stood for a moment mentally tracing the paths between mirrored and patterned tiles. For all this, though, it was difficult to make out what exactly the mosaic depicted, whether text or image.

He realised, momentarily, that it was not this that was the point of it, however, and sank to the ground, crossing his legs and watching about him as the very presence of this intricate beauty overwhelmed him. He remained, thus, in a wash of faded, reflected colour, each instance an echo of those before it, and created and recreated over and over as the sun slowly ebbed away in entirety.

It was until a ludicrous hour in the morning each day over the next week that Regent Polertrony worked in his attic office, poring over the angular text in the book and consulting a series of dictionaries and grammars he had pulled from a rotting wooden crate. The Voda's damp breath seemed to pervade everything, causing generators to short circuit, books to weep and moulder, and clothing to sweat seemingly spontaneously. The rooms on the ground level of the house were often clammy, particularly in the morning, as though spritzed with a fine layer of silty mist. Usually the attic escaped this, and remained relatively dry, but a telling, dark stain had begun to spread across the ceiling like a grasping hand. Similar stains marred the fleur de lis wallpaper that had been thickly and hurriedly applied to the walls.

Regent stretched his arms over his head, listening for the dull click of his shoulders and elbows. The Voda outside was tinged a faint green from the belching gas it released as it settled overnight. Every now and then, a Mora would break the surface, cabbage-like brain pulsing in its open cranium, and dash after a particularly large dragonfly or the skimming trail of a hapless fish swimming carelessly by.

He lowered his arms and stacked his reference materials in a neat pile, doing the same with the looseleaf paper on which he was jotting down the book's dimensions and concordance. He was not getting anywhere with it. The task was entirely beyond him: he was unfamiliar with the language — and what a language it was, as though deliberately designed to be as ambiguous and puzzling as possible. Which it probably had been, he thought, tying the silk sash around its leather cover and yanking it tightly enough that the edges of the cover bore shallow marks from the effort.

He switched off the generator powering his desk lamp, which was fading and flickering anyway, and went down the stairs, grasping at the slick banister with one hand, and clutching the book in the other.

Downtown University existed half in the new city, and half in the old. It was not that it had come out of the flood unscathed as such, but rather an enormous effort had been invested into draining the floors and buildings that now found themselves below ground level, and in building glass-walled partitions between the precarious structures so that they might be more easily accessed.

Regent found himself taking the familiar route down to his erstwhile office — left past Anthropology, down on to the Esoterics division, down again, right through Geomatics, and down again into the Linguistics and Culture rooms, the ones that seemed to have grown organically from the curved spool of the library wing. He glanced into the library, along the rows of musty writing desks that flanked the massive shelves that trembled slightly each time a Mils crewboat roared past or a ferry rumbled by, churning the water propping up the university walls like milk.

As he had hoped, and half suspected, Fenton White was bent over the desk farthest from the eastern entrance, working under the old-fashioned paraffin lamps and clattering away at his typewriter like a man possessed. This particular attribute probably had something to do with the fact that he was, in fact, a man possessed — although he would never volunteer any more information than that he had been self-experimenting at the request of a certain Mils High Commissioner.

Fenton looked up as Regent approached, but continued his mad touch-typing, switching the alphabet on the keys between those of three languages seamlessly. After transcribing an additional page or so, he ceased typing, and steepled his fingers together, resting his slender forearms against the fat black body of the typewriter.

"A challenging assignment, I take it?" he said knowingly. Regent almost expected him to rub his bony hands together in glee.

Fenton had the kind of memory that seemed to be perfect in all regards: he could recite verbatim entire books that he had read years past, and transcribe from memory conversations between multiple parties, but was most evidently gifted in languages, being able to master completely foreign socio- and pragmalinguistic norms with minimal effort. Regent, a renowned onomastician, but fluent in only three languages and passably knowledgeable about several dialects, found that his jealousy was lessened if he ascribed Fenton's gift to more Mils-funded self-experimentation.

"Maddeningly so," concurred Regent. "I've been at it all night. I've exhausted all my resources at home, and well, I have to admit that my proficiency with this language isn't what it should be."

"Well, it isn't really your area of research as such, is it, though?" He held out his hand to Regent, indicating that he should like to take a look at the book. Regent gladly gave it to him.

"It really seems quite impossible," Regent said, rolling his stiff shoulders back and forth. He had forgotten how the cold in here had made him ache. "Old Silthan. The word boundaries are entirely ambiguous, and appear in dozens of different formations throughout the text, making a lexical concordance near impossible, and both the case system and verbal inflection system use portmanteau forms that are half the time underspecified, meaning that any equation I write is either too generalised or too precise. It's like I've thrown a rounded off version of Pi into the first step of a problem."

Fenton nodded, taking up Regent's despairing argument and kindly pointing out the sheer hellishness of the language in question.

"Twelve cases," Fenton continued, "four moods, dual, tri, and multiple plural systems, and inflection that can vary according to the position of a letter within a word, that word within the phrase, that phrase within a sentence, that sentence within the paragraph..." He trailed off, exhilarated by the brilliance of the language they were discussing.

"It's like a language of fractals. There seems to be an immeasurable number of permutations. Each aspect of each equation that I write overrides the last."

"How long do you have?" asked Fenton, skimming over the pages of the book and tapping out notes on his typewriter as he read.

Regent seated himself backwards on the chair of the next desk along, hugging its curved wooden back. "Three weeks yet. But I have nothing: no clue as to the name. The number of syllables? The letter with which the name starts? The prevalence of vowels, and which vowels? The phonotactics? Everything I try seems to be filtered through a layer of obscurity." He unfurled his arms from around the chair, realising that he had been grasping it so tightly that long spiderwebbing marks caused by the pressure had begun to sprawl down his flesh. He dabbed at his brow with the back of his hand, and wished he could do the same for the clammy underneath of his knees.

Fenton, already immersed in several pages of notes pertaining to the book, glanced up over the long, low frames of his spectacles. "It's nearing dawn, Regent. I'd suggest that you take a break. Go down to the Noodle Road Snuggery or the Markets. Or even back to your own bed. I'll send notice if I come up with anything in your absence."

Regent wanted to protest, but knew that doing so would be only out of the fear of Fenton's making the sort of advance in the work that Regent held no hope of doing — which would be an inevitable outcome, anyway. He stood, straightening out his trousers so that they skimmed the tops of his narrow shoes.

The nerve passage running through his brow was stabbing sharply at his forehead, causing black spots to drill against his vision. The pain had spread through to the back of his skull and his neck; even his jaw was stiff. He did indeed need to rest: he was exhausted, in fact, but the pull of the Snuggery, at Fenton's suggestion, no less, was far more appealing. Both for its proximity and the soft opium haze that made its name so apt.

Boy remained in the old church for most of the following month, venturing out during the day for a roll of smoked meat or a handful of lychees and starfruit, but avoiding the analytical stares of the bustling citizens and tourists. As he gradually grew used to the city and its abundance of muddled together cultural and class groups, he found that everyone moved with a fierce focus, in a linear fashion.

At one point he bumped into a newsprint vendor with the most vividly black skin Boy had ever seen, who thrust a ragged-edged sheet at him. The vendor's fingers were swollen from arthritis, with his knuckles standing out like the thick wooden keys of hamlet flutes.

"The Mora!" bellowed the man, his tongue slavering from his mouth, covered in a thick yellowed paste. "Don't you want to know about the Mils and the Mora?" He caught Boy's arm, and Boy wondered whether those knotted fingers would grow into his flesh like roots.

Boy shook his head. "I don't read," he said simply. "I come from the hamlets."

At this, the man's gnarled fingers carved at Boy's pale skin, leaving a series of jagged raw crescents like demented notes on a musical stave. His left pupil swam mistily back and forth beneath the shell of a cataract, and his right overcorrected as he sought Boy's gaze. "Then how do you expect to know anything?" crowed the man, flashing filed-back gold teeth.

Boy pulled his arm away, rubbing at the vicious score printed into it. He dashed across an arched bridge heavy with mangoes and starfruit that had fallen from two entwined trees yawning up out of the Voda. An elephant-boy crawled about, a basket in either hand, selecting the darkest, softest fruit from the ripe mounds of pulp.

Boy ignored him, and leaning with his arms against a faded wooden balustrade, stared at the well-heeled patrons in a tri-level cafe carefully laughing and sipping at their drinks, and thought about what he knew.

His trek to the city, on foot and then the terrifying linked, open platforms of the rail-line that met the walls of the city before drowning beneath the black Voda water — this trek had been of such importance to him. Insightful, reverential, enlightening; time alone with himself, the book, and the teachings that coloured hamlet life from one's very first days. It was this, this and the time he spent in the sad, anonymous church, that was sharply marked for him. Indeed, this city to him was a furious, seething mass of seemingly unconnected people, things, places, all nameless, all unknown; but little by little, it revealed itself to him, evolving from chaos into a perfect, clockwork whole.

And there was not only this, but the thought that he, a bastard, after all, had no name, yet he was he not perfectly capable of comprehending himself?

Regent lay on his back across a metal book trolley. If he jiggled his legs, its castored wheels shivered from side to side. He suspected that movement enough on his behalf could send it crashing into a bookcase.

He finished tallying up his results, and said glumly, "Three hundred and forty-six." He waited not so patiently for Fenton to enlighten him as to his own number.

Fenton squinted myopically through his spectacles. He hesitated a moment before replying, drumming his spindly fingers against his typewriter. The ringing sound caused by this took a few moments to die away, but even once it had, Regent could not shake the eerie feeling that it somehow remained. "Six hundred and forty-three, I'm afraid."

Regent closed his eyes momentarily, biting down hard on the inside of his cheek. It had been six weeks, and though the hamlet boy had not yet returned, the two men had done little else than work on the problem of this holy book. Regent had taken to brewing his poppy tea and cooking up his fen (his latest indulgence) here in the library between parses of the text.

"We'll have to compare results. Is it possible to alphabetise them?"

Fenton grinned. "But of course." He snatched Regent's list, lined it up with his own, and clattered about on his typewriter for no more than ten minutes before pulling out a long, unbroken sheet of onionskin paper from the glossy machine. Regent was not entirely sure as to how he felt about this disturbing efficiency.

The two pored over the lists for several hours, aligning values and matching up vowel harmony and consonant mutation patterns. The sheet was soon marred with a mass of inky scrawlings and scratchings-out, and Regent found he was holding his breath as a glimmer of understanding danced tantalisingly before him before leaping away again.

Fenton, of course, beat him to it.

"They're opposites, in every way. Our results. Mine contradict yours —" he jabbed at Regent's seventh word, and scored at his own seventh last with a ragged fingernail "— but worse, mine contradict my own —" he slid his finger up to his own seventh word. "There is no harmony here. We've produced a ridiculous cacophony of random sounds, pathetic musings. If one takes a step away, looks less closely than we have been, one can see that these results are indeed related, but in such a way that they dance uselessly around some central notion that it is impossible to grasp. We cannot reach consensus, not even in ourselves, because there is no consensus to be found."

Regent found that he was clutching one corner of the page so tightly that greasy fingertip-shaped pools of sweat were soaking through it. The bookshelves, heavy and musty with books swollen from years of student borrowing and water damage, seemed to be edging ever closer, and each breath he took seemed too shallow to be satisfying.

"I'll return the book to the boy," he said, his voice calm, but as brittle as a tenuous drawing of a bow across strings. He picked it up, gingerly, as though it were soft and helpless in his grasp—although he knew it was anything but. His taxonomy remained, dog-eared and smeared, on the desk at which he had been working. As Regent went to leave, Fenton caught at his shirt-cuff, pinching it sharply between fiendishly malnourished fingers. He said nothing, but his eyes were feverish, haunted, his thoughts clearly, finally, mirroring Regent's.

Regent heard the sound of the paraffin lamps fading as he left, and he found himself wondering if there would be any library at all the next time he returned.

Regent's fountain pen-scarred work desk was the kind that boasts myriad flamboyantly decorated drawers and crannies—many too small to be of any use whatsoever beyond holding a single eraser or pen nib. However, it did contain several large enough to hold some of the enormous cardboard folders in which he maintained photographii of each item the inherent name of which he had determined, and that name itself, carefully embossed in a sharp-edged font in the lower left hand of each photographia. His notes and calculations he kept in separate files again, and it was these he consulted now. He rifled through thousands of equations, deductions, and solutions, confirming that his methods had indeed been true to the rest of his work.

There were over sixteen thousand items categorised and named — an enormous amount even for a considerably established onomastician such as himself. Sixteen thousand items that he had painstakingly solved for and given a name, given a place in this world. Yet this book, this terrible tome, with its foul language that obfuscated and mocked, this book had no such thing. In its leather-bound simplicity, this book was the most threatening, terrifying thing across which he had yet come.

As Regent wrote out a telegram to the Mils department of religious affairs, he could take solace only in the fact that without a name, the book simply could not, did not, exist.

THE ONE THAT GOT AWAY

Mark Teppo

haven for raconteurs and fabulists, the Alibi Room was a velvet-lined sanctuary where suggestion and persuasion were the watchwords and truth was such a devalued coin that it couldn't purchase a condom from the dispenser in the men's room. Once through the unassuming door and the voluminous coat check where racks of costumes, disguises, and false uniforms waited, the patrons redrafted their pasts and invented possible futures. The promise of altered company meant that everyone — the regulars slouched on the narrow stools at the mahogany bar, the graceful and discrete staff, the liars grouped around lacquered tables or sprawled on plush couches — everyone could pretend the world beyond the rust-colored brick and the old growth timber was the fantasy. The only reality that mattered was the invented one wrapped in velvet drapery and limned with orange light.

The Alibi, with its womb darkness and ambient embrace, held Colby tight. Whispering gently to him with the forgotten white noise susurration of his mother's bloodstream, the Alibi cared. The accounting analysis he did for Emphir Financial Services had merit. His study on corporate paper waste was important; his solution, an aggressive recycling program coupled with a carefully calculated ratio of premium bond paper for external communications to recycled pulp for daily consumption. The savings to the company would never be significant — barely two-thirds the salary of one accountant — but the paper reclamation would save several hundred acres every year. That won't be ignored, the Alibi said to him. Someone would notice, someone would call down to the Fifth floor where the bean counters and money handlers worked their precarious magic. Someone would —

"Hey, Colby. Your turn."

Colby roused himself. "What?"

Jack waved at the waitress, a slender girl with short pigtails and a Celtic tattoo curling around her wrist. "Pay Jennie and tell us a story."

Slowly extricating himself from the Alibi's grip, Colby fumbled for his wallet. Thumbing through his cash like he was trying to separate blades of glass, he tried to think of a good lie. This was the way their game worked: buy a round, tell a story — the others would be a receptive audience, alternately fueling the liar's tale or expressing mock outrage, false as everything else at the Alibi. Colby tried to compose something as he fumbled a twenty out of his wallet, but all that he could think of was dead trees.

Jennie smiled at him, an ivory gleam in the midnight of the room, and took his drunkenly offered bill. She spun around, her pigtails whipping against her lean neck, and smartly marched off to the infinitely distant bar.

He stared at his wallet, his thumb and forefinger rubbing the corner of a second twenty dollar bill. He couldn't think of a decent story — other than the one whispering in his ear. *Your report will be a catalyst.* The voice was a lover's mistral, a persuasive wind that cajoled and seduced, telling him what his yearning heart wanted to hear. Like an organic infection that spreads to each tree — transferred through root and branch — the impact of the document would spread throughout the entire system. *One branch, one nut, one sprout: eventually the whole forest is changed.*

Deeper in his body, somewhere in the region of his gall bladder and the poison collecting in his liver, a different story was taking hold. No one cares. *There was no short-term shareholder value in long-term ecological stewardship.*

On the tourist maps, the rounded hillock at the center of Windward Park was labeled "Gloriana's Uprising." The name was an abandoned epitaph for a matriarch no one remembered, a truncated geological marker christened by a scientist who knew stone and rock but not history. Glory — as the name was abbreviated by the locals — was a rounded mound: verdantly carpeted with wildflowers in the spring, a naked dome with splintered bones of ragged stone poking through in the winter. Stone lion heads — half-buried, their mouths choked with long liana dotted with red flowers — ringed the base of the dome.

In the previous spring, something broke beneath the uprising. Prosaically, it was a ruptured pipe, one of the heavy conduits that ran water from the recirculation plants along the coast near Sweetlow to the downtown corridor and Ludtown to the south beyond the industrial flats of Harbor Island. But, at the Alibi Room, "prosaic" is unsustainable.

Ancient wells, capped centuries ago when the land was barren of hand-tooled stone and shaped steel, had broken open in the wake of the latest seismic tremors that periodically rattled the silverware and dishes. Artesian waters, freed, sought a way out of their earthen prison. That spring, said the whispers at the Alibi, the lions began to drool.

By mid-summer, the heads were vomiting. And the waters, long preserved beneath the scarred and tormented surface, were so pure they caused the plant life at the center of the park to eruct.

The floral eruption spawned such a cloud of pollen and miasma of rotting fruit that strange creatures were drawn to the wild park, lured out of their hidden demesnes and secret valleys by the redolent paradise's scent. By the time creeping honeysuckle began to grip the paint-flecked sign of the old Rialto Theater at the corner of Glacier and 17th, anecdotal sightings were part of the pub-speak at the Alibi. Cats the size of huskies and as black as a starless night. Flying monkeys that clustered like ravens on the broken fire escape railings. Rabbits and gophers that walked upright. Hypnotic serpents, exothermic lizards, slick-skinned nereids, birds that molted gold leaf: the stories grew more fanciful with each passing week, just as the green crept further and further into the houses and streets ringing the traditional boundary of the park.

Winter froze the spread of the trees and vines, arresting their invasion of the brick and stone. The moon floated low over Glory during the cold months, its icy gaze layering rime and ice on the rounded hump. Pathways to the heart of the park became blocked and redirected, hiding the frozen paradise so that it became a sanctuary for the fantastic creatures that had been drawn to the city.

When the unicorn's side was pricked, it fled back to the hidden heart of Glory. Bloody spatter, stark and black against the frosted ground, was the precious trail that led the hunters through the icy maze of Windward Park.

David knelt and touched the red smear on the whitened ground. His face knotted with disbelief and uncertainty, he showed his stained glove to the others. "It's blood," he said.

Jack grunted as he reset his crossbow. "I told you I winged it." He fished another metal bolt out of the nylon pouch on his belt and slipped it into the groove of the stock.

"Winged what?" David asked. "There was nothing..." His voice faltered as he smeared the blood between two fingertips, feeling the sticky lubricant slide between his gloved fingers.

"It was standing right here," Jack said, pointing at the ground. "Colby saw it too."

Colby hunched his shoulders as David looked at him. "I saw something," he muttered. "Looked like — "

"A fucking unicorn," Jack interrupted. "Come on. Say it. You saw it." He mimed the presence of a protrusion from his forehead. "You saw the horn."

"I don't know what I saw, Jack," Colby said. "I mean, you were shooting at it before I could really be sure what it was."

"Oh, that's such bullshit." Jack scuffed the ground, throwing up a spray of ice slivers. He turned to the fourth man for support. "Did you see it, Hurley?"

Hurley, his gaze focused on the David's stained gloves, swallowed heavily and shook his head. Colby noticed his hands were tight on the stock of his crossbow and his breathing was shallow and quick.

Jack shook his head. "I know what I saw. It was all white, and its mane was like glass. It was standing right here."

Colby looked at his feet instead of meeting Jack's fervent gaze. His eyes ached, and his tongue was thick and heavy. Words seemed like bricks, too unwieldy to shift with his fat tongue.

"You wanted this too, Colby." Jack's face had the feral gleam again, that focused rush of the adrenaline talking. He crouched beside David and swiped his fingers through the spray of blood. He smeared unicorn blood across his forehead and down his cheeks. "We could have come without you, but you're the one that wanted something more than just a made-up story for the Alibi. You wanted something real." He stalked away, following an irregular path of crimson dots that led deeper into the park.

David's eyes followed Jack, and Colby saw him register the irregular spatter that Jack was following. "I didn't see anything," he said to Colby, his voice low enough that Jack couldn't hear it. "Nothing but shadows."

"Shadows don't bleed," Hurley said, stepping close to the other two as if engaging them in a conspiracy. "There was something there, wasn't there Colby?"

Colby touched his throat, rubbed his gloved hand across the cold skin of his neck as if he was trying to massage out the stuck words.

"You did see something," David said. "Just like Jack."

Colby nodded, still reluctant to speak of what he had seen. The unicorn had been nearly invisible against the backdrop of frosted tree trunks. But once Colby had been able to distinguish the difference between unicorn horn and tree branch, once he realized the distinction between ice-bleached bark and sleek hide, he had been able to see the creature without any difficulty.

Jack's crossbow bolt had caught it high on the right hip. Colby had watched it rear, moonlight twisting its pearlescent horn, and he had almost closed his eyes. As if such a denial would undo what he had witnessed.

Hurley arrived in time to pay for the next round of drinks. He gave a credit card to Jennie and then stared at the rocking motion of her backside as she walked away. "Man, it's like clockwork," he said, making a "tick-tock" noise with his mouth. "I never get tired of watching that."

Jack and David laughed, an eager audience response to the "Laugh Now!" marquee powered by Hurley's ego and wit. A gregarious salesman, he was well on his way to becoming a florid man; his ready smile and loosely hinged jaw spread his features toward his ears. His hands were large enough to stretch around the gravid circumference of his stomach, and his reach was like the open wingspan of a heron.

"You will not believe the day I've had," Hurley started. When Colby, the designee to be vocally incredulous by virtue of being on Hurley's right, said nothing, he spread his hands wide like he was reaching to hug the entire table. "It was pretty incredible."

Jack dismissed Colby's vacant stare. "Some report he turned in. Got him in a funk. Ignore him. Tell us."

Hurley's grin stretched as wide as his hands. "Okay, so there's this Executive Assistant who works for the Vice-President of Sales. I hear she's, like, nearly fifty or something. You'd never believe it. Toned, tight — must spend four hours a day at the gym. Just an amazing piece of ass.

"Anyway, we're in the elevator today — coming back from some meeting on Four — just her and I, and she catches me sneaking a peek at her tits. Know what she says? She says — "

"'Take me back to your office and fuck me'?" Colby surfaced from his reverie, revenant rising from an ancient tomb, drawn back to the table by Hurley's story.

Hurley's smile faltered, real-time erosion stripping away the edge of a cliff. "Hey, Colby, come on."

"You always tell the same story." Colby looked at the others, inspecting their faces for a sign that they, too, were aware of the persistent core of Hurley's tales. "Aren't you tired of it?"

"It's not the same," Hurley countered.

"Oh, what was last week's?" Colby asked. "An intern in the copy center who wanted to get copies of your dick. Was that it? And the week before — something about a car wash?"

"Come on, Colby, we're at the Alibi." David put a hand on his arm. "Does it matter?"

Colby shoved his hand away, drunkenly missing his wrist and having to use his whole arm to push the other man away. "Yeah, maybe. Maybe if we're going to lie to each other — to ourselves — we ought to be a little better at it."

"Who pissed in his drink?" Hurley groused.

"No, damnit. I'm serious. Aren't we getting too old for this? How long are we going to keep coming here and telling the same banal lies?"

"I thought that was the point." Jack raised an eyebrow.

"What are we hiding from?" Colby countered.

Jack reached for his drink. "Well Colby, since you're the one pissing in the stories, why don't you tell us. What are we — *what are you* — hiding from?"

The room lurched beneath Colby as if Jack's words were punctuated by a quake — tremors rumbling through the manmade bluff of the city's edge, threatening to calve off the Alibi Room and throw it down into the bay. A muscle in Colby's cheek twitched as if he had just been stung by a wasp. Does it matter?

Does any of it matter? An existential black hole lurked in wait for him. The velvet womb of the Alibi tried to hide him from this pit, tried to keep him from spilling into the limitlessness of...

"Nothing," he muttered.

"Then quit spoiling it for everyone else."

"So, are you a virgin?" Hurley asked Colby as they walked along the path beneath the frozen branches.

"Excuse me?" Colby said.

Hurley stopped and put his hand on Colby's arm to slow him down. "The unicorn can only be snared by those who are innocent of sin. You know the story: virginal maids sitting out under trees, waiting for the unicorn to come lay its head on their laps. Maybe that's why they were bait; they could see the animal." He shrugged. "Ergo: since you can see it, does that mean you're a virgin?"

Colby looked at the ice-fused branches of the poplars and birch overhead. As a child, he had chased squirrels in the park, laughingly pursuing them into the thickets of trees until they darted up the knotted trunks. It had been a long time, but he remembered always seeing the sky: blue through the partially interlocked puzzles of the leaves. Now, winter linked the trees in the awkward embraces of estranged cousins at familial funerals. It was like being inside a cathedral, a sacred place where confessions were heard and one's holy worth was considered. *Are you a virgin? Are you worthy of God's embrace?*

Suddenly colder, his spine reacting to an impression — a latent memory that was more instinct than personal recollection — Colby shivered and looked away from the dome of ice.

Ahead of them, David and Jack tracked the unicorn's trail, eyes watching for the chaotic pattern of each successive spatter.

"Listen," Hurley said, "It's not a big deal if you are, but — "

"What about Jack?" Colby interrupted, indicating the two men ahead of them. "Is he a virgin too?"

Hurley opened and closed his mouth several times. "Maybe. I don't know."

"By your argument, non-virgins can't see the unicorn, which would explain why long-time studs like you and David can't see it. You're blind because you shook your dicks at too many girls over the years. Is that how it works?"

"It's just an idea — "

Colby cut Hurley off with an abrasive laugh. "Maybe I've not had the 'office romances' that you've had, but I lost my virginity when I was fifteen, Hurley. And I've slept with a few women since then."

"Fine," Hurley snapped. "You got a better explanation?"

"We should be asking Jack. He seems to be the resident expert."

"Right," Hurley snorted. "David would know better. He's been hunting — "

"What?"

"Maybe that's what it is." Hurley grabbed Colby's arm. "Listen, maybe it's like that thing where every story changes with every telling. You know, like that game we did in school where we'd all line up and the teacher would whisper something to the first kid. He'd pass it along to the next, and the next to the next, you know, on down the line. The last kid then says aloud what he is told, and it is always different. Maybe the myth of the unicorn is the same thing. After all these generations of telling the story, the details have gotten muddled. Maybe it's not about being a 'virgin' but about being innocent."

"Innocent. How?"

"You ever been hunting, Colby? Have you ever killed anything?"

"No. Jesus, Hurley." Colby grimaced. "I've never even held a crossbow before tonight."

"Right. And David and I have. He's taken me bow hunting with him a couple of times. This isn't my first time."

"But that would mean that Jack is innocent too." Colby glanced at the receding pair. Until Jack found his quarry again. *Until they caught up with the wounded animal.* His chest tightened as if a python was squeezing his ribs. "What happens to the unicorn if we kill it?"

Hurley hefted his crossbow, getting a better grip on the stock. His eyes were bright and clear, unstained by alcohol. "Maybe that's when it becomes visible again. Maybe that's the only way the rest of us will ever see it."

The waitress replenished their drinks, removing the ice-filled glasses as if she were clearing the detritus of an expired ceremony. The four men made no eye contact with one another for a moment, their faces turned in random directions like a quartet of demagnetized compasses. The foursome, cast adrift from their collective mood by Colby's outburst, sought other distractions. Hurley stared after the waitress; David grew fascinated with the play of light on the half-moon of his fingernails; Colby's eyes roved around the room as he tried to pretend he didn't feel the feral burn of Jack's gaze.

"Are you tired of listening to us, Colby?" Jack asked. "Is it too much of an effort to have a beer and play along for a few hours? Have we bored you that badly?"

Colby stared at his glass, unwilling to raise his head. "I'm just tired," he said. "Long week. It's got nothing to do with anything."

"Yeah, 'nothing.' Is that the whole problem? You woke up this morning and realized just how empty your life is. When was the last time you got a decent raise? Or had a date? What friends do you have outside the three of us? Are you still living in that shithole in Parkway, or did you ever manage to save enough for a deposit on a place across the bridge?"

Each question was a psychic blow that collapsed more of his body: his lungs grew tighter, his stomach knotted, his throat constricted to a tiny hole. Each question externalized an interior complaint Colby had been fighting, had been dismissing these last months as he had focused on his report. As if everything would be resolved with the release of his findings; as if his document was a life-affirming manifesto instead of a study in paper consumption. Jack's questions were delivered as if he was trying to push Colby into the existential blankness that filled the void behind the inconsequential truth of his report.

Colby tried to brush them off, tried to dismiss them with a wave of his hand. "Forget it," he said. He struggled to get out of the plush comfort of the chair. "I'm done. I'm heading home."

"You need to do something," Jack said. "Something real. Jump out of an airplane, race a motorcycle. Something like that."

Colby paused, one arm partially snared in his coat. Against his better judgment, he turned and looked down at Jack. "Now?"

"Why not?"

Colby had a show of looking around the room. "Because it's the middle of the night. Because I — "

"Because you're scared? Because it's easier to talk about doing something than actually doing it? Because you'd rather bitch about us telling the same old stories than actually go out and make a new one?"

"No — "

"It's just an excuse, Colby. Whatever you're going to say. It's just a lame excuse to do nothing again."

Colby flushed. He shoved his remaining arm in his coat. "What the fuck do you care?"

"Because I think you're right. Because Hurley does tell the same damn story every time, and I'm sick of it too. But is that his fault? Is anything we fail to do here any fault but our own?"

"Jesus, Jack," Hurley snorted, stung by his words.

Colby's tongue was dry, and he licked his lips as if to find moisture on them. "What did you have in mind?"

Jack smiled. "There's a unicorn in Windward Park."

Hurley laughed. "Ah, shit, that's a good one, Jack." The others looked at him. "What? It's a good setup for a story. Giving us all grief for being boring and then hitting us with..." He faltered. "What? You believe him?"

David nodded. "I heard it too. From someone else."

"Oh, and that makes it true?" Hurley shook his head and reached for his drink. "Everyone could be telling the same lie here. That doesn't make it true."

Jack was still staring at Colby. "So let's go find out. If you're so eager for something true and hard and honest, then let's go. Let's go out there right now and find it."

"Why?" Colby asked, the only word he could manage.

"Why not?"

"That's not a reason."

"Isn't it?" Jack raised his chin towards the wall behind Colby. "David and Hurley have enough hunting gear to outfit all of us. Let's go bag ourselves a unicorn and get the head stuffed. Mount it right there on the wall behind you so no one forgets." He laughed and looked at the others, spearing them with the fervent gleam in his eyes. "Fuck the stories. Let's go make our own."

The ground was slick and icy near the lion statue, and Colby nearly fell. His hip caught on the angry mouth of the statue where he regained his balance, leaning against the cold stone for support. Behind him, Jack shouted incoherently, giving voice to the bloom of pain from the shattered bones in his shoulder.

The unicorn thundered up Glory's slope, its hooves cracking against the frosted hillock. Colby pressed himself against the stone lion, stealing a glance upslope as the animal passed. Silver twinkled in its mane, its horn a glittering spike. Blood streamed down its white flank from Jack's earlier crossbow bolt.

"Where is it?" Hurley was in a panic. "Where the fuck is it?"

"Look for Jack's bolt," David shouted. Standing in the open meadow at the base of Glory, he sighted carefully through the sights of his crossbow. *The experienced hunter*, Colby thought, transfixed by David's patience, *waiting for his prey to come into range*.

The unicorn charged down the slope past Colby, head lowered.

But he can't see it.

David squinted and fired. The unicorn flipped its head up, horn rising. The metal bolt struck sparks — a cascade of falling stars — as it ricocheted off the hard horn. Galloping past the stunned hunter, the unicorn dipped its horn down. David spun, trailing a thin arc of crimson, and then he was facedown on the ground.

Hurley hesitated, caught between trying to do something for Jack's shattered shoulder and his fallen friend. Colby found himself wondering how surreal the scene must be for the florid salesman. First, Jack had been knocked down and trampled and now David, throat cut, was a crumpled shape on the white ground. All the while, Hurley hadn't seen the animal that had dropped two of his companions. Like fighting a ghost.

The unicorn wheeled near the tree line and pounded back across the field. Colby braced his back against the cold statue as the animal charged towards him. His crossbow lay on the ground not far from him, but he didn't dare move from the statue, as if he could meld himself into the stone and disappear.

The unicorn pulled up short of Colby, rearing back on its hind legs. Up close, its hooves were huge and flashed like the blade of a headsman's axe. The blood streaking its flank made its ribs appear like dusty shadows under its pale skin. Its eyes were stark and white with panic, and its chest heaved like massive bellows.

Colby was sucked into the winter whiteness of the unicorn's eyes, suddenly pulled into a pure void bereft of shadow and darkness. As the animal towered over him, the panic and fear flowed out of Colby as if a plug had been pulled out of him and all the emotional tension drained out of his body. He floated in the opaque purity of the unicorn's gaze, and instead of being lost against this background, he was a single dot upon the white sea. A nut. A seed. A catalyst.

The unicorn blinked, a shuttering of souls, and Colby was snapped back into his own body. The animal lowered its horn. Not as an antagonist, but as a gesture of recognition and kindness. Of understanding. Colby raised his hand, his fingers reaching for the tip of the unicorn's horn.

The unicorn bleated and took a drunken step to Colby's left, and he saw the fresh crossbow bolt jutting from its side just behind its shoulder.

Jack, leaning against Hurley, lowered his crossbow, a triumphant grin working through the pain wracking his face.

The animal staggered on the uneven slope of Glory. It shook its head, twisting its neck in an effort to see what was biting its flesh. Colby took a step towards the wounded creature, hand still outstretched. He reached for the bolts jutting out of its sides instead of the horn. If he could just touch the bolt, he could draw it out before the unicorn expired. He could stop the flow of blood.

The unicorn's front legs buckled, and it fell heavily against the slope. Its head lolled on a weak neck, and Colby laid a hand on the heaving animal's flank. His fingers tightened against the hot and sweaty flesh.

An irrational urge to press against the animal's flesh shuddered through his arms — a foreign desire to dig his fingers deep into its damp skin as if by tearing into its flesh he would understand its secrets. As if the flesh under the quivering hide was a communion of sorts, a meat more divine than his own flesh. As if the animal was life itself, bleeding out onto the white ground. The unicorn was real — it was the only thing that was and could ever be real, its flank hot and shaking under his hand and cheek.

"Get out of the way, Colby!" Jack shouted. He had Hurley's crossbow and was pointing it at Colby and the unicorn. The tip of the bolt shivered as Jack's adrenaline-charged muscles twitched and jumped.

With a clarity like the white field he had seen in the unicorn's eye, Colby knew Jack would fire. Even if he laid his body across the animal in an effort to block Jack's shot, he knew such a sacrifice would be ultimately fruitless. Jack — or Hurley — would just shoot him, reload and fire again, unobstructed.

The unicorn snorted beneath him, a sighing exhalation like a furnace expiring. He could feel the ebb of its shivering breath. Colby stretched his arm across the back of the animal, and as he turned his head, his gaze fell on his discarded crossbow. The bolt was still in place, ready to fire.

"Colby — " Jack started, a grim finality in his voice.

He could stop the flow. In a winter-frozen moment of time, Colby understood how to stop the flow of the unicorn's blood. It was an act of sacrifice. A single act: like a single thought or a single shot. The rest was just how the story played itself out.

Colby scrambled for his crossbow, scooping it off the ground. He lifted it with one hand and pulled the trigger.

Jack quivered as the bolt struck him, his expression softening into something akin to dismay. The tip of his weapon drooped, and he coughed. Blood spattered the feathers of his bolt, and his face crumbling with a weak cry, he stared down at the metal bolt sticking out of his chest. He tried to look at Hurley, but his knees failed, and he fell.

The unicorn blew air again, struggling to its feet. Its head drooped, and its knees were locked, but it remained upright. To Colby, it was already fading: opaque through the withers, crystalline shine bleeding through its tail and mane.

I'll never see it again, he realized. His sacrifice was to be a different sort of blooding.

Hurley was reloading the crossbow Jack had given him.

Colby did the same.

"That's a pretty sad story." Jennie tugged on a pigtail, hair woven through the tangle of her long fingers.

Colby's mouth was dry from the telling, as if the words had all dried up in his throat.

"I've heard a lot of unicorn stories recently — it's the popular meme right now — but that one..." She shrugged. "It's different. Most of what I hear are tales of wish-fulfillment. You know, sex stories for stunted adolescents."

Colby nodded.

"Yeah." She clucked her tongue once, punctuating the thought, and tapped her tray against her leg. "So, seriously, are your friends going to be joining you tonight?"

Colby unconsciously put his left hand on his hip where the skin was still scabbed and sore. "No," he said. "I'm the only one."

ALEX AND THE TOYCEIVERS

Paul Meloy

Alex and the Toyceivers is the opening chapter in a novel which continues, pulls together and completes a cycle of stories which tell of the struggle between the Firmament Surgeons and the Autoscopes, warring supernatural beings who want to maintain and perfect Creation on the one hand and destroy it through entropy and despair on the other. The stories *Black Static, Don't Touch the Blackouts, Dying in the Arms of Jean Harlow*, and *Islington Crocodiles* contain the characters and developments which lead into this story of Alex and his first confrontation with the Autoscopes' malign beasts, *the Toyceivers*.

lex went through the cottage to the kitchen and packed a few things in a bag for the day. As he was checking a cabinet for something to put in a sandwich, a shadow passed by the window and he heard a scraping sound from above, on the roof. Some shingles rattled on the path outside, and he thought he could hear a clicking sound retreating down the lane. Standing up quickly, he peered out of the window. Rain blew across the village in fine sheets, causing the view to flutter and drain of colour; it was like looking through a billowing net curtain.

Alex gasped. There at the end of his garden, standing on the tallest pair of stilts he had ever seen, was a small figure. The rain blew and made it impossible to make out any features, but Alex got a distinctly bad feeling from seeing it standing there with rainwater running off it and down its slender stilts in rivulets.

Suddenly, it lunged forward and swung its right leg out and over the garden wall. The stilt swept through the air like the hand of an enormous clock and came down with a wet thud in the ground beneath the windowsill. Alex stepped away from the window, feeling threatened and scared.

Somehow, the creature at the top managed to swivel its hips and sling the other stilt over the fence. Its arms windmilled, and it threw its body forward, bringing the two stilts together outside the window. Alex could see them clearly, and they looked old and splintered and stained.

There was more scraping from the roof and then to Alex's shock, a large chunk of guttering crashed to the ground.

"Hey!" He shouted, and from up there he heard a dreadful rasping chuckle.

Alex felt suddenly disorientated; he had been preparing for a good day out a moment ago and now he was under attack. Alex rummaged in the toolbox beneath the sink and found a small-handled axe. He threw on his jacket, hauled on a pair of boots and opened the back door.

He had to squint against the rain and narrowly avoided getting his head knocked off by a downfall of roof tiles, which exploded on the step by his feet. He circled the rickety stilts and looked up. The stilts were embedded in the ground and reached into the sky. The creature had jumped from them and was now standing on the roof, tugging and pulling at the tiles like a vandal, giggling that horrid cracked laugh. Bits of shingle spattered down like hail.

Infuriated by this incursion, Alex approached the stilts and swung his axe. The creature saw him, shrieked and hurled a roofing slate. Alex ducked and whipped the axe round in an arc. It crunched into the stilt and sent splinters flying.

The creature shrieked again and leapt from the roof. It caught hold of the stilts in both hands and glared down at Alex, who wrenched the axe free and made to swing again.

It braced its feet on the stilts and, to Alex's amazement, shinned like a monkey to the top. It wobbled briefly, clamped its feet into odd, stirrup-like fitments and, before Alex could chop at the stilt again, was away.

It all happened so quickly. With two strides it was off, over the garden wall and down the lane. By his feet, two steaming holes beneath the window were the only evidence Alex had that it had been there. He looked up and there it was, a little shaking figure atop its enormous legs.

"*Pak-Pak!*" It shouted, in a grating high-pitched voice. "*Pak-Pak!*"

Alex felt like hurling the axe at it, but before he could do anything, he heard the strangest noise.

From behind the cottage came the rhythmic sound of rusty springs creaking.

Alex spared Pak-Pak one last look, then ran back into the cottage. He belted up the stairs and went through to the back bedroom.

Just in time to see an ugly blue face drop out of sight.

He went cautiously over to the window but, before he got there, heard that rusting *spang!* again and that face appeared, grinning with malignant glee. It pulled back its arm and threw a fist-sized rock at the window. There was an enormous smash, and the glass blew into the room. The rock carried through and crashed against the wall behind Alex. He leaped aside to avoid the flying glass, skidding on the floorboards and crashing against the wardrobe.

He went back to the window and threw it open.

Spang!

The creature rose up before him, and he saw a look of surprise on its face. It was a horrible thing, fat and slimy, with little stumpy arms and legs sticking out. Its skin was blue, and it was totally bald. It held an armful of rocks, but its shock at seeing Alex leaning out of the bedroom window prevented it from chucking any more. It dropped out of sight, gawping.

Alex reached out and slid a drawer from the bottom of the wardrobe. He heaved it round and pushed it out of the window, holding on tight to the heavy brass handles.

Spang!

The creature flew up and smashed face-first into the underside of the drawer. The wood buckled and splintered and Alex heard a muffled cry. The drawer leaped in his hands and he yanked it back in, threw it on the bed and peered out over the ledge.

Beneath him lay the creature, spread-eagled and cursing. Beside it stood a small, circular trampoline. The fabric looked gray with dirt, and it was laced across in places with big clumsy loops of stitching, where it had been repaired and patched up. The ring of springs connecting it to the rickety frame was ancient with rust.

As he watched, the creature staggered to its feet. It shook its head and rain flew off it in cold heavy droplets. It stood and stared up at Alex.

Alex had been feeling fairly charged up with all the action, but standing there with his head leaning out into the rain, he saw an expression on the creature's face and a look of utter hatefulness in its eyes that shook him and filled him with a sense of cold dread.

From the back of the house Alex heard a sharp cry, and before he could react, a stilt soared up and over the roof and plunged down into the dark wet grass of the back lawn.

With one stride Pak-Pak stepped over the cottage. It looked down at Alex and made a rattling sound in its throat. In response, the other creature gave Alex one last glare, waddled up to its trampoline and grabbed it by the frame. It yanked the trampoline out of the grass, turned and began dragging it across the garden towards the gate.

Pak-Pak spun on its stilts and with enormous strides, stalked away towards the Welts. The trees were thin at the bottom of the garden but thickened and towered as the forest drew away over the hills. This bitter winter had thrashed them of their leaves completely, so as Pak-Pak trod its way deeper into the woods it looked like something doggedly dodging mighty claws.

The gate banged shut, and Alex watched the creature with the trampoline drag it into the Welts. It turned once and Alex heard it make a thick snuffling sound as it met his eye. Then it turned and was gone.

Alex stood there for a moment longer, watching the wind moving amongst the trees, washing them down with that cool, fine rain. The garden gate swung back and forth on its old iron hinge, creaking softly.

He closed the window, careful of the broken pane and made his way back downstairs. He felt shaken but pleased that he had seen the creatures off. What had they been doing here, wrecking his home? He went into the kitchen and grabbed his bag from the kitchen table then went out to the shed to get his bike, a big old three-wheeler with a basket on the front. As Alex wheeled it out, Bong, his cat, came flying over the garden wall. He skidded to a stop at the back door, saw Alex and leapt straight into the basket.

He stroked the top of Bong's head, glad to see him and he nuzzled Alex's hand with an uncommon urgency. His tail curled and flicked and he peered up at Alex with a look of fright in his pale gray eyes. His ears pricked up suddenly, and he pulled away. He stood rigid, front paws up on the rim of the basket and the hackles went up all along his back. He hissed sharply.

Alex followed his gaze.

From out of the Welts came a cry. It began as a low note, and Alex felt it blanket his bones with chill and misery. It began to rise in pitch, gaining in volume, and it was the most awful sound he had ever heard, a sound that wanted to hurt you.

Alex felt like screaming it was so awful. At once, all the birds for miles rose up out of the forest and filled the sky with wheeling black static. They flocked in great pulsing blotches against the low white cloud, but what made the event so unreal was that they flocked as one regardless of species. Crows and doves, woodpigeons, starlings and magpies all turned and shoaled together in total and flawless formation. It was as if the sky kept folding and unfolding itself. They swarmed overhead, and Alex saw nightjars and wrens; herons, ducks, kingfishers and owls all in profusion above him. But the thing that shook him, which made the whole spectacle so upsetting was how they all looked. They all appeared terrified, as if this whole thing was out of their control. Their beaks gaped, and their little eyes bulged. And throughout it all, that screaming drove them, welling up out of the Welts.

Alex patted Bong's head down into the basket and tucked a cloth round him. He jumped on his bike and pedaled off down the path to the gate.

Alex suddenly needed Hemog's friendly face and kind words more than anything, and his vision blurred with more than just the rain. He stood up in the saddle and pushed hard on the pedals. They flew down the lane to Hemog's cottage.

As Alex reached the end of the lane and cut along a path worn into the earth at the outskirts of the Welts, the weather changed. Snow began to fall. Great flakes like rose petals swirled down from the darkening clouds. He rode through a dense and thickening blizzard, aware that the snow was settling quickly on the hard, churned earth and skeletal branches around him. Flakes drifted into his face and spattered against the back of his neck. Bong caught a flake the size of a potato crisp on his tongue and spluttered, burying his head under his cloth.

Mercifully, the dismal screaming had stopped and the birds had taken roost against the snow, a storm of dark particles replaced by sweet purifying whiteness. Alex thought all this had been too much for Bong, who in all the time he had known him had never been one for birds.

Eventually they arrived at Hemog's cottage and came to a stop at his gate.

As Alex climbed off his bike, the front door opened. Bong sprang out from the basket and landed softly in an inch of snow. He looked up at Alex, saw him nod and leapt over the fence and streaked down the path. As he reached the door a large white bull terrier appeared. Bong skidded to a stop but was too late. The dog was on him in a flash, teeth, tongue and gums grinning down on him, gnashing.

Bong slid in the snow, head down and somehow managed to glide beneath the dog's bandy front legs. He rolled over, recovered his footing and pounced on the dog's back.

The dog yelped, but Bong had an ear in his mouth and sensed victory. The dog bounded around the garden with Bong stuck to its back but couldn't shake him off.

Alex opened the gate and walked up the path. Although the door was half open, he knocked anyway, vaguely aware of a dog with a head like a chalk anvil bundle past him and get tangled up in a honeysuckle vine, a small cat hanging off it like a scarf.

As Alex was about to push the door open and go in he glimpsed something move in the Welts behind him. He paused and looked back down the path, and as he did so two horrid looking beasts charged out from the cover of the trees and threw down the gate.

Alex gasped. Bong saw them and, instead of tormenting the dog, grabbed its collar in his mouth and began pulling, freeing it from the tangled remains of the honeysuckle. The dog, who had been writhing and munching at the tendrils, sprang to its feet and advanced down the path towards the creatures, snarling. Bong leaped into Alex's arms.

One of the beasts was low to the ground and scaly. It had a human face and unearthly curly blonde hair, as if someone had stuck a doll's head on a Gila monster. It walked on all fours, although all four limbs were arms with long-fingered hands. It had spines like knitting needles in a ring around its neck.

The other creature had left the path and was circling the dog; a cluster of eyes like a spider's high on its forehead glittering maliciously as it stalked. It walked upright but with a terrible kind of caution as if it had recently recovered from a near fatal accident. It had a face as round and pale as a pudding bowl, featureless apart from that handful of eyes. It wore a dark, pinstriped suit, which was smothered in mud and blotchy with mould. For an awful moment of stillness it stopped and stood there, swaying slightly in the snowfall, and marked Alex. It reached out an arm and pointed at him. It made a gesture with its thumb and index finger like a pistol and mimed a shot at him. Alex felt a rush of air along his cheek, and a small hole appeared in the doorframe behind his head.

Alex cried out and dropped the cat, ducking instinctively. It only got off one shot. The dog twisted away from the advancing lizard-thing and threw itself at the taller figure. It made to fire on the dog but didn't get a chance because the dog had seized its wrist and was tearing at it like a hambone. The creature shrieked and made a desperate imploring gesture to its companion. The doll-faced thing blubbered, rolled its haunting blue eyes and scuttled across the grass to assist. The three fought in the snow, Pinstripe on his back with the dog savaging its gun hand, lizard-dollboy circling and slapping and whining. And all the time the snow continued to fall and it was like watching monsters dance in a dream.

Then, from behind Alex: "Alehouse!"

A hand landed on Alex's shoulder, and: "Hello, Alex. *Alehouse!* Leave them *some* dignity!"

Alex looked up into Hemog's kind, strange face and let him usher him into the warmth of his cottage. Outside, Alehouse was backing away from the creatures, issuing a low, protective growl. He reached the doorstep and stood at Hemog's side, huge barrel chest filled out with pride. Hemog fussed the top of his head.

The thing in the pinstripe suit lay on its back in the snow, arms and legs splayed out. It appeared dead. The other creature ran around it in circles, flakes of snow caught in its blond curls. Its hands were blue with the cold, but it didn't seem to notice. Then, suddenly, pinstripe sat up. It fixed Hemog and Alex with its tiny cluster of beady eyes, and something seemed to unzip beneath its chin. Fluid dribbled out down its tatty shirtfront, and then two huge wicked looking fangs like shards of glass slid out. It lifted its gun hand.

"Inside!" Said Hemog and shut the door.

Alex was too shocked to say anything and went through to the sitting room. Alehouse followed. He went over to the window, which faced onto the garden, and put his front paws on the windowsill and looked out. Alex stood beside him.

There were no shots though, only a terrible shriek of fury. The creature was on its feet again and was holding its shredded wrist in its good hand. It flapped it and tried to point it at the cottage, but it was useless. Alehouse chuffed contentedly beside Alex, who patted his head and watched as the two beasts turned and stalked away. They disappeared back into the Welts.

Hemog came into the sitting room. Alex looked up at him. He smiled and suddenly Alex was crying.

Hemog came over and gave Alex a hug. His huge paws patted Alex's back, and he could smell the good smell of sawdust and varnish on his overalls. Alex snuffled and felt Alehouse nuzzle the back of his knee. Eventually he pulled himself together. Alex straightened up, sniffed and coughed. He wiped his nose on the back of his hand.

Alex looked up. Hemog was smiling.

"I'm okay," he said softly. Hemog ruffled his hair and stepped over to the window. The snow was falling less dramatically now and had yet to cover up the scuffed tracks in the grass where Alehouse had seen off the beasts.

"Who are they, Hemog?" Alex asked. "Why are they here?"

Hemog was silent for a moment. Behind them the fire roared.

"Drivid and Stemp." He said. "The Basilisk and the Marksman."

Alex didn't know what to make of these frightening sounding names. "There were two others. They attacked my cottage before I came here. One on stilts and one with a rusty old trampoline."

Hemog nodded. "Pak-Pak and Quetapin. Toyceivers."

Hemog turned from the window. Behind him Alex could see the Welts disappearing into the distance, bare trees like spines on the back of an ancient, cold, cold beast.

"Have they come for me?" Alex said in a quiet voice.

"Yes, Alex." He said. "And others like them. That's why you have to be brave. We must leave soon. Twilight will bring them all, and already the sky is darkening"

Alex looked past him again, and sure enough, the strip of sky above the Welts was purpling down to night.

Hemog put his hands on Alex's shoulders. "There's much to tell you, Alex."

But before he could say anything else there was a sudden and awful explosion of noise from the Welts. It sounded like a circus load of animals blundering around tearing up trees and bushes.

Alehouse snarled. "Right," said Hemog. "This is it. Let's get to the cellar."

Hemog and Alex went through the cottage, locking up and fixing shutters. Alex spared a moment to look out of the front bedroom window, but all he could see was a stand of trees at the end of Hemog's garden dimly lit by light from the coach lamp over the front door. The few lit trunks looked like the bottoms of thick silver cables, which reached up into the darkness, tethering something vast and unknowable, somewhere above. The snow-covered grass appeared as smooth and mysterious as the wide white screen of the picture palace he had visited once as a little boy.

Then, like grotesque images projected onto that screen, they began to come, edging onto the whiteness from the dark border of the Welts.

Alex banged the shutters closed and locked them then returned to the top of the stairs. His heart was hammering in his chest, and he felt sick with fear.

He paused in the stairwell and looked down. Hemog was by the front door pulling on a pair of boots. He was speaking soothingly to Bong, who was winding himself around Hemog's legs. Courage, Alex, he told himself and went down to join them.

Beneath the stairs was a small wooden door. Hemog opened it and reached in to find a light switch. The light revealed a rickety flight of stairs. He gestured for them to go down, but before they could something hit the front door with enough force to splinter the frame.

"Down we go," Hemog said. His voice was as calm and steady as ever, but there was a different look in his eyes to any Alex had seen before. Something like anger and regret together with a fierce look of great and unfathomable protectiveness. It made him look stronger than ever.

Above, Alex could make out a now familiar sound. Someone was on the roof, battering at the tiles: Pak-Pak.

Something crashed against the front door again, and suddenly cold night air was blowing in and something was out there on the porch craning in at them. It had a thick, gray neck and a tiny head, all teeth, like a cricket ball studded with fishhooks. It made a sound unlike anything Alex had ever heard before, like paper endlessly tearing.

Alehouse snarled and leaped at the beast.

The creature reared up, its body wedged in the doorway. Alehouse hit it low down, and they both tumbled out into the garden. Alex could hear snarling and mighty barks and the sound of a terrible struggle. He looked up at Hemog, who shook his head.

"We must go now, Alex." He said. Bong was standing in the doorway, tail flicking back and forth. His ears were back, and he looked caught in two minds.

"Bong," Alex said. "You coming?"

He turned his head to look at them, standing in the hall by the cellar door, uplit by the soft yellow light. Outside came the sounds of growling and roaring, things slithering and purposeful. Something with a head the size and shape of a marrow waddled into the light carrying blades.

Bong hissed but had to dodge as it slung a blade at him. It flew over Bong's rump as he leaped aside and embedded itself in the bottom of the banister rail. Bong skidded on the wooden floor and bounded past us down the cellar stairs.

Alex followed him. Then Hemog ducked under the lintel and closed and bolted the door behind him. They went down into his cellar.

The cellar was Hemog's workshop. In the middle of the floor was a huge workbench made of ancient pine. It was littered with bits of wood and metal, cogs and clockworks, oilcans, drill bits, engine parts and electronic circuits. There were tiny motors, resistors, amplifiers, test tubes, canisters and beakers. Against the wall Hemog had installed a lathe, a sanding belt and an angle grinder. Beneath the stairs stood his band saw, his pride and joy. The walls were hidden behind cabinets and shelves full of tools and equipment, and the whole room was sweet with the smell of varnishes, linseed oil and paint.

Hemog went over to a hook on the wall and took down an old, oil-stained tool belt. He buckled it around his waist and began moving around the cellar taking things from drawers and boxes and putting them in the loops and fabric pouches on the belt. When he was satisfied, he turned to Alex.

"Take anything you want, Alex. We've got a journey ahead of us, so anything might be useful."

Alex looked around. He took a few things, tools mostly, a pot of glue, a few rolls of wire and tape, stuff he didn't think Hemog had selected. He still had his short handled axe in his bag along with some apples and a thick slice of bread he'd grabbed from his kitchen earlier.

He hefted the bag. Not too bad. He slung it over his shoulder.

"Ready to go?" Hemog asked.

Go where, Alex thought. Upstairs he could hear the sounds of things moving through the house. Something flickered past the cellar door, its shadow darkening the gap between the door and the frame and a line from a very old poem, read to him by Hemog many years before — a verse which had chilled him deliciously at the time — came suddenly to his mind, with its strange and haunting rhythm:

Stay sharp when the shadows flex in the lines between the doors.

And then, hard on its heels, another:

Something of the town not seen since childhood.

Not there, Alex thought. Oh, please, not *there*.

Hemog went over to the far wall. "Give us a hand, Alex," he said. He began to push against the side of a tall glass-fronted cabinet. Together they slid it across, revealing a hidden door in the wall. Hemog unbolted it and pulled it open. It juddered against the floor, so old and swollen was it. Beyond stretched a dark tunnel.

"It comes out beneath my shed at the bottom of the garden," Hemog said. He unclipped a torch from his belt and switched it on. He squatted down and shuffled into the cramped corridor, the beam of light swaying ahead. Alex went in after him and pulled the door shut with some effort. In the dim light he could make out two heavy iron bolts, one at the top of the door, the other at the bottom. He slid them home and went after Hemog.

At the end of the tunnel a trapdoor was built into the ceiling. Hemog again slid back bolts and pushed up the trap. He said, "Do you mind?" and lifted Bong up into the shed. "Alex," he said and cupped his hands. Alex stepped up and he hoisted him up. Alex took the torch from Hemog and shone it down into the tunnel. Hemog stood fully upright and pulled the rest of him into the shed.

In the torchlight Alex could make out lots more tools and a smaller bench with a couple of vices bolted to the side of it. There was a smoky-looking wood burning stove with a blackened flue in the corner, with a small pile of apple wood logs stacked beside it.

Hemog went to the door. "Put the torch out," he said. They were plunged into darkness as Hemog silently opened the shed door and peered out. He stepped onto the path, and Alex and Bong followed. They looked up towards the back of the house.

It was swarming with beasts. Great things with wings beat at its roof, things humped and segmented writhed and jabbered at ground level, throwing themselves at the walls and windows. From somewhere Alex could hear the unmistakable sound of Quetapin's trampoline creaking and flinging him skywards. And above it all, shaking with whatever emotion drove him, atop his monstrous stilts, quivered the figure of Pak-Pak. The cottage looked like something held between old splintering tweezers.

Hemog turned his back on the devastation and trod quietly around to the rear of the shed. Alex went after him and found him rooting around in some bushes. There was a creak and a hole in the fence was revealed as Hemog lifted some planks. They crawled under the fence and stood looking out onto the edge of the Welts. Alex risked turning the torch back on and played the beam over the perimeter. There did not seem to be anything too threatening out there, so they began to edge into the cover of the trees. Hemog took one look back and Alex saw sorrow appear momentarily on his face, no doubt for Alehouse, his mighty companion. Hemog sighed, and then together they went into the Welts.

Alex had never been into this part of the Welts. This was where the forest grew wildest and thickest, and somewhere beyond and within lay old dark towns, mostly industrial, linked by a single railway line. Further, many miles away, was the sea. Alex had never seen the sea. Some evenings, when they were sitting by the fire playing Senegal checkers, Hemog would tell him about the glorious town of Quay-Endula. A town spread throughout the steep hills surrounding a great blue bay. A place of turrets and spires and fabulous follies, rambling pavilions, markets full of billowing pastel tents and gazebos. Quay-Endula had fountains like cathedrals; it had plazas and parks, open-air theatres, carnivals, trams, cable cars strung between great glittering pylons and a pier like no other could compare.

The pier of Quay-Endula is a mile long, so they say, stretching out into the sea. It has its own fairground with a Ferris wheel the height of a skyscraper. It has helter-skelters and rocket ships that fly round on gleaming metal arms. It has buildings full of pinball machines and shooting galleries. All this built on a wooden raft held up on fragile iron legs, barnacle-brittle above an ever-swell of blue-green ocean.

Alex really wanted to go to Quay-Endula.

After some time of walking, they came to a break in the trees. Alex thought it might be a clearing, but it turned out to be a railway cutting.

They slithered down the bank and stood by the side of the rails. In the distance, a mile or so away down the track Alex could hear something approaching. He turned to face the direction of the sound and saw, as the tracks bent away through the forest, a deep orange glow like a bonfire. But this bonfire *groaned*.

He looked up at Hemog and saw that he was smiling.

The fire grew closer, the noise building and thrumming. They felt the ground beneath their feet tremble with its approach. Breathless, Alex waited. And saw it rumble into the cutting.

It drove a great caul of sparks before it, firefly debris from its shearing wheels. It was an iron bulk, a locomotive salvaged from a crusher. It was a square-backed, steam-driven thing of lonely nightlong industry. Driverless it thundered, following its midnight magnet through the forest. It had no lights, just the blazing cloak of molten swarf, which cooled and twinkled over its channeled flanks.

Rail Grinder uproared past them, a dreadful, gorgeous machine, and it steamed and bellowed and reaped the rails of rust.

"Come, on," Hemog shouted over Rail Grinder's terrible noise. They ran down the tracks, following the stately rocking of the locomotive's back end.

Hemog scooped Bong up and swung him onto the footplate. Alex didn't need a lift this time, just threw himself, whooping, on behind him. Hemog trotted along beside Railgrinder, grinning, then grabbed a rail and joined them in the open cab.

They stood there, rocking and bathed in firebox heat, the whole world full of clangs and ferment and turbulent row. The night stank of coal dust and engine oil, hot pistons and sparks.

Wherever they were going, they would arrive there in style.

GODIVY

Vylar Kaftan

t's a jungle in the office here, with all the administrators in heat. They're mating with the photocopiers and producing children born for office work. Dull, duplicate grayfaces attached to each other — they know the horrors of office work, but they were bred to it. Their fathers raised them suckling on espresso in plastic-nippled bottles. Softly the photocopiers whisper a legend: Espresso Nipples are a popular drink at the strip club. You pay a stripper twenty bucks and she shoots espresso from her nipples into your mouth.

This is how Jared starts his day, in a taxi's back seat. He takes a stripper to work and drinks from her nipples each day. She fake-moans at his touch, but he's thinking of the photocopier he'll fuck later. There's been a territorial fight lately with the photocopiers at stake. The Director wants to fuck Jared's favorite photocopier, but Jared won't let him. Jared's risking his job. But his photocopier is special. She's the mother of his first hundred duplicates, and only one of them is smudged. She's good for breeding and he likes that about her.

Today's stripper in the taxi is the color of espresso. Ivy grows from her head — a genetic alteration, or perhaps her mother was an office plant. Green vines flow over the seats, lengthening as he watches. She stares up at him from his lap, her nipples exposed to his thirst. She'd make a nice photocopier, Jared thinks, but she's merely a stripper. He calculates the formulas needed to become CEO. He must have X years of experience, Y degrees of beauty in his wife, and Z number of kids. XYZ = CEO. Jared's XYZ increases every time he touches his photocopier.

The stripper covers herself with her hair. Jared flicks the ivy away with a finger. "Hey. I want more espresso."

"You're cut off. I'm tired."

"I'm paying."

"Whatever."

Jared pauses. The taxi lurches sideways. She's watching him — a Lady Godiva in leaves. He'll call her Godivy. Underneath the leaves is espresso, and Jared wants more. "I'll pay triple the usual."

"Don't need the money."

"You're a stripper."

"I'm a mermaid." She stretches on the vomit-scented taxi seat. Jared looks at her legs. Two feet poke out from the leaves like an unearthed corpse. She has no toenails — only ten green scales. Godivy says, "I know, you're wondering where my tail is. Well, I don't have one."

"All mermaids have tails," says Jared. "Otherwise they'd just be women."

"Not black mermaids. Betcha didn't know we existed."

"I've never seen one."

"Blame the artists. No one painted us in the nineteenth century because they said we weren't even people. Not that mermaids were people anyway — just mouths, with tits. A sailor's dream. To take without giving."

Jared shrugs, thinking of his photocopier. She's gray and boxy, and her children resemble her more than himself. He wonders how he'll stave off the Director's advances. It'll be a careful black-and-white chess game. There's no room for an ivy-haired stripper. But Godivy watches him with ocean-blue eyes. He asks, "Why aren't you in the water?"

"I've got a mission."

"Which is?"

"Nothing you've paid for."

Jared loses interest. She's just a stripper, but his enemy is a Director. His XYZ is at stake. The taxi docks outside the building, and he pays with a handswipe over a panel.

"You're dismissed," he tells Godivy, extending his hand. He expects her to shake it and complete the transaction.

"Don't you want more espresso?" she asks. She lifts just enough ivy to reveal one perfect nipple.

Jared is captivated. "I thought you said I was cut off," he says, thirsting.

"Take me upstairs. I'll give you something."

"No. I can't take you inside."

She smiles. "You were interested in taking me anywhere you could have me. Something's changed. Are you ashamed? Worried about what I'll want in return? Or just afraid I smell like fish?"

He scowls. "Get out of here."

Godivy gathers her hair and lifts it out of the taxi. She steps into her green heels and walks away without a word. Jared watches her smooth brown hips as she disappears around the corner. No fish can walk like that. She's a liar, like the thieving Director.

He banishes her from his mind and concentrates on the game at hand. He must checkmate the Director today and save his photocopier. He's a rook sweeping through the front door, a bishop angling up the stairs. Jared the king steps into his throne office. The paneled walls prove his XYZ to the identical office cubes. The grayfaces bow at his arrival, and drift away on their business.

His photocopier stands in its corner. He strokes its open lid with the back of his hand. The photocopier whirs and beeps red, three times. "I'll protect you," he says softly. He unzips his pants. The photocopier spits out page after page: a plant, a plant, a plant. Jared looks at his photocopier's smooth face. Someone has left a ceramic pot on the glass. Inside is a tiny plant.

Jared suspects a plot by the Director. He throws the pot out the window and hears it shatter three stories below. Ivy bursts from the shards. Green vines explode towards Jared and tangle through the window. He tries to run, but the ivy wraps his wrists. A leafy ocean sweeps him to the floor.

Someone laughs. Jared turns his head. The Director stands there, tall and skinny and brown. Jared has never noticed his green hair before. The Director is motionless, his twig fingers extended toward Jared's photocopier. Godivy stands behind the Director.

"Who — what — are you?" asks Jared. The vines resist his struggles and tighten their grip.

Godivy steps forward. "I told you. I'm a mermaid on a mission. And this — " She gestures towards the Director. "This is a plant that I left here."

"Don't take my photocopier," Jared cries.

"Too late. She's not yours anymore." Godivy places two fingers in her mouth and whistles. It sounds like the ocean in a shell. The photocopier quivers and stretches itself. A long green tail grows from its paper tray. The tail reaches four feet long, then splits to form fins. Jared's office smells like the beach.

Godivy leaps out the window, and the photocopier swims through the air after her. Jared strains against his bonds. He hears splashing from the other offices. More photocopiers swim through the air, their tails flashing green as they escape out the window. They dive down the ivy waterfall and vanish. Jared's bonds melt into seaweed sludge. He lies on his office floor, next to the rubber tree he knew as the Director, his face gray and empty. The nearby cubes are silent. The photocopiers swim towards the open sea, their buttons flickering green in the sunlight.

♫

PAINTING HAITI

Michael Jasper

I n spite of the tinny sound of the alarm blaring in her cramped room for the past ten minutes, Claudia kept on working, thinking: just one more dab of color here, one more brush stroke there, just a bit more shadow in the background. She needed a little bit more, of everything: time, colors, inspiration.

Maybe one of these nights she'd give up a shift and just paint all night and sleep the next day until noon, and eat a huge breakfast just up the road at Big Ed's. Pancakes, grits, country ham, and all the coffee she could pour down her throat. But she knew that would never happen. Money. She needed the money, and so did her family back home.

"*Malpwòpte*," she muttered, glaring at her cheap alarm clock and then at her painting. With a sigh that turned into a laugh, she realized she wasn't sure which one she was labeling a piece of shit. Probably both, she figured, turning off the alarm clock with a bit more force than was necessary.

On her canvas, something was finally taking shape there in the dark-hued lines of her oil-based cityscape after almost three hours of painting and scraping and repainting the yellow streetlights, shadowy alleyways, and chain-link fences overrun with weeds. She'd been close to giving up on this one, and she couldn't afford to waste paint. Not with rent due on Friday for her room here, in a house ten blocks from the Capitol Building.

Repeating the Creole curse word, savoring each spitting syllable, Claudia pulled off her old flannel shirt and scrubbed her paint-spattered hands with it. Dark red, deep blue, and black paint smeared onto her brown skin.

As she stared at the swirling tattoo of tacky oils on the back of her right hand, she felt her eyes unfocus. The shape reminded her of something she'd seen late the other night at work. Something glimpsed from the corner of her eye as her speeding taxi zipped down a one-way street downtown. A blurred figure wearing a black hat and a dark blue jacket, disappearing down a red-bricked alley. Moving fast, chasing someone down or running away from someone, she couldn't tell.

With one last glance at her current painting — "broken" was the word that came to mind when she looked at it — she pulled on a faded NC State sweatshirt, dropped her short-handled baseball bat into the pocket of her winter coat, and locked the door to her rented room.

The hallway creaked as she hurried down it, betraying her to the whims of Ferdie, her next-door neighbor. Ferdie was from the Balkans and was a writer, which meant he looked for any excuse to leave his room and socialize.

"Claudette!" he called. "Going to the work?"

A real master of the obvious, Claudia thought, though the guy never got my name right.

"I'm *late* for work," she said, trying to detour around him, but Ferdie slide-stepped to his right to block her. He knew his rugby moves.

"But you must listen to this story," he said, pulling a crumpled page of *The Raleigh News & Observer* from his brown bathrobe he wore over his dress shirt and black jeans.

"Really late, Ferdie." Claudia considered ways around the thick-armed Serbian, but reconsidered. When Ferdie was into a story, it was best to let him run his course. Her boss at the taxi company had an understanding about tardiness, but Claudia didn't want to stretch that feeling of goodwill too thin.

"Only take a minute. I find this buried on the back of the Metro section, just two paragraphs. Listen: 'Raleigh police are investigating a series of petty crimes taking place in the Oakwood neighborhood of downtown Raleigh. Drug paraphernalia was found in an abandoned home along with material for arson. In addition, three cars have been vandalized, and an undisclosed number of homeless people have apparently been the victims of assaults.'"

Claudia forgot about being late and listened to Ferdie's booming voice. He smelled like sausage and typewriters.

"And you notice," Ferdie said as he paced up and down the hall in frustration, "you notice that the talk about our people comes *last*, after they talk of the property being vandalized. As if houses and cars are more important than humans!"

Ferdie was shouting, and Claudia was now twelve minutes late for work. She rested a hand on the big man's shoulder. He stopped pacing and took a deep breath.

"Letter to the editor?" she said, eyebrows raised.

"Yes!" Ferdie grabbed her and kissed her cheek, scratching her skin with his whiskers. "You are genius, my friend. Always knowing the right thing to do. I know just the tone to use..." Ferdie continued muttering even after he'd rushed back to his small wooden desk and fed a new page of paper into his ancient typewriter.

Jogging down the steps and out into in the snowy, late-February darkness, Claudia kept her right hand tight on the handle to her bat and tried not to think about Ferdie's story. Driving a taxi was hard enough, being a woman as well as an immigrant. She didn't need the added worry of becoming a victim of violence. She wouldn't be another statistic; that was why she'd left Port-au-Prince over a decade ago.

The Raleigh Taxi Company was tucked away in an alley off of Blount Street, next to a five-story parking deck and a closed Irish pub. The sign out front was covered in fresh snow, so Claudia gave the piece of metal a good pop on her way past, and most of the snow fell to the ground. She regretted it immediately — her hand stung and was covered in cold wetness dropping from the sign.

She was about to wipe her bare hand on her coat and pulled up short when she saw that the smudge of paint had returned to the back of her hand. Claudia had thought the paint had all flaked off. Now the smudge was mostly black and brown, like a healing bruise, almost hidden against her dark chocolate skin.

Looking at the smudge, Claudia thought of her grandmama again, and wondered what the old lady from the Haitian capital would make of this. Surely she'd think it was some sort of sign. Claudia simply shrugged and walked inside the relative warmth of the dispatch office, fifteen minutes late.

Lenny Akinebosoom, a Nigerian man with skin so black it shone, was waiting for her inside. With his wireless headset strapped to his bald head, he spoke rapid-fire into the mouthpiece. Lenny gave her surly look, pointed at the clock, and handed her a fare box and a list of customers, all while talking into his headset, reassuring the fare that their ride would be there in less than a minute.

Claudia's first fare was due at the Raleigh-Durham International airport at 7:00 p.m., a twenty-minute drive from downtown, probably closer to thirty if one of the city's few snowplows hadn't cleared the interstate.

"Better hope the plane's runnin' late 'cause of the snow 'n' all," Lenny said, his hand on the mouthpiece of his headset. "Claudia," he added, his voice softening, "be safe tonight. People been actin' *crazy* in this area."

Claudia gave him a nod and began pulling out air fresheners for the taxi she was inheriting from big Jake, who always left her with a cab reeking of body odor.

After ten minutes, with two more rides now backed up behind Claudia's pickup at the airport, Lenny gave up trying to hail Jake on the radio. Cursing in his native language, he dug out a blue plastic key fob in the shape of a number one and tossed Claudia the key to Bessie.

Yes, Claudia thought. My luck's changing tonight.

She loved driving Bessie. She always thought of Bessie as a yellow tank topped off with a dusty yellow Duty sign. She skipped across the stained concrete of the garage into the last stall where Bessie sat, collecting dust and cobwebs. As always, the twenty-year-old Crown Vic started on the first try, and with a roar forward, Bessie turned the dispatch office into a blurred shadow in her rearview.

Zipping past the few cars on the road, dodging the occasional parked car on either side of the narrow street, Claudia pointed Bessie in the direction of the airport. Snow was falling again, dotting the wide expanse of the cracked windshield. With the cold wind and dropping temperatures, not even the crazy drivers were out testing themselves on the unfamiliar snow and black ice. Heat had finally started to sputter from the vents when Claudia saw the red lights a block away on her right.

Just keep going, she thought at first. But Claudia knew this neighborhood, just half a mile from the interstate. She had friends living in the row houses here, had dropped off riders here almost every shift, people too poor to afford car payments. Something about the way the red lights of the cop car ahead of her played with the shadows made her think of the blurred shadow she'd seen off of Bloodworth the other night, a figure that had worked its way into her dreams every night since.

She turned right and touched the brake with a glance at the stubborn smudge of paint on the back of her hand. Something flickered in that mix of red and blue and mostly black paint, catching the lights of the Wake County police car parked in front of the yellow Raleigh Taxi resting on its side.

"Jake," she whispered, killing Bessie's engine. She stepped outside and lost her breath immediately in the wind.

The cop stood hunched over the taxi, looking through the spider-webbed windshield with his flashlight. The cop's radio screeched something, mixing with the howl of the wind. She could smell the sickly stink of something harsh, like burning oil. Underneath it was a familiar whiff of body odor.

And then she heard Jake's voice, screaming.

"Get him out — " she started to yell at the cop, her anger taking her back over a dozen years, to Port-au-Prince, shouting at the rebels and then hiding from them, and then later yelling at the U.S. Marines with their guns and their agendas.

Claudia never finished her sentence. The cop straightened up in one fluid movement from next to the overturned taxi. Claudia's gaze went from the cop to the fat white hand pressed against the inside of the ruined windshield.

"Move 'long," the cop said. "Nothin' to see here, miss."

She had to force her gaze away from that hand to look at the cop. He was easily six and a half feet tall, and his black face flickered in the red lights of his sedan. Something about the man's face was familiar, a tiny detail she couldn't make out in the darkness. She stumbled back to Bessie, numb with cold.

What made her punch the gas pedal hard was the sound of the cop's voice. It had carried easily over the wind, touching her ears like a freshly remembered nightmare.

He'd had a Creole accent.

The soldiers arrived just a week shy of Claudia's twentieth birthday, heavily armed, but the neighborhood leaders had a plan to keep everyone safe. At first she balked at the ludicrousness of the concept, but once she saw the death-black guns cradled in the arms of the Haitian men and then the Marines, Claudia had been more than happy to spread the rumor that there was a mad witch in their building. She told anyone who listened, including the men with guns, that the witch sat on a stockpile of magic powders in her apartment, and she was burning tiny effigies of American soldiers in her bathtub.

The myth was ridiculous, of course, just as silly as her grandmama's fervent belief in voodoo, yet the horror stories helped keep away the Haitian men on their way to Aristides' stronghold, as well as the U.S. Marines following them.

But one of the Marines wasn't buying the story.

His skin was deep black, much darker than Claudia's, and he wore a helmet and body armor like the other soldiers. His helmet looked like a child's play toy on his big head, and his flat belly was left exposed under his too-short vest. He walked straight up to her as if he'd smelled her deception instantly.

In spite of the series of tiny earthquakes going on inside her chest, Claudia did her best to ignore him and turned back to the occult design she was chalking on the sidewalk.

"Cross shouldn' have such a long base. An' your pentagram's all outta pr'portion."

She looked up from the doggerel she was chalking on the sidewalk, symbols grandmama had recommended to her (though Claudia knew she was mangling them in her shaking hands). She felt a curse on her lips, fighting the urge to swing a fist at the man. But the soldier had already moved on. She never forgot that deep voice with its Haitian accent and its tone of knowing disdain.

After the soldiers left, she'd continued scratching more symbols onto the asphalt and concrete, her head swimming with anger at the soldier's contempt and shame at her own inability to draw the magic symbols properly.

Claudia vowed not to tell her grandmama about any of this.

After a couple hours of sleep under three layers of her heaviest blankets, Claudia was back out in the wintry cold, on her way to the shelter with her brushes and paints in her backpack. Her sleep-fuzzed mind kept going over the events of that night, from seeing the cop and the wrecked taxi to when Lenny finally reached her to tell her about Jake's accident.

"The guy was always drivin' too fast. He hit some black ice and flipped," Lenny said in a careful monotone. "Cops said he died immediately." He sighed. "Careful, Claudia. Be careful out there. You can come in if you want."

Claudia's tongue was glued to the roof of her mouth as she forced out the word "No," feeling like she was sliding on ice herself, even though Bessie was stopped at a red light.

The cops, she thought as she crunched through the snow. Accent. What did they know? What do the men with guns ever know?

Half a dozen of her students were waiting for her in the small second-floor workspace above the homeless shelter on Fayetteville Street Mall. Claudia unloaded her paints and chatted about the snow with Briana and Derron. Teaching here kept her in paint and canvas; Marlene, the program director, looked the other way when Claudia occasionally took home extra materials for her own painting.

Within a minute of her arrival, her students had turned to their canvases, dabbing at them uncertainly as if afraid to waste the tiniest bit of paint. Claudia was just about to give a talk about perspective when Marlene popped into the room, the small white woman's face pinched with concern. She beckoned Claudia outside.

"Go ahead and get started," Claudia told her students on her way out. "No lecture for today."

She left the room to a sarcastic round of cheers accompanied by the magical sound of brushes touching canvas.

"There's bad news," Marlene whispered after she'd closed the door to the painting room. Marlene always whispered. "Someone from the shelter was killed last night."

Claudia closed her eyes as a chill ran through her. Once again, she thought about Jake and the overturned taxi, and the big cop hunched over him, waiting.

"Who was it?"

"Mr. Archer. They found him last night next to a dumpster behind the Side Street Café."

Mr. Archer — Archie to Claudia — was a crusty old white man, skinny as a rail and mad as a hatter. But he was always a gentleman in her class, and some of his painting styles were inventive, if not near genius.

"Claudia?" Marlene touched her hand. "I'm sorry. At least Mr. Archer is at rest at last, away from all the ugliness."

"Yeah," Claudia said, wiping a tear from her eye.

When she lowered her hand, she saw the smudge of paint again, even though she knew she'd scraped it off this morning with a brush and a bit of turpentine. This time, the dark colors kept swirling when her hand stopped moving.

"Claudia?"

When she raised her eyes, she realized she was now sitting on the floor, with Marlene hovering over her.

"Claudia. I'll cancel class for you, and you can get some rest. You work too hard — when was your last day off, girl?"

"Mmm," Claudia mumbled. "What month is it?"

A few minutes later, after Marlene had told everyone in the classroom to come back tomorrow, Claudia entered the now-empty room. She couldn't stop shaking. She was starting to think she'd come under some kind of curse that had caused Archie's death and Jake's accident.

Then she noticed the paintings. Everyone in class seemed to have hit upon a similar theme.

She walked past the first canvas stained with so many blacks and browns that the subjects — an outstretched hand and the neck of a guitar — were almost completely obscured. In the shadows of the background she could see light glinting off guns as well as the hint of a familiar brick building. That painting was Briana's.

Next to her dark artwork was Derron's somewhat abstract take on Raleigh's two skyscrapers. Just a few days ago the piece had been a bright landscape with streaking blue and red cars crisscrossing on busy one-way streets. Now, the cars had been replaced by tanks and humvees churning through a dark brown river edged in dark blue and rust colors. The blocky gray heights of the BB&T building and the slick black Capitol Center were striped red and ringed with fire.

All the other paintings had undergone similar changes: light replaced by dark, shadows overtaking the subjects like rot on a piece of fruit that had been fresh only a day ago.

The lone canvas that she couldn't see had been turned away and covered. Archie's. He'd always preferred that corner of the small room, close to the window and as far from the other students as possible. She took a deep breath before touching the thin cloth hiding his forever-unfinished painting from her.

In spite of the heat, Claudia hugged herself in her grandmama's apartment, wondering why she was putting herself through this. The walk over here from her parents' house had taken forever, and she was convinced someone would knock the canvas from her hands or pull the thin towel from the top of it, exposing her painting to the world before it was ready.

She set the canvas on a rickety card table in front of the tiny black and white TV set. Her first serious painting.

"Ready?" she asked her grandmama, who sat in her rocking chair about six feet from her. Just the right viewing distance.

"Almos'," grandmama said, lighting a fresh cigarette.

Inspired by her incident with the Marine, Claudia had been working for over a week on what she thought of as her new, adult style. She'd filled this canvas with as much detail as she could, including a small squadron of Marines in the lower left, advancing on a four-story apartment similar to the rundown one in which she now stood above her grandmama, while the green sky filled with warplanes mingling with doves and bats. The distant ocean's blood-red waves were tipped with yellow foam.

"Ready," grandmama said, exhaling a plume of gray smoke.

Claudia lifted the old towel from the canvas and closed her eyes. She smelled spicy food on the stove, making her mouth water. The radio played a song popping with accordion music when she turned to her grandmama.

"What do you think, grandmama?"

The thin old woman was not smiling. She kept the cigarette in her mouth as she inhaled and exhaled. She looked as if someone had told her soldiers were coming for her.

"No, child," she said at last.

Claudia tried to find her voice. "What do you mean?"

"You don' know 'nough yet. Don' fool wit dese pictures 'til you're ready to deal wit' the consequences of your work. You don't comprehend, child." She stubbed out her cigarette. "This ain't your callin', I t'ink."

Burning from the inside out, from betrayal and anger and a lingering sense that her grandmama had been right, Claudia had packed up the painting and run down the steps from her grandmama's apartment before the tears of betrayal and anger forced her to stop. With the firecracker sounds of gunfire in the distance, she'd thrown the painting into a garbage can next to the apartment building, breathing hard to get the flavors of her grandmama's cooking out of her nose and mouth.

Over twelve years later, Claudia blinked away the stinging memory of her grandmama's harsh critique and flipped the piece of cloth from the front of Mr. Archer's painting.

The piece had been composed using only black paint with brown highlights. Archie had spread on the paint so thickly that it had a three-dimensional effect, like the topographical maps of mountains Claudia had once seen in the library. There was no pattern to Archie's work, just angry coats of paint.

The brown and black ridges and valleys called out for her to touch them. She used her finger to trace the most prominent ridge of brown paint, and she felt a tiny shock with the contact. She saw the pattern, now, with physical contact.

Hidden inside all that paint was the outline of a face. Eyes glittering with anger, dark with need. Hunger. Claudia fingered a tiny sliver of white on a ridge of the face's cheekbone, like a scar made by the beak of a small, angry bird.

She jerked her hand away from Archie's painting as if it had burned her. Pulling the cover back over the painting took most of her strength before she turned her back on it and walked out the door of the tiny studio.

Like a stain on her vision, the brown and black shadows that had overwhelmed her students' paintings now tainted everything that she saw on her way home from the shelter.

She felt like she was walking under dark clouds even though the day was clear and the sun was out. Most of the snow from the storm yesterday had either melted or been cleared from the sidewalks. Still, all Claudia could see was a growing darkness.

A tattered page of the *News & Observer* blew against her leg as she was crossing Wilmington Street. The torn and wet piece of newsprint nearly shouted at her: "U.S. Marines Enter Haitian Capital." The page was dated two days ago, from Tuesday's paper.

She looked at the photo of the Marines in dark camouflage, handing equipment off the back of a truck. Brownish shadows filled the background of the photo, obscuring all other details. Claudia squinted and blinked at the newsprint. On the flip side was a short headline with the words "Street Killer" in it.

What if the chaos back home was like a virus? Claudia wondered. And it had finally caught up to me here?

She dropped the wet piece of newsprint and saw, to little surprise, that the smudge of paint on the back of her right hand had grown larger, stretching toward her fingers and wrist.

She turned into the wind and hurried past the empty block of brown grass and park benches that made up Moore Square. She was nearly running by the time she got back to the house on Oakwood Street. She kept her right hand buried in the pocket of her coat so she wouldn't have to look at it until she got home.

When she finally set down her brush and turned to her clock toward her, she gave a grunt of surprise: 11:41 p.m.

Her feet and back hurt from standing hunched over her painting for so long, and her hands ached from gripping palette and brush. She was done.

She stepped back before looking at the canvas a final time.

Swirling black and brown shadows highlighted a streetlight, a brick wall, a car wheel. Chalk-white symbols were scribbled onto the stained concrete. Slightly off-center to the left was a bent figure whose head was just beginning to lift, exposing a narrowed set of white eyes just below the brim of a black hat. A hat that could have been a helmet. Or a policeman's cap.

The eyes gazed off into the distance, and she knew she'd put just the right amount of shadow around the face. Other than the tiniest bit of white for the eyes and a thin white scar matching the one on Archie's painting, the only other colors she'd used had been dark red, midnight blue, and a muddy brown.

He was waiting for her there, she realized, in an alleyway off Bloodworth. The soldier, the cop, the hunter. He was her responsibility now.

"Now you know it, girl," she whispered in a voice like her grandmama's. "And maybe now you're starting to *comprehend*."

On a sudden impulse, she reached back for the old piece of white chalk on her dresser before she closed the door behind her, thinking of her grandmama. The old woman would have loved the sight of Claudia leaving home at just a few minutes before midnight, on her way to meet someone on a street named Bloodworth.

She'd been painting all day in her grandmama's spare bedroom, hiding her work from the old lady while trying to keep an eye on her, when she heard the kids yelling outside. Paintbrush still in her hand, she went out to stop them from throwing rocks at the Marines and Haitian soldiers patrolling the area. The local men cheered on the kids.

A storm was brewing in the sky as well as on the street, and Claudia could barely breathe for the electricity in the air. The weather was much too hot for October. It made people crazy.

Including her grandmama. Pulling two skinny boys off the street, Claudia saw at least two rifles point up at her grandmama's window the instant she heard her grandmama's voice.

"Ged on outta heah," she was screaming, her voice cracking with rage. Claudia realized, too late, that she should never have left her grandmama alone.

"The witch," one of the Haitian soldiers said, pointing.

Behind her, the local men swore at Claudia for stopping the kids and their fun. In front of her, the big Marine who'd critiqued her pentagram stepped up to the Haitian soldiers and put his hands on the barrels of their rifles, lowering them. The big man always seemed to be around whenever something bad happened in the neighborhood, especially if there was a shooting or a death. He never raised his gun, however. He was just always...there.

At that instant, little Daniel Blaise threw the last rock that would be thrown that day. With a dull slapping sound, the rock hit the big black Marine square in the helmet.

The Marine took a step back, but he never went down. His eyes went wide and white, then they narrowed as the street filled with Grandmama's mad, cackling laughter.

"Move out," he hissed.

His voice barely carried to Claudia across the square, above her grandmama's laughing. The soldier looked up at Grandmama for a moment, and his eyes narrowed. Her laughter came to a sudden stop, followed by a panicked scrabbling sound at the windowsill high above them. Then the old woman fell out of her window.

Claudia let go of the young boy she was holding back and tried to move under her grandmama, as if she could cushion her fall somehow.

The too-loud thump of her grandmama hitting the pavement silenced the crowd more effectively than a pistol shot.

The Haitian soldiers took one look at her grandmama and hurried off down the street after the Marines. Claudia kneeled next to her motionless grandmama, rocking back and forth over the old woman's broken, lifeless body.

Soon a shadow smelling of gun oil fell over her. The big Marine had taken a knee next to her. With her vision blurred with tears, Claudia saw his dark face flicker with emotion for a moment, followed by a sickening expression that looked to Claudia like satisfaction.

"We tried to help," he muttered. "But now, you people are on your own. You people chose this outcome."

His thick fingers rested on her grandmama's shoulder, sausage-like fingers kneading her flesh.

Claudia's hand moved before she realized what she was doing. The brush still clamped in her fisted right hand swung out in an arc that ended at the big Marine's cheek. She wanted to kill him for touching her grandmama like that. As if painting on a slick, glistening canvas, the brush left a three-inch-long line of white paint on his dark skin. Claudia's only regret was that she hadn't been holding a knife.

The soldier reared back as if he was going to swing his fist at her in return. But at the last instant he dropped his arm and stood up.

He muttered "you people" once more, like a curse, and moved away. The other soldiers followed him in the now-silent street. Claudia was left with her lifeless grandmama, the smells of her cooking spices fading, replaced by the coppery scent of blood.

When she touched her grandmama again, the old woman's flesh was colder than the bite of the ocean in February.

Outside of Bessie's heated interior, the icy air hit Claudia's face like a slap. The streetlight gave off a weak light tinged with brown and black smudges, as if the light itself in this area had been corrupted by the evil in the air. She inhaled a metallic smell of guns and something burnt.

And then the wind relented, and Claudia caught a whiff of what smelled like cloves, mixed with fresh basil and her grandmama's favorite: thyme. The memory gave her the courage to enter the darkened alley.

Crouching next to a dumpster, the big man waited for her.

This time, Claudia could see the white line of paint on his cheek in this shadowy alley.

"Go back home," Claudia said, her voice cracking.

"You t'ink it that easy, girl?"

His voice was deep as the night before, filled with the same bemused confidence she remembered from their first meeting. Wearing old jeans and a green army jacket, he looked much older now. He was quivering like a junkie, full of unhealthy need.

"Wasn't my grandmama enough for you?" She moved closer, anger and indignation growing with each step.

"We all have to eat," he said, rising to his full height. "I just come to where the eating is...richer. Easier."

As he did, Claudia lifted the piece of chalk she'd kept with her from that day in Haiti. She held it in her drawing hand, the same hand stained from last night's painting. In spite of the reek of the garbage, Claudia could still smell a trace of her grandmama's spices. She wanted to take a turpentine-soaked rag to the man's cheek, scrubbing away the mark she'd left on him years ago.

"There always has to be a victim," he said in a chiding tone, as if talking to a child. "Look at the killer here, in your neighborhood. Taking *your people*."

"Killer?" Claudia almost lost her grip on the chalk. "*You're* the killer."

"Nah." The man shook his head so hard he rattled the dumpster again. "I just follow after her, get what I need when she's done."

Without taking her gaze off him, Claudia went to one knee. She wiped snow from the alley floor and looked down long enough to draw a long white line that separated her from him. The rumble of Bessie's engine at the end of the alley calmed her and kept her hand from wavering. The chalked line became a cross.

"Girl," he said. "You doing more art? Don't you know better, now?"

She continued drawing, his words encouraging her. She thought she heard him flinch back when she finished drawing the first symbol of power her Grandmama had taught her.

"That's *enough*, girl."

Claudia continued drawing. She wondered if he remembered what she had chalked into the street that day in Haiti, even if she hadn't believed it herself then. She knew better now.

As she drew, Claudia thought about her home, her true home. She wondered if there had been so much suffering in Haiti these days that a death there just wasn't special enough for this creature. So he'd come here, hungry for a new kind of death.

The next symbol became a pentagram. The connection made all those years ago in Port-Au-Prince had to be broken.

"Y-You not doing that right," the man began.

"I didn't ask for an opinion," Claudia snapped. "What I need from you is to take care of whoever's killing our people. Feed on the *killer's* suffering instead of feeding on us."

"Stop," he hissed, dropping to both knees.

"Do what I ask, and I'll release you. If not — " Claudia moved her hand over the chalked symbols. "If not, I erase you."

"Do you think...it...that easy?" the man whispered.

A sudden flow of warm air scented with her grandmama's spices touched Claudia, and she closed her eyes to make sure she caught every last hint of cloves and basil and thyme. When she opened her eyes, the big man was gone.

"Yes, *Malpwòpte*," she said. "It *is* that easy."

Somewhere in the cold night, as close as a few blocks away, she thought she heard a scream filled with surprised betrayal. The magic practiced by her grandmama was potent, nothing to toy with as she'd done all those years ago, and it worked quickly. The black man, the feeder of the dead, had taken care of the killer stalking her friends here in downtown Raleigh.

I *comprehend*, Grandmama, she thought as she wiped away the chalk symbols as fast as she could, erasing the feeder from existence now that he'd caught the killer. And I miss you.

From the safe confines of Bessie's still-warm interior, Claudia looked up from where she'd been staring at the empty patch of skin on the back of her right hand as the sun rose. She couldn't even see the slightest trace of paint there, not even a sliver of dried red or dark blue stuck to her.

She hoped Big Ed's restaurant opened soon — she was looking forward to a big breakfast and a mug of strong coffee more than anything else, even if it would never compare to a meal prepared for her by her grandmama.

And after she took her own sweet time eating her meal and drinking her coffee, Claudia would sketch out her next painting, something that would use the colors in her palette that she'd been ignoring for far too long.

THE FUNERAL, RUINED

Ben Peek

t was the weight that woke Linette. Her weight. The weight of herself.

The flat red sky above Issuer was waiting when she opened her eyes. Five hours before, when she had closed her eyes, it had been a dark, ugly brown-red: the middle of the night. Now it was the clear early morning red, and a thick, muggy warmth was seeping through her open window with the new light. There would be no rain today. Just the heat. Just the sweat. Just that uncomfortable, hot awareness of herself that both brought. The worse was Linette's short, dark hair, dirty with sweat and ash. The ash that had come through the open window during the night. It had streaked her face and settled in her mouth and she could taste it, dry, burnt and unappealing in her gums. Her left arm, with its thick, straight scars across the forearm, felt heavy and ached; but it always ached. It was a dull, lazy ache in the heat, and a sharp, pointed pain in the cold, as if, with the latter, the brittle weather was digging into her fractured bone to snap it. Her feet, tangled at the bottom of her coarse, ash stained brown sheets, sweated uncomfortably, and her long, straight back could feel the sweaty outline of the bronze frame beneath the thin mattress that she lay on. There was no end to herself, Linette thought, and she would never be able to sleep again, so aware of it was she.

Her dreams had not been a sanctuary, however. In them, Linette had lived under a different part of the red sun, wrapped in heavy brown clothes, wearing pieces of light bronze armour, and holding a short, wide-nosed gun. Around her, clouds of black ash spewed from the back of bronze, grey and silver coloured machines. Cages of crows peppered the ground and, inside, the black birds sat silently, waiting. They were not real, she knew. They never had been. The ground the fake birds lay on was mud and ash and the waste of brown and red trees that had been torn down to make the circular camp she lived in. The wastage clung to her boots, leaving a trail to its centre behind her. There was a man beside her, but she couldn't make him out. He had been asking her when she planned to read the letter, but she had responded by telling him to be quiet. Two men had escaped, she said. They could be anywhere. They could be watching —

They were, but she had awoken before that.

It didn't matter: she knew the outcome, had lived it, didn't need to experience it again.

The letter, however, was not part of the memory. The letter was part of the muggy heat and her life in Issuer. It was sitting in her tiny kitchen, leaning against an old bronze kettle: thin, straight, pristine and white. A perfect set of teeth to speak with. Her name was printed in messy letters on the front, and though a young, clean skinned man she didn't know had delivered it, she knew the author.

Slowly, Linette pushed herself up with her good arm. Her left was a dead weight in her lap. It would take a shower and exercise for it to gain full movement. Two months out of the hospital, out of the army, and a month living in Issuer and her arm had only just begun to improve to the point that she could use it properly. But it took time, still. She slid across the bed that was big enough for two, but held only one, and placed her feet down on the cool stone floor of a room so bare that a visitor would have thought no one lived in it.

The room's possessions lay in the hallway in a disorganised jumble. Linette had thrown them there last night. The large, bronze framed mirror that had, once, sat on the far wall to give the room size now leant against the wall with cracks around the top. Near it lay a brass clock, and next to that a stocky bronze fan with bent blades, followed by a dozen tiny mechanical devices that she had been unable to stomach the thought of having near her as she slept. The way that each simulated a natural event, or imposed an artificial meaning...she had been disgusted by them, just as she had been by the way she had treated each with easy familiarity at one stage in her life. In anger, she had thrown them from the room and opened the window so that the muggy, ash stained breeze could enter.

She had not yet opened the letter.

My Dear Linette —

I do not know how to begin, but I do know is that there is little time left for me to write. In half an hour, the operation will begin. I am apprehensive. My hand trembles. I have always prided myself on clean, simple letters, but look at them now. They cross lines. They mix against each other. They slope one way, then another. They fall outside the neat order that I have cherished so much. I suppose, given what is about to happen, that is the way things should be. Nothing in life is neat and contained.

She tried to eat, but the taste of ash lingered in her mouth, even after she had rinsed.

From her chair at the kitchen table, Linette swallowed her half-chewed piece of apple, then tossed the remaining half into the bin next to her sink. The apple was small, brown, and made an unpleasant, soggy slap as it hit the brass bottom of the bin. Silence followed. The tall woman, now wearing black pants and a long sleeved black, buttoned shirt, had not allowed a sound to escape her mouth since waking up. She had left the bedroom rubbing the scars on her arm, disgusted by the way sweat gathered around the thick, puckered flesh. She had stepped around the mess in the hall, entered the toilet, pissed, showered, scrubbed herself with hard movements, worked her arm until it moved like the other, then dressed and picked up the apple. The only noise had been her feet on the slowly warming concrete floor.

Not so long ago, the mornings had been filled with sound: men and women she knew in smoky, hazy camps, talking about bad food, about operations, about people back home, and those they knew now. Before she had left, and when she had lived in Ledornn, there had been conversations about what kind of toast she would prefer, and who would come up with dinner. Insignificant, shallow, domestic conversations...

Linette gazed through the dirty window of the kitchen. The tall, dark shadows of windmills lined Issuer's morning skyline, a few turning slowly, but most that she could see were still. The empty red of sky hung above them regardless, still and oppressive.

She did not think consciously for the half an hour that she sat at the table, her fingernails clicking on the bronze top every now and then. Her mind had drifted and, in a mix of fragments from conversation, bits of song, parts from books, and even scenes from plays that she had seen, her mind turned itself over until, finally, she began to focus on a man. He was blond, slim, and his teeth were crooked, and he had been an unlikely lover for her as much as she had for him. She did not want to think of him, and when her arm began to throb again, either with real or symbolic pain, she knew that she had to stop before her thoughts turned into a morbidity that crumbled her resolve for the day.

Quietly, Linette entered the small, pale grey painted living room. There was a long brown couch in the middle, while a slim bronze table and brass and silver lined radio sat on top of it in the far corner. A box of outside opinions pushed aside. On the floor, however, were a pair of old, scuffed black boots, which Linette picked up. Holding them, she sat down upon the couch, and there, paused again.

In the kitchen, the letter sat, still, against the kettle.

"I have been to too many funerals," she said, as if it could reply to her.

It could not, of course, but the fact that she had spoken to it both frustrated and upset her. With hard yanks, she tightly wound the frayed black laces of her boots up. On the right boot she missed a hole, and on the left, two. She ground her teeth together harshly both times, but retied carefully, wiping her hands free of sweat.

Finished, she rose and crossed the tiny kitchen, to the back door. Her strides were quick and purposeful: the walk of a woman who had an unpleasant task ahead of her, but who would meet it without flinching.

Are you angry?

That day when I first met you, you were angry. Nearly two years and that is what I remember about you most. It is not your beauty, not your smile, not your habits...No, for over the years, I have realised that these do not define you. They are secondary to your anger — that brilliant, burning anger that exists because the world is not right. The anger that exists because you must fix it, somehow. The first time I saw you was from afar, standing beneath a bronze parasol, while you stood at the front of the Anti-War rally in Ledornn, and it was there that I saw that anger. You demanded to know why Aajnn mattered so much to the Shibtri Isles? Why the Queen and her Children were such a threat?

You told us that they lived in cramped cities beneath the earth, away from our red sun, and with the bones of crows around their necks to catch their souls when they died. They were full of superstition that made the men and women who had Morticians tattoo their life into their skin for God seem at the forefront of science and logic.

What impressed me most (and everyone else, I imagine) was that you were not a person off the street, but a career soldier. You stood in front of us in the straight, light brown pants and suit of the army, your medals and rank displayed for all. You were proud of who you were. You were proud of what you had done for the Isles. You were proud to be in service.

But now, you were angry, and that anger would not allow you to be silent, no matter the consequences. It was an anger to fear and, I am afraid to say, I did — and do — fear it.

The pear shaped Ovens of Issuer dominated the city's horizon, though they were easily an hour away by carriage.

Lately, the twin ovens had a tendency to blur around the edges for Linette, but even with the beginning of her deteriorating eyesight due to her thirty-eighth year, the immense girth and height of the creations meant that they were unable to be passed over when she looked at Issuer's skyline. In contrast, the hundreds of long, bronze windmills that rose out of the city could — and did — fade from her awareness. The Ovens, however, lurked on the horizon like a pair of dark, hunched watchers outside the city, covered in a layer of soot as a disguise. If you managed to forget them (and Linette doubted she ever could), then you would be reminded each Friday when they belched tart smelling ash, and plumes rose out of each to signal the burning of the weekly dead.

Outside of her house, Linette spent a moment in morbid contemplation of the Ovens. It was where she would finish her mortal journey, she knew: a friend, a family member, perhaps even a Mortician, would take her body wrapped in white sheets up to the silent monks who lived beneath the ovens. There, she would be bathed, cleaned, and finally, placed in the giant pits that never fully cooled, and which would ignite at the end of the week, consuming her. There was nowhere else where she would prefer to end. She would not be buried in the ground, not given — or sold or stolen — to a Surgeon's workshop...what was left of her would be burnt away. She would be given freedom.

Her small house sat at the end of Issuer, surrounded by other small, cheap, red brick houses. Packed dirt worked as a road around them, but within minutes, she had stepped onto the paved streets of Issuer proper. There, the tall windmills turned at a variety of paces, powered by electricity that was strung from house to house. Issuer had never been big: it was a transient's city, organised in an ordered grid, with street names that indicated purpose. Everything in it was designed to make it easy for the visitor, of which Issuer saw many. It was a city — more a town, really — where men and women arrived for a few days, a week, and after they had seen the Ovens burn and their duty was done to family and loved ones, they left.

The windows to the private houses Linette passed were shut, the boards pulled closed. Inside, bronze fans circulated the air, but the impression of personal lives being closed off was not an illusion. The people who lived in Issuer kept to themselves for the most part, and it was only when you entered the middle of the city, where the public stores, hotels, and other places of business were, that an openness existed. There, windows were open. There, fans sat on the streets, blowing, while larger windmills — the largest in the city — turned above them. There, men and women, mostly young, presented the smiling, happy face of Issuer to visitors. Everywhere — and everyone — else, Linette believed, looked like a coffin: closed in, quiet, and still.

Death was the commodity of Issuer. Alan Pierre, a black man who had come to the Isles as a child and made a fortune as a body snatcher, had founded it. When age had finally driven him into looking for a way to settle, he had looked at the makeshift tent city that had existed outside the Ovens and sunk his considerable, ill-gained fortune into turning it into something more lasting. It wasn't long until hotels were built, Surgeons and Morticians arrived, as did the other trades that had attached themselves to the industry of death. The people, like Linette, who drifted into the town, drawn by their own morbid frame of mind and the internal struggles that each had, had always been part of it.

Linette herself did not know, exactly, what it was that drew her to Issuer. Her pension provided enough for rent and food, but very little else. In another city, she might find work, and earn more, but while her life was mean, she did not dislike it. The heat bothered her, but it was not as bad as the cold. She was lonely, but —

No.

No, that was wrong: she was not lonely.

She had not been lonely since she moved here and had been able to gaze upon the Ovens daily.

I am not a soldier, and I do not pretend to know what you went through, or why, indeed, Issuer allows you to sleep more calmly than you did in Ledornn; but I like to think I have been supportive of all your needs. That I have tried, as much as I possibly can, to be supportive of you.

It has not been easy, Linette. It is true, yes, that I have not been in the best health, but your hatred towards the advancements in our society have made our lives — our illnesses and injuries — more difficult than they should be. Neither of us can heal with your attitude.

For you, it is your arm that bothers you. Why would it not? The machete of an escaped prisoner splintered the bone and it is now held together by steel rods. It will take years to heal, if ever it does, and it bothers you greatly. The obvious solution to your injury was a replacement, which was offered by the army Surgeons, but you rejected this — and you have since rejected anything that the Surgeons have been able to offer that takes away what you are born with. You tell them (and you tell me) that it is unnatural, that it is not right.

But what is right, I ask? Tattooing your body for God? Wearing a charm around your neck to capture your soul? To believe the Ocean is a living God? To believe the hundreds of other, unexplainable things in this world? Are these somehow more acceptable to you now than the science that has been developed, the advancements that will allow us to live long, healthy lives?

Though Linette did not believe in a God, she made her way to the men and women who traded in that belief on the Morticians' Avenue. Specifically, she made her way to the long, straight building of the Mortician Yvelt Fraé, which was made from caramel coloured bricks. It had a dark, brown tiled roof, and was the largest building in the street, lying curled in between a dozen smaller houses of varying brick colour. Her building had three bronze windmills around it, two on the roof, and one larger piece cemented at the back, and which towered over all others on the street.

At the bronze door, Mrs. Fraé, whose hair, it appeared, had only been freshly dyed a red-brown, greeted Linette. Her skin, however, sagged around her jaw, wrinkled over her face, and continued to do so down her neck until it was covered by the brown gown she wore. Beneath the tattoos across her body there was no tautness of youth, and so the illusion created by dying her hair seemed ridiculous and nothing more than a vanity.

"Linette, it is pleasure to see you." Mrs. Fraé's deep voice sounded as if it should emerge from a larger woman. "Linette? Are you — "

"He's dead."

"Ah." A pause, then, "I'm very sorry."

"There was a letter." Her voice was short, clipped. She could feel the emotion in the back of her mouth, threatening to spill out over her words. "He — he wasn't there yesterday."

"Come in, come in," Mrs. Fraé murmured, stepping back from the door to allow her entry.

The inside of the house was lit in a warm orange and divided by a set of thick, bronze doors. Over each panel of the door was a pattern of angels and devils at war, naked and carrying weapons. The figures on it were ridiculous: sexless for angel, sexual for devil, and posed in mid-action. Behind the twisting battle, Linette knew, lay the private residence of Mrs. Fraé and her family, who were also part of the Mortician trade. She had never seen behind the door, and never would, but expected it to be different from what she saw now. The side of the house she stood on was plain, but expensively decorated with a floor covered in wooden boards and cushioned lounges made from pale brown leather. There was a real, ash-wood table at the end of the room, with a ledger that was used for appointments and payments. A feathered quill lay on it. It looked as if one of Mrs. Fraé's angels had made a table out of the dead for her, and left one of its own feathers to write with.

"Would you like a drink?" the elderly Mortician asked.

"No, I — " The emotions from before welled up, threatened her, and she swallowed them. "I'm fine. I would just like to start, if possible."

"Of course."

Linette had known that there would not be a problem. She had left early, before Issuer fully awoke, and arrived when she knew that Mrs. Fraé would be awake with the early morning vitality that the elderly had. Had she arrived later, and the woman had been engaged, she would have had to wait, for once a Mortician began leaving his or her mark on you, another would not touch you until the first had died. Linette knew that she did not have the patience to wait today.

Mrs. Fraé led her to a small room where, with a click, white electric light flooded its darkness. In the middle lay a chair made from bronze and with thick cushions on it. The bolts and screws and dials in it ensured that while the chair was ugly, it could be folded into a number of positions. Mrs. Fraé flattened the chair into a board before turning to the trays that lined the side of the room, filled with needles and pots of ink.

Linette had received her first tattoo shortly after she had moved to Issuer, when her arm had been mostly useless, but it was the memories of the war that damaged her mostly. She had been in the army for twenty-one years and had seen men and women die, just as she had killed, by her reckoning, more than thirty in various battles. Psychologically, death was nothing new to her. She had always been able to rationalise it, to make it part of her job...at least until the campaign against the Empress and her Children began, and she found herself fighting men — always men — armed with mining equipment and rusted machetes and muskets so old that they wouldn't hurt anyone but the owner. It was impossible to look at those men and see a threat. After she left the army with her injury, she had struggled with that awareness, and how to deal with it.

On her back were one hundred and thirteen names in the neat, elegant script of Mrs. Fraé. They were the names of soldiers: friends, some, but a large portion were men and women who she had fought with, peers and comrades before friends. Each one of them, however, had died fighting the Empress and her Children. Each one of them had died needlessly. Died pointlessly. Died for nothing but the greed of their own country.

"Do you still want this outside the others?" Mrs. Fraé asked, referring to the new tattoo. "On the small of your back?"

Linette nodded.

She did not need to speak his name, for which she was grateful. Climbing on to the bench, Linette pulled her shirt up, then curled her arms beneath her chin, and waited. The puckered flesh of her bad arm was uncomfortably warm against her and she could feel her muscles tensing in anticipation of the moment when her skin was pierced —

"So."

A voice. *His* voice.

"So," he said, repeating it, drawing it out, letting his very familiar voice sink into her. "This is my funeral."

I am dying.

Soon, I will be taken into a chamber where two giant tubes hang from the ceiling, and I will be submersed in a green liquid. There, I will die. There, I will be put into a new body. There, I will return. I will return without these weak lungs I was born with; without the holes in my heart; without the pains that stop me from being able to travel this world of ours without having oxygen next to me. When I awake, I will be, for the first time that I can remember, without pain.

You would rather me die. You said that to me, only a week ago, stroking my hair as I lay in our bed, exhausted by the muggy heat, and unable to draw a good breath. You would rather me die than return a man made from bronze and silver and skin. You would rather mourn me than celebrate me.

You defend the right for the Empress and her Children to worship and live as they wish, but it strikes me that their beliefs are not so different than mine. For them, they return in a new body, reborn into their family by a sister, brother, daughter, or son. Perhaps even their own parents. The men and women who believe in God, and who we share our cities with, believe they will be reborn too — given a new life in Heaven (or Hell), after their life has been judged by God. So why is it that I cannot return?

You will be angry, I know, when you read this. You will see it as betrayal. I do not wish for you to do so, but you will.

If I —

I will find you, Linette. I will talk to you — the Surgeon is in front of me right now, and she is urging me to finish, so I must. But I will find you, after — I will.

For a moment, he looked just like the man she remembered: slender, pale, blond, with a blade of a smile that revealed his crooked, yellow teeth. Except, of course, that they were not crooked, and therein the truth was told. They were straight, and white, and he was, she knew, dead.

The room was quiet with the pause between words and action. Linette (and, she assumed, Mrs. Fraé) could hear the faint murmur of machinery that surrounded the man before her, much in the way that insects create a susurration of noise in the evening. If allowed, it would slip into the background, become a familiar, normal buzz; if it could be allowed, that is. To Linette, the sound only served to remind her of the fact that, beneath his pale skin, he was no longer bones, no longer blood, no longer all the things that she was. Instead, he was bronze and brass bones circled by copper and silver wiring and with a complex motor in the centre of his chest. The skin, like the pale red pants and black shirt he wore, was just another piece of clothing — a piece of fashion, to allow him to look as if he were part of the world.

"Nothing to say?" he said, finally. He remained standing in the doorway to the room, the orange light behind him bathing him in an artificial warmth. "I came all this way — "

"You should leave." Her voice was hard. "I don't want you here."

"Linette — "

"*No.*"

"I — "

"Mrs. Fraé, please." Linette turned to the elderly Mortician, who had been watching the exchange calmly. "Can you do nothing?"

"Don't look to her," he said, a hint of smugness in his voice. "How do you think I am here? She left the door open. She agreed to my plan to meet you here."

Mrs. Fraé smiled faintly, apologetically, and Linette felt the betrayal deeply. It was true that she did not follow the same faith as the Mortician, and that her tattoos were about grief, not God. Her words were a closure she could not get elsewhere else in life, but she had begun to trust the older woman as she trusted few. As the work on her back drew to an end, Linette had felt a bond with Mrs. Fraé, and to feel that connection severed so sharply, so quickly, so instantly, hurt her more than she would have ever considered.

"I thought seeing him would help," Mrs. Fraé explained. "You have an irrational — "

Linette jumped off the table and stalked towards the door. Her body was tense as she approached him, but her gaze held his, and she knew, *knew*, that if he touched her, she would lash out.

"Linette, please, listen — " The murmur of his body grew louder when he opened his mouth. "Please. Stop. Listen to us."

His hand moved to her, but she reacted quickly, slapping it aside. "Don't touch me," she hissed. She could feel her grief and anger mixing, close to hysteria, and she fought it back as best she could to retain her control. "Don't ever touch me. *Never*, do you understand? *Never.* Don't come anywhere near me. I know your kind, and you may think you're someone I know, but you are not. You're not him. He's *dead*. You're just the copy of him. You're nothing but a tool — an object. Something to be used. Something to be sent in to kill men with. Something that can pretend that it's dead so that you can sneak in like an assassin and kill them without remorse. Something that can switch off every emotion because it is just a wire. Something that lets me switch off my emotions. Something that lets me kill one, kill ten — kill fifty! Something that allows me to kill as many people as I please because — "

"*Linette.*"

"*Because* you make death meaningless."

Silence. His mouth opened, the hint of growling mechanics growing into an artificial shout, but she shouldered past, bashed past him, threw him off balance with his new, heavy weight, and his voice did not emerge. Her damaged arm throbbed in a sharp, renewed pain. Good, she thought. Good. She wanted to feel the pain. The pain would stop the tears, would hide the hurt, the betrayal, and if, perhaps, while she stalked along the streets of Issuer back to her house...if perhaps tears slipped out from the corner of her eyes, then she would know it was the pain in her arm, and nothing else.

For all the differences we have, for the all the difficulties that we have faced since your return, Linette, I want you to know that I am still dedicated to us. To preserving us.
Antony.

The tears had stopped by the time Linette reached her house, but her body was covered in a sheen of sweat, as if it had begun to weep silently now that her eyes were dry.

She was conscious of the twin shapes of the Ovens behind her, and the finality that they represented. It was a small comfort, and as she stood at the side of her house and gazed back at Issuer, with its barely populated streets that were threaded together by shadowy lines of electricity and punctuated by bronze windmills, she took that comfort for as much as she could. Even though the city had betrayed her — no, not Issuer itself, but a part of the city, part of its trade, its life — the Ovens sat, unmoving, waiting, the period that put everything into perspective for her. The period that gave her security. She took from the Ovens everything that she could, and when she entered the house finally and saw *his* letter, leaning against the kettle just as it had before, her previous anger and hurt failed to rise.

She could throw it away, and knew, perhaps that she should. She could rip it, cut it up, drown it, burn it...

And yet, despite herself, she did not.

Down To The Silver Spirits

Kaaron Warren

The looks of pity were bad enough, but it was the advice we grew sick of. Eat this, take that, go there, buy this. And the don'ts, as well: don't have hot baths, don't drink tea or coffee, don't take anti-depressants. All this from smug women with babies on hips.

"Why don't they shut up?" I said one morning after a particularly bad shopping trip.

My husband Ken said, "You shouldn't let them upset you." He showed me some research he'd done on the internet, about eating only eggs for a month to boost your chances.

"I like eggs," I said, so we ate omelette, scrambled eggs, boiled eggs and fried for eight weeks, and still I didn't fall pregnant.

I tried to stay positive. I kept looking. I told Ken, "The Tarot told me that June 12 would be good, if I wear red all day and don't fuss with small things."

Silence.

"At least pretend to be supportive."

"No, it's just that... I wasn't going to tell you about this, but someone at work told me about a woman who might be able to help us at a spiritual level. He and his wife went to her after their daughter was drowned, and it was a sanity saver, apparently."

"We don't have any dead children," I said.

"I know," he said patiently. "I know that. But it might help."

It did help.

Maria Maroni changed our lives.

Ken asked me if I wanted him to wait in the car.

"No!" I said. "This is about you, too. This is us." He took my hand and squeezed it, then we walked to Maria Maroni's door.

"You knock," I said.

A tall young man opened the door. He smiled, an open-mouthed smile which showed broad, white teeth.

"I'm Hugo," he said. "Mum asked me to show you through."

His hand warm on the small of my back, he led us along a mosaic-floored hallway.

"It's beautiful," I said. He didn't respond, and I wondered if he was the artist, pretending modesty.

I thought Maria would be matronly, kindly, make us cups of tea and let us talk. But she was tall, blonde hair in a high bun with soft wisps down the side. Her features were sharp but beautiful, highlighted with cleverly applied makeup. She wore a black singlet with a see-through blouse over the top, and tight black pants and high heels.

"You're here!" she said, and took my elbow. Her voice was strong, and she made me think of those women who spruik out the front of dress shops, clothing for every size inside, they say, 50% off, today only. She gave us each a glass of brandy and took one for herself, then led us to a small, white-walled room. There was no furniture; she knelt to the floor and gestured us to do the same.

"Are you okay?" Ken whispered in my ear. He doesn't like anything as esoteric as this. He likes chairs and tables, and doctors with tests.

I looked at him and nodded. "Are you?" I said. He nodded also, but I could see he was concerned. He would never say so, but he thinks I'm vulnerable to vultures, that they can take advantage of me if he isn't there to watch over me. I don't really need his protection, but it comforts me to have it.

Maria tapped on one wall, and I thought we were beginning, that she was summoning her spirit. I closed my eyes and waited.

But she was calling her son. "Drinks, Hugo."

"What would you like?" he asked me.

"Just a glass of water, thank you."

Hugo wrinkled his nose as if I'd asked for a glass of pig's blood. I wondered if he was one of those who despised anyone who turned down an alcoholic drink.

As he left the room, Ken said, "You've got him well-trained."

"For now. It won't be long before he's the boss."

I couldn't make sense of it; perhaps it was a mother-son thing, which I would know one day.

Maria Maroni stared at me for five minutes or so. Then she said, "You have three shining silver balls spinning around your head and shoulders." I looked over my shoulder, and up, and she laughed.

"It is a gift I have, to be able to see them. They are vessels," she said. "The spirits have moved on, but the vessels will stay with you always."

"Where are their spirits?" I whispered.

She closed her eyes. "I don't know. It may be they have not yet found a home."

I said, "But I've never been pregnant. It's never got that far."

Maria nodded at me. "Oh, yes, it has." She lifted her chin to indicate upwards. "Three times."

Ken sucked in breath, bracing himself. He knew what was coming. I wept for those lost babies, crying till I was sick and had to run for the toilet. Maria gave me a glass of something green and sweet, and when I'd swallowed it I felt no better, just calmer.

She squeezed my hand and looked into my eyes. "Usually at this point I counsel people about the eternity of existence and the surety of fate. But with you, I am compelled to direct you in a different way. I know a small group of potential parents like you," she said. "Lovely people, every one of them. It might be good for you to meet them."

Hugo came in, the long-forgotten water on a tray held before him.

"Am I too late?" he said.

We had been to groups before, but never found the right one. Some had given up any hope of becoming parents, accepted childlessness and thought us obsessive. Some seemed to think it was fine being around people with children. They could stand seeing happy families.

This group was not like that. We gave each other the strength to do what had to be done.

It was wonderful to be among people who understood. We had all suffered in similar ways, though Julie and Wayne had had four miscarriages and three stillbirths, and I couldn't stop crying to hear of her pain. And Nora and John had the record for the most IVF attempts; Fay and Frank, who, at sixty-five, would be considered by most as too old, but not by our group; and Susan and Brent, who didn't talk much about their experiences. Susan usually cried.

It was good to talk, to compare methods and chances taken. But it was sad, too, the failure of us all. That was hard to deal with in a group.

Ken and I had been attending weekly meetings for three months and it was our turn to host. I still saw Maria Maroni on a professional basis every two weeks, just to hear her talk of what could be. She asked me about the group, and shook her head to hear of empty wombs and lost souls. I invited her to the meeting at our house, because she had brought us together and I wanted to thank her with some nice food and brandy. She was reluctant at first, saying strangely, "I'm not sure if you're all ready."

"Ready for what?" I asked, but she shook her head.

"I'll let you know," she said.

She called me on Tuesday morning, saying, "I've spoken to Hugo, and we've decided you are ready. We've decided it's time to try something new."

"What is it?" I said, my heart beating. There had been nothing new to try since the eggs. I had a feeling it would not be anything dietary.

"I'll tell you all tonight," she said.

They arrived at nine, when most of the nibbles were gone and we were close to the end of the brandy. She seemed agitated, excited.

"Sit down," I said. "Have a drink."

Maria accepted a glass and swallowed most of it before looking at us. "How are you all?" she said.

"Maria!" Nora said, "Please! Jen told us you have something new, something for us to try. Please!"

Maria nodded. "I've brought my son today. All of you have met him."

Hugo seemed different, though. There was a magnetism about him, a handsomeness I hadn't seen before. Very different from the sullen, resentful young man.

"What's he going to sell us?" Ken muttered, and if I'd had a knitting needle I would have stabbed him for speaking.

Hugo sat down with a beer in his hand, and we made small talk until Julie slammed down her cup in agitation.

"I don't care about how long your taxi took!" she said. "Why are you here?"

"I'm here because Mum has asked me to come and tell you what I know of the place where I was conceived. A place called Cairness. You won't have heard of it; it's a well-kept secret. Mum learned of it from an old man who traded the secret for a lot of money."

One of the husbands sighed. I'm not sure which one.

"This is not about money, though," Hugo said. "This is about Cairness, and what it can do for you."

"But what is it?" Nora said. "What do you mean by Cairness? What is it?" The word 'conception' ensured our attention.

"Mum didn't tell me till recently that she'd had trouble conceiving. It's not the kind of thing you inflict on a child." He smiled beautifully at Maria.

"No. I kept it quiet for a long time. But then you wanted to know. You needed to know. And with you, your heritage is everything."

"It is. Knowing where I'm from changed the path my life will take."

"This is making no sense," I said. "What are you talking about? What is Cairness?"

"Cairness lies beneath our lake. Below this very city. It was an ancient city destroyed by flood and built upon, forgotten by the cities that followed. It's down there." He gestured, to help us see.

John said, "I vaguely remember hearing about it, now. When they engineered the tunnel beneath the lake. They didn't get far, did they? Before it flooded?"

"That's it. That's Cairness."

"But it's flooded. All of it. I heard they accessed it using SCUBA gear, but nothing was found."

"There is treasure, for those who will look."

Frank said quietly, "But we are not interested in treasure. You've been misled. Not one of us here has any interest in treasure."

Maria said, "You're telling this badly, Hugo."

He gave her such a look. "There is one great room there, one deep, protected room. This is where the treasure hunters reached. But they returned empty handed and terrified. The bodies were long gone, many, many thousands, they think, all drowned and gone to rot. But there are ghosts. They left their souls behind. No one is sure why. Would you like me to tell you what I think?" Hugo asked.

"Please," said Nora. "Please do." Her voice always sounded on the verge of panic, as if any minute wasted made a difference to her chances. He took a sip of beer and grimaced.

"It's gone warm," Ken said. "I'll get you another." Hugo handed his bottle up.

He said, "I think they are the souls of the babies never born. The ones in the womb when the city drowned. I think they are desperate to live a life."

"And we are desperate to have them," Nora said. We chattered excitedly, the other women and I, about the possibilities of it all. The men slipped away one by one, and I caught them in the kitchen, whispering.

Ken looked guilty, kissed my forehead and said, "Hello, darling."

"What are you men talking about?"

They exchanged glances.

"We're discussing what he's said," Ken said.

"You mean Hugo. He has a name." I went back to my friends. I didn't want to hear the husbands' negativity.

I shivered as Hugo spoke. I looked at Maria and she was nodding at him, smiling.

"I've been into the city," Hugo said, "and walked through the first tunnel. I did not believe in ghosts; all I saw was metal, boxes, furniture pieces. Then we entered a larger, more open space. I saw nothing but decay, until my guide said to me, *try to shift your focus, like you're looking at one of those 3D pictures.* I stared at the back of a ragged chair until the room around it blurred. I let my gaze slip and saw them. Hundreds of them, crowded in the room like it was the hull of an old transport ship, squatting on the floor, shifting, moving. They plucked at me and my guide, pulled at us. He said, 'They hate us being here. I think they want women.'"

Fay choked a little. "What is this? What are you telling us?" We are not patient story listeners.

Hugo said, "I went back a number of times. My friends couldn't understand why I went, they'd say, *Aren't you afraid of the ghosts?*"

Maria said, "And what would you say to them?"

"I'd say, 'I'm going for the ghosts.'"

"But what sort of a city was it? Do they know?" John said. The men had rejoined us. Ken handed Hugo another beer.

"It was a good place," Hugo said. "A place of great learning and charity. Of absolute equality. I can tell you that much. I took friends there, showing the place off, I guess."

"And just by chance the connection was made," Maria said. "A couple, who'd tried everything for ten years, got pregnant. It was a miracle. It was discovered that the spirits are ready to be reborn. That is, if a woman comes with a womb to fill, there will be a silver spirit ready for her."

We all looked at Hugo. "You?" Julie said.

He nodded. Hugo drank his beer. None of us spoke. "There is no real record of who the silver spirits are, and we cannot guarantee your own children's souls are there. But we do know that these spirits are benevolent, regardless of who they were in life, and that most clients report a moment of absolute knowing." He nodded at us. "Recognition."

The bribes were huge, he told us. That's where most of our money would go. We didn't care, though. None of us cared about the money. We wanted those silver spirits.

We wanted one like Hugo.

My husband squeezed my knee. "We'd like to give it a shot," he said. I loved him for believing, for accepting the possibility. Twenty-five years was too long to wait for a child; soon we'd be fifty-five, too old, too old to start that life.

Maria said, "I just want you all to be clear about what you will be giving up, beyond the financial sacrifice. You will not be the same once you are mothers. The men will notice this and may choose not to care. But you will not feel about them the same way."

We all nodded, barely listening.

Hugo said, "Only those who are truly serious make it, I'm telling you. The dedicated ones. The ones willing to make sacrifices."

I felt proud to be such a person.

We all met the night before in an expensive restaurant right in the centre of the city. Views of the Lake. I didn't like it there, never felt safe, felt ugly and old, out of place. Julie loved it; they lived in the city. Hang the expense, she always said.

"Maria?" I asked.

"She won't be joining us," Hugo said. "She wishes you all well."

It was a little shocking. I was relying on Maria for support.

Susan and Brent weren't there. They didn't like the idea. We'd had a difficult meeting when they told us they weren't coming. Brent had said, "I've been asking around about Cairness. It seems that local legend has it the parents trapped the children and then flooded the city. That's what people say. That it was no natural disaster."

"Brent!" Nora said. "Don't ruin this for all of us by listening to gossip."

"Nora, they say the spirits are of the drowned children, not the unborn babies." He looked at us all as if wanting us to understand. "You need to think about why the children were murdered by their own parents. Why would any parent do such a thing?"

Fay's husband Frank was ill. Some men just don't have the stamina. Wayne wasn't there, either, but Julie wasn't bothered. We all knew they had an 'open' marriage. I watched her flirting with our handsome young waiter and cringed.

"We're starving!" she told him.

We all chuckled over our delicious meal. The unity of it made me want to cry. This was how it should be. This was where I was supposed to be.

"The men will need to wait at the entrance. We've talked about that, right?" Hugo said.

"Aren't they coming with us? I said.

Hugo shook his head. "No. No. This is a woman's place. The silver spirits like women. If the men go down I can't guarantee a result."

"I don't know if I can do it without John," Fay said.

"And me without Wayne," Julie said, although of course she could.

"And me," I said.

"It's not up for discussion. As far as I know, it doesn't work if the men go down there. It's up to you. The risk is yours." He looked at the ground. "You will need to leave your men behind."

For a moment I almost gave up. Then Ken said, "There's no need for discussion. This is what we came to do, this is what we'll do."

"So do you want a boy or girl?" Nora asked. My husband and I smiled at each other.

"We don't mind," I said, "So long..." and the whole group interrupted me then, saying, "... as it's healthy." Everybody laughed. Sometimes you laugh for the joy of being the same, those rare moments when a group of people think alike.

We sat up late, talking softly and enjoying the night. We didn't talk much about the next day and I was glad. I didn't want to think about what lay beneath. What we would be seeing. I wanted that part done with, and my baby in my arms. I could almost smell that baby scalp smell.

I woke up in the morning to my husband's bare, downy back. I stroked him gently, his shoulder blades, his neck, his back. He stopped breathing for a moment then started up again, and I knew he was pretending for fear of stopping me. It struck me suddenly how wonderful he was, all he did for me. I kissed his back gently and he stopped breathing again. I pulled at his shoulder to turn him over and we made gentle love without speaking.

Hugo was at our door early, making sure we were okay. "You're looking flushed, Jenny," he said.

I blushed. Ken laughed. Sex had been a matter of timing for us for a long time. Spontaneity seemed like a waste. It was as God intended, sexual relations for procreation, not pleasure. My husband made sad little jokes about it to his friends, "We're trying as hard as we can," winking at them. No one ever laughed.

All the husbands except Frank made the joke, we realised when we got together. Not one of them mentioning the hard work of it, the routine. Frank found it all offensive, every last mention.

We spent the day exploring the city, buying presents for the babies, our arms laden with generosity. Hugo didn't join us.

John waited in the bar that evening while we got ready in the hotel room Hugo had booked. We giggled like brides and did buttons and zips. It was odd, such sensible, serious women acting like girls, but we were so very excited. We had all brought beautiful dresses to wear. It was the most important day of our lives, and we were going to look our best. Ken was jealous and finally stomped off to the bar to join John. "You never dress like that for me," he said.

"This is not about you," I said.

"It never is," he muttered.

We giggled when he left. It's hard to take men seriously. Julie joined us last; she can't go a day without a run. She thinks her obsession with fitness will help her keep a baby. We had just opened a bottle of champagne when Hugo knocked at the door. We squealed like teenagers, and Julie let him in.

"We need to get moving," Hugo said. "It's a long walk down and back up again."

I hate walking at night at the best of times, but here? In this city? I wanted a police escort.

The others kindly told stories to distract me. John spoke about his brother, who bathed his kids at Nora and John's house.

"Can you imagine?" John said. "The whole bathroom smelt of children for days."

"That's so cruel," we said. Most of us rarely saw the relatives with children. They were so smug, so pleased with themselves.

As we walked, we talked a little about expectations. All of us were terrified. We were headed for a community of ghosts, and no matter how benevolent Hugo said they were, we were frightened. We walked quickly to keep up with him. He didn't look down, watch his step, as we all did. He seemed to float, almost oblivious to the city. He reminded me of my Indian Guru, stepping on those who didn't get out of his way.

We reached the lake's edge, and Hugo stopped under the ramparts of the old bridge. He seemed to pant like a frightened dog.

"What is it?"

"Not keen on water. It's okay. I'll be fine."

John said, "I love it here. Testament to man's stupidity. Why build on a flood plain? It doesn't make sense."

"Cities have been destroyed by flood here many times. Each is arrogant enough to believe they will be the ones to avert the waters." Hugo shrugged. "This city is over two hundred years old. It's doing okay. You live here, John. You chose this flood plain."

"What if the child is like him?" Ken whispered to me.

He could be a hateful man.

Crowds walked by, shouting, and beer bottles landed at our feet. One glanced off Fay's arm, but she rubbed at the spot and said nothing.

Hugo led us down under the rampart. It stank of rubbish, wet dirt. He pulled some gloves from his pocket and squeezed his fingers into them. He swept a pile of rubbish away to reveal a manhole, which he lifted and shifted.

He gestured me inside.

We climbed down. It was quieter. The smell of it: Wet, hot concrete. Urine, vaguely, as if the piss had been mixed into the concrete when it was poured. There were steps, steep, with rusty railings. Nora twittered away, frightened to hold the railings in case they collapsed.

"Hold onto me," her husband said.

Rust covered my hands. I wiped them on Ken's shirt a dozen times.

Hugo seemed jumpy. Eager to please.

The walls felt very near. We began to sing to distract ourselves; "It's a Long Way to Tipperary" petered out and someone started on the National Anthem, which made us all laugh.

"Are we close?" Julie said. Her voice was faint. We were all tired. I didn't even want to think about the climb back up.

"I should never have brought you here," Ken whispered in my ear as we stepped over a pile of reddish refuse.

"You didn't bring me" I hissed. "I came! I came of my own accord." He lifted his arms up, a favourite gesture of retreat, and at that moment I wanted him gone. He supported this without really believing it, and I would leave him if he ruined my chance at motherhood.

"Is that the entrance, sealed with the rock?" he said.

This practicality distracted the men, and between them they rolled the rock aside. We didn't talk. Each one of us women knew we would do this; we would walk through a pit of fire for our babies.

We heard a low groaning sound.

"What's that?" Ken asked.

"The air sounds different down there. It's enclosed, and there are walls and things. You'll be all right," Hugo said.

"I can't do it," Fay said. At our group sessions, she was always the tensest, wanting to know the truth but terrified of it at the same time.

"It's all right," Hugo said. "It's the silver spirits calling. They won't harm you. Ghosts aren't malevolent when they're in the majority. They tend to be calm, and feel like they're at home. In heaven, perhaps."

He looked at us, standing back.

"You're all here because you've been to hell and back. You want children, right?"

We nodded.

He spoke very quietly. "They're waiting. Go find the one you love."

A sound of babies crying and a smell, the smell of babies came to me. I clutched Ken's arm. "Can you hear that? Smell it?"

He shook his head. "I can't. I'm sorry."

I stepped in first. I was tired of waiting; I wanted that baby.

I expected underground to glow silver. Hugo had told us it was cold so we were rugged up, but the iciness of it still surprised me. The smell was bland, a little metallic, a little earthy. Someone had rigged lights up, and we could see the rubble and debris of a fallen city.

There were sockets in the wall, where the hinges of the main gate had hung.

"I can't believe the archaeologists haven't cleared this place out," Fay's husband called from the entrance.

"Look at this wall." Nora touched the clear flood marks. "You can see where the water stopped." She bent down and picked up a handful of dirt, then sifted through it to show us a silver coin. "I can't read it in this light."

"We'll look at it later," I said.

"What do we do?" Fay said. "Just stand here?"

"I say we walk. They must be further in," I said.

We moved in close formation, tripping over bricks and rocks as we made our way deeper into the city. The floor was very damaged, but you could see the beauty it once was, the remnants of a magnificent mosaic.

The room was very deep, probably five times my height. On one wall (and again, it was terribly damaged) I could see an amazing family tree, each child below its parents, all with that same broad smile Hugo wore.

There was movement to our left.

"What's that? Is it someone?" Fay said.

It was grey, drab. "It can't be. It's not silver," Nora said.

Then the grey thing lifted its head, and we saw a face of such terrible anger we all screamed.

"Move on! Move on!" Nora shouted.

"No, back. Back!" Fay said.

"I'm not leaving without my baby. I've come this far. I'm not leaving," I said.

I stepped forward and shouted, "We're here. Where are you?"

Hundreds of the grey, drab creatures appeared, slouching towards us like wolves. Their faces were drawn, sad.

"This can't be them," Nora said.

The groaning grew louder as they approached.

"I don't want one of them! They don't look like babies," Fay said.

Some of them seemed twisted, bent. I couldn't look them in the eye.

We turned and tried to run, but they surrounded us.

"Maybe this is how they're meant to look," Julie said. "They'll change, won't they?"

Their faces were deformed, ugly. They snarled with transparent teeth and floated above us, spinning so fast we grew dizzy watching them.

I felt drawn to one, it's true. For a moment it paused and cocked its head, as if assessing me. Then it stretched its hand out to me.

"No, Jen, no!" Fay said.

It was too late. The ghost stretched out with both hands and thrust its long fingers into my eyes. I was blinded, but felt no pain. I felt it crawling into my head through my eye sockets, dragging itself through, sliding down my throat and into my womb, where it curled up, waiting for a body to grow into.

Fay covered her eyes, crouching on the ground. "Fay," I said. "You will be so sorry if you don't do this. Come on. Look, I'm all right." I pulled open her arms and she looked up. Five of them surrounded us, peering down. They jostled to reach her, their fingers grabbing at her eye sockets and tugging until she screamed. One slid its index fingers in and the others flew off, leaving the silver spirit to enter her as mine had done.

I turned to see Julie being filled as well, and Nora. My throat constricted as if swollen, and we walked silently back to where the men waited. The other ghosts flew around our heads, ducking over us, making us flap at them as if they were birds.

The sight of those dear husbands made me cry. Ken looked like a stranger, as if he'd aged ten years since I'd been in Cairness.

"What happened?" they said. "Are you all right?"

We all touched our bellies, feeling life wriggling there.

"We're all right," I said. There was no point telling the men. No point. What could we do? You can't kill something already dead and we all wanted children so much.

"And now you know why my mother will never return," Hugo said, quiet in my ear.

Fay brought her famous potato salad again this year.

"I roasted the potatoes," she said, as she passed me the dish. "Isn't that naughty?" I watched her three year old son, already stripped to saggy spiderman underpants, sawing at my bench with the bread knife. He danced around us, his tiny penis jiggling, his flabby white stomach quivering. I smiled, thinking, "*You look like a worm. Or a fat white adder who's just swallowed a child.*"

He stopped dancing and paused, cocking his head at me. Then he hissed like a snake.

"Very naughty," I said. Fay's husband Frank kissed me dryly on the cheek and smiled. He didn't say hello; every year the tiredness takes him more. He placed three bottles of red wine on the bench.

"Are we the first?" Fay asked. Ken entered the kitchen, carrying our three-year-old daughter, flopped as if boneless in his arms.

"Punctual as ever," he said. Fay flicked her gaze to my daughter, then to me. We shared the look, the look we Cairness mothers share, then bustled to get drinks and nibbles ready. Ken bent to place our daughter down, but she screamed, as she always did, clawed her way up and onto his shoulders. She stuck her long index fingers into his ears and pressed her face to his hair. He bent with her weight and said, "Who else are we expecting?" He is quiet now, and pale, like he's an extension of her, a growth from under her arms with legs and part of a brain. She likes to be carried. Looked after.

Hugo and Maria, there early to help set up, kissed her.

"Four new families are coming today. Back from Cairness a year ago," Maria said.

"So the children are three months old?" Fay said. We exchanged our Cairness mother's glance again and knew we would not ask the women any questions. We wouldn't say, "How was Cairness for you?" and we would pretend not to notice their babies' eyes, silvery grey, all of them, all of the children's eyes that silvery grey we knew well but that the husbands didn't recognize because they never entered Cairness with us.

Nora arrived with her family. Their son vomited red and purple lollies, half-digested, in the entrance, and we cleaned it up. His arms were covered with carefully drawn naked pictures of his mother. Nora caught me watching and pulled his sleeves down. "He's talking now," she said. "He's got a vocabulary of fifteen words."

"That's very good," I said. I didn't ask her if she could understand the words he spoke or if, like my daughter, the language sounded like something not quite English. It started to rain and we watched our children shiver inside, hide their eyes. To a one they hate water. We can't teach them to swim, can't take them to the beach. Fay says it's because of the terrible story Hugo tells them again and again. We can't stop him, though. He says it's family history. He loves the children, each one of them. He gathers them to him like disciples.

"The parents of Cairness were the meanest you ever saw." He spreads his fingers, drawing the children's eyes to his. "And they trapped their dear children, tricked them into a room, and they let go the sluice gates. Those children drowned, choked with water in their lungs, no air. Can you imagine?"

Oh, the children could, all right. The others hated the story, but Ken saw its importance. "She'll want to know where she came from. When she's older."

"She's our child. That's all that matters."

"It does matter, though. All adopted children want to know."

"She...is...not...adopted." I could barely stand the sight of him.

The new families arrived, bringing store-roasted chicken and packets of chips. Their babies cried and fussed, wriggled and cried.

Fay said, "Don't worry, it gets better," but we watched the three year olds and we knew it wasn't true. Her son crawled around, picking the sleep out of the babies' eyes with his long fingernail.

We'll keep in touch. We see Susan out sometimes, and she looks insane, her furious envy making her shake to see our lovely littlies. Our children are so close in age, and our shared experiences tie us together. Two boys and two girls. All of them difficult in their own way, cold about the eyes and lacking in innocence. But they are our children and we love them. As they grow we will watch them and wonder: What will they do to the world when they are adults, and what are the words we will use to justify bringing them to life?

THEY WOULD ONLY BE ROADS

Darin C. Bradley

P rester fingered the chain — he'd pulled it from the tank behind one of the commodes downtown, in Idio, the old feed-mill turned nightclub near the depot. The chain had absorbed such faith in the dank water, pulling endlessly as expected — as the clubbers believed it would. Prester imagined each flushing synapse exhausting its neural blast all the way through the chain and into the water, where it rippled gently into the lime-scarred porcelain. Idio's clubbers had no doubt empowered the chain to degrees that, no matter how he found his gnosis, Prester would never fully measure. The tarnished scars on the delicate chain's aged links reminded him of flowers, complete with rusted stems and lines of calcium like pale roots.

He took a deep breath as he eased out of his reverie, now acutely aware of his apartment's water-stained breath. With a cough, he eased the chain back into his pocket — it had invaded his thoughts with decay enough for now.

"I'm going to need more charms," he said aloud, the phosphor glow of his computer monitor rendering his fingers blue.

"aLan," he called.

The screen on his link-pad blinked at his elbow, its colors momentarily negative as the slender machine stirred awake.

Prester glanced at it. "Sorry, thought you were in the box."

Lacking speakers to respond, the pad blinked its patience as Prester linked it up to his stationary computer.

"You set?" Prester asked after a moment.

"I'm here," aLan's androgynous voice said.

"I need more charms," Prester told it. "A *lot* more."

aLan thought for a moment, its status bar slipping across the monitor's screen. "You have two hundred inactive," it reported.

Prester looked at the diagram tacked to his wall. The newsprint had yellowed in the last six months, and the storms that had softened the city last weekend had curled its edges. In lines of colors, twisting, arranged in Solomonic sigils, yoked together by strands of brittle yarn, his ready charms littered the page: names, addresses, e-mail servers — they all promised power in different guises. Some signified chain letters still sleeping in his filing cabinet; others were acronyms for the various forwards in his e-mail inbox. A few were rumors he hadn't yet started. Each carried its own charm, the granted wish it promised for spreading it around. Prester didn't have enough — not to make this new rite capable of generating the wishes it would need. He needed at least enough to diffuse the Levites' anger, should an uninvited wish or two slip past the protective rite and into their sanctum. Prester didn't care what it was they wanted so badly to secure — he just wanted their money.

"No good," he finally concluded. "I already set most of them in the rite: counter-charms." He scratched his head. "And I need the few spares to get out of here later."

aLan did some more thinking. As familiars went, it was slow, but Prester had counted on it for so long, he didn't want to summon a new one — not with today's risks on the web. There was too much at stake now to open himself up to whatever strange programs would answer his call.

"Taylor," aLan eventually reported, "has released eighty charms in the last five days."

Prester wheeled away from the computer, the chair's hissing casters sighing his frustration. With enough active to release that many so quickly, Taylor wouldn't surrender any for cheap.

But what had she done with them?

"Why do you need so many?" Taylor asked. The Pipeline was making something digitally husky of her voice. Prester recalled with a shudder how long it had taken him to separate the glamour she'd created for herself in the 'line from how she'd sounded in the bedroom.

Prester pushed aLan's headphone deeper into his ear. "It's for a job — I've got a deadline."

"You can't farm your own?"

"No."

Taylor paused. "This isn't about the New Levites, is it?"

Prester didn't say anything.

"Didn't I tell you not to take that job?"

"Yeah."

"And you took it."

"Yeah."

"Well, fuck you then, Prester." He could hear the cigarette smoke in her voice — he was still quit, ever since they decided to do it together that Christmas.

He decided to hold his tongue, decided not to tell her that not every charmer could still pull college-money from dad. With a record like his, he had few options. He hadn't held an identity long enough in the past two years to put any real-world equity into it, so the best job he had found had been cleaning toilets for the scensters at Idio.

Prester steadied his voice. "Taylor, please. Let's just do this — just business."

"Fine," she snapped — he could tell she wasn't doing business, not the kind he wanted. "I'll get you the charms, but I'm going to have to pull them from what's available."

He could tell where this was going.

"Short notice leaves you without many options, Prester — it's gonna take a theft to get what you want."

Damn. He'd only just gotten used to this identity.

"Andrick," he realized.

"Yep," Taylor snapped, exhaling. Her smoke seemed to send static crackles through the 'line. "And he's got clients itching for a hit on their South African."

Prester held his tongue. He thought everyone had abandoned the South African — no one believed in benevolent bankers looking to give away money anymore. At least, so he'd thought.

"All right," he said. aLan's task bar paced across the computer screen, looking rather judgmental, Prester thought. "Forward it along, and I'll respond."

"The money's got to be legit," she warned.

"It is — there's just not much of it."

She paused again. "You want this, you deal with the headache. No reports. Nothing."

Prester ran a hand through his hair. It was too oily, he realized. How long had it been since he'd showered?

"I'll play to the scam," he promised. "Just send it along and Pipe the charms to aLan."

"Have you got a new face ready?" she asked.

He nodded. "Been doctoring it for a few months — figured something would come up sooner or later."

"New security number, birth — credit rec — "

"It's covered, Taylor. I'll give your South Africans a week of transfers and then tank the old face."

"You're going to regret this, Prester."

"I know."

"They're aligned," aLan reported.

Prester stirred awake. Dumbed by fatigue, he took a pull from the mug on his desk, forgetting the effects of naps on coffee. He swallowed with a grimace. aLan had aligned Taylor's charms with the new rite and was slipping the results through the aged plastic lips of Prester's printer. He thought it looked like the machine was gumming the page — a pair of waxy, chapped jaws, trying the alignment out, hoping, perhaps, it was edible. No doubt the printer was as hungry as everything else in Prester's apartment, including himself.

He sat up, groaning with the chair, and started re-arranging his yarn. Taylor had been good for it — aLan's printout had forwards on it that Prester hadn't seen yet, each one promising a different route to the same miracles, the same desires that suckered the charms into life in the first place. Ten friends, ten minutes, three wishes in an hour. Dumb as it had once sounded to Prester, there were enough people who'd try — just in case — and ship the idea along to their friends, families. Things had been different when charmers had relied only on chain letters, but the principle had been the same. Internet had only sped things up. The Pipeline made them insane.

Prester pulled scraps of paper from the piles of envelopes and petitions on his desk. After a few minutes, he'd scribbled out the names of the new charms and pinned them to the wall. He was almost out of yarn, but he had enough to track the new charms' positions in the rite. Different threads for different wishes — ribbons on these, sketches on those, braids for counter-charms. Once aLan got the rite moving, Prester'd sell the wall again. He hoped the Arts Council was still into gutter collage.

"Right," Prester said, stepping away. "Open the reserve charms."

"To whom?" aLan asked mechanically.

"Doesn't matter," Prester told it. "I'm not looking for fireworks here, just a coincidence."

"Set?" he asked after a moment.

"Ready," aLan reported.

Prester closed his eyes. He only needed a few gallons — a minor wish, as it went. He tried to keep Taylor out of his thoughts, tried to keep everything she had and he didn't from souring the charm. It didn't matter; he could feel his resentment staining the small rite. Taylor never had to worry about how many gallons she had in the tank — her father had been buying her metro passes as long as Prester could remember. Had been forking over credits for new clothes, a better pad.

New furniture. Prester hadn't held a pass in weeks, and there was no telling how much longer he could keep the Bel Air running. He couldn't even remember what new things smelled like.

"Send," he ordered.

Outside, he smiled. The pad was warm in his pocket — heated by aLan's now-smug computing. Prester had seen the truck parked next to his car in the lot before, but it was always much further down, closer to the pool — nowhere near Prester's dolorous efficiency.

He thumbed open the truck's battered tank-flap and traced a finger over the gas cap. The paint wasn't rusted in here, and the sun hadn't gotten to the cap's dark plastic. He unscrewed it, slipped in his hose and started sucking. A few moments later, the truck bled its noxious fuel down the line. Prester only took a few gallons — he didn't want to push the charms. Having only sent ten to effect the coincidence, he feared things would go bad quickly if he tried to take more than he'd earned.

Afterward, he slid the hose into his trunk and coaxed his old car to life. He'd hoped to get moving earlier, when the sunlight meant the dim, left headlight wouldn't make any difference. Now, he just hoped that the night would slip itself over the car, shrouding as best it could the old thing's derelict complexion. He didn't want to attract attention.

Downtown rolled past his windows in phantasmal lumps, its many signs and streetlights casting multicolored gazes across Prester's windshield. Every building stared at nothing, each doing its neon best to be looked at in return but self-blind to know if it was working. Artificial barge-boards clung lamely to the rooflines, their finer details brightened by gap-toothed Christmas lights like lines of glowing birds. People slipped in and out of clubs below, smoking at each other, wandering with the traffic, looking smooth and going hurriedly nowhere. Compelled. Saturday was the excuse they gave themselves, but Prester knew there were charmers behind the crowds — there were good reasons why the corner mart's business went dead when it did, why Ladies' Night worked better here than there. Someone wanted a hold-up — another needed a club full of pockets to pick. Charmers made their own opportunities, and different places, different circumstances, decayed as ordered.

When he cleared the avenue and maneuvered through the tree-line, he could only see the city in its paranoid glare atop the misted spruce trees — those that had grown high enough to stare back. Gated communities lifted their parental, wrought-iron fingers as Prester passed — there'd be no decay behind their gates, they promised. Stucco and sheetrock and windows with fake casements — these places had the medical teams that downtown didn't, effecting with their trowels and nail guns the cosmetic surgery that didn't need neon, that didn't blind itself — it only layered scars, and no one here looked for those.

At length, he passed the furthest-adventuring suburbs and moved down the old logging road toward the Levites' estate. Their gate was open when he arrived, and the motion of the moonlight across the shadowed drive looked like an inhalation. Prester looked up at dozens of pairs of laced-together shoes dangling from the Levites' wind-swinging Pipeline cable. He wondered what the old wack-jobs thought they had accomplished.

Prester stretched his feet, reclining across the chair's tucked and pleated leather. The parlor had the same black and white domino floor that he saw in all these enclaves. He wanted to roll his eyes, wanted to carve something pithy into the yantras and mandalas and god-damned horseshoes tacked above the dark wainscoting.

But he didn't. aLan worked sedulously on a mahogany lowboy at his elbow, porting Prester's rite into the Levites' aged terminal.

"This looks fine, young man," the Levite said. Prester didn't know his name, didn't think they had names.

Prester smiled. "I've done my best, sir."

"Our terminal reports that many of these...*charms* are new." The old man studied Prester through his spectacles, the light of faux gas lamps dithering across his pate. "That will make the rite more potent?"

Prester leaned forward. "Yeah. My rite will keep your database secure, and the new charms mean it will learn faster. The more it encounters, the sooner it will mature — the better it will wish." He glanced at aLan — it was almost finished uploading. "It should be fully itself within a month."

"Very good," the old man smiled, hunting and pecking at his keyboard. "I'll just see to this transfer then. Your...*familiar* should be able to validate the funds shortly."

Prester swallowed, fishing a slip of paper from the lapel of his battered coat. He offered it to the Levite. "Use this account, if you don't mind."

No sense putting his new money in the old account, just in case any of the South Africans were checking.

The old man squinted as he took the paper. "Of course."

Prester took the cigarettes angrily and stormed through the shop's doors. He felt guilty about smoking, but what did it matter? Who would care? Taylor certainly wouldn't, much as he wanted her to.

Back inside his car, he jammed the cigarette lighter into its nest and accelerated out of the lot. aLan sat coolly on the naugahyde beside him, as blue and uninterested as the light slicking Prester's dash. He was glad he'd be switching faces in a week — the tickets that damned community-cop had tossed at him would have eaten everything he earned from the Levites...and then some. At least now he'd only lose a quarter of it on a more authentic set of new plates. He could use the rest to get the jump on next month's charms. Maybe, for once, people would be calling him.

Down the road, he eased the Bel Air into one of Idio's narrow parking spaces. The lot winked at him in rainbow flashes, the oils in its pavement awakened by the mist and the moonlight. Prester shoved his pad into his pocket and picked up the cigarettes.

Inside the club, he pulled a pile of cheap placards from another pocket and started handing them out. They promoted a fake show — a band he'd come up with last year — and asked their bearers to spread the word through graffiti and Xerox. The show, Prester's placard promised, would make their wildest dreams come true, but only if they'd spread the word.

At the bar, Fidence, the tender, thrust a meaty finger in Prester's face. "Stop handing that shit out, Prester."

Prester didn't want a fight. He shoved the remaining placards back into his pocket. Later, he'd count them again so he could tell aLan how many he'd released.

He spread his hands placatingly. "Just want a beer, Fid."

"Out," Fidence reported sourly.

"You're out?" Prester challenged. "Of beer?"

"Floated the last of it ten minutes ago," Fidence said. "Damned if Bachs didn't run inventory just last Wednesday. We're gonna lose at least a thousand tonight without it."

Prester's shoulders tightened. First the cop, now this. It was absurd. Idio had never run out of beer, and Prester hadn't pissed anyone off recently — not any charmers. Who'd be throwing wishes at him?

Prester looked around uneasily. "Well, all right. I just came to celebrate."

"Go somewhere else, then," Fidence grunted.

Prester left, unnerved. Outside, a rivet fell from one of the gantry-towers spanning the rail line behind the club. One of the metros chimed its way over the tracks on the other side of the avenue, its over-lit riders like stage-painted extras inside. Prester could see a few looking at him as they slid by.

He had to get to Sixx — Taylor was usually there, and he was starting to worry. Maybe Andrick's charms were no good. Maybe he'd white-washed some old ones, and Prester's security-rite was trying to harness dead wishes. He flinched. That always meant trouble.

He eased into his car, stunned when he glanced into his mirror to see a gutter-thread scenster standing at the back of the car. The guy looked like he had sheet-metal skin, like his hair was just head-rust and lichen. The kid's eyes shone with the homogenized orange glow of the surrounding city lights.

Prester turned, but the people he could see crossing the lot looked normal — normal for Idio, anyway. Though he looked, he didn't see anyone in his lane.

He lit another cigarette as he picked his way out of the lot, brakes squealing their distaste.

Sixx wasn't as crowded as Idio. Prester even liked the music better — they played things downtempo here. He could only take so much drum-and-basc from Idio.

Taylor was with some corduroy kids in a corner booth. Prester bummed a light from a passing bearded guy and hurried toward the booth.

He'd broken the guy's lighter.

"Hey, Taylor," he said, anxious.

She looked up, the light from her pad throwing venomous, green reflections across her glasses.

"Get that one moving tonight," she told the others.

The kids slid out of the booth, clutching their pads. Prester sat.

"Hey yourself," Taylor said, cinching her shoulders. "Get your rite off?"

"Yeah," he said. "Money's good."

"You're a goddamn idiot," she said, the air-filter clicking in the rafters overhead.

He swallowed. "Yeah? Why?"

"Just wouldn't listen to me, would you?"

He'd play along — decided he *had* to play along. "About what?"

She leaned across a cluster of empty beer glasses. "You've been took."

"By the Levites?" He tried to keep his eyes out of the abyss of Taylor's plunging neckline.

"Designed a security-rite for them, didn't you?" she pressed.

"Yeah."

"They already had one."

"No they didn't," Prester scoffed. "aLan marked their entire grid before I even started collecting charms."

"Yes," she said, "they did. I tried to warn you off, but what the hell do you think I can say over the 'line? Christ, they've got familiars listening everywhere."

He swallowed. Maybe they had other servers, remote units that didn't splice from the Pipeline as the main grid. He shook his head. Even so, aLan would have picked up their relays. No familiar can keep quiet for that long.

She grabbed his hand. "Maybe if you ever came out instead of just calling me when you need favors, I could have given you the jump." She lit a cigarette. "Now you're just fucked."

"Let's say you're right." He palmed the sweat from his brow. "Me laying a new rite over an existing one doesn't mean anything. Nothing wrong with redundancy."

"Except," she said, exhaling rooftops of smoke, "you're the test. You've set yourself up to be screwed and screwed and screwed. You laid out the code, loaded their terminals with your rite, and then empowered it with your own charms. Fine. Except now, as the charms' suckers forward and sign and mail to their wishing-hearts' content, they're keeping your rite alive, meaning the old one will keep feeding off it."

She took a drag from her cigarette. "Eventually, it'll track the charms back to their source and decide that you're a better target. Hell, it may have figured that out already."

Prester rubbed his face. "Wait."

She folded her arms across her chest.

"Who coded it?" he asked.

"I did. Two months ago."

He scooted closer. "Well, Christ, Taylor — call it off!"

She lidded her gaze. "You think I've got ties to it? Don't be a dumb ass. I took precautions."

Prester could feel the tiny fans in his pad powering up, venting the machine's mechanical heat. "How, then?"

"Damn you," she said, scooting out of the booth. "Come on."

"No," he said, pulling away, "let's take my car."

Taylor reached out and grabbed his hand again. "You're lucky you made it this far in it," she hissed. "If you want my help, you're coming with me. By now, the brake fluid's gone, the plugs are corroded — who knows?"

Prester relented and walked with her toward the metro. He thought about the cop outside of town. About Idio. Taylor's rite had figured him out — he knew it had.

"I can't believe I'm helping you," she muttered. The mist had congealed into rain, and it was now gathering in shimmering beads on her mostly bare shoulders. "This is stupid."

Prester held his tongue.

On the sidewalk, they picked their way brusquely through the opposing crowd. Everywhere he looked, Prester saw people slicked by the rain, their wet skin and clothes reflecting the city back at him. Neon curves and brickwork smears gathered in the dampened shadows of the walkers' dark faces. He saw the walk-sign white men pacing *through* people, stop signs in flashes across wet cheeks. Power lines and metro cables tangled in hair.

One walker slammed into him, his many-ringed fingers crunching against the pad in Prester's pocket — he hoped the stranger hadn't scrambled aLan.

Dragging him onward, Taylor pulled him through a trio of night-outers: long-haired girls in clean sweaters from the campus down the lane. They glared at him with eyes like street signs.

He couldn't be sure if he lost his balance or if a nearby light pole had taken a swipe at him.

When they passed the entrance to the metro, Prester tugged. "Train?"

She jerked back, flashing a look of wet annoyance at him. "We're walking."

"Where to?" he asked weakly. One of his fake placards flopped from the crowd into a puddle at his feet. Absently, he slid a hand over the pocket where he'd stashed them, but he suspected that this one had come back from elsewhere.

Taylor dragged him without answer, slamming him into person after person, banging his shins against smooth-bricked, sidewalk flower gardens. As the traffic thinned, and the buildings stared less at the people and more at each other, Prester started to relax. Here they had shadows, corners and abutments and alcoves without neon, without windows. Places where facades had long since succumbed to the stains of old coal smoke and weak mortar. Prester imagined that these, in the great municipal decay, were only architecturally aware of *themselves*. Aware that, at some other point, there'd been others. A time when they, the buildings, had directed the realities in town. When the integrity of their girders and the strength of their re-bar had dictated at what pace things would change. Now, they knew only that entropy was coming at them from different angles. That things fell apart when they shouldn't, that styles matured and moved on before their time. That, ultimately, they would only be roads.

Prester looked up, watching the rain cascade from a length of the Pipeline between the gutters of two buildings. Its insulation had been agitated bare by the data stream, he could tell — and when he planted his palm against a pock-marked ashlar to brace for Taylor's sharp turn into the alley, he could feel the 'line humming through the stone, animating the self-blind building beyond its time, into tasks it couldn't contain.

He heard things walking behind him as they cleared the alley. Looking over his shoulder, he saw diamond-plate elbows and dumpster-green eyeballs sucked out of his view by the fall of new shadows. They looked now like their metaphors: trash bins and fire escapes. The dark places were groaning in the rain. Taylor's rite was piecing its agents together with from the city's dying body parts.

Taylor wheeled about — they were standing now in a bricked lane. Coffee shops and book stores lined the far side of the pedestrian mall, and oak trees stretched in stylized planters, their leafy fingers foaming with green-wet light under the glare of nearby security lamps.

"Check the air," she ordered.

Obediently, Prester fished out his pad. Its face had cracked in the collision with the ringed walker, but it had life enough to glow aLan's thoughts. Prester hammered a few quick commands into the pad's rubber buttons, but aLan couldn't detect the Pipeline's wireless gaze here.

"Atmospherics," he reported, looking up. Taylor was tapping at her own pad.

"Let's hope so," she said, her hair now flat against her neck, dark ribbons tracing the bluish veins just beneath her pale skin. Prester's own hair was guiding rain in cold runnels down his back.

"So what now?" he asked, squinting.

Taylor cinched up her shoulders. "By now, your accounts have been reabsorbed — your new faces are gone. I expect your apartment might already have burned down, but the rain may have delayed that."

"Christ," Prester said.

She looked at him. "My rite is bouncing forwards and routing letters by the dozens every minute. It's got chat bots spreading ideas in rooms all across the 'line. It's not that hard for it to get people's wishes aligned," she said. "It just has to encourage the right ones in the right order. I mean," she paused, "none of the wishers knows they're helping it get you when they wish for a shift in road maintenance or a clearing-out of the tenements on your side of town."

"Coincidences," he realized.

"Results, rhetoric," she continued, waving a hand. "The rite can *encourage* them to wish what it wants. Vague is good when you're talking about thousands to harness. The rite only has to harvest them up and send them where it needs."

Prester laughed. "You mean at me."

"Well, your work, really."

He looked at her. "So why are we here?"

She pointed. Prester followed her arm. They had approached it from a different route, so he hadn't recognized the place, but he could see it now. The Arts Council, smug and clean at the end of the mall.

"The collages," he realized.

She nodded. "Bait and switch."

Prester started dragging *her* this time. If the place was still open, and if he could find some 'line for aLan, they might be able to reuse some of Prester's old rites. Their effects had long since died off, and he could only remember a few of them: job opportunities, a nice table downtown — a carburetor with a longer life. If he could salvage even a few of the charms out of the old yarn-and-newspaper rite-maps, he could set Taylor's rite on a dead trail, send it chasing work down causal lines that no longer existed. Like the buildings around him, Prester would decay himself out of the rite's starving reach. He would reduce himself to dead art: a collection of strings and paper that had long since lost its meaning. A road that went nowhere.

"You're thinking," she said.

"My new face is my old one," he said back, feeling everywhere upon him the harmonics of the rain. The sidewalk hummed beneath its aquatic massage, the gutters sang — the old buildings could hope once again that the sky might wash away some of their entropic scabs. Things were breathing while decay stared at itself with unblinking neon eyes.

He would kick his way into the Arts Council if he had to, if Taylor didn't have any charms that she could work on a forgetful night watchmen and the rotation of the lock. And once inside, he would replace the chain in one of the place's brushed steel commodes with his aged length from Idio. He would let visitors and custodians flush his old chain's power into the walls, back into the art. It would buy the ruse some time.

"Come on," he said, pulling her to him under a nearby awning. He held his breath, hoping that the cigarettes in his pocket would still light.

Taylor laughed, playing along, and thumbed the cigarettes afire with her lighter. They smoked, safe for now, exhaling together into the rain. Giving it back what it was giving them.

TASER

Jenn Reese

e got a whole pack of demon dogs watches out for us, led by this fierce half-husky we call Taser. They hang around and eat our food, sometimes bring us guns and drugs in their toothy mouths — tails wagging, tongues lolling, and sending us in this direction or that, to steal or fight, or just to break.

Me and Keys, we climb the telephone pole. I can see him looking at the scars on my arms and legs as we go, can feel his jealousy. We get to the top and toss a pair of Markus's sneakers over the wire. Markus got shot two weeks ago, and now his Nikes'll keep the goddamn birds away from us and ours while we smoke and do our planning. Those fucking pigeons will tell everything they see to the packs of girls that gather where we're not. But the shoes are like piss, marking our spot, and they got a deep magic, buried in sweat stains and dirty rubber.

We shimmy down and Taser is waiting for us, sitting on the asphalt like it's some kind of throne. He wants us to do something. I feel Keys staring at me, can hear his breathing coming ragged near my ear. The dogs always come to me. They know I can get it done, whatever it is they want. I've climbed in small places and broken into cars and stolen for them. I've distracted the cops and the store owners and boys from the other gangs. I've sat out in the darkness keeping watch for hours and hours, and I'll do it again when they ask me.

Taser's eyes flash. His tongue rolls out over pointed teeth and he pants, grinning. When he gets up and trots down the street, we got no choice but to follow.

Keys calls back to the others, tells them we're headed out after Taser. I can hear the pride and the fear in his voice. This is his first trip, his skin still dull and ordinary. Rick Z., who calls the shots these days when the dogs let him, nods and goes back to his weed. We made a big score two nights ago, and it'll be another couple of days before any of us does much of anything besides smoke and eat. Even the guys old enough to catch pussy will keep their dicks to themselves while we got enough pot to stay high.

We follow Taser through a tangle of streets and alleys, all dark and smelling of drunks and garbage. Taser's nails click against the black road. His tail wags from the motion of his jog, not from any real joy he gets from leading us this way. I suppose maybe he does take some happiness in us, maybe even some pride, but he sure as hell won't let us know if he does, and not by some lame-ass tail wagging.

Keys is younger than me, but bigger. Taller by two inches, maybe. I gotta look up at him when I talk, but that's true with most of the others, too. I'm shorter than all but the youngest of us. As the night creeps colder and we ball our fists at the shadows, Keys throws me a lot of looks, a lot of questions with his eyes. Taser never pulled him from the group before, and he's as like to shit in his pants out of fear as excitement.

I don't look at Keys, don't tell him not to worry. I relax my shoulders, take bigger steps. This is my zone, and Keys needs to know it. Needs to feel it. Needs to tell the others every fucking detail.

Taser keeps on going, till even I start to lose track of where we are. The apartments flatten out into duplexes, the duplexes split into houses, then grow into bigger houses as we walk. The people change color, too. I never been this far from home, from the territory we cover. Birds fly overhead, and there's no sneakers to guard us from their seeing out here. Even the dogs in the yards we pass have dead eyes. Their mouths have never tasted the cool metal tang of a gun, only some tasteless, dry-ass kibble crunched up from a plastic bowl. They're nothing like Taser.

The sun falls. There's growling in my gut from lack of food and too much weed. Keys is going crazy behind me, trying to act like he's not. Taser takes us to a strip mall. Maybe he wants us to take one of the cars — there's a sweet little Mustang I already got my eye on — but then we walk through the lot and around back. A streetlight sputters overhead, and it's like someone keeps flicking the switch on the sun for the way it's fucking up my eyes.

Trash bins and bottles, cardboard boxes and the smell of rotten fruit. The stuff we always find in alleys. The stuff that makes this place, no matter what neighborhood it's in, more ours than theirs. And then, up ahead, scuffling. A whimper. Taser steps to the side and sits, tongue hanging out his mouth in that twisted smile of his.

I don't have a piece, but fuck, I wish I did. Taser never asked me to fight for him, but there'll be a day when he does, and I got nothing but my knives when that shit comes down.

Another whimper, and a gurgle. No thug in the world could make that noise, so we're probably not headed into a fight. Behind me, Keys goes, "Huh?" But I say nothing. I got to keep cool in front of him and Taser. I take a few steps forward till the shadows sink into their true shapes.

There's a woman, a baby, and a dog.

Woman's pale as paper except where there's dirt, and there's a lot of dirt. But her eyes shine wide and scared, and she starts pulling at the baby.

The baby's on the ground next to the panting dog — a brownish bitch, maybe a Shepherd — and is sucking hard against the dog's belly. Goddamn nursing, is what it's doing. Keys steps up, almost beside me but just behind, and mutters a bunch of the words I'm thinking.

"What are we supposed to do?" he whispers.

I look at Taser. Most dog's faces are hard to read, except when they're begging or humping, but there's something in Taser's eyes, something dark and tangled, that speaks directly to my mind in a way stronger than words.

Abomination, he says to me. *Kill it dead.*

Christ. I suck in my breath before I can stop myself, and Keys notices. I turn my back to the woman and the doomed kid, and tell Keys what Taser wants, steeled for his outrage and his fear.

But Keys only looks over my shoulder, at the baby, and nods. "Yeah, we can do that easy," he says. "No one around. We can probably do the woman, too."

My palms are sweaty. "No, just the kid," I say, not too fast, but slower than I want. I never spilled blood before, except with my fists or my feet, and I never killed. Maybe Taser thinks I'm ready. Maybe this is a test. I refuse to turn my head and look at him again. I'm not that weak, and I don't want to look like I am.

Jesus, I can only imagine the scar I'll get for doing this. The harder the job, the harder the dogs bite into flesh, tearing and marking and scarring. My arms and legs are covered in punctures and lines, but they're shallow, might even fade away to nothing when I grow. Then I'd have nothing to show for this life, nothing to stop the others from playing with me like I was just a smaller, weaker piece of shit.

"I'll hold the woman," Keys says, again looking over my shoulder, "and you can take the kid."

He's offering it to me. He knows his place, and he's respecting me, honoring me — not trying to take what he knows he doesn't deserve yet. There's no way Taser would have picked him for this job without me, and Keys knows it, is showing me he knows it. Only...*shit*.

I rub my palms against my pants, buying some time so I can think. I got my knife, and it's more than sharp enough to kill a baby. No issue there, except for keeping the blood off my clothes as it dies. Keys'll take care of the woman, cover her mouth with his hand until the kid is dead and there's no point in her screaming. She's got enough dirt on her to know how to shut up after it's done.

But doing it. Jesus. I never slid my knife into a person's flesh before. I thought about it plenty of times, while the others pounded me into my place, before the dogs started favoring me. But I always thought I'd do it while I was fighting — no time to think, just time to thrust. Slash. Twist. Pull away.

Taser growls, a low rumble that sets my teeth grinding, makes me feel like pissing in my pants. I look at the woman. She clutches that little baby to her chest, almost smothering it. The Shepherd bitch is still lying on the ground. I can see little brown blobs — maybe six — curled near her white-furred belly. Her pups. Not moving. The woman probably killed them to make room for her kid.

That makes it easier. She killed off the dog's babies, and all Taser wants now is paybacks. Revenge is as big a part of us as the urge to find food or jack off. I take a step forward. That's all Keys needs. He walks fast and grabs the woman. She struggles, tries to scream, but she's slow and clumsy from whatever shit she's on. Keys silences her with a rough hand and whispered threats in her ear. Her eyes grow wider, darting from side to side in their sockets like mice in a cage.

I wipe my palms again, swallow, step. All I can hear is blood pounding in my ears. I pull at the baby, but the woman holds it tight. Keys yanks her head back a little, whispers something through cruel teeth, and the woman lets go, surrenders as much as she has to, but no more, to keep on living.

The baby wails. Goddamn thing is heavy in my hands. Not real heavy, just heavier than I thought. Real and warm and breathing and smelling of spoiled milk. Ugly as sin, too, with its twisted up pink face, eyes screwed shut, and too-big head. But Jesus. It's breathing and moving in my arms, like something alive.

I pull out my knife, and Keys heaves the woman back another few feet. She struggles, and I can tell Keys is enjoying it. His left hand, the one not over her mouth, is pressed heavy against her breast.

Then that fucking baby goes and opens its fucking eyes. Sky blue eyes look up at me, squeeze shut, open again and stare.

It's not supposed to be like this. It's not supposed to feel this way. It's supposed to feel like you're fucking the world when you stab someone. Like you're winning the biggest pissing contest ever. Instead, I want to vomit. Maybe, even, I want to cry.

I step over the dog and turn around, so Keys and Taser are both in front of me.

"We're not killing it," I say, my voice growling out of my throat, my knife ready, hilt nestled in my hand.

Taser pops to all fours, his teeth bared, his eyes full of hell.

"What the fuck are you doing, man?" Keys says.

Taser turns his muzzle towards Keys, maybe just noticing him for the first time, and something passes between them. Keys hesitates. He starts to look at me, but remembers where I am, what I'm doing. Then his knife is out, flashing across the woman's throat as he pulls his other hand away. A splash of red and she falls, gurgling, to the ground.

"We got to kill the kid now," Keys says. His eyes glow like Taser's. He keeps turning back to look at the woman. His body is shaking, vibrating. He looks like he just fucked the world.

Taser steps closer. He's only a few feet of dog, but he feels like a bulldozer. My hand with the knife shakes. The more I try to stop it, the more it wobbles.

I drop down to one knee and hold the knife over the prone Shepherd. I keep my eyes on Taser. Keys moves, but stops at one sharp bark from the demon dog. This is between him and me, and he lets Keys know how it is.

Nothing happens, and so much. Taser and me look at each other, and I feel like all the heat of a furnace is blazing against my skin. I want nothing more than to look away, to lower my head from his disdain. His disapproval. His hate.

But Lord, if I back down now, then I'm nothing. Maybe not even that much. I stare back into those deadly dog eyes, and then, somehow, the knife stops shaking in my hand. I reach a new place, the peak of some mountain, and on the other side is calm strength to fill me up and chase out the weakness.

Taser stares at me with his husky eyes. He could kill me. We both know it. But there's something going on here, something different. I'm not challenging him for dominance of the group. I'm just after dominance of myself. His power sears me, prodding, poking, testing me. And then, just as I'm getting ready for another wave, Taser backs off. My heart is beating so hard that it makes my chest ache. I lift my knife from the dog's throat.

Taser turns, walks to Keys. With that lightning strike of understanding, Keys drops to his knee and offers an arm. Taser looks at me as he opens his mouth and drives a fang through Keys's skin. Keys yells, part agony, part joy, and Taser rips his flesh, deep and true. It'll make one hell of a scar. But it's to remind me, as much as Keys, of this night. I'm sure of that as I'm sure of anything.

Taser's expression changes as he looks at me, and now it's disgust in his eyes, as if he was looking at trash instead of his once-upon-a-time most faithful. He releases Keys and starts trotting back towards the street. Keys, grinning and clutching his bleeding arm, stumbles after him.

I follow, too, a good number of feet behind, and drop the baby on the doorstep of one of them fine houses we pass along the way. I got no idea what will happen when we get back to the others, or what kind of a place I can make among them now, after tonight. Shame crawls over my skin, burrows its way towards my heart, and I let it. I fucked up and I gotta pay, maybe even with my life. That's for Taser and the rest to decide. But if I live, I'll be more me than I ever was, and that'll run deeper than any scar.

THE SOMNAMBULIST

David J. Schwartz

The somnambulist brakes at the intersection of two suburban streets — Ivy Something Lane, Something Creek Road. Her headlights illuminate the 2 A.M. silence. She leans over to open the passenger side door, and her husband, in the body of a grey squirrel, jumps in. He's been gone twelve days, in a double-door trap, in a coma, trekking across astral space and chemically treated lawns. Earlier today his human body died. The somnambulist cried herself to sleep; salt tracks have dried upon her face.

She pulls the door shut and sits up. The squirrel-husband hops over to her, his tail arcing after him like an echo. He climbs the arm of her teddy bear pajamas and perches upon her shoulder.

The somnambulist — her name is Judy when she's awake — has been married for ten years. Her husband calls himself a trader, and this is perhaps the best description of what he does, but he has been called other things: magician, sorcerer, devil. Within the profession these terms have little meaning. He traffics in power, which is more or less what Judy has always believed.

"The hospital," says the squirrel-husband. At least, she hears a voice, and the squirrel is the source. The somnambulist turns towards the highway.

Judy believes that her husband — his name is Donald when she's awake — is a sweet but dull man who compensates by taking her on trips all over the world. She knows nothing of the role she plays in his work, of how he relies upon her. She doesn't know that he is not dead and only she can save him.

When they met, Judy had a job where she worked with a phone and not with her hands. The age difference had bothered her at first — she was in her twenties, and Donald was in his forties. But she was fascinated by his casual knowledge of baseball and fairy-tales, disarmed by his unabashed interest in her. Her sleep-walking didn't bother him; he hardly remarked upon it, although it had been worsening for some time.

Judy worried that he didn't have enough friends, but it wasn't long before she had moved into his small world. Her sister didn't approve. "It's like you're turning into him," she said the last time they spoke.

Judy had planned to keep her job for a while after they married, but he had money, and he wanted her to travel with him. They went to Morocco and Thailand and Portugal and Ecuador and Patagonia. She had the most exhausting dreams when she traveled. She dreamed that she carried a fire-tipped lance astride an eight-legged horse, that she excavated bones from the floors of ancient cathedrals, that she climbed the inner walls of ruined fortresses long since given over to tourists and pulled amulets from behind loose bricks. Sometimes she killed faceless things that crawled through wind or flew upon currents of sand. She developed calluses on her hands, woke up sore after sleeping on silk sheets. Her nails never needed to be clipped.

Doctors could not diagnose her fatigue. At home she spent days in bed, and Donald made frequent trips up from his basement office to feed her comfort foods: tuna melts, spaghetti with gooey slices of mozzarella, macaroni and powdered cheese. He worried for her so.

She ate while he told stories where an enemy transformed the hero into a beast and sent him far away from his beloved. To return he must travel through the kingdoms of rival beasts, across rivers and mountains. The beloved always wore a diamond on a pendant the hero had given her. She kept it close to her heart. (Donald never gave her a pendant like this, though she always expected he would.) There were always ladders in the stories, which no one ever climbed. In the end the hero and the beloved lived happily ever after.

The stories were all true, all but the last part. Sometimes Donald shed tears when he told them. She believed that this was because he was so caught up in the telling, and she found it both endearing and off-putting.

She drives better in her sleep. She does many things better in her sleep — speak Urdu, play the harp, *krav maga*. She moves in sacred space, the dimension behind the frontal lobe where she speaks the language of beasts and climbs to heaven to drink with the gods. Sometimes she feels like a walking blade; on planes her body sings out like a tuning fork, sending her teeth chattering.

The squirrel-husband, the trader, is explaining where he has been. His trade is in scraps of life and power. The exchanges are done in astral space, souls buying and selling radiance. He offers near-dead idols for sale, sacrificial skins with the faintest stains of blood, and his rivals fear Death too much to pass them up. They pay in secrets and maps, things they cannot expect to live to profit by. The trader uses this information to find the hidden reserves of power. With sleeping Judy as his aide and assassin, he takes all he can, selling the dregs for more. The others hate him.

The trader fears Death as much as any of them. More, perhaps. He was the first to cheat Death, has known Death since before the rift opened between earth and heaven. Once he feasted with Death and all the gods, but now the sins and fears of his stolen years weigh upon him. He tells himself that he will climb to face the gods when he is strong enough. But it is too soon.

Twelve days ago he lay in a trance, trading radiance in the ether, when a consortium of his enemies had slid through the shadows of his defenses and severed the silver cord which tethered him to the physical plane. His body lay dying, his heart stranded.

Panicked, he had thrust his soul into the first displaced creature he found. The squirrel was in shock — a neighbor had trapped it in his attic, and its soul was already in confusion. With a flick of his mind the trader set it adrift and moved in. Even so, he hardly knew what form he had taken before he was released in a riverside park, territory unknown both to him and to the memories of his new body.

Beasts know borders humans cannot see, and the squirrel-husband had become an interloper. For twelve days he fought and fled his way through hostile lands, beset by warrior-kings fierce in the defense of their treetop kingdoms. More than once on his journey he encountered the avatars of death. Rabid hounds and infected raptors have pursued him. He bears wounds behind his ear and upon his belly, and his breath is ragged above the hurtling of his heart.

He stands on her shoulder, one tiny forepaw resting on the side of her head, the other tucked behind her earlobe. Her long, dark hair brushes against his tail. Her scent is strong in his new nose; its effect is almost narcotic. He inhales the dried salt of her grief, shuts his tiny eyes and nuzzles up against her ear.

At the hospital the somnambulist parks in an empty corner of the lot. Still bearing the squirrel-husband on her shoulder, she picks the lock on a side entrance and descends to the basement. She unbuttons her pajama top, slips it off her left shoulder, and draws a five-foot sword from her collarbone.

She pads barefoot down the hall.

The death of the medical examiners is unfortunate. Even the squirrel-husband feels this, more so in fact than his wife, who is only having a dream she expects to forget soon. She is as he has built her, her bones imbued with alloy, her muscles trained for his needs. But she is not just a Swiss Army knife of useful skills — bodyguard, mechanic, dragon slayer. He has to love her for any of this to work, because love is pain is change is magic.

There are two men working in the morgue, and sleeping Judy kills them before they can wake her. The sword cuts them, but there is no blood.

The squirrel-husband senses where Donald's body is kept. He whispers to sleeping Judy, who opens the cooler and slides out the drawer to reveal him, shriveled and naked and cold and all but empty.

Once, on a trip to Colorado, they went to the Cliff Palace of the Anasazi. The guide took them inside a ceremonial chamber accessible only by descending a ladder. Donald had made it down without any problem, but when it came time to climb out he panicked. They eventually had to lift him out with ropes and a harness.

Judy had asked him if he had a fear of ladders. A phobia, perhaps. She told him she was terrified of lizards, but for some reason that made him laugh. It was just a panic attack, he said. But she'd never known him to have a panic attack before.

Once, in Arizona, she'd dreamed that she was dancing around a rope which hung taut from thundering clouds. Her husband was shouting into the night sky, first angry, then pleading. Death's face had appeared in the clouds. It was not a terrible face, she had thought, but her husband was afraid.

When they fucked (she never thought of it as making love, although there was love all around it) Donald walked his fingers slowly up the notches of her spine, and sometimes incredible heat followed his path, rising towards her skull until she thought her brain would boil.

The somnambulist sheathes the sword inside herself and picks up a small rotary saw. She cuts through Donald's scalp and directly into his skull, all the way around, until a cap of bone can be pulled away to reveal his brain.

The squirrel-husband still clings to her shoulder. He is still telling her secrets, not because she needs to know but because he doesn't know how to say goodbye.

"My heart is not my heart," he says. "My heart is a diamond. I took it ten thousand years ago, when the gods were neighbors."

Sleeping Judy sets the cap of bone on the steel table. She flexes her fingers and pries open the folds of Donald's brain.

"My heart loves perfectly, and its clarity is unmatched." The squirrel-husband, the trader, looks down at Donald and remembers loving him. He has never been able to decide whether keeping the stolen bodies, being able to look into a mirror and see the faces of the ones he has loved, is a solace or a penance.

The contours of Donald's frozen thoughts ooze under Judy's fingers and cause them to slide away from their target. The inside of her own skull hums, resonance of sword and sight. She believes this is a nightmare. She is only a few steps from waking in terror.

The body of the squirrel clings to her lapels; his vision fuzzes at the edges. He has accomplished the transfer under worse conditions, but he cannot know until the last moment whether it will succeed. The fate of his heart lies within hers.

The somnambulist's fingers grasp something small and hard and round. She pulls it from the ruins of his old house, the roof-hole through which he fears to climb alone.

"Swallow it," he tells her.

She sets the diamond, frosted with gore, on her tongue. It burns away the barriers between sleep and waking. Its clarity is a lamp shining through her eyes, and in the light she sees a ladder rising through the cage of her dead husband's chest, rungs like ribs. The ladder extends through a hole in the ceiling of the morgue.

"Swallow it," he says again.

It is always a gamble at the end. For more than ten years he has worked toward this moment. Every gift, every touch, every indulgence of her passion for cheese — all intended to capture her love and cage it, so that she will put him ahead of her at this moment when she is privy to all his secrets, when she is Judy and the somnambulist both, capable of either saving or destroying him.

She does not love him.

She doesn't understand the implications of this in the moment she realizes it, but she does not do as he commands. She holds the diamond in her mouth and looks down at the ruined body of her husband. She mourns him, but she will not be a vessel for his heart. She takes hold of the ladder, illuminated by the diamond light, and begins to climb.

The squirrel drops from her shoulder, shrieking. The desperate, scratching sound reverberates through the steel and diamond inside Judy, and for a moment she is stunned. She recalls other things her husband cooked for her, broccoli and cheddar casserole, omelets sloppy with Swiss. She recalls lazy mornings spent curled naked together. But instead of affection she feels anger. She left so many things behind to be with him: her job, her family, her independence. And to him she is only a suit of armor. She resumes her climb.

He is so proud of her. She has the quality that all somnambulists share — she thinks herself incapable of all she does for him when she dreams. And yet she is doing what he fears to do, climbing the ladder.

But all his work, every lumen of power he has profited, has gone into preparing her to become his vessel. He abandons the squirrel and becomes a pillar of wind and lightning. He pummels her as she climbs with hammers of air, fists of current. Her hair lifts like a halo, and her skeleton glows blue through her skin.

The ladder is longer than it appears. If Judy falls she will die. Perhaps he hopes he will be able to jolt her into swallowing his heart, her last breath becoming his first. But she grips the rungs with the steel cage of her bones and climbs. Judy accumulates time as she ascends, gathers divinity. It settles on her like dust and she takes it into her bones. Eons: the wear of mountains, the appetite of rivers. The diamond rattles against her teeth like an earthquake.

From here she can see heaven. Heaven is the back deck of a chocolate-brown lake cabin that needs repainting. Death sits with the other gods, drinking beer and listening to a baseball game. The lake is endless. On the lawn between its banks and the deck, squirrels journey up and down the trees.

The trader — life-thief, storm-husband — howls at her ears, *dontyou lovemedontyouloveme* as he tries to send her plummeting to the hard floor below. She doesn't. She pities him — but she is as he has built her: more than human, and too strong for him.

At the top of the ladder she takes the diamond between her teeth and bites down with jaws as old as creation. The trader's heart trickles from her mouth like ash, and this, at last, is judgment.

THE AGE OF FISH, POST-FLOWERS

Anna Tambour

ust when you think you've killed them all, others impossibly wriggle over the wall. Or bore through it, some say. Or worse — though this might be another rumor — breed within.

As for the sounds, there's lots of speculation, some of it pretty noisy itself. Are the sounds some new tactic to get rid of the orms? We in the corps have argued about that, most of us too scared to want to talk about it, or to want to hear it discussed; but (and it could be a pose) a few loudmouths insist on spouting daily assurances that the Sound, as they say it Capitalizedly, is the Newest Advance in our age. This might be convincing if they, the optimists, weren't doing the mole act along with the rest of us, and running downstairs as fast as they can when the first sounds rumble in the distance every forsaken morning. They answer *collateral damage, possible risks, someone will tell us, never you mind* and the sun will come up sunny one day.

Today we got another report closer to home. An orm, a relative baby though thick as a man's thigh, its dorsal fin tall as his waist, and its mane thick and coarse as cables. Just a block away, it was caught in the act of engorgement, two legs waving from its maw.

The story goes that a man in blue shot it with his harp-net. The orm's tail wasn't properly caught, and it smashed the guy's stomach to pulp, but the mib had already called the orm squad. The person in the orm (unknown sex) was already a lost cause. That orm would feed a hundred New Yorkers, maybe plenty more from outside. That's what Julio says because he saw someone who saw the squad load it into their omni. All just speculation on my part. I'm not a knower, and I don't know anyone who is.

The sounds and craters are something else. The sounds come always at dawn. In them are elements of rumble, drag, shear, and I would imagine earthquake, all in one indefinability, just the sound to make you wake shaking from a dream, though this isn't one. Correction: wasn't one before. The real has exceeded dreams — former dreams, that is.

The sounds have patterned our waking. We all run down to the drypit (though none of us has slept enough) and huddle there feeling the building tremble (or is it just us?) till the day calms, relatively.

It's still raining. We passed the forty days and forty nights mark long ago, thankfully longer ago than anyone in our corps cares to harp about. No one left amongst us is the quoting type. I don't remember the last time the moon shone.

Two levels of underground carpark in our building are now nicely filled with water. So we don't have that to worry about. Power could have been a problem but for our resident genius, an arrogant creep otherwise. Julio is the only person who can relate to the guy, but as long as Julio stays with us, we're laughing. (Must keep Julio happy!)

Julio is a genius, too, but a different kind. He named us "The Indefatigables," but that is really he. He found it in a book, he says, in his self-effacing way, but he is the one. I have never been able to figure him out. I thought perhaps it was love, and of who else but Angela Tux? But she left almost at the beginning and Julio stays. He says we give him purpose and that he loves the Brevant, and maybe we do and he does. I certainly must give him purpose, as I don't think I could live without what he's done for us.

The Indefatigables, properly the coop of the Brevant Building, "the corps" as we call ourselves, would be happy as clams these days (no irony intended) if we could only get more dirt. George Maxwell goes out for it instead of just wishing we had more. He went all the way to 51st Street yesterday to find a dirtboy with real dirt.

He was so upset he didn't mind the danger, he said. I think that he was so upset he didn't *think* of the danger. I've never sought a dirtboy. Too frightened of being killed for my seeds. George, though, is a big guy, played varsity at Yale (people say it's still around, where the knowers are). George is one of those guys whose muscles get more tough with age, as does their stubbornness. We've got quite a collection here now in our little group, none as brave as George or useful as Julio, but we like to say *each has something to offer.* The building used to be filled with useless types — hysterical, catatonically morose, or verbally reminiscent, but they died out or disappeared. I'm proud and I admit, lucky, to be part of our corps now.

From Julio, the super, we hear rumors. He was the one who told us to fortify, though in the end, it was only him and George Maxwell who stuck broken glass and angle-edged picture frames and sharpened steel furniture bones into the outside wall, one man sticking, the other man guarding the sticker with a pitiful arsenal of sharpened steel. For the steel, it surprised us all how many of us had Van der Rohe chairs. I got mine at a ridiculously cheap price from a place in Trenton, though the delivery, by the time they were all installed in my apartment (I had to get three at the price) was ridiculous. I was glad to donate the chairs. They had always seemed to unwelcome my sitting in them, and gloat when I left them alone. Until the defenses project, I had never been able to part with them, but the prospect of them being torn asunder into ugly scrap gave me the best day I could remember in this age.

So few diversions. The Wall now, you'll want to know about. Walls, really, I don't rightly remember when. Sometime in the first years of the age. The orms were only part of the reason then, but the part that motivated public pronouncements on the Wall project. Where the orms came from, we'll never know. Norwegian cruise ships were blamed for dumping the "freshets," as the spawned babies are called, with the ballast, in both Miami and New York. The Norwegians protested, saying *these are not orms*, and anyway, theirs are mythical (though plenty of Norwegians disputed that). But the mayors and the President said "orms" in their announcements, and so that is what we've called them since. It doesn't matter about the name anymore anyway, nor how they got here, nor to us, how far they have traveled inland. There are rumors that they reached the Great Lakes long ago, and the Mississippi, and that they can travel overland for many miles before they need water. We used to speculate, but as George pointed out, why? We're probably the safest in the country because we protected first, and we have the most organized (not to mention mechanized) protection force in the country, as far as we know, and also we still have both wall-workers (we hear) and men in blue.

The Wall. The first place of building was the hardest: New York Harbor. Then the Wall encompassed more and more of the boroughs, then out to formerly exclusive burbs. The greatest achievement of mankind — it can be seen from outer space. It had massive public support, and became a focus of both civic pride and hope. I remember the feeling.

The Navy sonared the sea to bejesus, both the harbor enclosed by the wall, and out to three miles. Then the army electrified the Wall wherever it was land-based. We slept easy for it must have been close to a year.

Then the first orm was found *inside*. I remember the headlines in the old *New York Times*: "Mib loses fight to orm; Mayor vows to beef force." Eleven feet long, it came up through a toilet in Flushing (yes, Flushing got in, though I don't know why, but maybe it wasn't Flushing, but they said so because it is funny, and let's face it. Anything funny runs like a nose in November). By the time the orm was hacked to death with a broken plate glass window stuck to a love seat (by the wife, a weight-lifter, I remember, but again, I don't know if this wasn't any more true than Flushing) the orm had (supposedly) bitten through the middle of a tall and muscular dry-waller (but again, he could have been a flabby accountant). Whoever-it-was's middle was found in the orm on occasion of the orm's post-mortem (orms were not then eaten by anyone). The fact is, an orm killed in a safety zone.

A massive eradication campaign was launched to kill freshets within the Wall and anything that had gotten into the sewer system. The subway was sealed, the vent covers replaced by cement plugs.

There was maximum publicity for effort and minimum information of results. Then media stopped, as there was thought to be no further public benefit to be gained from it. The orms kept coming for a while and then, as far as we heard, died off. Julio says they never died off, which is why we and anyone else of wealth isn't connected any more to the sewer or to any other municipal system (if indeed, there's anything left).

In one respect we feel secure. Now neither people nor orms can climb our walls, nor gain entry through our two doors (our genius designed that protection).

"Be prepared" — our motto for when we do have to leave the Brevant. Each of us has to on a rostered basis, for at least a little time. George (the health nut) makes us. "You need the air," he says. He doesn't add, *You need gut-building*, but he could. Both muscles in the gut like George, and some of the guts that gave him the courage to fortify our building. Each of us has to deal with the dealers. That spreads the load. And sometimes, one of us doesn't return. We all mourn the loss of the corps member and whatever it was that was lost as pay to the dealer. The most valuable pay is of course, seeds. Dealers being who they are, there are those who think only of a shot of energy — and they want meat.

Next to seeds, the next most valuable commodity for forward-thinkers, is dirt. The dirtboys are just that — boys, and dirty. They are the second fastest natural things in the city. They are the only ones who know where dirt is. Mibs kill them if they can corner them because dirtboys dig holes in the Wall to go outside to get dirt. That's what's said. I don't know, but they carry the dirt in their clothes. They strip and you've got to put the dirt into *your* clothes. Tied-off pants and shirt arms are a giveaway, so there's many ingenious ways that dirtboys hide their load. If we're caught with dirt, we don't get killed, but we do get drafted to volunteer. I've never known a volunteer. Part of Julio's job is to keep us from being volunteers, and so far, the Brevant has been left alone. What we have that is valuable to the mib besides our seeds, I never know, but Julio does. He usually asks us for old electricals: a shaver, some extension cords, a bread-making machine — and we always give him the stuff. Someday maybe we won't have the means to pay, but so far we do. Why the mib don't just take what they want, I don't know. Maybe they are designed to serve.

Lately I've been thinking of other things. Like these craters Julio told us about. Every crater open to the sky is a breeding ground, he says, and he also says it is a matter of time. Since the orms adapted to the electrification of the wall, the electricity had to be disconnected and sharp spikes mounted porcupine-style all over the wall. And this means that with rain, danger is increased, as the streets are slick and every pothole is a pool. An orm and you and water — and as soon as the orm feels your presence, your body will spit like a frozen freedom fry dropped into boiling oil.

The craters are the most recent crisis in our age. I've never seen a crater, but Julio has, blocks of them on the Grand Concourse in a stripe that is so fat it took away the Jerome Avenue El. Poe Park, he said, is now a *much* bigger park (and he laughed in a spine-crawling way), and that little house is gone, he said, which is too bad, but the El being gone makes a much nicer vista, he said. How a whole elevated "subway" could disappear along with all the buildings, we were trying to comprehend when he said it all made the neighborhood look much better, and he laughed again, *even with the craters* where all those stubby brick apartment houses had been. *Alexander's final closing down sale finally finalized*, he chuckled, and then he nearly choked himself pointing to us and cracking up, doubled over like some comedy antique. It was rude of him to make a joke that only he understood. But then his happiness is infectious, and we all ended up laughing anyway. Julio has a way that can bring you out of your cares! He always looks on things in his own way. I wish I could, as I had nightmares for a week from that trip of his to the Bronx, especially the *where did everything go* part.

George saw a cleared area in Queens with lots of holes where basements were; and oddly, so did Fey, who once traveled further than anyone. Must have been his daydreaming that let him get that far, and luck that brought him home.

I could worry during my waking hours, but where would that get me? That sounds heroic, stoic maybe, but I can only worry about so much, and at the moment what I worry about — what keeps our whole corps awake at night, is this: Does anyone know about our sunflower?

The corps celebrated when this sunflower took — the only one of five precious seeds from George's last (strictly illegal) seed expedition. (The only trade that is legal is to work for "food" as a volunteer. I can't eat that "food" from what I hear of it, and I don't want to sacrifice myself to the Wall any more than anyone with a smitter of choice left.). Perhaps these seeds came from the botanical gardens in the early days of the Transition. George assures us that, as he was assured, this sunflower plant will grow to have a flower with real, fertile seeds. Regardless of the pictures in books in the Brevant collection, we have to see those seeds to believe them, and then we have to see *them* make new seedlings. Our books are all *old*, bought way back when because they *were* old, even then, when seeds were seeds for the generations, and books with pictures were for collecting and not trying to get some information, *any crumb of useful information* to live by.

Mrs. Wilberforce's ancient poodle paid for the sunflower seeds, and we were lucky that that dealer was crazy with hunger, or he would have asked for the poodle *and* seeds in return.

Orm. You'd think it would have a nightmarish name, but it doesn't need to. That horse-shaped head. The mane, its congealed, tangled mass; the gasping mouth, as wide as a garbage bin and fringed with triangular, razor teeth. The eyes of a shark, pitiless. A voracious appetite for flesh. Just to see it move is terrifying. The humping fleetness of it over walls, up brick, galloping across intersections once so clogged with people, buses, cars, honking yellow taxis. That was in the early days when there were pictures of them in the news. I've never seen an orm in real life.

But back to the sunflower. Our future relies on this plant — our fortune and salvation. Few people have the water, the dirt, and the power to grow indoors, and also, have the social organization to not destroy their riches. We have all that, which makes us *very* rich, potentially. Seed dealers are low-quality thinkers. They think only of the present. Meat gives them a present. We want a future.

We are not alone. There are a select few who think as we do. Which is why there are dealers, thank goodness. We paid our last meat for these sunflower seeds, if no one is brave enough to hunt orm. Even Julio and George aren't that brave. "Yet," says Julio.

Our cucumbers failed again. Sterile seeds again. Or maybe fake. The mushroom spawn won't take. That was a terrible (and costly) blow.

None of us have gone sidewalk-harvesting. Too much danger for too little reward. The little shoots of grass that spring up are so small by the time they get picked. The other weeds disappeared years ago. Didn't get to bud stage. As for the parks, they disappeared early, their danger recognized and paved over. We'd read that we could eat bark, but all the street trees were burnt that first winter.

Everyone has responsibilities. Old Mr. Vesilios has the dwarf apple tree, as he was allowed to keep it. It was his to begin with. He loves it. He calls it "my wife." And what would you expect someone with the name Luthera Treat to have? And by the way, she looks like her name. I thought "prunes," but it was chickpeas and something she calls black salsify. How would she have gotten chickpeas, ones that weren't sterile, let alone salsify, you ask? She grew them in her windowbox back when we kept windowboxes. She says she got the chickpeas from a trip to Egypt when she was young, and had kept them for luck. She says luck, but I am positive: romance. She says she planted them because she couldn't stand the look of any more flowers, but if that's true, then I'm the Easter Bunny of Times Past. The chickpeas are nutritious, but they're beautiful, and she turns red if anyone asks her about their origin. I can't complain about Luth, though. By the way, she hates being called that, she says, but we call her that because George says she secretly likes it. Actually, I'm sure she hates it, and furthermore, wishes she were a Genevieve or Helena and a beauty — her outside matching her inner soul, which is truly *beautiful*. I would say that even if there were still beautiful women left here, because it's true. Luthera's manner fits *Luth*, though. With her looks, it wouldn't do for her to show romantic notions, thus her embarrassment over the chickpeas (and their carved, exotic windowbox). She hardly needed to be interested in food crops on a personal level, even if she was big in the funding of some food-donating NGO, as Julio once said.

As for the rest of us, we've had to learn to like to eat "purple pillow" and "espresso" geraniums (tasting like a pillow of mothballs and nothing much — certainly not coffee), clove-tasting carnations, revoltingly sweet violets, fartish marigolds, tulips that look like candy canes and almost taste like food, *almost* — all that flowerbox stuff that distinguished the Brevant. It was once recreational to eat ornamentals, Luthera said, and when she did, I remembered a time when philanthropy dinners stunk from what looked like soggy, forgotten corsages dropped into every course. At that time Luthera "in revolt" threw out her tulips and lobelia, and planted her windowbox with salsify and those chickpeas. More than any other person's efforts in our corps, her revolution has kept flesh on our bones. The salsify, we particularly have grown to enjoy, though the yachties used to complain that it tastes too much like oysters — "oysters dying over the beach fire, and the juice running down salty arms, bottles of beer, and sun." The yachties are all gone now, thank god, having left in a group. Luth's sourness is more popular than the yachties' reminiscences any day.

There are other crops now, also. We have never been able to get potatoes that would grow. We tried, even though the dirt cost was phenomenal. We haven't been successful with any of our so-called organic wheat grains, brown rice, lentils, or any other of the healthy stores that most of us had in our pantries, mostly untouched before they were recruited as crop seeds. We grin and bear other ornamentals, and they haven't killed us, like when Kate in 4C gorged herself on her own impatiens, rather than give it up to the corps.

For generosity, the prize if we had one, would go to that gray-skinned shaking relic of a rocker, Fey Klaxon. Real name John Smith *really*, he told us the day that our corps got down to its present number, eight.

At the end of our first corps meeting (25 present) to set up the new order, he told us to please wait, which was unusually polite for him. We were so shocked, we did. He soon appeared staggering under a huge potted bush. Its leaves are only plucked on special occasions (and then, only a precious few), such as when anyone leaves the building, and when we are all huddled in the drypit listening to those sounds. We tried to propagate more with cuttings, and failed. Our attempts to grow from seed have failed also. For my money, this is the most valuable possession of our corps, though Fey's food store would be more sensibly considered the biggest valuable, now almost vanished.

It seems that all of us have in our own ways, liked good buys. The Moores on the first floor collected Ming, but what they paid for each piece was their biggest joy. It wasn't how much. It was how little. Unusual in the art world, but then Mr. Moore's business was smell-alike name brands. For Cordell Wainer, it was shoes. For Mr. Vesilio, it was olive oil. He used his wine room to store olive oil, and hated wine. For me, it was canned goods. Not having any guests, I had lots of room. I shopped sensibly. Delivery was a problem, so I stocked the spare room and the bath in one delivery. When the first intimations of a new age began, I decided that the dining room could again be put to use, and filled it, too. It was a comforting sight — all my cans. It was crowded again, like when I was a child and my parents filled the rooms with guests and laughter.

I received my last can from the corps about a year ago, but it made me feel good thinking how long my can supply lasted everyone with good management (my own, as I have been from the first, in charge of the food stores).

Fey did better than I, though. He had become chronically shy. I would be, too, if I looked like he, and had looked like he had looked. His health was a constant worry to him. He had been on Dr. Etker's mucousless diet for years, and that didn't do any good. His colon troubled him. Crystals didn't work. He worried about fungus. He didn't trust practitioners any more, so he devised his own regime. He stocked up and then planned not to leave the building ever again. What he bought was canned English-style custard powder "with pure vanilla and pure cornstarch." At the time of our first coop meeting, he had lived on that as a pure food, just adding water, for six months. His apartment is larger than mine, being two joined together for rampageous entertaining. One, he had filled with his provisions. The custard ran out last month.

We are all still healthy relatively speaking, though no one carries excess fat, and you can count everyone's ribs and vertebrae, a little more delineated each day. We still have a varied diet, though it needs to improve pretty fast now, as nothing miraculous has turned up. Everyone but Fey admits to craving meat. I know I do. None of us has tried orm. We don't talk about what other people outside the Brevant eat, although we know that rat is traded practically legally. I could *never* eat rat! Orm at least, is a fish.

The sunflower is our most valuable possession now. It is our future, should no better future shine upon us.

-2-

We do think of a better future, you know. Not for our children. The Brevant is not for children. But because, why? Mr. Vesilios gave a beautiful talk last night about the number of colors he has counted in the blossoms on the apple tree, and his talk gave me a dream that I didn't want to wake from.

It is now dawn again, when most of us habitually wake. That sound is beginning. I should rush down to the drypit.

The sunflower. The sunflower, though still a sprout, is breathing in, exhaling oxygen or whatever it is plants do. In, out. Just like us, but the sunflower calmly breathes all day and sleeps all night, every night, in its rare earth. And is loved. To be so loved.

That sound. Its muffled quality only makes it more terrifying. I always make a racket of noise rushing to get down the stairs as fast as I can. I make as much noise as I can, to cover up the sound. Today, for some reason, I listen — don't let myself move.

One of Fey's leaves. Is it possible to imagine chewing a leaf? A gob of them? The bitter spit, that pinch of plaster that Fey and Julio figured out as the strange accompaniment to the leaf. The leaking of ease and happiness into my blood, my heart, my thoughts. It lasts such a short time, but in that time, even the sunflower doesn't matter.

I listen, and imagine being George Maxwell. Being Julio. Being more than them because they rush down to the drypit, too. I imagine being like someone in the old days — strong, brave, heroic. Like men in blue were back when they were real men in blue.

The sound is louder now but still far away, I think. Crashing bangs and slides? I'm sure if you were underneath, you could only feel, not hear, because your eardrums would explode.

I am going. I am going. I wish I hadn't stayed in bed this long. Moving is all the more difficult. Usually I run, but now it's all I can do not to flatten myself and crawl, hugging the walls. Ashamed, I force myself to walk calmly, an insane compromise.

In the vestibule, a tiny opening high in the barriered window lets in the dawn light, pink as a young rose. When did I see this light before? It's been so long. Back in the time of roses, when I used to wake to pigeons cooing against my window. Then, on with the tracksuit, out to the park. One lap, and a cool-down in the rose garden when the dew lay in the petals.

Now, roses in the sky just makes it all the worse to dive like a mole as day breaks. My stomach twists. Wouldn't it be funny to describe the reasons why, as in the old days. *Doctor*...

And the solution to my problems? Clumps of cintered powders.

That sharp bar of rose-colored light enters my right iris. I should be a mole-rat now, huddled in the drypit with the rest of them. Eyes, unnecessary, as we sit out the monotony of our daily terror.

Perhaps it is my stomach, or maybe the color of the rose.

I lower my head and quickly perform all the tasks needed to open the small exit door.

Its *swish-clunk* at my back speaks for me. I can't hear it, but I feel it against my body. Felt it.

Dawn is dead.

The Sound that blanketed the Brevant's door-thud, is *alive*. So, alive, it runs between my teeth like a mouse. There is nowhere to go. I threw off my moleskin when I touched the door, so I do what I imagined — step into the street. Now's the time to lift up my head... and that feels *good*.

Searching the skyline, where is the source? The Sound is so loud now that it crowds into the me-ness of me, or would *like to*. It is so loud that I can't tell which sounds I hear. Originals or echoes.

The sky is now the color of wet cement, with a slick of blood in it. Peer as I do, I can't see anything through the murk.

Looking out...looking up...

Something.

Two thin cables (?) though each could be at least as thick as a city block. I can't tell distance.

They fall parallel from a point of infinity to a jagged horizon.

Scrapes and crashes. Distinct. Sharp. I saw for a moment, but all that's left is the Sound now, as the cables disappear in the wool of a grey sky again.

I haven't heard of anyone installing anything above the city, but I told you already — I don't know any knowers. It would be so much safer up there. Maybe they didn't want us interfering, and that is why they make that noise. What are they doing? Maybe this is the cleanup they spoke about. They took their time!

Even on my tiptoes, as far as I can see, I am the only person watching. My whole life, nothing like this.

This is the best thing that has ever happened to me.

Wallace Evian Sturt IV. Little Wally. I'm not little. It's just the fate of IVs. My great grandfather would have sunk all his money, spent it all on whores and horses if he knew that it would have trickled down to the likes of Dad, and I'm no throwback. There was something to the grands. More than just living to make contacts, make money. I've overheard people refer to me as "nice" back when my parents were alive.

I need to concentrate on what's happening. They promised us years ago to do something, but never specified, and then they didn't bother to make announcements any more because all we did was complain.

Well, we *did*.

The Sound pummels the air now. It's rising in shudders from the ground. It's personal now, like when a dentist punctured the roof of my mouth. I can feel the Sound from my soles to the roof of my mouth, to the roots of my hair. I can't properly *see*, dammit.

A smudged cloud rises and then falls and as if it never left us, the sun comes out and shines down like the sun once did. The sky in the area of the chains is now old-fashioned innocent-flower blue, and that grayness is unmistakably clouds not made by moisture, but made by what we've made, for they rise from where the chains disappear into the skyline. I am *not* going to move.

The cables (or chains?) are even bigger, and the grinding crashes get closer, and I stand where I am, chewing on the inside of my cheek till I can taste metal. My own blood. But I can coolly taste it and report the taste to myself.

Another cloud puffs, and then a spate of crashes, crisper than before, closer than ever. My cheek twinges, awash with blood.

I can see the end of the cables. They are attached to what looks like a giant open mouth of a net. They're pulling the net upwards... full. Fat power station cooling towers bulge out the shape, bits of highway, buildings, spires poke through the holes. What must be bridge cables hang down from the bottom like the angel hair spaghetti of my childhood hung from a fork. As the bag rises, more of the mass becomes visible. A ball — that Earth sculpture that had once been so big. Huge unmistakable broken blocks — the Wall!

Bits fell at the beginning of the pull. Those were the last crashes.

I wonder how many orms they caught in the net.

Now there is no sound. Rather, there is a startling reverberation of hush as the bulging base of the bag is hoisted high. I can see that its enormous bulge at the base would be wider than Yankee Stadium. Many times wider. The long, long bag ascends — into the brilliant sun. I couldn't see where they ascended to, for the glare. And now, though it is blue where I've looked, raindrops stab my eyeballs — a monkey's wedding, I think it's called. Sun and rain. It's over for the day, anyway, I know. So I uncrick my neck and turn around for home.

I didn't even think about an orm, that whole time. I don't even know how long it was.

That was close. I do know that. I have seen.

I will tell about it, and I know I won't stutter even once. Wallace isn't a good name, but it's better than Little Wally, and a darn sight better than Luthera. Maybe my name will be changed.

Others could have been me. There were rumors, but no one believed them. I didn't, and Julio laughed. George said it didn't matter. He just said, "Get out. Get your air."

Build guts? Did George know, but had undeveloped guts himself when it came down to the choice of being a mole every morning, or throwing off that shameful animalness and striding out as a man, biting himself to bravery?

Now, at least somewhere, there is no Wall. That must be a good thing — the breakthrough we've been waiting for, but were too cowered to realize.

Anyway, I will tell of what I saw — I who ventured.

And what to do, now that the Sound has been identified? I would advise: As long as we go underground, we should be protected during the sweep.

Can I insulate myself with painted canvas and make myself a spear, or have we used up all our chairs?

What does orm taste like?

What would Luthera think if I brought one home? *When* I bring one home. I hope they don't clean up everything before I catch one.

But there I go again. Might as well have been stuttering still, such was the Little Wally mindset. Sure, it would be great to be the hero of the corps. But throughout history, any man worth his sword thinks higher than a Luthera.

The Last Escape

Barth Anderson

ere's what was about to happen: The Scarab would be handcuffed and put in a three-lock safe, and that safe would be sealed in a crate, and that crate would be hoisted by a winch on the marina's primary pier, and three massive harbor-charms commissioned from the Brotherhood Itself would enchant the winch.

He can get out of anything, but he couldn't possibly escape that, could he?

We argued for weeks about whether or not the Scarab could do it. Some people, fortunetellers on the wharf, thought he could actually escape, and hoped he would because they hated the Brotherhood Itself

The rest of us weren't so disaffected. The Brotherhood Itself wrapped our city and harbor in cocoons of conjured mist. It protected us from conjured diseases spiraling out from the archipelago, ruthless inland bandits, and insurrection. A mouthy foreigner like the Scarab in his silly beetle costume with a red sash across the belly — well, the Brotherhood should trump that.

It was hard to say which magic would prevail, though, because we didn't know who or what the Scarab was. A Catalan mystic, perhaps? A Micronesian medicine man? Rosicrucian? About three months ago, around the time that plague ship first anchored off-harbor, this escape artist started working the crowds on the wharf, right along with the smokesters, glass jugglers, and lavish dumb shows of Pericles in Delaware. There was a translation problem fouling him up from the beginning. His hand-painted sign announced:

"He disobeys bindings as unto a beetle!"

"You will be unpredictable!"

"Why don't you instantly probe his desire!?"

The Scarab's first audiences consisted of passing shark boaters, more interested in that odd sign than his tame escapes.

But the Scarab quickly earned a reputation for squirming out of any headlock. Crouched like a wrestler, he'd call out to passing teamsters, "Come and hold me! You there. Hold me!" Bored, they'd bet him that they could pin him for a twenty count. On that first day, it became apparent that the Scarab might be for real: Small as he was, one or two men weren't nearly enough to pin him. Five? No good. The Scarab would lie prostrate, his red cape splayed, and ten or eleven beefy gorillas, stripped to their union suits, would get a grip on him. Thrashing and grunting ensued. Bets were placed among the circle of wharf rats that always formed, and, then, from under that scrum of massive buttocks and tree-trunk thighs, the Scarab would slither loose.

Those poor sots paid up their wagers with a grin and a snort, but they hated the Scarab, and all of them wanted revenge. So next their union stewards came down the wooden steps to the wharves from the machine shops and shipwright halls, and the Scarab, in a single, sweaty afternoon, cleaned out the union. He cleaned out management. He cleaned out the Iron Works who made a special livery of soldered gauntlets (palm to palm), a torso in the shape of a giant beetle's thorax, and legs that were bolted in place after the Scarab was put inside. We streamed down in crowds, flooding into the wharf district to watch the latest phenom. Though, of course, the upper crust from Whale Oil Hill wouldn't leave the polished, wooden stairs connecting their neighborhoods to the docks. Adventurous ladies with costumed retinues and magicians of the Brotherhood Itself in powdered wigs stood on the bottom landing in distress, as if attending a hanging, not a man struggling out of a metal bug suit.

That one gave the Scarab trouble, and after a painful length of time, the metal bug was pried apart to reveal that the escape artist wasn't there. The carapace was empty and the eager silence stretched as we stared at the lack of a Scarab. One person in the audience clapped. It sounded sarcastic in the quiet, so we turned to see who this was and found the Scarab standing among us, face bloodied and costume torn.

That's when we knew he was a force to reckon with, and we were dying to know what would happen next.

As a result, the Scarab was enshrined in the local lexicon, too, because each time he escaped, he'd clap his hands together once and shout in his unplaceable accent, "No, no! I am incorrigible!" This entered *wharfese* almost immediately. Any time you'd get away with something (a hat trick in freedeck, a run-in with your boss) you'd turn to your friends, clap once and you'd all shout, "I am incorrigible!"

About this time, that galley flying its black flag came sailing into our inlet. The whole marina paused as halibut merchants put up their oars, and fingers tarried over unplayed hands of deck, wondering at this sad turn of events.

At the Scarab's usual spot was a tableau of raised hammers over a hastily lidded coffin, nails pinched in winced mouths. The cluster of seven men almost had the Scarab trapped inside, when they saw the black flag. Too bad for them. As they looked away, a force from below them shoved upward, and suddenly, the men slid from the coffin lid and the Scarab stood alone, in red-caped beetle costume, gazing out at the plague ship.

There was never much to watch when a plague ship arrived. Mysterious infections were always escaping from the new islands forming in the Atlantic and shipped in from far-flung cantons. Disfigured victims apparently told tales to the Brotherhood Itself of plagues carried by merchant marines in mismatched gear, diseases that split feet into cloven hooves, and bent human voices into bleating. When a plague ship arrived, our Port Authority would semaphore the ship to drop anchor off-harbor, away from the shipping lanes, out where the floor of the ocean plunges deep. Then the Brotherhood Itself would sail into position in order to communicate with the crew or whoever was left aboard, saving whom they could. Within a day, the ship would be sunk by canon fire.

So while a member of the Brotherhood Itself stood in the prow of a twenty-foot Port Authority skiff, starboard of the plague ship, the Scarab, still standing in his coffin, started shouting in his native tongue. He seemed indignant to the point of panicked, but then, he fell quiet, looking down at the men he'd just bested and those immediately around him, searching faces perhaps for an expression of recognition or familiarity.

"You half-witted comedians believe this bedevilry? What is desperate for you, wonderers?" He was heard to shout. "Do you know what that boat *is?*"

When we didn't answer him, he stiffened and muttered to himself in an angry whisper, kicking coffin nails away and walking to the Siren Inn, red cape whipping.

None of us understood his anger. Those near enough to see his face said he was looking at the magistrate in the prow of the skiff, but beyond that, no one could parse his reaction or what "half-witted comedians" meant.

Sensing an opportunity, a smock-maker clapped and shouted, "You are incorrigible!" Which drew an easy, comforting laugh.

But something was different now. The Scarab's pitch changed the very next day. He continued calling out businesses, unions, or individuals to capture him, but on his sign was now written:

"No half-witted bedevilry can hold him!"

We all passed the marina every day on our walks to market and church, and we saw it out there, the plague ship, its black flag raised against the omnipresent wall of enchanted fog beyond. But no survivors were shipped to shore. No medical boats skimmed out to help. No war galley came to sink it with a blast of cannonballs. We were dying to know what would happen next.

Two days after the arrival of the plague-ship, the Scarab's sign changed again. The word *bedevilry* had been crossed out and *Brotherhood Itself* was written above it.

Could the Scarab escape the Brotherhood Itself's magic? Our doubt was delicious, and we devoured it with griddlecakes in union kitchens and drank it in our bubbling beer.

The Brotherhood Itself at last rose to the bait, after the term "bedevilry" had become a synonym for "Brotherhood" in dockside vernacular, and agreed with the Scarab about a wager. The fortunetellers flipped their silver sticks and clucked, "See? The Bedevilry Itself wants to discredit him publicly. He's a threat."

Several magistrates met the Scarab on his dockside stage and attempted to hold him down with Brotherhood manacles and leg-shanks. Winter winds were beginning to bite, but the event drew a sprawling crowd to watch the magistrates stand stern as pillories after cuffing the foreigner, their powdered wigs freshly dusted and unmussed by the weather. Once shackled, the Scarab was put into a heavy, canvas sea bag, and then the magistrates sang their all-for-naughts, lock-me-tights, knitknots, and nighty-nights. But the Scarab shrugged the manacles and the spells from his body and bounced before his audience with his barrel chest thrust out.

"I am incorrigible!" We all shouted on cue.

There were three more contests, and at each meeting between the Scarab and the magistrates, the bet was doubled, so that by the time the Big Show was announced, where the Scarab would be suspended in a safe over the harbor, the Bedevilry Itself was into the escape artist for quite a bit of treasure. Which of our two heroes would prevail in the end?

Sadly, the temperature plunged for two straight weeks, and vicious winds from the mountains came shrieking against us. Foreign ships rowed away to avoid ice-lock, and the big contest between the Scarab and the Bedevilry Itself was delayed.

This incensed the Scarab but not for want of the wager. Rather, he seemed afraid of something, confused or angry, though it was difficult to understand why since he had so much treasure. "They can't arrest that infection," he told some of us at the Siren's bar. "Let's filch a galley and subvert that sick boat with cannon fire ourselves. Come! Who will carry me?!"

A group of toothpullers plied the Scarab with another round of archipelago lager. Certainly, the plague ship was no longer a threat, they told him. Certainly, any plague carried on that boat had devoured its human food supply weeks ago.

"I try to roll you out of bed, because, attend, this Brotherhood Itself has no witchery," he said. "That black flag outside your harbor, don't you observe? That ship! There's true bedevilry out there, a fast threat, but your Brotherhood Itself can't arrest it."

"Nothing bad ever happens here, Scarab," a toothpuller said. "The real question is, can you pull off this escape tomorrow in the Big Show?"

The Scarab laughed in derision. "Oh, I'll escape," he said, drinking and slamming down his glass. "But without doubting, I am singular and uniquely."

He probably said some other things, too, but that saloon crowd was already bored with him and didn't remember much more. How tiresome the Scarab had become, we decided — just like the fortunetellers and their preachy resentment of the Brotherhood Itself. We liked him much better when he was weaseling out of bug armor.

That night, the eve of the rescheduled contest, with the harbor waters steaming under the frigid winter air, a boy took the Scarab's dinner to his room at the Siren. After repeated knocking, the serving boy and the decrepit concierge let themselves in, and, as reported in the more reliable broadsheets, the Scarab was gone, his rooms in curious disarray. His beetle costume was shredded, but his clothes were still neatly folded in a steamer trunk. The room smelled dangerous with flammable oil from a spilled lamp, and a little curlicue of blood was written on an unbroken windowpane, while two full glasses of cognac sat sparkling on the mantle. The ancient concierge told the Port Authority that the Scarab had received a visitor earlier in the day, a tall man cloaked in archipelago medicine-man style (bear fur), but beyond that, he couldn't account for the Scarab's whereabouts.

The Port Authority immediately barred the roads going in and out of the wharf neighborhood, and the Brotherhood Itself announced that they were dropping two enchantments on us, preventing anyone from exiting or entering the city. Finding the Scarab for his own safety was suddenly the mission of every magistrate in town.

Deep winter frosted our doors shut, and the cobblestone streets became so slippery that only the watch's heaviest draft horses clopped over the ice. Was this magic? Was this weather built by the Brotherhood Itself, or was this winter? We hoped it wasn't merely winter. Again.

We woke the next morning to see that the harbor had completely iced over, freezing the last galley in place: the plague ship. The day cleared, showing a cruel, cold sky and a broken sun. No delivery carts rattled in the snow-bound streets, and the docks were rimed with thick blankets of ice and sea salt. That night, a fat moon lit the harbor blue, and a small team of shark-boaters sneaked out into the perilous cold to whittle at a few bottles of vodka together. Their work was summer work, rowing kegs of rum and fresh water from general stores to ships in port, so drinking late, even on nights as cold as this, wasn't unusual for their lot.

Under the light of this cold, severe moon, one of the shark-boaters looked out at the distant plague ship and saw figures standing near it on the ice.

"Hey, look out there."

As the shark-boaters watched, twenty or thirty people dropped onto the ice from the plague ship's high gunwales.

"What're those idiots up to? Don't they know that boat is dangerous?"

"I heard the Brotherhood Itself already disinfected that ship days and days ago," another said.

In an almost ritualistic dance, the figures gathered on the ice, clustering. Then they began walking together across the wide, frozen harbor toward the marina. The cluster drew ever closer, and in the passing swoops of a lighthouse's beam, their long shadows were thrown like ink across the pale blue ice, again and again.

"It's a team of priests returning from consecrating the plague ship's dead," the captain of the shark-boaters said.

"Maybe they're shipwrights examining the hull for ice damage."

"Could they have survived the plague?"

"With no supplies?"

"I wonder what they are."

The long moment was drawn out as the dense cluster slowly walked past the ice-paralyzed buoys and entered the marina. As these strange figures drew closer, it became apparent that they were wearing the mismatched uniforms and long dress-coats of various foreign navies.

Empty bottles clattered on the icy pier. The shark-boaters stood with hands raised, as if prepared to stop the advance of this impossible crew. The youngest was sent running to tell the Port Authority what they'd seen, but when he arrived at the oak-pillared hall, graven with ships and maritime symbols, he found it completely empty. No precinct sergeant on duty. No tables of officers playing freedeck. No bunk beds of sleeping troops awaiting a call to arms.

The young boatswain ran to the Magistry of the Brotherhood Itself with its colonnade of bone-white columns. But no one was there either. No stodgy house lord scolding the boy for knocking. No magistrates milling behind stained glass in the trifectory.

No members of the Brotherhood Itself anywhere. No one.

Across the frozen marina, the cluster of sailors from the plague ship broke ranks. They ran. They scattered this way and that, scrambling up onto small docks and rocky banks, their boot heels tapping on cold planks and paving stones as they all vanished into the shadows between our shops and sheds.

For days, we watched from the safety of locked and bolted windows, waiting for someone to tell us it was safe to go outside. It was lonely in our quarantine, maddening, but we all knew that fear would make us careful. Our hands, now hooves, stamped upon kitchen floors. Tails lashed in fright. Our throaty voices grew hoarse, vainly braying questions.

But we had more than our fear and regret, in that moment, of course, because, oh, we were still wickedly curious about what would happen next.

PALIMPSEST

Catherynne M. Valente

16th and Hieratica

fortune-teller's shop: palm-fronds cross before the door. Inside are four red chairs with four lustral basins before them, filled with ink, swirling and black. A woman lumbers in, wrapped in ragged fox-fur. Her head amid heaps of scarves is that of a frog, mottled green and bulbous-eyed, and a licking pink tongue keeps its place in her wide mouth. She does not see individual clients. Thus it is that four strangers sit in the red chairs, strip off their socks, plunge their feet into the ink-baths, and hold hands under an amphibian stare. This is the first act of anyone entering Palimpsest: Orlande will take your coats, sit you down, and make you family. She will fold you four together like quartos. She will draw you each a card — look, for you it is the Broken Ship reversed, which signifies perversion, a long journey without enlightenment, gout — and tie your hands together with red yarn. Wherever you go in Palimpsest, you are bound to these strangers who happened onto Orlande's salon just when you did, and you will go nowhere, eat no capon or dormouse, drink no oversweet port that they do not also taste, and they will visit no whore that you do not also feel beneath you, and until that ink washes from your feet — which, given that Orlande is a creature of the marsh and no stranger to mud, will be some time — you cannot breathe but that they breathe also.

The other side of the street: a factory. Its thin spires are green, and spit long loops of white flame into the night. Casimira owns this place, as did her father and her grandmother and probably her most distant progenitor, curling and uncurling their proboscis-fingers against machines of stick and bone. There has always been a Casimira, except when, occasionally, there is a Casimir. Workers carry their lunches in clamshells. They wear extraordinary uniforms: white and green scales laid one over the other, clinging obscenely to the skin, glittering in the spirelight. They wear nothing else; every wrinkle and curve is visible. They dance into the factory, their serpentine bodies writhing a shift-change, undulating under the punch-clock with its cheerful metronomic chime. Their eyes are piscine, third eyelid half-drawn in drowsy pleasure as they side-step and gambol and spin to the rhythm of the machines.

And what do they make in this factory? Why, the vermin of Palimpsest. There is a machine for stamping cockroaches with glistening green carapaces, their maker's mark hidden cleverly under the left wing. There is a machine for shaping and pounding rats, soft grey fur stiff and shining when they are first released. There is another mold for squirrels, one for chipmunks and one for plain mice. There is a centrifuge for spiders, a lizard-pour, a delicate and ancient *machine which turns out flies and mosquitoes by turn, so exquisite, so perfect that they seem to be made of nothing but copper wire, spun sugar, and light. There is a printing press for graffiti which spits out effervescent letters in scarlet, black, angry yellows, and the trademark green of Casimira. They fly from the high windows and flatten themselves against walls, trestles, train cars.*

When the shift-horn sounds at the factory, the long antler-trumpet passed down to Casimira by the one uncle in her line who defied tradition and became a humble hunter, setting the whole clan to a vociferous but well-fed consternation, a wave of life wafts from the service exit: moles and beetles and starlings and bats, ants and worms and moths and mantises. Each gleaming with its last coat of sealant, each quivering with near-invisible devices which whisper into their atavistic minds that their mistress loves them, that she thinks of them always, and longs to hold them to her breast.

In her office, Casimira closes her eyes and listens to the teeming masses as they whisper back to their mother. At the end of each day they tell her all they have learned of living.

It is necessary work. No family has been so often formally thanked by the city as hers.

The first time I saw it was in the pit of a woman's elbow. The orange and violet lights of the raucous dancefloor played over her skin, made her look like a decadent leopardess at my table. I asked her about it; she pulled her sleeve over her arm self-consciously, like a clam pulling its stomach in.

"It's not cancer," she said loudly, over the droning, repetitive music, "I had it checked out. It was just there one day, popping up out of me like fucking track marks. I have to wear long sleeves to work all the time now, even in summer. But it's nothing — well, not nothing, but if it's something it's benign, just some kind of late-arriving birthmark."

I took her home. Not because of it, but because her hair was very red, in that obviously dyed way — and I like that way. Some shades of red genetics will never produce, but she sat in the blinking green and blue lights haloed in defiant scarlet.

She tasted like new bread and lemon-water.

As she drifted to sleep, one arm thrown over her eyes, the other lying open and soft on my sheets, I stroked her elbow gently, the mark there like a tattoo: a spidery network of blue-black lines, intersecting each other, intersecting her pores, turning at sharp angles, rounding out into clear and unbroken skin just outside the hollow of her joint. It looked like her veins had darkened and hardened, organized themselves into something more than veins, and determined to escape the borders of their mistress's flesh. She murmured my name in her sleep: Lucia.

"It looks like a streetmap," I whispered sleepily, brushing her hair from a flushed ear.

I dreamed against her breast of the four black pools in Orlande's house. I stared straight ahead into her pink and grey-speckled mouth, and the red thread swept tight against my wrist. On my leather-skirted lap the Flayed Horse was lain, signifying sacrifice in vain, loveless pursuit, an empty larder. A man sat beside me with an old-fashioned felt hat askance on his bald head, his lips deeply rosy and full, as though he had been kissing someone a moment before. We laced our hands together as she lashed us — he had an extra finger, and I tried not to recoil. Before me were two women: one with a green scarf wrapping thin golden hair, a silver mantis-pendant dangling between her breasts, and another, Turkish, or Armenian, perhaps, her eyes heavily made-up, streaked in black like an Egyptian icon.

The frog-woman showed me a small card, red words printed neatly on yellowed paper:

You have been quartered.

The knots slackened. I walked out, across the frond-threshold, into the night which smelled of sassafras and rum, and onto Hieratica Street. The others scattered, like ashes. The road stretched before and beyond, lit by streetlamps like swollen pumpkins, and the gutters ran with rain.

212ᵗʰ, Vituperation, Seraphim, and Alphabet

In the center of the roundabout: the Cast-Iron Memorial. It is tall and thin, a baroque spire sheltering a single black figure — a gagged child with the corded, elastic legs of an ostrich, fashioned from linked hoops of iron — through the gaps in her knees you can see the weeds with their flame-tipped flowers. She is seated in the grass, her arms thrown out in supplication. Bronze and titanium chariots click by in endless circles, drawn on runners in the street, ticking as they pass like shining clocks. Between her knock-knees is a plaque of white stone:

IN MEMORIAM:
The sons and daughters of Palimpsest

who fought and fell in the Silent War.
752-759

Silent still
are the fields
in which they are planted.

Once, though the tourists could not know of it, on this spot a thousand died without a gasp. Legions were volunteered to have their limbs replaced with better articles, fleeter and wiser and stronger and newer. These soldiers also had their larynxes cut out, so they could not give away their positions with an unfortunate cry, or tell tales of what they had done in the desert, by the sea, in the city which then was new and toddling. Whole armies altered thus wrangled without screams, without sound. In the center of the roundabout, the ostrich-girl died unweeping while her giraffe-father had his long, spotted neck slashed with an ivory bayonet.

Down the mahogany alleys of Seraphim Street, clothes shops line the spotless, polished road. In the window of one is a dress in the latest style: startlingly blue, sweeping up to the shoulders of a golden mannequin. It cuts away to reveal a glittering belly; the belt is fastened with tiny cerulean eyes which blink lazily, in succession. The whites are diamonds, the pupils ebony. The skirt winds down in deep, hard creases which tumble out of the window in a carefully arranged train, hemmed in crow feathers. The shopkeeper, Aloysius, keeps a pale green Casimira grasshopper on a beaded leash. It rubs its legs together while he works in a heap of black quills, sewing an identical trio of gowns like the one in the window for triplet girls who demanded them in violet, not blue.

At night, he ties the leash to his bedpost and the little thing lies next to his broad, lined face, clicking a binary lullaby into the old man's beard. He dreams of endless bodies, unclothed and beautiful.

I can be forgiven, I think, for not noticing it for days afterward. I caught a glimpse in my mirror as I turned to catch a loose thread in my skirt — behind my knee, a dark network of lines and angles, and, I thought I could see, tiny words scrawled above them, names and numbers, snaking over the grid.

After that, I began to look for them.

I found the second in a sushi restaurant with black tablecloths — he was sitting two tables over, but when he gripped his chopsticks, I could see the map pulsing on his palm. I joined him — he did not object. We ate eels and cucumbers thinner than vellum and drank enough clear, steaming sake that I did not have to lean over to kiss him in the taxi. He smashed his lips against mine, and I dug my nails into his neck — when we parted I seized his hand and licked the web of avenues that criss-crossed so: heart and fate lines.

In his lonely apartment I kissed his stomach. In his lonely apartment, on a bed without a frame which lay wretched between milk crates and cinder blocks, the moon shone through broken blinds and slashed my back into a tiger's long stripes.

In his lonely apartment, on a pillow pounded thin by dozens of night-fists, I dreamed. Perhaps he dreamed, too. I thought I saw him wandering down a street filled with balloons and leering gazelles — but I did not follow. I stood on a boulevard paved with prim orange poppies, and suddenly I tasted brandy rolling down my throat, and pale smoke filling up my lungs. My green-scarved quarter was savoring her snifter and her opium somewhere far from me. I saw the ostrich-child that night. I smelled the Seraphim sidewalks, rich and red, and traded, with only some hesitation, my long brown hair for the dress. Aloysius cut it with crystal scissors, and I walked over wood, under sulfurous stars, trailing dark feathers behind me. The wind was warm on my bare neck. My fingers were warm, too — my bald quarter was stroking a woman with skin like a snake's.

There were others. A man with a silver tooth — a depth-chart crawled over his toes. With him I dreamed I walked the tenements, raised on stilts over a blue river, and ate goulash with a veteran whose head was a snarling lion, tearing his meat with fangs savage and yellow. He had a kind of sign language, but I could only guess correctly the gestures for *mother, southeast,* and *sleep.*

There was a woman with two children and a mole on her left thigh — between her shoulder blades severe turns and old closes poked on an arrondissement-wheel. With her I dreamed I worked a night's shift in a restaurant that served but one dish: broiled elephant liver, soaked in lavender honey and jeweled with pomegranate seeds. The staff wore tunics sewn from peacock feathers, and were not allowed to look the patrons in the eye. When I set a shimmering plate before a man with long, grey fingers, I felt my black-eyed quarter pick up her golden fork and bite into a snail dipped in rum.

There was a sweet boy with a thin little beard — his thumb was nearly black with gridlock and unplanned alleys, as though he had been fingerprinted in an unnamable jail. He fell asleep in my arms, and we dreamed together, like mating dragonflies flying in unison. With him, I saw the foundries throwing fire into the sky. With him I danced in pearlescent scales, and pressed into being exactly fifty-seven wild hares, each one marked on its left ear with Casimira's green seal.

Lucia! They all cry out when they lie over me. *Lucia! Where will I find you?*

Yet in those shadow-stitched streets I am always alone.

I sought out the dream-city on all those skins. What were plain, yellow-lined streets next to Seraphim? What was my time-clock stamping out its inane days next to the jeweled factory of Casimira? How could any touch equal the seizures of feeling in my dreams, in which each gesture was a quartet? I would touch no one who didn't carry the map. Only once that year, after the snow, did I make an exception, for a young woman with cedar-colored breasts and a nose ring like a bull's, or a minotaur's. She wore bindi on her face like a splatter of blood. Her body was without blemish or mark, so alien and strange to me by then, so blank and empty. But she was beautiful, and her voice was a glass-cutting soprano, and I am weak. I begged her to sing to me after we made love, and when we dreamed, I found her dancing with a jackal-tailed man in the lantern-light of a bar that served butterfly-liquor in a hundred colors. I separated them; he wilted and slunk away, and I took her to the sea, its foam shattering into glass on the beach, and we walked along a strand of shards, glittering and wet.

When I woke, the grid brachiated out from her navel, its angles dark and bright. I smiled. Before she stirred, I kissed the striated lines, and left her house without coffee or farewells.

Quiescent and Rapine

There are two churches in Palimpsest, and they are identical in every way. They stand together, wrapping the street-corner like a hinge. Seven white columns each, wound around with black characters which are not Cyrillic, but to the idle glance might seem so. Two peaked roofs of red lacquer and two stone horses with the heads of fork-tongued lizards stand guard on either side of each door. They were made with stones from the same quarry, on the far southern border of the city, pale green and dusty, each round and perfect as a ball. There is more mortar in the edifices than stones, mortar crushed from Casimira dragonflies donated by the vat, tufa dust, and mackerel tails. The pews are scrubbed and polished with lime-oil, and each Thursday, parishioners share a communion of slivers of whale meat and cinnamon wine. The only difference between the two is in the basement — two great mausoleums with alabaster coffins lining the walls, calligraphied with infinite care and delicacy in the blood of the departed beloved contained within. In the far north corner is a raised platform covered in offerings of cornskin, chocolate, tobacco. In one church, the coffin contains a blind man. In the other, it contains a deaf woman. Both have narwhal's horns extending from their foreheads; both died young. The faithful visit these basement-saints and leave what they can at the feet of the one they love best. Giustizia has been a devotee of the Unhearing since she was a girl — her yellow veil and turquoise-ringed thumbs are familiar to all in the Left-Hand Church, and it is she who brings the cornskins, regular as sunrise. When she dies, they will bury her here, in a coffin of her own.

She will plug your ears with wax when you enter, and demand silence. You may notice the long rattlesnake tail peeking from under her skirt and clattering on the mosaic floor, but it is not polite to mention it — when she says silence, you listen. It is the worst word she knows.

The suburbs of Palimpsest spread out from the edges of the city proper like ladies' fans. First the houses, uniformly red, in even lines like veins, branching off into lanes and courts and cul-de-sacs. There are parks full of grass that smells like oranges and little creeks filled with floating roses, blue and black. Children scratch pictures of antelope-footed girls and sparrow-winged boys on the pavement, hop from one to the other. Their laughter spills from their mouths and turns to orange leaves, drifting lazily onto wide lawns. Eventually the houses fade into fields: amaranth, spinach, strawberries. Shaggy cows graze; black-faced sheep bleat. Palimpsest is ever-hungry.

But these too fade as they extend out, fade into the empty land not yet colonized by the city, not yet peopled, not yet known. The empty meadows stretch to the horizon, pale and dark, rich and soft.

A wind picks up, blowing hot and dusty and salt-scented, and gooseflesh rises over miles and miles of barren skin.

I saw her in November. It was raining — her scarf was soaked and plastered against her head. She passed by me, and I knew her smell, I knew the shape of her wrist. In the holiday crowds, she disappeared quickly, and I ran after her, without a name to call out.

"Wait!" I cried.

She stopped and turned towards me, her square jaw and huge brown eyes familiar as a pillow. We stood together in the rainy street, beside a makeshift watch-stand.

"It's you," I whispered.

And I showed my knee. She pursed her lips for a moment, her green scarf blown against her neck like a wet leaf. Then she extended her tongue, and I saw it there, splashed with raindrops, the map of Palimpsest, blazing blue-bright. She closed her mouth, and I put my arm around her waist.

"I felt you, the pipe of bone, the white smoke," I said.

"I felt the dress on your shoulders," she answered, and her voice was thick and low, grating, like a gate opening.

"Come to my house. There is brandy there, if you want it."

She cocked her head, thin golden hair snaking sodden over her coat. "What would happen, do you think?"

I smiled. "Maybe our feet would come clean."

She stroked my cheek, put her long fingers into my hair. We kissed, and the watches gleamed beside us, gold and silver.

125*th* and Peregrine

On the south corner: the lit globes, covered with thick wrought- iron serpents which break the light, of a subway entrance. The trains barrel along at the bottom of the stairs every fifteen minutes. On the glass platform stands Adalgiso, playing his viola with six fingers on each hand. He is bald, with a felt hat that does not sit quite right on his head. Beside him is Assia, singing tenor, her smoke-throated voice pressing against his strings like kisses. Her eyes are heavily made-up, like a pharaoh's portrait, her hair long and coarse and black. His playing is so quick and lovely that the trains stop to listen, inclining on the rails and opening their doors to catch the glissandos spilling from him. His instrument case lies open at his feet, and each passenger who takes the Marginalia Line brings his fee — single pearls, dropped one by one into the leather case until it overflows like a pitcher of milk. In the corners of the station, cockroaches with fiber optic wings scrape the tiles with their feet, and their scraping keeps the beat for the player and his singer.

On the north corner: a cartographer's studio. There are pots of ink in every crevice, parchment spread out over dozens of tables. A Casimira pigeon perches in a baleen cage and trills out the hours faithfully. Its droppings are pure squid-ink, and they are collected in a little tin trough. Lucia and Paola have run this place for as long as anyone can remember — Lucia with her silver compass draws the maps, her exactitude radiant and unerring, while Paola illuminates them with exquisite miniatures, dancing in the spaces between streets. They each wear dozens of watches on their forearms. This is the second stop, after the amphibian-salon, of Palimpsest's visitors, and especially of her immigrants, for whom the two women are especial patrons. Everyone needs a map, and Lucia supplies them: subway maps and street-maps and historical maps and topographical maps, false maps and correct-to-the-minute maps and maps of cities far and far from this one. Look — for you she has made a folding pamphlet that shows the famous sights: the factory, the churches, the salon, the memorial. Follow it, and you will be safe.

Each morning, Lucia places her latest map on the windowsill like a fresh pie. Slowly, as it cools, it opens along its own creases, its corners like wings, and takes halting flight, flapping over the city with susurring strokes. It folds itself, origami-exact, in mid-air: it has papery eyes, inky feathers, vellum claws.

It stares down the long avenues, searching for mice.

Author Biographies

EKATERINA SEDIA lives in New Jersey with the best spouse in the world and two cats. Her new novel, *The Secret History of Moscow*, is coming from Prime Books in November 2007. She is currently working on *The Alchemy of Stone*, due from Prime in 2008. Her short stories sold to *Analog, Baen's Universe, Fantasy Magazine*, and *Dark Wisdom*, as well as *Japanese Dreams* and *Magic in the Mirrorstone* anthologies. Visit her at www.ekaterinasedia.com.

FORREST AGUIRRE won the World Fantasy Award for editing the *Leviathan 3* anthology. He has edited several other anthologies, including his most recent anthology, *Text:UR, The New Book of Masks*. His fiction has appeared in a variety of markets including *Polyphony, American Letters & Commentary*, and *Notre Dame Review*. His short fiction has been collected in *Fugue XXIX* and his first book-length release, *Swans Over the Moon* is available from Wheatland Press. He lives in Madison, Wisconsin with his wife and four children.

BARTH ANDERSON's imaginative fiction has appeared in *Asimov's, Strange Horizons, Clarkesworld Magazine, Polyphony,* and a variety of other quality venues. Regarding his first novel, *The Patron Saint of Plagues* (Bantam Spectra; 2006), Salon said, "Anderson has some serious writing chops, and he delivers a page turner that is at once a medical thriller, cyberpunk romp and provocative tease." His second novel, *The Magician and The Fool*, is forthcoming in 2008. Barth lives in Minneapolis with his wife and two children.

STEVE BERMAN grew up on an unhealthy diet of Saturday morning television. It affected his lower brain functions and now he cannot help but have delusions of being a writer. He imagines he has sold over 80 articles, essays and short stories. Maybe a young adult novel. Or edited some anthologies. He thinks New Orleans might once have been his home. Or Philadelphia, which does resemble the Fallen Area if you turn to the right UHF channel on Saturday mornings. He can be channeled at steveberman.com.

DARIN C. BRADLEY is the fiction editor and designer for *Farrago's Wainscot*. He holds a Ph.D. in Poetics, specializing in the mechanics of "weird," and has placed work with *Electric Velocipede*, *Strange Horizons*, *Polyphony 6*, *The Internet Review of Science Fiction*, *Abyss & Apex*, *Astropoetica*, *GrendelSong*, and *Bewildering Stories*.

STEPHANIE CAMPISI's work has appeared in *Fantasy Magazine, Farthing, Shimmer*, and more. She is currently working on a novel set in the same world as this story.

HAL DUNCAN was born in 1971 and lives in the West End of Glasgow. A long-standing member of the Glasgow SF Writers Circle, his first novel, *Vellum*, was nominated for the Crawford Award, the British Fantasy Society Award and the World Fantasy Award. The sequel, *Ink*, is available from Pan Macmillan in the UK and Del Rey in the US, while a novella is due out in November 2007 from Monkeybrain Books. He has also published a poetry collection, *Sonnets For Orpheus*, and had short fiction published in magazines such as *Fantasy, Strange Horizons* and *Interzone*, and anthologies such as *Nova Scotia, Eidolon* and *Logorrhea*.

MICHAEL JASPER gets by on not enough sleep and too much caffeine in Wake Forest, North Carolina, where he lives with his lovely wife Elizabeth and their amazing young son Drew. Michael's fiction has appeared in *Asimov's, Strange Horizons, Interzone, Fantasy Gone Wrong, Heroes in Training, Aeon*, and *Polyphony*. His story collection *Gunning for the Buddha* came out in 2005 from Prime Books, his paranormal romance *Heart's Revenge* (writing as Julia C. Porter) came out in 2006 from Five Star, and his novel *The Wannoshay Cycle* is due out from Five Star in January of 2008.

VYLAR KAFTAN writes science fiction, fantasy, horror, slipstream, and cleverly-phrased Post-It notes on the fridge. Her stories have appeared in *Strange Horizons, ChiZine*, and *Clarkesworld*, among other places. She's appeared in Spanish translation in the Argentinian magazine *Axxon*. She lives in northern California and has a standard issue tie-dyed T-shirt to prove it. A graduate of Clarion West, she volunteers as a mentor for teenaged writers with the online group Absynthe Muse. Her hobbies include modern-day temple dancing and preparing for a major earthquake. She blogs at http://www.vylarkaftan.net.

JAY LAKE lives in Portland, Oregon with his books and two inept cats, where he works on numerous writing and editing projects. His current novels are *Trial of Flowers* from Night Shade Books and *Mainspring* from Tor Books, with sequels to both books in 2008. Jay is the winner of the 2004 John W. Campbell Award for Best New Writer, and a multiple nominee for the Hugo and World Fantasy Awards. Jay can be reached through his blog at jaylake.livejournal.com.

PAUL MELOY works as a psychiatric nurse in a crisis team in Bury St Edmunds. In 2005 his story *Black Static* won the British Fantasy Society Award for best short story. He has had stories published in *The Third Alternative, Nemonymous* and *Interzone*. TTA Press will be publishing his collection, *Islington Crocodiles* in late 2007.

JESS NEVINS is the author of the *Encyclopedia of Fantastic Victoriana*, a guide to the characters and concepts of 19th century genre fiction. He is a librarian at Sam Houston State University and is currently writing the *Encyclopedia of Pulp Heroes*, a guide to the characters and concepts of 20th century genre fiction.

RICHARD PARKS lives in Mississippi. His fiction has appeared in *Asimov's SF, Realms of Fantasy, Lady Churchill's Rosebud Wristlet, Fantasy Magazine, Weird Tales*, and numerous anthologies, including *Year's Best Fantasy and Fantasy: The Best of the Year.* He has two books out in 2007, a novella titled *Hereafter And After* from PS Publishing and a story collection, *Worshipping Small Gods*, from Prime Books.

BEN PEEK is a Sydney based author. His short fiction has appeared in *Leviathan 4*, edited by Forrest Aguirre, *Polyphony Six*, edited by Deborah Layne and Jay Lake, *Agog! Ripping Reads*, edited by Cat Sparks, as well as *Aurealis, Fantasy Magazine*, and various Year's Best volumes. He is the author of *Twenty-Six Lies/One Truth*, released by Wheatland Press, and *Black Sheep*, released by Prime Books. He keeps a lo fi web presence at http://benpeek.livejournal.com

CAT RAMBO lives and writes in the Pacific Northwest with her charming spouse, Wayne. She is a graduate of both Clarion West and the Johns Hopkins Writing Seminars. Among the places in which her work has appeared are *Fantasy Magazine*, *Subterranean*, and *Strange Horizons*. "The Bumblety's Marble" takes place in the seaport of Tabat, a setting shared by several of her stories as well as the novel she is currently completing, *The Moon's Accomplice*.

JENN REESE has lived in various suburban landscapes most of her life — Illinois, New Jersey, Maryland, and upstate New York — but now makes her home in Los Angeles. It's a sun-bleached desert city of freaks, and she absolutely loves it. When she's not writing or at work, she's studying martial arts, playing strategy games, or sitting in traffic. You'll find a list of her publications, including information on her first novel, *Jade Tiger*, at www.jennreese.com .

DAVID J. SCHWARTZ's fiction has appeared in such venues as *Strange Horizons, Twenty Epics,* and *Fantasy: The Year's Best*. His first novel, *Superpowers*, will be released in 2008.

CAT SPARKS lives on the south coast of New South Wales, Australia, where she works as a graphic designer and runs Agog! Press with her partner, author Robert Hood. In 2004 she was a graduate of the inaugural Clarion South Writers' Workshop and a Writers of the Future prizewinner. Cat has accumulated seven DITMAR awards since 2000 and was awarded the Aurealis Peter McNamara Conveners Award in 2004. She recently became a member of SFWA

ANNA TAMBOUR currently lives in Australia. Her collection *Monterra's Deliciosa & Other Tales* & and her novel *Spotted Lily* are Locus Recommended Reading List selections. The adventurous might also want to visit the ormless lands of Anna Tambour and Others at www. annatambour.net, and Medlar Comfits, a blog http://medlarcomfits. blogspot.com.

Most days, **MARK TEPPO** lingers at Calliope's Coffee House and Bookstore, perched in a comfortable chair near the front window. He'll be nursing a cinnamon double ristretto while watching for patterns in the flow of traffic through the intersection of Mission and 14th. Occasionally, a meeting of the Fourth Foundation Society will dislodge him from his favorite seat and he'll spend the afternoon in the park, chasing squirrels. If you have access to the Internet (or an aversion to squirrels), you can find him at www.markteppo.com. During 2007, Farrago's Wainscot has serialized his hypertext novel (www.farragoswainscot.com).

CATHERYNNE M. VALENTE is the author of the *Orphan's Tales* series, as well as *The Labyrinth, Yume no Hon: The Book of Dreams, The Grass-Cutting Sword*, and four books of poetry, *Music of a Proto-Suicide, Apocrypha, The Descent of Inanna*, and *Oracles*. She has been nominated for the Pushcart Prize and is the winner of the 2006 Tiptree Award. She currently lives in Ohio with her two dogs.

GREG VAN EEKHOUT's fiction has appeared in places such as *Asimov's Science Fiction, Magazine of Fantasy and Science Fiction*, and *Realms of Fantasy*. Several of his stories have been reprinted in year's-best anthologies, and his story "In the Late December" was a finalist for the Nebula Award. He is an instructional designer by trade, an avid coffee drinker, and an enthusiastic if not terribly skilled martial arts student. Greg keeps a blog at writingandsnacks.com/blog.

KAARON WARREN's short story collection *The Glass Woman* will be released by Prime Books this year. The Australian edition won three fiction prizes. She has a story in Ellen Datlow's *Year's Best Fantasy and Horror 20* and lives in Fiji.